DEAD TIME

Between Two Evils
Book Three

DEAD TIME

D. L. ORTON

Between Two Evils Series

Book Three

ROCKY MOUNTAIN PRESS

Between Two Evils Series
Book Three
BetweenTwoEvils.com
Published by Rocky Mountain Press (USA)
RockyMtPress.com
ISBN: 978-1-941368-16-9
Paperback Edition (v1.3)

Written by D. L. Orton
(dlo@dlorton.com, @DL_Orton)
Illustrations by Micah McDonald
Edited by David S. Taylor (thEditors.com)
Cover by Andreea Vraciu
Book Layout by Fernando Urbina
Line Edits by Deanne Charlton
Proofreaders: Keith Moser, Jenny Dwight Dip. Edit.,
Lynn Worton S.A.C. Dip, & Michael Golvach
Airplane Consultants: Mike Kutz & Richard Merrill

The text was set in Adobe Dante, a serif typeface originally
cut for use on a hand printing press.

TABLE OF CONTENTS

Front Matter

Dead Time

End Matter

DEAD TIME

D. L. ORTON

A
book
is
a
time machine,
a magic mirror,
a flickering candle,
a friend, a lover,
a wormhole to
another universe.
It's a memory of a
place that doesn't
exist outside the
pages.
This book is dedicated to those who believe in
the power of a story to change the world.

To love or have loved, this is enough.
Ask nothing further.
There is no other pearl to be found
in the dark folds of life.

Les Misérables
Victor Hugo

CHAPTER 1

Shannon: Till Death Do Us Not-So-Much

I stand with the rain pelting my helmet and watch the Cessna ascend into the stormy sky—my last chance to go home disappearing before my eyes.

When the airplane vanishes into the dark clouds, I close my eyes and let the tears fall. I imagine myself sitting next to my puppy, Bearhart, in the backseat of the plane, wondering if the boys at C-Bay will be nice to me, or if the girls will think I'm dank. I can almost see Mr. C gripping the armrests and looking nervous as we fly through the rough air. I smile and tell him not to worry. We've got Madders at the stick, and Professor Matt Hudson is the best pilot in the whole wide world. He'll get us out of this mess, no *problemo*.

A flash of lightning brings me back to reality.

The wind is ripping at the loose tabs on my biosuit and hurling huge raindrops against me like projectiles. I have thirty minutes of O$_2$ left in my tank and one emergency air canister. My sketchpad is tucked inside a pocket of my suit, along with the lucky seashell Mr. C gave me, but that's it. I take a sip of my dwindling water supply and turn toward the dilapidated biodome, feeling anxious and scared.

Just turned eighteen, and my life is over.

Mom always says that bravery is being the only one who knows you're afraid.

I'm trying to be brave, Mom, but it's harder than I thought.

All the jeeps and other equipment are gone now, and I count four dingy biosuits slogging toward me through the downpour. I gaze up at the sloped wall of the massive bio-dome, wishing it didn't look so… alien.

What would Madders do?

He'd be collecting data, not blubbering like a D-2 who fell off a swing and scraped her knee.

Identify the problem, engineer a fix, and Bob's your uncle.

I force down a sob and get to work.

I'd estimate this biodome is twice the diameter of the Bub. So that means it must be…

I have to force my brain to do the calculations.

Four times as much floor space and almost as big as C-Bay. Holy—

Someone shoves me hard in the back. "Let's go, girly."

"Okay." I start moving toward the man-made mountain. "No need to be rude."

"When the air runs out," he says, "all the good manners in the world ain't gonna save you."

But neither is being rude.

I blink back tears and continue walking.

Maybe if I focus on the outside, it won't hurt so much on the inside.

I make a mental note of the distance between airlocks, the algae-covered fishpond, and a huge pile of trash and discarded junk. And then I remember the hole in the bio-dome that was visible from the plane. It's way up on the top of the dome. I slow my step and lean back for a better look, trying not to be too obvious.

Mr. Rude—Mikey, I think they called him—decides it's a good time to give me another shove in the back. "You best be keeping your head bowed and your eyes on your feet, if you know what's good for you."

I do as he instructs, but not before I notice that the damaged spot on the biodome isn't sagging at all. Maybe they patched it from the inside but didn't bother to fix the outer shell?

Which means the repair is only cosmetic—and the minute the inner skin fails, everyone will be dead.

After Mikey turns away, I glance up and notice that the door to the main airlock is wide open.

Do these people have a death wish?

Failing to shut the exterior door on any airlock is a big no-no, but leaving the one on the main airlock open could get everyone in the biodome killed. In any sort of an emergency, there would be no way to get out. When the external door is open, you can't open the internal one—not even with the manual override. People would be trapped inside—just like they were when that biodome in Arizona burned to the ground nine or ten years ago.

The thought fills me with panic.

The CO_2 alarm in my suit goes off, and in my haste to locate the puncture, I lose my balance, nearly falling down.

Someone grabs my arm, jerking me upright. "Watch it!" The voice is shrill and nasal. "The clumsy don't last very long out—"

"I… I can't breathe!" My faceplate is fogging up and my air is getting thinner.

The man with the high-pitched voice glances at the

flashing orange light and shouts, "Her biosuit's busted!"

The others hurry over, searching for the telltale wisp of vapor that signals a breach. But it's raining hard, and I'm all wet. Hands grab at my sleeves and pants, searching in vain for the leak.

This time, you're going to die.

I bend over, trying not to pass out—and count down the seconds.

Mikey laughs. "Hey Sporus, they scramble your brains when they cut off your nuts? Kid's having a panic attack, is all. CO_2 got too high and the filter couldn't keep up."

The alarm goes silent.

"Bet she pissed her pants and ruined that nice suit a' hers," Sporus says, and they all laugh.

Breathe, Shaz. Just breathe.

"Okay, girly. Fun's over," Mikey says. "Let's get a move on. I don't like the looks of that storm."

I watch all but one set of boots shuffle away—and then a hand reaches out.

"You alright, princess?" The voice is deep and gravelly.

I look up into the sunken eyes of an old man, his face covered in whiskers and his helmet stuffed full of tangled hair.

"A bit too much excitement is all," he says and helps me stand up. "Can you walk?"

I choke back a sob and nod.

Mikey's voice fills my helmet. "You ain't going all soft on her now, are you, Grizzly? She may be a cute cub, but she'll grow up to be a killer just like all the others."

"Pipe down, Mikey. You're scarin' her," Grizzly says. He touches his helmet to mine. "Don't listen to him. He's got a bit of an ax to grind." He chuckles to himself. "Never mind. Keep your eyes on the airlock and don't breathe too fast." He starts pulling me toward the biodome. "You'll be fine. Plenty of folks get queasy the first time they're Outside."

His words make me feel like some lolo D-2, and I'm grateful Mom and Madders weren't here to see me fall apart at the stitches.

I force myself to take slow, even breaths.

You can beat this, Shannon Malia Kai. Mom won't let these people get away with kidnapping you. As soon as Madders gets to C-Bay, he'll put together a rescue party. You just have to figure out a way to survive until they get here.

We're heading for a small, two-person emergency airlock. It's wide open, and rainwater is running down the side of the biodome, curling around the tiny roof and pouring into the room.

When I get to the door, I stop and stare at the mess. The floor inside is a muddy jumble of decaying leaves, plastic bottles, and bits of trash floating around in the ankle-deep sludge.

Mikey shoves me from behind, and then all four of the patched and faded biosuits squeeze in with me. It's too many people for this small space, and I'm forced back against the wall. My boot slips and I lose my balance.

A hand steadies me. "Careful, miss." It's a new voice, deep and soft. "You don't want to fall down in all this muck."

I twist around to look at him, my heart still pounding. "Thanks," I manage to say—and realize he's only a kid.

He nods in acknowledgment, his eyes taking me in. "We're not monsters, you know. We're just—"

"Stop blabbering and help me get the damn door shut," Mikey says.

The kid averts his gaze and squeezes past me.

The electricity seems to be off. So they have to close the door by hand—which explains why they left it open.

My heart rate settles a bit.

With my helmet pressed against the inner wall, I can hear metal grating against metal as they work the rusty door mechanism. If I had to hazard a guess, I'd say the last time they did airlock maintenance was when I was still in diapers.

Mookers, I get in trouble for throwing my clothes on the floor. Mom should see this place!

They have difficulty getting the outer door to seal, and with so many bodies crammed into such close quarters, my suit is overheating.

Just when I start to feel light-headed again, the inner portal slides open. I half-trip, half-step through the doorway and stop in my tracks.

Oh. My. God.

Dim light is filtering through the translucent biodome walls, and as far as the eye can see, the place is littered with piles of garbage and discarded junk. It's like a scene out of some low-budget, post-apocalyptic movie where only the idiots survived.

"Hustle up, miss. Don't want that exterior door to fail, now do we?" Someone pokes me in the back.

I shuffle out of the way, my eyes focusing on the billowy gray cloud rising from *inside* the biodome. It takes me a minute to figure out what it is.

Smoke. From a fire. Burning inside *the biodome.*

Before I have a chance to work through the long list of reasons why that is so *wrong*, someone unlatches my helmet and pulls it off, dumping out the last of the drinking water.

"What about the decontamination procedures required after manual airlock flush?" I ask, unable to believe these careless people are still alive. "There could be pockets of air containing the virus in any number of—"

Mikey snorts. "Welcome home, princess."

The stench of unwashed bodies and decaying biomass accosts me. The air is so foul, it makes my eyes water.

But before I have a chance to address my captors, I'm blindfolded.

"Get her out of that thing," Grizzly says.

Rough hands pull off my biosuit, leaving me shivering in shorts and a thin T-shirt.

Mikey lets out a wolf whistle. "Will you look at them curves? I could poke her so deep, whoever pulled me out would be king of all Eng—"

"Shut it," Grizzly says. "You gotta wait your turn like everyone else."

Someone tugs on my ankle, and I step out of my biosuit.

"Mm, mm," Mikey says, his mouth next to my leg.

I feel something warm and wet slide up my thigh—and let out a yelp when I realize it's his tongue.

He laughs. "Don't worry, blondie, there's more where that came from." I hear him kick my suit out of the way.

"Hey," I say, blindly reaching out for my biosuit. "You need to hang it up or it'll—"

A smelly rag is stuffed into my mouth, and then they tie my hands behind my back.

"No time for that," Grizzly says. "Don't want to be late for your nuptials."

I'm not sure what that word means, but I don't think it's good.

"Let's go," Mikey says as he yanks my arm forward.

A tear slips down my cheek. I wipe it away with my shoulder, but another one takes its place.

"And enough with the blubbering," Grizzly says. "You're a grown woman. You best start acting like one."

The five of us—Mikey, Grizzly, Sporus, the quiet one, and me—spend the next hour working our way through some sort of maze.

I try to keep track of the lefts and rights until someone grabs me by the front of my shirt.

"Don't you be getting any ideas about escaping," Mikey says, ripping a tear in the thin fabric as he spins me around.

"I just as soon shoot you as see more of that pretty little bra you're wearing." He squeezes my breast so hard it hurts. "You hear me?"

I let out a frightened squeal and then nod, feeling sick to my stomach.

A few minutes later, they stand me up against a wall while they open some sort of complicated bulkhead. I hear a heavy door squeak open, and they force me through and reseal it.

The air is noticeably better.

"Home sweet home," Sporus says. "The land of the free and the home of the brave."

They lead me down a long hallway, our footsteps echoing, and into a stuffy room. The door closes behind me and someone forces me down into a chair. I hear muffled voices and the sort of music they play in old vampire movies coming from somewhere nearby.

There must be a lot more people in there!

The moment they take the gag out of my mouth, I yell, "Help! I've been kidnapped!"

A bony hand covers my mouth, mashing my lips against my teeth and pressing my cheek into the back of the chair.

"Stop that hollerin'!" Grizzly says, his scratchy beard brushing against my ear. "The Prez don't want you to see how we get in and out, but we ain't gonna—" He starts coughing, the reek of his breath making me recoil.

"We ain't gonna hurt you or nothing," a younger voice says. "We ain't no rapists."

"The kid's right," Grizzly says, suppressing another cough. "'Round here we do things by the Good Book. You ain't got no reason to fear us." He nudges me in the shoulder. "You hear me?"

I nod, and he loosens his grip a little.

"If I let go, will you behave yourself?"

I nod again, and he releases my mouth.

"We should take that blindfold off her too," Grizzly says. "Don't want the fine, upstanding folks in the chapel getting the wrong impression."

"I thought she wasn't allowed to see me until the ceremony!" It's the boy who kept me from falling down in the airlock.

Grizzly grunts. "What's she gonna do, call the po-leece?" He laughs at his own joke, but it turns into another coughing fit.

"You sound like you need a doctor," I say.

The kid pulls off my blindfold. "We ain't got no doctors."

"Don't matter," Grizzly says, his beard covering nearly all of his face and his thinning hair wild. He sits down on a wooden crate. "Ain't nothin' they could do anyways. It's like a caved-in coal mine here, and there ain't no cure for that 'cept dyin'."

"The Giver says it's God's punishment for desecrating the Garden of Eden," the kid says, not sounding convinced. He looks to be sixteen or seventeen, tall and skinny as a snake. His skin is a gorgeous shade of coffee—but his curly hair is a little orange. "She says if we follow the righteous path, the Lord will save us."

"How many folks you met who made it out of a coal mine alive?" Grizzly asks, his mouth twisting into a sneer.

The kid shrugs.

"What's a coal mine?" I ask.

Grizzly snorts and shakes his head, obviously annoyed by my question.

I turn toward the boy and raise my eyebrows.

"I don't rightly know," he says, not meeting my gaze. "But it must be something horrible because everyone in here is sick from the bad air."

I hold my breath, wishing I had grabbed one of the

rebreathers from the airplane.

Grizzly laughs. "Best get used to it, princess. This here's your home now. It may not be gay Pair-ree, but it beats the heck outta getting strangled by Doomsday."

I look around. The room is small and windowless. One wall is lined with cabinets, and there's an empty bulletin board on another.

"What are you going to do with me?" I ask.

The kid glances down at his hands and then shakes his head. "I'm sorry they forced you to come here."

"You are?" I ask, my voice breaking. I look over at Grizzly. "Then why don't you let me go? Kidnapping is a sin, you know." I'm not positive about that, but I think I must be right, because the boy jerks his head up, his eyes wide.

"You ain't no kid," a voice says from behind me. "So it ain't no *kid*-napping."

I crane my neck around. Mikey is standing behind me, peeking through a door into another room. He's shorter and thinner than I imagined, and his teeth are bad.

"But it's still wrong," the skinny kid says. "To take someone against her will, I mean." The boy's hair is long and tangled, and he has a bad case of acne.

"If you dab your face with vinegar," I say, "it'll help clear up the pimples."

He turns toward me, his eyebrows furrowed. "You a doctor or somethin'?"

I shake my head. "More of an engineer, but my mother's a doctor—one of the best in the country."

"Maybe we should invite her over for tea," Mikey says, "I've never done a lady doc—"

"Shut it," Grizzly says, "or I'll report you."

"Then you'd be good as dead, old man." Mikey shuts the door and steps around in front of me, flicking open a pocketknife with one hand and closing it again.

"I ain't"—Grizzly stifles a cough and then spits on the floor—"got much longer either way."

The kid ignores them. "Vinegar, you say?"

"Yeah. Any kind will do, but apple cider vinegar works best." I turn and look at Grizzly. "And you should cover your mouth when you cough, or you'll spread your germs and more people will get sick."

"Lord in heaven!" Mikey says, pointing the knife at me. "Now I remember why we didn't want no womenfolk here."

"Well I think she's nice," the kid says, standing up straighter. "And pretty too."

"Thank you," I say without thinking, "but my mother says you should look for brains over beauty." I feel my face flush.

Shut it, Shaz.

"What a load of crap," Mikey says. "All the brainy women I ever met had a smart mouth to go along with it. Give me a dumb blond any day."

"Just because I'm blond, doesn't mean I'm stupid," I say. "And there's nothing wrong with being educated."

"Hush now," Grizzly says, wagging his finger at me, "or you'll be giving the boy notions."

The kid narrows his eyes like he's wondering what notions he might be missing out on.

Mikey laughs. "I told you, old man, giving blondie to that pansy is a waste a good tits and ass. He wouldn't know what to do with his pecker if God hisself—"

"How old are you?" the kid asks.

Mikey hurls his knife at the boy's head, narrowly missing him—and me. I scream and try to move out of the way, but I'm still tied to the chair. All I manage to do is tip over.

I lie there on the cold, dirty floor, too frightened to speak.

Mikey steps over me and pulls his knife out of the bulletin board. He wrenches the chair—and me—back upright.

"You do somethin' like that again," Grizzly says to Mikey, "and I'll kill you myself."

Mikey laughs and runs the back of his hand across my cheek. "You sure do scream pretty, girly."

The boy swallows, his face unreadable. "So how old are you, miss?"

"Eighteen," I say, trying to keep my voice from trembling.

"Well, Romeo here is nineteen," Grizzly says, pulling at his bushy eyebrows. "So it ain't such a bad match."

"As long as you ignore his limp dick," Mikey says and snorts. "In any case, they'll be wanting us to bring her in soon." He flicks open his knife and uses it to lift up my chin. "And it'd go better for you if I didn't have to drag you in kicking and screaming."

"Drag me in where? What are you planning to do to me?" I look at the boy, but he won't meet my gaze.

"Ah, shit," Mikey says. "I forgot to get the dress. Stall 'em until I get back." He pockets the knife and slips out the door.

I slump back in the chair and breathe a sigh of relief.

The moment the door clicks shut, the boy starts untying my hands. "I'm letting her go. She's not some slave girl you can order around, even if she don't believe."

"Believe what?" I ask. "What's going on?"

"Your funeral, kid," the old guy says and stands up. "Which is pretty much the same ceremony as a wedding any—" He starts coughing again, but this time he covers his mouth.

"Wedding?" I say, rubbing the circulation back into my wrists. "I think you should tell me what this is all about."

The kid's face turns the same color as his hair.

"And thanks for untying me. My name's Shannon." I offer him my hand, but he just stares at it.

"He ain't never touched a girl before," Grizzly says. "His mother died when he was a whippersnapper, and the

28

women here don't let no one touch them except during the Culling—and Romeo here ain't made it through one yet. Seems his pecker don't work right." He smacks the boy on the shoulder. "Where are your manners, kid? Kiss the lady's hand like a proper gentleman."

The kid doesn't move, and for a moment, I think he might start crying.

"I'm sorry about your mother," I say. "And you don't have to kiss me. Where I come from, people shake hands."

He gives my hand a quick squeeze, and Grizzly rolls his eyes.

"What's your name?" I ask, surprised at how big his hands are given how skinny he is.

He swallows, still looking embarrassed. "Peter."

"Nice to meet you." I force a smile. "You seem like a nice person, Peter."

"Petey here is the Prez's son," Grizzly says, "our one and only *dauphin*."

Peter rounds on him. "I'm not no fish."

Grizzly lets out a snort. "It's French, you retard—means you're the next king."

"Oh," the boy says, looking embarrassed.

"You shouldn't make fun of people who aren't as educated as you are," I say to Grizzly. "Besides, Peter's not the one who fucked up the world. You are." The old man's eyes get big, so I bet he knows what I mean. "And anyway," I add, "it's America. No one cares about dolphins—or silly old kings."

Peter half-smiles.

"Thank you," Grizzly says dryly, "for the history lesson, but I suggest you keep your colorful language to yourself in the future. Most folks around here ain't as... *tolerant* of uppity womenfolk as Ol' Griz. I'd hate to see that pretty little face of yours get beat up over a few bad words."

They hit people for swearing?

The door opens and Mikey strides back in. He glances at the chair and then at me. "So you decided to cooperate, did ya?" He runs his gaze leisurely down my body, his lip twitching. "Good. Makes it easier when it's my turn."

I stifle a cry and shuffle closer to Grizzly.

"Well it ain't your turn," Grizzly says, "so keep your pecker in your pants."

Mikey's carrying a bundle of fancy white cloth, and I notice that his right hand ends in a stump. He's missing all four fingers.

I try not to stare.

"Take off your clothes," he says and tosses the bundle at me. "And put that on."

I barely manage to catch it. "What?"

"You heard me," he says and hides his disfigured hand behind his back. "Do it, or I'll do it for you."

Grizzly steps between us. "Put the dress on over what you're wearing. Lord knows it ain't much."

I stand up and slip the full-length dress over my head, grateful to have something to cover my torn T-shirt. There's one long zipper on the side—something I've never seen before—but I manage to get it zipped up by myself.

The dress is decorated with the pearls and the sparkly things Miss Lucy wears on her fancy hats... *sequins*, I think they're called. It fits well—except the hem drags on the floor.

"It'll do," Mikey says, his eye twitching.

"As you may have guessed," Grizzly says, inclining his head toward Peter, "you are this young man's fiancée."

The blood rushes to my feet. "His what?"

"His bride-to-be, princess. Only yesterday, the Prez prayed for a grandson, and today you fell right out of the sky."

"I didn't f-fall out of the sky," I say, struggling to stay in control. "My plane ran out of fuel." My chest is so tight, I can scarcely get the words out. "You can't make me marry someone I just met. It's unethical!"

Mikey laughs. "You say the damnedest things."

A door opens, and loud organ music floods into the stuffy room.

Mikey grabs my arm, dragging me toward the door, and when I jerk away from him, he slaps me hard across the face.

"That's enough!" Grizzly says.

Mikey gives him a treacherous look and then grips my arm again. "Don't matter what you want, girly, long as you can bear children." He pulls me toward the oppressive music. "You got forty days with limp dick, here, because the law says so." He glances at the boy's pants and shrugs. "And then you'll be gettin' a visit from me." He uses his stump of a hand to turn my face toward his. "And if you don't submit, well then, we'll be pushing you out of the coal mine a bit early."

"Lordy me, they found the plane!" Lucy calls from the clinic hallway. She rushes in, her pillbox hat in hand. "Jack says they'll have more information any minute..."

I drop the bed sheets I'm folding and run out the door.

Shannon!

I sprint across the darkened expanse of Central Park toward the radio room, my lungs on fire.

You never should have let her go. You never should have trusted Mr. Miracle.

When we first got word that the Lou had failed, everyone was worried sick: a biodome full of people forced to evacuate and the closest help hundreds of miles away. We were told that someone had spoken to Madders—and the plane was headed back to KC.

That was over twelve hours ago.

When Kansas City hadn't heard from them by midnight, we all feared the worst: The plane had run out of fuel and gone down God knows where. KC assured us they would send out a search party at first light—and that there was nothing else to do except wait and see.

Please let my daughter be alive.

I rush through the door of the radio room and narrowly avoid crashing into Mindy's father, Jack.

"They've spotted the plane to the east of C-Bay," he says and gives me a hug.

I nod, still trying to catch my breath. "Shannon?"

"Everyone on board is fine, but they're low on fuel." He switches to speaker mode. "Ted," he says into his headset, "I've got Lani here. Can you give us an update?"

"Sure thing," the guy at C-Bay replies. "We have them on visual, and we're tracking their approach."

"Oh, thank goodness," I say, tears of joy streaming down my face.

Before you met Diego, you hadn't cried in years. Now it seems that's all you do.

"They're about thirteen nautical miles out," C-Bay says, "and Mr. Kirk is scrambling a rescue boat even as we speak. He's on the other line and will talk to you just as soon—hold on a sec..."

I glance over at Jack. "David sent a rescue boat?"

"Yeah. Pretty much everything up and down the East Coast is underwater—and has been for more than a decade. Last time I was there, the place was crawling with crocs."

"Probably alligators," I say, "but that's not much comfort."

"Well there's no need to worry, Doc," he says and squeezes my arm, "C-Bay is well above the high-water mark—including their runways—and the whole area is surrounded by a military-grade security fence."

The radio is quiet for another ten seconds and then crackles back to life. "Bub, I've just been informed that they are attempting a dead-stick landing on an old section of raised freeway. Stand by." The connection light goes out.

"What's a dead-stick landing?" I ask, my brain full of scattered parts, mangled bodies, and crazed gators.

"No engine power," Jack says. "But it's no big deal. Madders has probably done it hundreds of times." The look on his face betrays his real thoughts.

For twenty-seven excruciating minutes, I pace back and forth next to the silent radio, afraid that my one and only daughter is going to be swallowed up by an alligator-infested swamp.

Finally, I can't take it anymore. "What the hell's happening, Jack? Can't you call them up and ask?"

"I'm sure they'll get back to us as soon as they have any new information," he says. "They're probably talking to the plane right now, and we would be getting in the way."

"But that's my d-daughter out there!"

The receive light comes back on.

"Hey, cupcake." The voice is warm and confident.

"David!" I nearly shout. "What's going on?"

"Calm down, doll. Everything's fine. The rescue boat picked them up a couple minutes ago."

"Thank goodness." I wait for my heart to stop pounding. "Can you put Shannon on the moment she gets through the airlock, please?"

"Yeah, about that... I'm afraid she's not with them."

"What? W-where is she?" I shut my eyes, icy coldness filling my chest.

"Look, I'm sure everything will be fine, Lani. I haven't got all the details yet, but apparently Shannon's still at the biodome in Catersville. That's in Tennessee."

Jack and I exchange looks.

"I know where C-Catersville is, David. That biodome was all over the news a few years ago when... when they killed all those women by pushing them out—" I feel faint, and the next thing I know, I'm slumped on the floor.

I feel Jack's hand on my shoulder. "What about Diego?" he says. "Was he on the plane?"

"Yes," David says. "He and Hudson are fine, but they were forced to leave Shannon behind."

"Leave her?" Jack says. "For crying out loud, what happened?"

"When they were refueling the plane, a couple of men spotted Shannon hiding in the back and forced her out at gunpoint."

I feel sick to my stomach.

Oh God, no!

"Come again," Jack says, reaching out to help me up. "They what?"

"They forced her out of the airplane and were planning to take her inside the biodome. Hudson says they couldn't do anything to stop 'em."

Jack offers me his chair and I collapse into it, struggling to breathe. "What do you mean they c-couldn't do anything?" I say, gripping the microphone with both hands. "Why didn't Diego try to s-stop them?"

"Easy there, babe," Dave says. "I'm going to head down there and—"

"Just tell me what happened, David!"

He exhales. "Crusoe did try to stop them, but Catersville had a fifty caliber machine gun aimed at the plane. Apparently, shots were fired. Hudson tried to reason with them, and when that didn't work, things got ugly. Crusoe went all action-hero on a handful of paramilitary, and they beat him up pretty bad. By the sounds of it, he and Hudson were lucky to get out alive."

"What in *Pele's* name were they doing in Catersville?" I say, my fear giving way to anger. "Everyone knows the p-place is a loony bin. Madders would never take Shannon there."

"With St. Louis out of the picture, they needed fuel, and Catersville was the only viable option. It was that or go down in the woods."

"*Oka fefe*, David, I don't want to hear this. You have to d-do something. You have to get her out of there."

"It's not as bad as you think, Lani. As soon as I heard what happened, I got on the horn to Catersville, and I expect to hear back any minute. I don't have any reason to doubt what Hudson says, but I'm sure CV will have a different story. It may not be a pinnacle of democracy, but one of the original founders of the sect was a good friend of mine, and that biodome is one of the best there is—fully automatic environmentals and more backup systems than you can shake a stick at. Shannon will be safe there until I can get to her."

"Safe? With a bunch of religious fanatics that kill women who don't submit to them?"

"It would have been way worse if the plane had gone down in the Tennessee woods, Lani. So take a deep breath and give me a chance to do some negotiating."

"I will not calm down until my d-daughter is safe." I wipe the tears off my face. "You need to send someone to get her out of there right now."

"Look, I've dealt with these guys before. They may be able to bully neophytes and little girls, but I can take them down at any time, and you can bet your ass they know it. I built their biodome. If they mess with me, I'll send them back to the Stone Age. If that doesn't bring them to their knees, I have enough firepower here to blow them to kingdom come—but that's a last option. No point in killing innocents if we don't have to."

I can't concentrate on his words anymore. All I can think of is my daughter being captured and raped by those brutes. They could be torturing her, forcing her to do horrible things. *Why did I let her go with them?*

"What if they don't cooperate?" Jack says. "You can't blow up the biodome with Shannon in there." He looks at me, his eyes huge. "After all, Catersville is the place where they shoved all those people out the air—"

"Whoa there, Jacky-boy. You're not helping the situation. Didn't I just say Plan A is to negotiate? I'm not charging in guns a' blazing unless I have no other option. I know there are lots of nasty rumors about that place, but they are not going to hurt her. They may not see things the same as us, but they're not monsters."

"Yes, sir. Sorry, sir."

"There's no need to worry, Lani," David says, his voice sounding strong and confident—like the man I once fell in love with. "I'll get her back, babe. I promise."

I take a ragged breath, wanting to trust him but unsure if he's telling me the whole truth. "You can't leave her overnight, David. She won't last a week with those animals. What if they do things to her? Force her to… Oh, God, I'm begging you!"

Dave clears his throat. "That whole mutiny thing was a bunch of hearsay, Lani. I'm sure Shannon is fine—probably a bit scared—but fine."

"How do you know? Have you talked to her?"

"No, but we know their computers can still access the Eastern Grid. I'm pulling up the data on their biodome now. They haven't responded to our radio queries, but that doesn't mean they won't. Like I said, they have a jeep-mounted M2. I can't just waltz in there and ring the doorbell. We need to give them some time to cool off."

"I don't give a crap if you have to lock up everyone in the

whole biodome. I want my daughter back!"

"And you will get her back, Lani, but it's going to take some time. You need to tread cautiously around these types."

My anger burns out and leaves despair in its ashes. "You have to help her, David. Please, I'll do anything to get her back. She's only a child. I can't even imagine how terrified she must be."

"Poor kid," Jack says. "Locked up with all those pervert—"

"Shut it, Jack."

"Yes, sir."

"It's too bad it wasn't me in that plane," David says. "I *never* would have let them take her in the first place. All Diego needed to do was threaten to punch holes in their bio-suits, and those morons would have been stumbling all over themselves to get back Inside." I hear his tired sigh—it's after 3am. "Sorry. I didn't mean that—heat of the moment and all. It's not Diego's fault. He did the best he could in a bad situation."

"I want to talk to Diego," I say. "I want to know why he left Shannon at that lunatic asylum."

"The guy's a mess, Lani. They beat him up pretty bad. Catersville has a history of playing hardball. So give Mr. Crusoe a day or two to recover before you attempt to murder him again."

"Damn him," I say through tears. "His name isn't Diego Crusoe, it's James Nadales."

"So you already knew," David says. "I dug up his passport after Bella recognized him in one of the photos you sent. She swears he's had some sort of plastic surgery, but I'll be damned if I can figure out where. He was mixed up with the NSA back before Doomsday hit. I'm sending Hudson up to DC to see if they can uncover anything more on who he is—or what he was involved in."

I don't know what to say.

"In the meantime, I'm sending over instructions to deal with the failing section of the wall. I wish I could replace it, but the Bub's a one-of-a-kind prototype, and I don't have the parts. I'm working on some new technology that might eventually help, but for now, I want you to follow my directions to seal it off. I'll send the supplies back with Hudson."

I stare at the microphone, not really listening anymore.

Diego is some sort of ex-NSA operative who changed his identity? I don't know which is worse: the time machine story he told me or this.

"I'll give you a call in the morning with an update," David says. "In the meantime, try to get some sleep. I know you're worried about Shannon—and so am I—but running around like a chicken with its head cut off isn't going to help. And like I said, nothing bad is going to happen to Shannon."

I press my lips together, unable to speak.

"Thank you," Jack says. "We'll get working on the repairs right away, Mr. Kirk. Tell Madders we said safe travels."

"Hang in there, Lani," David says. "I'm doing everything I can to get your daughter back safe and sound. As soon as I have any new information, you'll be the first to know. And get on those biodome repairs ASAP."

"Will do, Mr. Kirk," Jack says.

"Good. And Lani?"

"Yeah," I say, my eyelids shut tight against the tears.

"Trust me, okay?"

He waits for me to reply, but it's all I can do to keep breathing.

I hear him sigh. "C-Bay out."

Chapter 3

Diego: Her

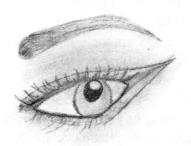

The sky is getting light when I stumble into the airlock at C-Bay still wearing Shannon's blanket from the plane. The others are already through, but C-Bay has me strip and breathe three minutes of bottled air to clear the virus out of my lungs. Then they make me toss my blanket and clothes out—and cycle the airlock again. I stand naked for another three minutes, shivering and waiting for the all-clear. Someone opens the inner door and tosses in some clothes. I put them on and limp through, wishing the wackjobs who beat me up had finished the job.

What are you going to tell Lani? You got her daughter raped and possibly killed?

Our rescuers are paramilitary, armed to the teeth with guns and Tasers, and there are more men in uniform waiting inside. Matt is already there, and the instant the door behind me shuts, one of the uniforms steps forward and gives me a crisp salute. "Welcome to C-Bay, Mr. Crusoe. I was told that you are in need of medical assistance. Would you like a wheelchair?"

I shake my head. "I've spent enough time in wheelchairs, thank you very much."

"Very well," he says. "I'm sure you're tired and hungry. So if you'll follow—"

"I want to speak to Mr. Kirk," I say. "About sending a rescue party to Catersville."

"I can assure you," he says, "that Mr. Kirk is well aware of Miss Kai's plight. Now then, if you'll follow me, I'll show you to your quarters."

Matt and I stare at each other, both of us feeling like something is… off.

"Mr. Crusoe," the uniformed man continues, glancing at his clipboard. "You have an appointment to have blood drawn at thirteen hundred hours, followed by a radiology exam, a biometric assessment, and a psychological evaluation." He turns to Matt. "Dr. Hudson, you are scheduled to fly out—"

"Excuse me," I say. "But I need to speak with Dave Kirk. Right now. Could you call him, please?"

"Mr. Kirk is a very busy man, Mr. Crusoe." The guy is short with dirty blond hair, and the huge mustache he's sporting—along with his knee-high leather boots—makes him look like a dime-store Civil War general.

Mierda, he looks like Custer. All he needs is the hat and horse.

"As I said," he continues, "Mr. Kirk is looking into the hostage situation, and I'm certain he will speak to you at his earliest convenience."

I start to protest, but he holds up his hand. "Although I understand your concern, Catersville is no longer your problem. As I'm sure you're aware, your ability to survive Outside is of the utmost importance to Mr. Kirk and everyone in this biodome. I have orders to let you sleep for five hours and then escort you to begin testing. I intend to follow those orders, Mr. Crusoe." He glances over at Matt. "Dr. Hudson, if you'll come with me."

Matt hesitates and then steps closer to me. "Commander Armstrong is it? I think your best bet would be to wake Kirk up and tell him we're here. He and I go way back, and I expect he'd want to talk to us in person. Pronto, if you catch my meaning?"

"I see." He nods at his men, and before I can react, they slap handcuffs on me.

Yep, Custer it is.

"We're all on the same team here, boys, and I sure wish you'd start acting like it." Custer turns to Matt. "Dr. Hudson, you're free to go."

Matt hesitates.

"I suggest you take advantage of it before I change my mind."

"Yes, sir." Matt nods at me. "I'll talk to Kirk and come find you later." He hurries off.

"Show Mr. Crusoe to his quarters," the commander says, stroking his mustache. "And get him something to eat."

Two men grab me from behind and start hustling me down the hallway.

"Wait," a muffled female voice says from behind us.

The uniforms freeze.

Something about her voice makes my throat tighten, but I'm too overwhelmed to sort it out.

"Let me see his face," she says.

"Of course, ma'am."

They haul me around.

The woman steps out of the shadows—tall and thin with a surgical mask over her face. Her limp blond hair is in a bun at the base of her neck, making her look like a middle-aged

Evita on her way to surgery.

"Bring him here." She speaks with undeniable authority, and the uniforms hustle to obey, dragging me along. We stop in front of her, the guards gripping my arms like I'm a traitor bent on murdering the queen.

She stares at me, her gaze like a floodlight. "Who are you?" Her voice is icy cold, but it makes my heart race. I'd recognize those eyes anywhere.

Isabel.

Custer answers for me. "Diego Crusoe, ma'am. We just brought him in."

"I know that, you idiot." She doesn't take her eyes off me. "What's his real name?"

He pokes me in the back. "Speak up, son."

I shrug. "I don't remember."

Above the mask, her eyebrows rise.

"I'm sorry," I say, staring into her stunning green eyes. "For everything." It's as if I'm speaking to a woman in another universe.

Christ, I've missed you.

She tips her head to the side, her eyes slits, and lets her gaze roam from my face, down to my chest and shoulders, and then back up to my mouth. "More like you don't want to remember." She grits her teeth, her eyes full of hatred. "And who could blame you? If you had even a shred of human decency, you would have stayed dead, James, and saved me the pain of remembering what you did to him—to us."

"To whom?" I say, my voice faltering. "What are you talking about?"

She slaps me hard across the face, and I stumble sideways into the guy on my right, tasting fresh blood.

A dog barks, and we all turn toward the sound.

"Is that what I think it is?" she asks Custer.

"Yes, ma'am. The puppy was in a pressurized cage in the

plane and just cleared quarantine. Cute little fella. I figure the men could take care of him. Feed him and train—"

"Let him out," she says, and a second later, Shannon's puppy comes barreling down the hallway, heading straight for me.

"Bearhart!" I say and lean over to greet him, but my captors restrain me.

Bella pulls off her gloves and mask, bends down, and puts her nose right up to the puppy's. "Bearhart, is it? What a sweetie you are!" She ruffles his ears, and a moment later he licks her face, his tail wagging his whole body.

She looks up at me, her eyes glossy. "I haven't seen a dog in decades. Where did you get him?"

"Matt brought him back from Seattle for Shannon Kai's eighteenth birthday. Shannon's the girl—"

"I know who she is," she says and stands back up, her expression hardening again. "It would seem you're an expert in felony child endangerment." She exhales through her teeth. "Get him out of my sight."

∞

I wake with a start.

A nurse comes in carrying a tray of food, her shoes squeaking as she power walks across the floor.

I wait for the cobwebs of sleep to clear enough to figure out where I am.

C-Bay. Without Shannon.

Mierda.

I have no idea how long they let me sleep, but it wasn't long enough. I feel like shit.

"Good afternoon, Mr. Crusoe. I've brought your lunch." The nurse sets a tray down on the bedside table and nods at a stack of clothing. "If you'd eat and freshen up, I'll be back in thirty minutes to change your bandages and escort you to have your blood drawn." She gives me a saccharin smile. "We can't sleep away the whole day, now, can we?"

"I'm not going anywhere until I talk to Captain Kirk."

She frowns. "I'm a nurse, Mr. Crusoe, not a magician. Mr. Kirk is a very busy man, and when he gets a chance, I'm sure he'll be over to speak with you. Until then, I suggest you cooperate. Handcuffs can be such a nuisance." She turns on her heel and walks out.

I haul myself out of bed, limp across the floor, and check the door.

It's locked.

Mierda, what have I gotten myself into?

One of my eyes is swollen shut, and my whole body hurts, but I manage to make my way into the small bathroom without incident. I splash warm water on my bruised face and then notice a pump bottle of liquid soap—something I never saw at the Bub.

What else do they have that the Bub doesn't?

After I dry off, I put on the clean clothes and comb my hair, tying it back with a rubber band I find sitting on my clothes. My backpack is in the corner. I take out Shannon's jaguarundi drawing and stick it up on the wall using Band-Aids from a cabinet.

I'm sorry, Shaz.

Lunch consists of three dry brown disks, a glop of greenish sludge that looks like bad guacamole, and a glass of tepid water with floaters. I take a sniff of the Soylent Green and almost retch. It smells like they scraped it off the bottom of a fishpond. I plug my nose and bite into one of the cookie-like things—and then spit it out, wondering how they get that heavy metal taste into salted cardboard.

I take a stale granola bar out of my pack and wash it down with my last bottle of water, feeling miserable.

At precisely one o'clock, Nurse Ratched comes in

pushing a wheelchair. Her eyebrows rise when she sees that I'm dressed, but fall again when she sees that I haven't eaten anything. "The seaweed baked with ground fish bones is very nutritious, Mr. Crusoe, and now it will go to waste." She clicks her tongue. "Need I remind you that we have lots of people to feed and very few natural protein sources?"

"Give it to them with my compliments."

She purses her lips and rolls the wheelchair around to the bed. "Are you going to cooperate, or shall I call security?"

"I don't need the damn chair."

"I was told to transport you in a wheelchair," she says and gestures toward the seat. "If you don't like it, take it up with the doctor."

I give up and sit down in the wheelchair, wondering if Lani knows about Shannon yet.

Christ, what am I going to tell her?

I spend the rest of the day being tested for diseases, deformities, and drugs. I'm poked, prodded, and pumped for information about my early childhood toilet training, but not one single person asks me about the biotech devices in my blood. Not one.

That evening, I'm brought back to my hospital room, where yet another round of inedible crap is waiting.

"Good night, Mr. Crusoe," Nurse Ratched says, tapping her foot as she waits for me to get out of the chair. "I will be back in the morning at eight o'clock sharp. I would appreciate it if you were ready." She pushes the wheelchair out, securing the door as she leaves.

The lights in the room go off at nine. I do ten push-ups, brush my teeth using real toothpaste, and then climb into bed. There's a light in the bathroom that I can't turn off, and I lie awake, staring at Shannon's jaguarundi drawing. When I finally fall asleep, my dreams are full of huge reptiles attacking her as I stand frozen, unable to do anything except watch.

In the morning, the lights come on at seven, and breakfast is waiting when I get out of the shower. It's the same crap as the day before, but I'm getting pretty hungry. I force down a bite. The salty glop hits my stomach like a rock, making me want to puke.

The nurse pushes in the wheelchair precisely at eight, takes one look at my tray, and gives me a disapproving look. "That's very wasteful, Mr. Crusoe."

"I wasn't hungry."

"Then I'll let the kitchen know that you won't be needing any lunch." She humphs. "Let's go. You have a very busy schedule today. First up, proctology."

Proctology? It's like someone is torturing me for shits and giggles.

"No," I say. "I'm done taking tests."

She stands there, lips tight, and I get the feeling no one's told her 'no' before.

"Goddamn it," I say, "you've done everything except chop me up into little bits to see if my legs regrow. I'm not submitting to any more tests until I speak to Dave Kirk."

She crosses her arms. "I'm sorry we're not living up to your expectations, Mr. Cru—"

"Now. So either call the guys with the handcuffs or tell Captain fucking Kirk to get his ass in here."

She snorts, her lips puckered. "There's no need to be vulgar, Mr. Crusoe."

"And would a goddamn bowl of oatmeal be too much to ask?"

"Unfortunately, this is a hospital—not a resort—so I strongly suggest you eat what you're served." She glances at the breakfast tray on my bed, and then turns the wheelchair around. "Things would go better for you if you kept that in mind."

Chapter 4

Shannon: False Pretense

The Giver of the Law, who has ink drawings all over her face and hands, is wearing black robes with an elaborate velvet hat.

She pins me with her gaze. "I said, do you take this man to be your lawful wedded husband?"

I've been kneeling on a hard wooden step for more than an hour, and my legs and back are cramping. Mikey has been standing behind me with his hand resting heavily on my shoulder while the woman drones on about *connubial fidelity, marital subjugation,* and *arrant submission.* I don't know what half of those words mean, but I can guess.

"Answer her." Heavy footsteps approach from behind.

I twist around and stare up into the pock-marked face of an older and meaner-looking white man—with Peter's reddish hair.

"Speak up, blondie," Peter's father says, his eyes narrowed and his hands twitching at his sides.

"I don't want to get married," I say, fighting back tears. "Not to Peter or anyone."

The man slaps me with the back of his hand, and I fall sideways against Mikey, my eyes watering.

No one moves to help me.

Peter's father steps closer. "I don't think I heard you right."

Mikey drags me back onto my knees.

"Say yes," Peter whispers, not looking at me. "Please."

"Beggin' don't become you, boy," Mikey says. He increases his grip on my shoulder. "But Petey's right, girly. Won't do no good to fight. Just get you killed—and that'd be a damn waste."

"Ask her again," Peter's father says, and the woman in the robes repeats her question.

I tuck my hand into a fold of the dress and cross my fingers. "Yes," I whisper, and Mikey releases me.

"Don't think the folks in back heard you," Peter's father says.

"Yes," I repeat louder, tears streaming down my face.

"I now pronounce you man and wife," the Giver says. "You may kiss the bride."

Peter leans over and gives me a peck on the cheek.

His father lets out a derisive snort. "You're gonna have to do better than that, boy, or I'll be taking her for myself."

I swallow and turn toward Peter. He shifts his weight, his face ashen. I meet his gaze and give a slight nod—and then shut my eyes.

He kisses me on the lips.

I open my eyes in time to see the Giver make a sour face. She turns and disappears through a hidden door in the wall.

Mikey snorts and drags me up off my knees, "Let's go,

girly. The sooner his pecker fails, the sooner I'll be poking you with mine."

I burst into tears.

Peter's father grabs my arm and jerks me around to face him, making me drop the fake flowers I've been clutching. "You stop that blubbering, woman, or I'll give you something to cry about."

I look up at him, my lips pressed together to keep from sobbing, and then the words tumble out. "Is that also by the Book? Forcing young girls to get married and beating them up if they refuse?"

I hear gasps from around us.

He lifts his hand to strike me again, but Peter steps between us. "She's my wife now," he says. "If she needs to be taught a lesson, I'm the one to do it."

His father laughs. "That's the spirit, boy. 'Bout time you started acting like a man. Bedding an unbroken woman will do you good, long as you don't spare the rod."

I gasp. "Are you going to hurt me, Peter?"

"Well?" his father says. "You gonna discipline her or not?"

Peter turns to me, his eyes cold. "You open your mouth again without permission, wife, and I'll beat that lily-white ass of yours to a bloody pulp. You hear me?" He leans over, his forehead almost touching mine. "I said, did you hear me?"

He's just like all the others.

"Yes," I whisper and drop my gaze to my socks.

"Yes, *sire*," Peter's father says.

"Yes, sire."

"And pick up those damn flowers," he says. "You a retard or somethin'?"

"Yes, sire," I repeat, glancing up at Peter. I scoop up the ugly bouquet, my hands trembling so hard I almost drop it again.

"You best put a son in her before the next Culling," the

man says to Peter, "or she joins the others, just like it says in the Commandments." He runs his hand roughly across my cheek. "Although I'm inclined to give her a lesson or two myself—no point in having the blind lead the blind, if you get my meaning."

"That's against the l-law," Peter says, his voice breaking.

"Might be necessary to invoke *Primae Noctis*." His father squeezes my breast like it's a loaf of bread. "Show you how to handle a woman who don't know her place."

"You promised she'd be mine," Peter says, his voice pleading, "I helped bring her in."

"I ain't gonna keep her," he says, laughing. "Just break her in for you." He drags his hand down to my crotch. "Grab me a little pussy."

"No!" Peter says and pushes his father away.

The man wheels around and seizes his son by the throat. "You lay a hand on me again, boy, and I'll cut it off—same as I did to that mouthy, insolent mother of yours."

"Yes, sir." Hatred flares in Peter's eyes—and disappears just as quickly.

"That mouthy bitch may be yours," his father says, "but that don't mean you can forget your place."

Peter lowers his gaze. "Forgive me, father."

The man grunts. "Still, I'm a merciful man. Since she's your first, I'll give you a chance to take her. Woman like that's gonna fight, and it'll do you good to break her in."

Peter nods, not even attempting to escape his father's grip.

"But the next time she disrespects me, I'll teach her a lesson she won't forget. You hear me?"

Peter nods, and his father releases him, leaving a ring of red flesh around his son's neck. "Speak up, boy."

Peter flexes his shoulders, but doesn't look away. "I heard you."

His father sneers. "You're just like your mother, and if you're not careful, you'll end up hanging from the same rafter."

The man raises his hand, and Peter shuts his eyes.

"Coward."

The men around us laugh.

Peter's father spits, and a fleck of saliva lands on Peter's face. "My only son is a spineless pantywaist, God help me." He whirls around and jabs his finger at me. "Take off that damn dress, blondie. You look like a tramp in a second-hand store."

I glance around at the gawking stares of the men. "In front of everyone?"

Peter's father reaches for me, the veins in his neck bulging.

"Do it, wife," Peter says, his eyes averted. "And be quick about it."

I step backward, unzip the dress with trembling hands, and step out of it.

"Whew-wee," Mikey says under his breath and yanks the dress out of my hands. "My pecker's ready."

Someone wolf whistles, and the crowd laughs.

I stand there in my torn T-shirt and shorts, my arms folded across my chest.

"You got forty days." Peter's father turns on his heel and strides out of the chapel, the rest of the men trailing like hungry dogs.

Peter wipes the spit off his face. "Follow me," he says, his voice wavering. "They'll leave us alone once we get to the Chamber of Release."

Chamber of Release?

I hesitate, afraid of what he intends to do to me.

"I won't touch you," he says, reading the look on my face, "long as you do what I say."

I nod once, wishing with all my heart that I had listened to Mom.

"And try to act dutiful," he adds, dropping his gaze.

I stare at him, fear paralyzing me.

He swallows and looks up. "I'm sorry about those things I said, but I didn't want them to…"

I nod again.

He exhales and then turns and strides down the aisle, his steps silent on the threadbare carpeting. "Follow me, wife," he calls out, his voice sounding hollow in the empty chapel. "And keep your head bowed or it will go the worse for you!"

I let out a soft whimper and obey, too overwhelmed to do otherwise.

Peter leads me down another long hallway and out into a deserted open area. It must have been a park once, but all that's left are tree stumps, dirt, and what I realize are hand-carved grave markers.

I hurry across the cemetery, rocks and twigs cutting into my feet through the thin socks. I steal a look at the roof of the biodome but can't see any signs of damage, only the dim glow of the crescent moon. Peter catches me staring up but doesn't comment. Instead, he quickens his pace, and I stumble after him, my head bowed and my heart pounding.

He strides down more hallways, opening doors with some sort of metal key and locking them again after we pass through. Finally, he stops in front of an ornate wooden door, a huge brass knocker hanging in the middle of it. He pulls the door open and waits for me to enter, his eyes downcast.

"It's Shannon," he says as he shuts the door and turns the deadbolt. "Right?"

CHAPTER 5

Diego: The Good Guys

Ten minutes after Nurse Ratched leaves with the Soylent Green, the man who haunts my nightmares walks in and offers me his hand.

"I'm David Kirk, head of C-Bay," he says. "I hear you wanted to see me."

I stare at him for a moment, unnerved by how much he looks like his doppelganger in my world—except this Dave Kirkland has less hair and more flab.

"Have we met before?" he asks. "Something about you seems familiar."

"No, I don't think so," I say and shake his outstretched hand. "Diego Crusoe. Thanks for stopping by."

"My pleasure, Mr. Crusoe. We're awful glad you made it here safe and sound."

"Thank you for your help." I say, shifting my bum leg and

sitting up straighter. "And please call me Diego."

"Certainly, Diego. I would have gotten here sooner, but I've been tied up looking through blueprints for Catersville. I know you must be worried about Shannon, but believe me, I want to get her out of there as much as you do."

"You know her?" I can't keep the surprise out of my voice.

Maybe the Dave in this world isn't such a dick?

He laughs. "Of course I do! Lani and I go way back, and there's nothing I wouldn't do to protect them."

Dave and Lani? Dave and Isabel?

Can't this guy find his own women?

He pulls up the chair and sits down. "I wish Lani had consulted me before sending Shannon out here with you and Hudson—I could have had my private jet stop by next month—but that's water under the bridge." He gives me a warm smile. "So what can I do for you, Diego?"

Mierda, he seems like a decent guy.

"I want to help," I say, feeling off-balance talking to him without wanting to throw something. "I mean help get Shannon back. I was hoping you were putting together an expedition to pull her out of there."

"I'm considering all options."

"Christ, Dave, they're a bunch of religious zealots, and they're probably planning to use her as a sex slave or—"

"Whoa there, Hoss." He holds up his hands. "You're right about the place being a bit unusual—and maybe you ran into a bad *hombre* or two—but they're still people. Some of them are old friends of mine."

"You know those guys?"

"Of course I do. I know pretty much everyone who survived."

"Right."

"Doomsday forced incredible hardships on all of

mankind, and it's only natural that some people..." He rubs his chin with his hand. "Well, that some people took different paths. Folks are naturally afraid of outsiders—and these days, it makes good sense. The disease vector in an isolated population is enough to make anyone piss their pants. Fear of dying makes you do some crazy shit."

"You mean like kidnapping teenage girls?"

"Easy there, cowboy."

All of a sudden, I remember why I don't like this guy.

"I haven't spoken with the head honcho yet," he says, "but word is, he took her for her own safety."

"What!?" It comes out as more of a croak than a word. "You think they dragged her out of the plane at gunpoint for her own protection?"

"Just because they're religious doesn't mean they're evil. They know right from wrong. Let's give them a chance to explain things before we charge in there with guns a' blazing."

"I can't believe you are taking them seriously. They kidnapped Shannon, and you're going to let them get away with it?"

"Of course not. PC estimates that Catersville is down to fewer than a hundred bodies, the majority of them men over fifty."

"Who the hell is PC?"

"Population Control. Where have you been for the last twenty years? I'm not saying it's a good thing they took her, I'm saying we should get all the facts. Despite what you may have heard, they're not a bunch of teenage hooligans thinking with their dicks."

"They damn well are. They took her against her will and beat the crap out of me when I tried to stop them."

"Pro tip, *amigo*: Speak softly and carry a big stick."

I stare at his thinning blond hair and ruggedly handsome face, trying to fit my Dave Kirkland into the savior of mankind—and failing. "So how are you planning to get her back?"

"Like I said, I'll find a way to persuade them to let her go."

"What the hell do you mean 'find a way'?" I say, knowing I'm starting to sound like a petulant child, but unable to stop. "I thought you already sent a rescue party."

"I built their fucking biodome, Domingo."

Ah, there's the Dave I know and love.

I resist the urge to correct him. "What does that have to do with anything?"

He looks annoyed. "I can hack their computers—and I have access to their O_2 and water filtration systems. In a week, they'll be begging me to come get her. But if it makes you feel any better, the moment negotiations fall through, I'm prepared to send in a few dozen badasses. I can get her out of there faster than a babysitter's boyfriend hightailing it when the car pulls up."

"I'll go with you."

He laughs again. "You got dog tags hiding underneath all that hair?" He reads the look on my face. "Didn't think so. The last thing we need is for you to go stumbling ass-backward into machine gun fire. Your job is here, where we can science the shit out of that magic in your blood."

I turn and stare at Shannon's jaguarundi, frustrated by my inability to do anything useful. "Shannon's like a daughter to me. I can't just stand around waiting for you to bring her back. She's my responsibility. I'm the reason she's in danger. Can't you understand that?"

"Believe me, I do. You have my word that I won't rest until we bring her home."

I don't respond.

"Look, the best thing you can do is stay here and help us with the biotech research."

I shake my head. "Not while Shannon is stuck out there with a bunch of weirdos. I can't live with myself, knowing what might happen to her."

"Hell, James, I admire your balls—but I can't have some amateur putting my men in danger."

"James?"

He laughs and rubs the back of his neck with his hand, his face getting red. "Like I said, you look like a guy I used to know—was my best buddy, actually. You wouldn't happen to have a sickle-shaped scar on your wrist, now would you? Something you got climbing on the Great Pyramid?"

It takes me a moment to realize he's serious. "Nope," I say and hold out my wrists. "I've never been to Egypt."

If my parallel self was gallivanting around the world with Dave, things went down a lot differently in this universe .

He looks doubtful. "To tell you the truth, you're the spitting image of him—James, I mean—except he would be twenty years older than you. I keep telling myself that it's impossible, but the likeness is uncanny."

"What happened to him?" I ask.

"He died in a car accident thirty years ago. Lost control on an icy bridge and drove into a river. His five-year-old son was in the backseat. Both of them drowned."

I'm dead, and I killed my own son?

I swallow. "Christ, that must have been horrible for his wife."

"Yeah, it was," he says, "but you're clearly not James." He laughs—which feels odd considering he just told me his best friend died in a gruesome wreck.

"So what happened to her—James's wife, I mean? Did she make it inside a biodome?"

"She did—thanks to yours truly. After their funeral, she moved back to California—tried to start a new life. A decade later, the Feds dumped that rogue nuke in the Pacific, and the biodome she was scheduled to move into ended up in the drink. When Doomsday mutated, I managed to get her into the Bub—and believe me, with over 250 pre-paid customers displaced by that damn tsunami, it wasn't a picnic."

So some of the events played out the same here—except they had Dave's biodomes to protect them.

I shake my head, remembering the night the nuke was launched. The roads were a mess, and when I finally managed to get to Isabel, I was forced to wait outside her building, hoping we'd all survive until morning. "I imagine it wasn't."

"But back to Shannon," Dave says. "Use your head, Diego. I got the largest, best-trained, best-armed army this side of the Urals, *and* I have the inside track on the life-support at Catersville. You got a guilty conscience and a death wish. Who do you think is going to have more success getting Shannon back?"

I take a deep breath, trying to put all the pieces together.

"You know I'm right, buddy." He gives me that condescending nod of his.

"Okay," I finally say, too beat down to continue fighting with him. "You're right."

"I knew you'd see it my way." He pats me on the shoulder like he's my dad. "Promise me you won't go running off after Shannon, and I'll persuade Bella to call off the dogs—get her to stop serving you that green crap." He nods at the breakfast tray. "God Almighty, even the pigs won't eat that shit."

"Sure," I say.

"Good man."

"Who's Bella?"

"She's the woman I was telling you about—James's wife. Like I said, the three of us were real close." He scans my face, looking for what, I don't know. "I married Bella a few years after he died."

Bella. Isabella. Oh my God. It is her—and she's married to Dave Kirk!

He rubs one eyebrow. "I was told you two already met—when my men brought you in."

"Sort of," I say, my thoughts racing. "She must have assumed I was James too—and she wasn't particularly happy to see him."

"Can't blame her for that. His death was pretty rough on her. And I think she blamed him for their son's death too—but it's not like he would have driven their car off a bridge on purpose, for Christ's sake."

"Right."

He stands up. "Why don't you join us for supper this evening? Straighten things out?" He glances at my clothes. "I'll have somebody drop off a suit and tie. How does seven-thirty sound?"

Suit and tie?

"Uh, fine, thanks. But I have one more question—a favor actually."

"Shoot."

"Is there any way I can talk to Lani, explain what happened—maybe try to apologize?"

"I'll see what I can do."

"I'd appreciate it."

He walks to the door and then turns back, half smiling. "So, *do* you remember anything? I mean, from before you fell out of that tree?"

I shake my head. "Sorry."

He nods and turns away, letting the door swing shut—and I hear him mumble to himself, "Probably best if it stays that way."

CHAPTER 6

Lani: Dead Wrong

I place the radio headphones over my ears and shut my eyes, determined not to cry.

"I'm sorry," he says, the sound of his voice tearing me up inside. "I can't tell you how sorry I am about Shannon."

I sit there, staring at the illuminated connection light, unable to move or speak.

"If I'd known," he says, "what was going to happen at the Lou—and Catersville—I never would have taken her. Everyone says it was a freak combination of bad luck and ill timing, but I take full responsibility for what happened. I made a terrible mistake."

I focus on my breathing, knowing that any words I say will be bent and torn by my stuttering.

He waits for me to speak, and when I don't he continues. "It was stupid of me, Lani. I shouldn't have assumed I knew what was best for Shannon. I'm sorry. I was an idiot. Can you forgive me?"

He remains silent for ten long seconds.

"Christ, Lani, say something."

I suck in a breath of air that seems too thin to sustain me. "How are you going to get her out of that hellhole, Nadales?"

"Well…" I hear him swallow. "Dave is working night and day to get her back. He's attempting to negotiate with Catersville right now." More silence. "And if that doesn't work, he's got a plan to send a team of hotshots in to get Shannon out—"

"I already t-talked to David," I say. "He called me the minute they spied your plane and again when Madders told him what had happened to Shannon."

"Ah. Right." He exhales. "So you know we're going to get her out of there."

"Are you going with them?"

"*Mierda*, Lani, I'm not much of a military man, and they need me here at the lab. Everyone involved thought it would be best if I stay put and—"

I let my anger strike like a coiled snake. "I don't c-care what the *kahuna* 'everyone involved' thinks, Nadales. 'Everyone involved' isn't responsible for getting my one and only d-daughter kidnapped by a bunch of religious lunatics who intend to rape her until she dies in childbirth or can no longer produce offspring."

I hear his sharp intake of breath.

"And now you're t-telling me that the most important thing you can do is lounge around the hospital cafeteria waiting for some intern to draw your blood while Shannon rots in a prison full of sexual predators? For Christ's sake, Diego, you're immune. Why didn't you do something?"

The silence is oppressive.

"I'm sorry, Lani. I fucked up. I don't know what else to

say."

"Yeah, I got it. Unfortunately, I don't have time to hang around and listen to you soothe your guilty conscience. My daughter's in mortal peril, and I've got a biodome full of panicked people trying to survive the next storm. It's been nice chatting with you."

"Lani, wait! What happened?"

"A section of the wall collapsed, but 'everyone involved' thinks it's not your worry. So why don't you toddle back to your coffee and donuts and stop wasting my time?"

"Was anyone hurt? Are you okay?"

"What the fuck do you care?"

He doesn't respond.

"And in case I'm not being perfectly clear, I don't want to hear your voice or see your face until I have my daughter back. And if those perverts have done *anything* to hurt her, Nadales, anything…" I take a slow, angry breath. "I'll fucking kill you."

I slam my fist down on the disconnect button—and then sit there and cry.

There's a knock on the door, and Jack the radio operator peeks in. "Madders just landed."

I nod and head over to the main airlock.

I stare out at the empty sky, unable to believe how much my life has changed in a handful of days. When Madders makes his way inside, he drops his stuff and pulls me into a bear hug.

"I feel terrible about what happened to Shannon, Lani. I'm so sorry."

I blink back tears. "I never should have let her go. I should have insisted that she stay here and…" The floodgates burst, and I sob against his chest. "Oh, Madders, I can't believe my baby's gone."

"We're going to get her back, Lani. David's a smart,

resourceful man, and he'll come up with a way to get her out of there. But you have to give him a little time. What with the Lou failing, the Catersville fiasco, and the Bub on the edge of failure, he's up to his eyeballs in emergencies."

He rubs my back, waiting for me to regain control, and then we go to collect his luggage. "Speaking of which, how is the repair effort coming along?"

"We started a couple of days ago," I say, "following the plans that David sent. The work requires cannibalizing pieces of the inner wall from the storage area. We reinforced it after the bomb, and we're using an extra piece from there to cover the hole."

"Yes," he says. "That's a good idea. Did it work?"

"Last I heard they were attempting to move the wall section into place and seal the edges."

"Good," he says. "Once they finish with that, we'll need to weld the struts that Kirk sent to reinforce things a bit." He glances out the window. "How long do we have?"

"Seattle says they can see a storm brewing over the Pacific. Probably be here in a week or so."

"Has the council come up with an evacuation plan?"

I look over at him, knowing that the chances of us making it to Salt Lake City are laughable. "They want us to take a thousand kilometer trek over some of the world's highest mountains."

"Bloody hell. Let's hope it doesn't come to that."

I put my hand on his arm, unable to wait any longer. "Madders, I need your help."

"Of course, Lani. What is it?"

"I need you to fly me to Catersville. Help me get Shannon out."

He frowns. "But—"

I put up my hands. "Please. Hear me out. David helped build Catersville, and he knows it like the back of his hand.

There must be some way to get in."

"Of course there is," Madders says. "Kirk had emergency airlocks built into all the biodomes. But you won't be able to sneak in. They're not connected to the biodome's electrical grid, but they are linked into the Breach Alert System. If someone opens the airlock, it's gonna show up on the monitors in big, colored lights."

"Not if they don't have access to the control center. I dug up an old satellite photo of Catersville taken right after the explosion. David says it's in that sector. If he's right, they won't have any idea we're there."

He rubs his chin with his hand. "I imagine it could be done."

"And we could take some meds to barter with," I say, "in case we get caught."

He exhales. "You know I'd do anything to get her back, Lani, but even if we could get in *and* find her *and* bring her back out, we'd be stuck there with no fuel for the plane. If you're counting on Catersville filling us up, I don't think—"

"I'm not. We can land at the Lou. I talked to Shelly, and there's a crew there now rebuilding the generator. They have a small section pressurized, and they're flying supplies in from Omaha. Shelly says they'll trade us fuel for medical supplies. We could fill up the plane at the Lou and then fly to Catersville and back on a single tank."

He closes his eyes, his lips moving as he does the calculations in his head. "I imagine it's possible—but it's a big ask, Lani. We won't be able to get inside without setting off alarms, and we already know they have lots of firepower. The fuel will be tight, and whether landing the plane close enough is even feasible—"

"Don't lecture me," I say. "I know it's going to be hard. Will you help me or not?"

He takes a deep breath, rubbing his hand across his

face. "Give me a chance to unload the plane and check on the repair. We can go over your plans this evening, and if everything checks out, we'll leave as soon as the wall is fixed, okay?"

I throw my arms around his neck, tears streaming down my face again. "Thank you."

He puts his hands on my shoulders and steps back. "Can you hear that?"

I listen for a moment and then nod, my chest getting tight. "Yes. It sounds like the groan steel makes when it's bending."

There's a loud screech of metal on metal, and the biodome shudders. A thin cloud of dust falls from the ceiling.

And then someone screams.

"Oh, bloody hell." Madders lets go of me right as Shannon's best friend, Mindy, comes racing around the radio building.

"There's been an accident!" she says, breathing hard. "In the construction area. They need a doctor!"

"What happened?" I ask as we rush back the way she came.

"I was babysitting some D-2s when that piece of wall they're trying to install fell on the crew. My dad's under the rubble!"

"Grab my bag from the clinic," I say to Mindy. "And have Lucy and Becky meet me there."

She nods.

"Go, go!"

She takes off running.

By the time we get to the construction site, the crew has managed to pry up the fallen section of the wall. Underneath are three unlucky men. Two of them are torn up pretty badly, but don't appear to have any broken bones. The third man is Mindy's father, Jack—our radio operator. His leg is crushed, and he's lost a lot of blood. His pupils aren't responding, and I think he may have broken his back in the fall. Thankfully, he's still breathing.

I have Lucy and Becky attend to the first two while I try to stabilize Jack.

There's a loud groaning sound above us, and I look up. The emergency patch they put up a few days ago is tearing loose.

It takes only a glance at Madders to see how dangerous that is.

"Everyone put on a mask!" he shouts and then turns to the crew leader. "Get everyone out of here as quickly as possible." He grabs one of the council members. "Go increase the air pressure to the max and start the sequence to seal off this sector of the bubble. Hurry."

"Are you sure?" The frightened woman's eyes are huge. "If we do that, we'll lose access to the filtration system and the communications center."

"Better than having the whole damn fishbowl contaminated. Send anyone you can spare to move the radio equipment out, and have someone set the filtration system to automatic."

As she scurries off, Madders turns back to the assembled crowd. "Get those damn masks on now! This is not a drill. If you are not helping here, get to the communications room immediately."

He looks down at me. "Can you get these blokes out of here without me?"

Jack moans as I work to stem the blood flow in his crushed leg. "Yes."

"Okay. I'm gonna see if I can reattach that patch." Someone hands him a rebreather and he puts it on. "Get your mask on now, Doc."

I nod and take the mask Shannon made for me off my

belt. "Be careful!" I call out.

"Always am." He takes a couple of the repair crew and hurries off.

I send two women to get a backboard from the pool. "Put those masks on now!" I yell after them.

I fit my mask onto Jack, securing it the best I can without moving his neck. Then I take a moment to search through the debris until I find the mask he was carrying on his belt. I put it on, wishing I had told Shannon how proud I am of her, wishing she could see how many lives her rebreathers might end up saving—wishing she were still here with me.

I hope you're okay, baby. I love you.

I see Lucy and Becky head for the clinic with their charges.

Good.

I glance down at Mindy's dad. "Don't die on me, Jack."

I flag down four D-1s who have been through a training rotation at the clinic and quickly check that their masks are on properly.

"We need to get him out of here as quickly as possible," I tell them, "but if his back is broken, any twisting movement to his spine will paralyze him for life. I need you to make sure his neck doesn't move while I get him stabilized. Okay, folks?"

The D-1s nod, their eyes wide.

"Once the backboard arrives," I say, "we'll lift him onto it and get him to the infirmary."

"Is he going to make it?" Mindy asks, her face pale.

"Yes," I say, determined to make it so.

We hear the announcement to put on a mask and exit the sector immediately, and a moment later, the wooden backboard arrives.

Just as the huge bulkhead door behind me clangs shut, I hear a desperate yelp from Madders.

"Shite!"

I glance up as the patch swings away from the exterior wall of the biodome, exposing a small sliver of deadly blue sky.

For the first time in twenty years, I can feel a soft breeze blowing against my skin—and then the breach alarm goes off.

I hope to hell they got all the bulkheads closed in time.

Those of us left in the contaminated room turn and look at each other. The faces staring back at me are frightened and silent, some of them Outside for the first time in their lives.

Counting the injured man, there are ten of us, all with Shannon's re-engineered masks on, and all still breathing.

I turn back to the D-1s, attempting to keep my voice level. "Keep your masks on and make sure that Jack's doesn't slip off. On three, help me lift him onto the board."

"We're ready." Mindy's hands are shaking, but her movements are calm and controlled.

"We're all going to be fine," I say. "We'll go out through the airlock in the storage area and get back inside through the main entrance."

Their heads bob again.

"One, two, three."

We manage to get him on the backboard without mishap, and a second later, Madders joins us, a nasty gash on his arm. I stare at the bright red blood, suddenly worried that the biotoxin will enter through the wound and kill him—even though I know the virus is airborne and can't survive in the alkaline environment of blood.

He shakes his head, reading my mind. "I'm fine, Doc. Let's get Jack to the clinic."

All eight of us lift the backboard and carry the man through the evacuated section of the bubble. As we pass the open doors of the communications room, I notice a body slumped on the floor in a puddle of frothy bile and blood. The sight brings back horrible memories, and I fight down the urge to panic.

Madders takes a closer look inside the room and then comes out with an armful of cables. He closes the doors. "It's too late. He should have heeded the warnings to use a mask."

We pass two more lifeless bodies in pools of vomit and blood. "Keep your eyes on the patient," I say using my doctor voice, "and avoid any abrupt movements. Saving this man's life is our priority here."

We carry the wounded man out through the open airlock and into the bright sunshine. I can hear sobs coming from the D-1s—and some of the adults too.

A minute later, we step inside the main airlock and press the *Emergency Cycle* button. As the outer door slides shut, I turn toward Madders, and he lets out a startled gasp.

"Are you okay?" he asks, his eyes wide.

"Yeah, I'm fine," I say, wondering why he looks so frightened.

"Your mask is broken," he says and brings his hand up to my faceplate. "You've been exposed to the virus."

"What?" I run my fingers across the fractured plastic. The gash in the faceplate is wide enough to get my pinky through. I stand there for a moment, waiting for the convulsions to start.

But nothing happens—except my mask fogs up from my panicked breathing.

"It must have been broken when I put it on," I say, trying to remember. "I gave Jack my mask and eventually found his. I was too busy to check it. I didn't—"

"It's okay, Lani," Madders says and steadies my arm. "You must be immune like Diego, or you'd be..."

"I'd be curled up on the floor in a pool of my own feces,"

I finish for him. "The most lethal virus known to mankind has somehow failed to kill me?"

"It would seem that way."

The airlock finishes cycling, but the inner door doesn't open and the *Virus Detected* sign continues flashing.

I reach around Madders, push the button to reverse the cycle, and pull off the broken mask. "If the virus is already inside my lungs, I can't go in with you."

The exit door slides open, and I step back Outside.

The D-1s are all staring at me with their mouths hanging open.

"Get Jack to the clinic," I say, "and then rig up the ultraviolet lamp—same as we did when we brought Diego in."

Madders nods. "I'll be back in a few minutes."

I lift the clear plastic cover on the outer wall, slap the *Start Cycle* button, and watch the airlock door slide shut.

The moment it's closed, I drop the broken mask and slide down the wall into the overgrown weeds. I take a deep breath and gaze up at the cloudless sky, my heart still racing.

All these years you were immune, your own DNA containing the key to going back Outside, and you never guessed.

I pluck a dandelion puff with a trembling hand, bring the delicate sphere up to my mouth, and blow.

The tiny parachutes float up in the cool breeze, twirling in the late-afternoon sunlight.

Life goes on.

Chapter 7

Diego: Ghost Busters

Bella opens the front door of what can only be described as the Kirk Mansion, her eyes red and her mascara smeared.

I take a step backward, my heart racing. "Hi."

She glares at me.

The difference between *my* Isabel and *this* Isabella is staggering. Bella is starvation thin and wearing a floor-length gold lamé dress. Her platinum blond hair is limp and straight, her lips are thin and tight, and her face is caked with so much makeup that I wonder if she spent the whole afternoon applying it.

"Um…" I say. "Am I interrupting?" I point over my shoulder. "If so, I can get some dinner back at the hospital…"

She stares at me, her swollen eyes devoid of life.

I glance past her, looking for Dave—and the significance

of that is not lost on me. "Mr. Kirk, your husband," I say, "told me about your other husband—I mean about your *first* husband, of course." I swallow, trying to get my brain to engage. "About what happened to James and your son."

Mierda.

"I'm so sorry about the accident," I say, my heart aching for her. "I can't imagine living through such a tragedy. It must have been terrible for you."

"You couldn't just abandon me?" she says, spitting the words out. "You had to take Lucas too?"

"What?" I step back, holding up both my hands. "Wait a sec. I—"

"And now you have the gall to come back and taunt me—looking *exactly* the same as you did the day you murdered my son?"

I exhale and lower my hands. "I had nothing to do with your son's death. I know I look a lot like his father, but it's a terrible coincidence. I assure you, I'm not him. I'm not... James Nadales."

Her eyes narrow, and she looks more closely at my face. "Then who are you?" she says, her nostrils flaring. "You have the same voice, the same eyes, the same damn—"

"Where are your manners, Bella?" Dave steps around his wife and offers me his hand. "Good to see you again, Diego. Please forgive my wife. She's convinced you've been on ice for thirty years and just now got defrosted." He chuckles at his own joke. "You know women."

I force a laugh and shake his hand, still trying to come to terms with Dave being my best bud and Isabel hating my guts. "Thanks again for the dinner invitation."

"Of course. Come in, come in." He puts his arm around his wife and steers her back into the house. "I told you, darling, he's not James. I agree there's a remarkable likeness—and he certainly had me going the first time I saw him—but last time I checked, cryogenic chambers haven't been invented yet."

"They never found the bodies," Bella says, keeping her eyes trained on me as her husband shuffles her inside and shuts the door.

"Do you honestly expect anyone to believe that James is still alive, Bella?" Annoyance spills from Dave's voice. "After nearly thirty years and all that's happened?" He lets go of his wife and turns to me, shaking his head. "God Almighty, if she doesn't get crazier every year."

I follow him into a foyer that is larger than Lani's whole apartment.

"By the way," he says, stopping in front of a glass and silver wet bar, "I did get a message through to Catersville. Ted is trying to arrange a meeting for tomorrow morning, and after that, I'll have more details on Shannon's situation."

"That's great news," I say. "Thank you." Dave can be a pain in the ass, but at least he's true to his word—and he did build all these biodomes.

Christ, if it wasn't for him, all the people in this universe would be dead—including you.

"How did your talk with Lani go?" he asks.

"Not so hot," I say.

Dave drops ice cubes into a glass. "She's taking the Shannon thing pretty hard, but I'm not sure why she blames you." He claps me on the shoulder. "It's not as if you had much choice in the matter."

Bella lets out a shriek. "How can you say that?" She glares at me. "He's a serial murderer!"

A pained expression crosses Dave's face. He turns to his wife. "No he's not. He was in the wrong place at the wrong time, and in any case, Shannon is going to be just fine."

"She's right to blame me," I say. "Lani didn't want Shannon to go, but I talked her into it. I convinced her it was the right thing to do." I decline the glass of whiskey he offers me. "It's no wonder she hates me. *I* hate me."

"There does seem to be a spate of that going around," Dave says and gives me a conspiratorial wink. "But a man's gotta do what a man's gotta do, right?" He glances at Bella—who is still standing in the doorway. "Bella, darling?"

She gives no indication that she's heard him.

"Come here, princess, and let me pour you a drink."

I cringe, knowing what *my* Isabel would say if Dave called her *princess*—but Bella shows no reaction. She turns like a ghost in a low-budget movie and drifts across the marble floor toward us.

Dave reaches past me, offering her a glass of scotch. But instead of taking the drink, she glances at me and then latches onto Dave's arm, pulling him into a long, deep kiss.

I stifle a gasp, and by the look on Dave's face, he's as surprised as anyone. He sloshes the whiskey out of the glass as he tries to free himself, his eyes wide.

I step backward, dodging the deluge.

He manages to break away. "Shit, I'm sorry!" He holds the dripping glass away from himself, Bella still clutching his arm. "Let me get you something to wipe that off."

"No need," I say. "It's only a couple of drops."

Dave reaches around Bella with his other hand, takes a stack of expensive napkins, and tosses them on the spill. "Bella, darling, what's gotten into you?" He tries to pry her off his arm, but she refuses to let go. "Diego is our guest. The least you could do is be civil."

I spend a moment mopping up the liquor while awkward silence fills the room. Finally, I toss the soiled napkins in the trash and reach across the abyss, offering Bella my hand. "I'm sorry we got off on the wrong foot, Dr. Sanborn. Perhaps you'll give me another chance? Mr. Kirk tells me you run the top research hospital in the world, and I'm looking forward to working with you."

Dave clears his throat. "It's Dr. Kirk, actually."

I put my hand back in my pocket and turn to Dave. "I'm sorry, I didn't realize you—"

"Not me." He nods at his wife. "Her."

"Oh," I say, feeling like I'm in a pinball game. "Dr. Kirk, then?"

She releases her death grip on Dave and floats out the doorway.

"Must be the new aftershave," he says with a shrug, and I force a laugh.

After he refills his glass, we follow her into an ornate, high-ceilinged dining room that smells like my grandmother's kitchen on Christmas Day.

I gawk at the elaborate display of opulence, my mouth watering.

A candelabra with lit candles is resting on a table large enough to seat twenty people, but there are only *four* place settings: white china with brass chargers, gaudy silverware, and crystal goblets. A bottle of wine sits in a silver bucket, a butter sculpture shaped like a dolphin leaps over a wave of ice, and fresh pineapple wedges surround a platter of real strawberries.

Mierda. The people at the Bub would kill for this spread.

Dave reads the look on my face. "I am permitted a bit of extravagance due to my position. It's a bit embarrassing actually, but the people insist. Please, have a seat." He gestures toward a chair, and I take it. "Our daughter should be joining us momentarily."

"Your daughter?" I say, my voice too high. "You have a daughter?"

"Yes," Dave says, his voice amused. "Last time I checked, it wasn't a crime."

"Right." I force another laugh. "Of course you have a daughter. Why wouldn't you?"

I can feel the sweat collecting under my tight shirt collar.

"So tell me," Dave says, "what's it like to be able to survive Outside? I'm sorry I wasn't there when my men brought you in, but Bella tells me it was quite a sight. I'd love to be able to feel the fresh air on my face again."

Before I can answer, the door swings open, and an attractive young woman steps through.

"Ah, there she is!" Dave says and stands. I follow his lead.

His thirty-something daughter has short curly hair, high cheekbones, and stunning green eyes.

"Soleil," Bella says, her face lighting up. "How are you, sweetheart? So nice of you to join us."

Soleil?

My heart stops beating.

Soleil kisses Bella on the cheek, "Hi, Mom." She steps over and gives Dave a hug. "Thanks for the invite, Uncle Dave, but I'm drowning in cell cultures, so I can't stay long…"

Uncle Dave? Christ, Nadales, she's your daughter!

Unbidden, an image of the twins' grave fills my head—cold stones stacked high on the wet earth, the rising sun filtering through the pine trees as I set the last rock on top. I see myself turn toward the cabin, Soleil and Lucas dead and buried, Isabel sick and dying, and me bearing the responsibility. An icy despair forms in the pit of my stomach—and I realize I'm staring at Sol.

"I'm sorry," I whisper, the words spilling out before I can stop them.

Soleil looks at me for the first time, and all the blood leaves her face.

"What is it?" Dave says, still standing with his arm around her waist. "Are you alright, baby? You look like you've seen a ghost."

Soleil steps away from Dave, her eyes huge. "Lucas? Oh my God, it's you!" She throws her arms around my neck. "I knew you'd come back. I just *knew it.*"

I stand there with Soleil's arms around my neck, trying to decide what to do.

Mierda. In this universe, she wasn't stillborn.

I clear my throat and place my hands lightly on her shoulders. "Uh…"

"I've missed you so much," she says, not letting go of me.

I put my arms around my daughter, overwhelmed. "I can't believe you're… here."

"He's not Lucas," Bella says, her voice icy cold.

Soleil glances at me and then backs away. "What?" She looks more carefully at my face. "Lucas?"

I take a step toward her before stopping myself. "I'm sorry, but I'm not your bro—"

"He's your father!" Bella lifts her arm, pointing a bony finger at me. "He's the man who murdered Lucas."

"No, I'm not," I say, absolutely certain that no version of me would ever hurt his family.

Soleil shakes her head. "Dad didn't murder Lucas, Mom. I've told you that a hundred times. He loved Lucas—and he loved us too."

Bella's arm wavers and then collapses onto the table. She looks up at me, her eyes pleading. "James?"

"Whoa there, ladies," Dave says, holding up his hands. "I think it's a case of mistaken identity all around." He puts his hands on his wife's shoulders. "Bella, darling, even if James managed to survive the accident—which he didn't—he would be in his *sixties* now."

"The biotech," Bella says. "It protects him against the virus, and it could stop the aging process too!"

"It could?" I say, the thought having never crossed my mind. "No, it doesn't."

At least I don't think it does...

"It's not him, Bella," Dave says. "It can't be. Show her your wrist, Diego."

I give him a confused look.

"The scar. Show her that you don't have the scar." He sits down next to Bella. "Remember when we were in Egypt for the twins' fifth birthday—the afternoon we climbed the Pyramid?"

"Yes," Soleil says. "I remember! That meteor went streaking right over us. It was loud and scary, and it made me lose my balance."

"Your father grabbed you so you wouldn't fall, and he cut his wrist on the rocks," Dave says to Soleil and then turns to his wife. "And Bella cleaned him up when we got back to the hotel, even put a few stitches in."

"So he had a scar," Bella says. "On his left wrist. Yes, I remember."

Dave nods at me. "Show her."

I undo my shirt cuffs and hold out my wrists.

Bella stares at them and then moves her gaze up to my face. "He's had it removed."

Dave makes an audible groan. "Give it a rest, Bella. He's twenty years too young and he doesn't have the goddamn scar."

"Then how did he know my maiden name?" Bella's voice is defiant. "He's James. I'm sure of it."

"No he's not," Soleil says. "He's Lucas. I've said for years that he's still alive."

"And he's not Lucas either," Dave says, sounding exasperated. "I had my guys run a DNA analysis. There were some... similarities, but no matches."

"What do you mean similarities?" Soleil asks. "The report should have said *exactly* how Lucas and this man are related."

"Well, the lab had trouble sequencing Diego's genome—probably due to the biotech—but they're absolutely certain he isn't Lucas. We don't have James's genome to compare, but it's pretty clear he isn't James."

"Maybe the biotech altered his DNA?" Soleil looks at her mother for confirmation.

"I presume it's possible…" Bella frowns. "But doubtful."

"Isn't it obvious?" Dave says. "James had another son—one none of us knew about."

Bella gasps. "By another woman? While he was married to me?" She drops her head into her hands. "It just gets worse."

No, of course he didn't! He would never have done that.

Everyone looks at me, and I realize I've said that out loud.

"I mean, give the man a break," I say. "There must be some other explanation…"

Soleil brings her hand up to her mouth, looking spooked. "So who are you?"

"Diego Crusoe," Dave says. "The guy who can survive Outside."

Soleil gawks at me like I have two heads, and Bella eyes me like she wants to chop one of them off.

You've gone from child-murdering psycho to cheating ex-husband's lovechild. So maybe you should count that as progress.

"You mean, *Tarzan?*" Soleil says, raising one eyebrow. "That naked man you were telling me about months ago—the crackpot who fell out of a pine tree?"

"That's the one," Dave says.

Soleil sizes me up again, her eyes darting from my face to my clip-on bow tie and back, looking less than impressed by my superpower. "I thought someone made that up," she says, glancing sideways at her adopted father.

"Well, that's what I thought too…" Dave says. "Naked

guy in a tree? Everyone assumed it was a joke."

She pins me with her gaze. "Are you immune?"

I shrug. "So far, so good."

Soleil jerks her head back, probably wondering where I'm hiding my horns and tail. "How?"

"We're hoping you can answer some of those questions," Dave says. "I've spoken to the medical council, and we're putting you in charge of Diego's case."

"You are?" Soleil says, her voice full of disbelief. She turns to her mother. "Why aren't you taking it, Mom? You're the genetics expert."

"She's already got too much on her plate," Dave says, referring to Bella as though she's a child. "And besides, it's time you stepped up. You've spent years researching Doomsday. This could be your big breakthrough."

"It's the opportunity of a lifetime," Soleil says, looking stunned.

Dave smiles and holds out his arms. "Nothing's too good for my little sunshine!"

Soleil rushes over and throws her arms around his neck. "Thank you, Uncle Dave. You're the best."

He kisses her on the forehead and then pushes a lock of hair back from her face. "And I'm sure your mother will be happy to help in any way she can."

"Of course, sweetheart," Bella says. "I haven't been in a lab in ages, but I can certainly answer any questions that come up."

"So, you must stay for dinner and celebrate with us," Dave says. "We hardly see you anymore…"

Soleil gives her mother a quick hug from behind her chair. "Of course I will."

Bella pats her daughter's arm. "You were always such a good girl."

"Well then, let's eat." Dave rings a tiny bell next to his

water glass.

Soleil tosses her keys and bag onto the polished wooden table, pulls off her sweater, adds it to the pile, and plops down in the chair.

Dave frowns but doesn't comment.

Soleil reaches for a strawberry, still glancing at me like she half-believes I'm Lucas, and half-believes I'm a monster.

"Where is that woman?" Dave says to no one. An instant later, a Latina scurries in, carrying a large serving dish.

She sets it on the table in front of Dave, whisks off the silver cover, and curtsies.

"Thank you, Sally," he says, not even looking at her.

The woman disappears, and a minute later comes back with more food—and then even more.

It's a feast fit for Caesar and his fifty generals.

Soleil notices me staring. "Don't worry, Sarita will send whatever we don't eat over to the barracks."

"Your Uncle Dave must be very popular with his men." I haven't eaten a decent meal since I left the Bub. I fill my plate.

"That's an understatement. He's pretty much a demigod around here." She glances in Dave's direction. "Mom and I owe him everything."

Dave nods at her like he's Mahatma Gandhi.

"Good for him," I say. "Who's Sarita?"

"Oh, that's Sally's real name. Uncle Dave thought Sarita sounded too foreign. So he calls her Sally."

"How nice of him."

Dave spends the next half hour telling us about how he single-handedly saved humanity while Soleil nibbles at the fruit and Bella scarcely lifts her fork.

The moment the plates are cleared, Bella pushes back her chair and stands. "Good night, David. I'll see you in the morning."

Dave—still chewing a dinner roll—struggles to his feet, and I follow suit.

Bella floats over and kisses Soleil on the cheek. "It was wonderful to see you, sweetheart. We should do this more often."

"G'night, Mom." Soleil leans back in her chair and wraps her arms around her mother's neck. "Will you be at the hospital staff meeting tomorrow?"

"I don't think so, dear. It's all too tiring. You'll let me know if anything important happens?"

"Of course, Mom."

Bella nods at me rather stiffly, "Mr. Crusoe," and floats out of the room. A few seconds later, we hear a puppy bark—and then toenails skittering down the hallway.

Bearhart comes racing into the room, bumps into a table leg as he tries to turn on the polished floor, and leaps onto my chair.

I smile and ruffle his ears. "Hey there, buddy! They taking good care of you here?"

He wags his tail and starts licking my plate.

Soleil laughs, but Dave smacks his hands down on the table and yells, "Goddamn it, Bella, will you get that foul-smelling mutt out of my dining room?" Dave grabs the puppy by the collar and drags him off the chair and back into the kitchen, muttering about dog hair. I can't recall Gandhi acting like that, but maybe my memory's faulty.

Soleil stands and picks up her belongings. "Welcome to our little fishbowl, Mr. Crusoe. I'll see you in the morning."

"I'm looking forward to it," I say, still standing up. "It was nice to meet you, Soleil. And I'm very sorry about your father and brother." I move to kiss her on the cheek, but she steps away.

"I don't mean to be rude," she says and offers me her hand, "but given the circumstances, I think it would be best if we maintain a strict physician-patient relationship, Mr. Crusoe."

"Of course, Dr. Kirk." I incline my head. "Please forgive me."

"It's Dr. *Nadales*." She turns on her heel and walks out.

CHAPTER 8

Shannon: The Room

We're locked inside a windowless chamber that smells of musky perfume, stale sweat, and cleaning solution. In the middle of the room is a giant bed with sheer curtains hanging from the ceiling like some harem tent in *The Arabian Nights*. There's a heavy wooden stool at the foot of the bed and a padded piece of furniture that looks like a headless horse along one wall. A tall, narrow chest of drawers stands next to the bed—its shiny red finish out of place in this dingy biodome.

Subdued light spills from lamps in each corner, casting eerie shadows on the paintings of naked women—and other creatures—in suggestive poses. Although I have no idea what all the metal rings on the ceiling and walls are for, it's pretty clear what we're supposed to be doing in here.

"Shannon?" His voice is a whisper.

I try to cover myself with the flimsy curtain. "What are you going to do to me?"

"No-thing," he says, his voice cracking. "Don't worry. I won't try to…" He looks away. "…you know, touch you or anything." He clears his throat and looks back at me. "Do you need to use the toilet?"

I nod.

"The door's behind the painting of the woman and the squid." He shifts his weight. "You're welcome to use anything you want in there, but don't drink the water."

"What's wrong with the water?" I ask and release the curtain.

"I don't know," he says. "But the people who drink it get sick."

"Don't you filter it?" I ask, shuffling sideways toward the bathroom, unsure what to make of all this.

He shrugs.

I stare at the painting of a woman with a squid in her lap, trying to figure out what the creature is doing. "I think it's an octopus," I say. "Squids have *ten* tentacles."

"I never looked at anything except the woman."

"Ah," I say, feeling like an idiot.

I pull the recessed door handle and peer into a lavish bathroom. "Wow."

"There should be a nightgown on the counter," Peter says. "And tomorrow someone will bring you clean clothes."

"Okay," I say, not really listening, and walk in.

All of the fixtures are golden, and the floor and counter are made out of some sort of polished white stone—beautiful but cold. After I use the toilet, I stand there staring at the huge shower area. It's bigger than my bedroom at home, and there's a raised bathtub at one end and six showerheads at the other: two at the top, two in the middle, and two coming out of the floor.

What could anyone possibly do with all that water?

My clothes smell and I could use a hot soak, but bathtubs are considered extravagant at home. Plus, I have no idea how to work the shower. So, I take everything off except my underwear and wash as best I can using a bar of soap that is hard and cracked. When I'm done, I splash water on my face and tangled hair, careful not to get any in my mouth, and then dry off with the largest towel I've ever seen. I wrap it around myself and rinse out my clothes—including my underwear—and then hang everything up in the shower to dry.

There's a black, lacy dress folded up on the counter, and it takes me a moment to realize it's the nightgown Peter mentioned. Back at home, I sleep in an old T-shirt. I've never seen anything so frilly, not even in the movies.

I slip it over my head and then stare at myself in the mirror. The girl looking back at me is a stranger. Her hair is a tangled mess, there are dark circles under her eyes, and a bruise is forming on her left cheek. I shiver in the thin nightgown and then notice that it's totally see-through—right down to the mole I have on my tummy.

I consider taking it off, but instead, I wrap the huge towel back around myself and sit down on a small stool and cry. When I run out of tears, I wipe my face on the towel, blow my nose on the wet washcloth and rinse it out again, and then spend a few minutes finger-combing my hair and braiding it into a single plait. There's not much more I can do. I make sure that the taps are all the way off, straighten the remaining towel, and take a deep breath.

Then I walk back out into the room.

Peter has his shirt off, and I notice that his shoulders are broad—but his ribs are all sticking out.

I clear my throat, and he lets out a startled yelp. He turns away and slips a clean shirt on—but not before I see the scars all over his back.

"Um," I say, feeling super self-conscious. "Did you want me to stay in the bathroom?"

"No, of course not. I... I didn't expect you to come out so soon." He backs away from me. "I mean, I wanted you to come back..." He stops talking and stares at me, his mouth stuck open.

It's like he wants to look at my body but is afraid to move his gaze below my bare shoulders. I cinch the towel up, wishing there was something less revealing to wear to bed.

"I like your hair that way," he says. "In a long, golden rope."

"Thanks." I edge over to the back side of the bed. "It's called a braid. My mom usually does it for me before bed." I drop the towel on the floor and dive under the covers.

Peter's eyes get big, and then he looks away. "Uh, would you like something to drink? A glass of water?" He opens some sort of hidden panel on the wall.

"Yes, please. Assuming it's not poisoned."

He jerks his head around. "No, of course not. I wouldn't try to—"

"I was kidding, Peter."

"Yeah. Right." He takes a plastic bottle out of the cupboard, opens it, pours water into two glasses, and then hesitates. "Shall I bring it over to you?"

"Yes, please."

He tiptoes around the bed and offers me the glass, his gaze averted.

I sit up and tuck the covers under my arms. "Thank you."

"You're welcome." He backs away.

"Tell me about your mother," I say. "Do you remember much about her?"

He shakes his head. "I was only a child when she died." He looks up at me. "Anyways, folks around here don't talk much about the past, except to mention how terrible it was."

"I'm sorry," I say. "About your mother, I mean. I'm sure she was very kind. Just like you."

He nods, looking uncomfortable. "How about your mother?" he asks, looking at my braid again. "I bet she misses you a lot."

I bite my lip, trying not to cry. "My mom's the best doctor this side of C-Bay, and she's smart too—smarter than me." I take a drink of water and spend a moment fighting back tears. "She didn't want me to come on this trip." I wipe my eyes with the back of my hand. "I miss her a lot."

"There's no way she's as smart," he says, "or as pretty as you."

I cover my face with my hands, unable to contain my tears any longer. "I want to go home, Peter."

"I know," he says in a whisper. "I don't want to live here either."

I sniff my nose and look up at him. "You don't?"

"Of course not. All those nasty rumors about us are true: We *are* monsters. My mother killed herself rather than submit to my father's brutality. She hanged herself in the chapel—the same place where they forced us to get married. I found her body hanging from a crossbeam. I was five."

"Oh, Peter. I'm so sorry."

He takes a deep breath, his gaze downcast. "And now that they have you, they won't let you go. If people try to rescue you, my dad will shoot them." He looks at me, his face drawn. "Grizzly was right. You're stuck here, Shannon. You can never go home again."

"I have my biosuit," I say, my heart pounding. "I'll find it and put it back on—and then I'll *walk* home."

He sits down on the bed, careful not to make me spill my water. "It's hundreds of miles to the nearest biodome. What are you going to do when your suit runs out of air? And even if you could find enough oxygen tanks—which you can't—you don't have any way to carry them. And it would take days, weeks probably. You'd have to go without food and hope you could find clean water and some way to filter it."

Better than staying here.

He tips his head to the side. "If you let me... I mean, if we, you know..." He glances at my bare shoulders, his eyes getting big. "Then I can protect you, keep the others from hurting you. But if they take you away from me..." He narrows his eyebrows. "They'll—"

"You're right," I say, pulling the covers up to my chin, "the biosuit is a bad idea, but I have a better one: I'll use a rebreather mask. I'll find one and fix it—and then use it to escape. Madders says they last for months."

"Even if you could find one, how are you going to mend it, Shannon? Nobody knows how to repair the old technology. Once something stops working, it goes to Oblation, and the Giver prays for a new one."

"Surely you have tools to fix things? Hammers and screwdrivers and stuff?"

"Sure. But it's forbidden to touch them—unless the Giver says so. She controls everything, and the men are all afraid of her—even my father."

"Then we'll have to be sneaky."

He scrunches up his eyebrows, looking confused.

"That means we won't let anyone else know what we're up to. I'm good at that."

"You are?" He looks surprised.

"Yeah. Do you know where they keep the spare parts for things: light bulbs, cleaning supplies, and extra gloves for the biosuits? Some sort of giant room full of stacked and numbered boxes?"

He nods. "Grizzly goes there sometimes, and he takes me to help."

"Good. I'm guessing you have hundreds of masks sitting

in boxes somewhere, just like we did. If we can find them, along with some silicone sealant and a couple of vises, I know how to make them work again."

"Vices?" he says. "You mean like pride and gluttony?"

"No, silly. Like vise grips. They're tools that help you glue two things together."

He gives me a blank look.

"Never mind. You must have a tool shop around here somewhere too. There'll be vises in it." I exhale. "But it might be harder to find the sealant."

"There's a big room full of bottles and jars," he says. "My mother used to go there to make ointments, and I used to go with her. I remember the bones painted on the door. People don't go in there anymore."

"That sounds like the right place. Do you think you could show me how to get there? Maybe draw me a map?"

"I can do better than that," he says, sitting up straighter. "I'll take you there. And I'll help you fix the masks so you can escape."

"Oh, Peter!" I squeeze his hand. "Thank you!" He pulls away, looking uncomfortable, and I let go. "Sorry."

"It's okay," he says. "You don't have to apologize. I knew it wouldn't last."

"What wouldn't last?"

"You staying here with me. I knew a girl like you wouldn't want to, you know, be with me." He gets up from the bed. "You're too pretty and smart to ever be interested in someone like me."

I cross my arms. "That is complete bullshit, Peter."

His eyes widen. "You think so?"

"Of course I do—not as your wife or anything, but still…" I shrug.

He nods and looks down at his hands.

"We'll make *two* rebreather masks," I say. "One for each

of us, and then we'll escape together. I can go east and you can go west, and we'll see who gets to safety first."

"Sure," he says, his shoulders slumping. He takes the empty glass out of my hand, careful not to touch me. "Would you like more water?"

I shake my head.

"Okay, then. I'll see you in the morning." He sets the glasses on the floor by the door, shuts the cabinet, and turns off the light. In the soft glow coming from the bathroom, I watch him sit down in the corner, wrap his arms around his legs, and put his forehead down on his knees.

I hop out of the bed, grab a pillow and a blanket, and take them over to him. I feel exposed in the thin nightie, but I'm hoping it's too dark to see anything.

"You're not a monster," I say. "I'm sorry I said that about you." I set the bedding down next to him. "And I don't hate you or anything, I just want to go home."

He doesn't respond.

I tiptoe back across the room and crawl into the huge bed.

"Good night, Shannon," he says. "Thanks for marrying me—even if you're only pretending."

CHAPTER 9

Diego: Drawing Blood

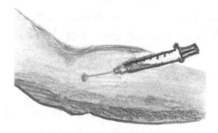

When Soleil enters the examination room the following morning, she's all business. "Good day, Mr. Crusoe. I'm officially in charge of figuring out how you survive Outside."

"Morning, doctor." I offer her my hand and then think better of it. I swallow and run my fingers awkwardly through my hair. "Uh, thank you for taking my case, and I apologize for last night. I had no idea my appearance would stir up such painful memories."

She looks at me, her lips pressed together, and shrugs. "That's neither here nor there, Mr. Crusoe, but I appreciate the thought."

Her resemblance to her mother is uncanny, and I have a difficult time not staring at her.

She clears her throat. "Mr. Kirk asked me to tell you

that he's contacted Catersville and will have an update on Shannon Kai soon."

"That's great news. Thank you." I steal a look at her hands, checking to see if her fingernails are more similar to mine or her mother's. Against my will, the image of those tiny hands wrapped in a blanket and buried near the cabin fills my head.

Why couldn't I figure out a way to save her?

The thought leaves me struggling with my emotions.

She holds up a thick manila folder. "It says in here that—with the exception of a slightly-elevated white blood cell count, the laceration on your left cheek, and some mild contusions—you check out perfectly normal."

I sit there staring at her.

"You're lucky," she says. "The doctor who put you back together knew her stuff. Most of the patients who come here from remote biodomes aren't so fortunate." She drops the stack of papers on the counter and crosses her arms. "So, what else should I know before we get started?"

The question makes my throat tight.

How much did Lani write down? The time travel stuff? The other universe claim? Or just that I'm delusional?

I swallow. "You're familiar with Dr. Kai's notes?"

"Yes. According to her, you fell from a height of twelve meters, broke twenty-three bones, and suffered a concussion. She offers no explanation for how you got in that tree, nor does she speculate on where you've been for the last twenty years. She did some testing on your blood, but only notes that you have the somewhat rare blood type O negative. Her final entry states that you are still experiencing some memory loss, but it seems to be improving." She doesn't even glance at the notes. "Would you agree with that evaluation?"

So Lani didn't reveal anything.

I gulp. "Yes."

"Good," Soleil says. "So why don't we start with how those biotech devices got in your blood?"

"Sure." I say, determined to stay as close to the truth as I can without saying the words *time machine*. "Back before Doomsday," I say, "I was part of a secret government project to investigate a hollow metal sphere of unknown origin. The thousand-pound ball fell out of the sky, going at Mach 8, and set a good chunk of downtown Denver on fire when it came down."

"I don't recall hearing anything about that. Are you sure it was in Denver?"

"Yes. I was there the night it happened. I nearly died in the resulting fire."

She looks more carefully at me, probably doing the math. "How old were you?"

"Thirty-eight," I say. "How old were you when they sealed the biodomes?"

She hesitates and then decides that the information isn't top secret. "Fifteen."

"*Mierda*," I say, feeling off-balance.

She was born when you and Iz were first dating. If you hadn't gotten angry and hopped on that plane…

She raises one eyebrow. "How old are you now?"

"Older than that." I slide my hands across my face, trying to hide my damp eyes. "To be honest, I don't know for sure, Sol."

"Please don't call me that," she says, her voice carefully controlled.

I stare at her, unable to get the image of her lying dead in Isabel's arms out of my mind.

She narrows one eye. "And I would appreciate it if you would stop staring at me like I'm some sort of unicorn."

"I'm…" I drop my gaze. "…sorry."

"So what was inside the hollow sphere?"

I force myself not to look at her. "Plans to build a biotech device. It took nearly a year, but a team of top-notch geneticists followed the instructions and created what they thought was a vaccine."

"For Doomsday?" She thumbs through my chart.

"Yes," I say and steal a glance up. "But when they tested it on a volunteer, he died in a matter of minutes."

Her eyes get big. "You tested a vaccine of dubious origins on a human?"

"People were desperate—and we were running out of time."

"So what made you decide to volunteer?"

I shrug. "I didn't really have a choice. I was abducted by two government agents and agreed to cooperate with them in exchange for medical supplies to be sent to my... wife. She was dying from an infected knife wound, and all the hospitals had been closed and looted by then."

"Did she receive the necessary antibiotics in time?"

I nod.

"And did she make it inside a biodome?"

I exhale. "I don't know. In my... area, there's only one biodome. It would have taken a miracle."

Or Dave.

She taps her pencil on the clipboard, the corner of her mouth twitching. "Do you have any other family? Any children?"

I stare at her, the word *children* stuck in my brain. "No."

She looks away. "So what happened after the vaccine killed the test subject?"

"Turns out, my name was also inside the sphere: handwritten on a sheet of pink paper. After the initial failure, the geneticists determined that the biotechs might have been designed for a *single* genome. When Doomsday mutated, I agreed to have the vaccine injected, hoping it might protect me. And here I am."

"Just like that, huh?" She reaches back and shuts the door. "Why does the vaccine only work on you? What makes you so special?"

"I wish I knew."

"So," she says, sounding like she's talking to a six-year-old, "you were thirty-eight when Doomsday mutated, and almost twenty years later, you look..." She tips her head to the side, squinting at me. "...about thirty-eight."

"Yeah."

She snorts, sounding exasperated. "So the biotech *does* affect your aging. Is that why you look twenty years younger than you are?"

I shake my head. "I don't know."

"You don't know." She crosses her arms. "How do you explain the age discrepancy?"

"I can't."

She glances down at my chart. "How did you end up in that tree?"

"A computer malfunction."

"Have you had a full physical since you arrived in C-Bay?" She glances at my stack of papers. "I didn't see one in your chart."

I shake my head. "Just tests—most of which had nothing to do with my injuries *or* the biotech devices."

"I'm going to need you to disrobe and lie on your side."

I stare at her, not understanding.

"I'm going to aspirate some bone marrow for my own testing." She walks over to the cupboard and takes out a pair of latex gloves. "Where is the lab that made the biotechs?"

"I don't know. I was unconscious when they took me there."

"They drugged you?"

"No," I say, feeling my face get warm, "I fell asleep."

She opens a drawer and takes stuff out, keeping her back to me. "Who were the geneticists?"

"I don't know that either. They were on a separate team." I watch her, still unable to process that she's my daughter.

"What was your team responsible for?"

"Building a computer."

"Where have you been living for the last twenty years?"

"In Colorado."

She turns, her hands on her hips—and then notices that I haven't taken off any clothes. "Did you want me to leave while you undress?"

"No. It's just that you're... I mean, I'm..."

Mierda.

"Never mind," I say and start taking off my shirt.

She watches me for a moment, her arms crossed again. "I assure you, Mr. Crusoe, the fact that I'm a woman will have no bearing—"

"Believe me, it's not that."

I spend the next ten minutes trying not to flinch as she sticks a long needle into the back of my hip bone.

"Okay, I'm done," she says, after swabbing and taping the site. "You can get dressed."

I sit up and start putting my clothes back on.

"I need to drop this sample off at the lab, and then I'll be back." She takes some papers off her clipboard and hands them to me, along with a pencil. "Please fill this out while I'm gone."

I glance at the first question:

Are there any genetic diseases that run in your family?

She labels the test tube, places it in a plastic bag, and exits, carrying the sample and the tray of used paraphernalia.

I give her thirty seconds—and then get up and start reading through my chart.

Except there's nothing in it but useless test results: "No

iron deficiency found" and "Results normal" and "Patient was agitated about testing but cooperated. FIT negative."

I set it back on the counter and peek out the door. Right across the hall is a closed door with "Dr. Soleil Nadales" on the nameplate.

Bingo.

I check the doorknob—it's unlocked—and then slip inside.

The walls are covered with family photos: Soleil and Lucas as toddlers in matching bear outfits. A pre-adolescent Soleil smiling and holding up a soccer ball with her brother standing behind her making a goofy face. Soleil as a baby asleep on my chest, her tiny hand wrapped around my index finger.

I stand there staring at the photo, my heart aching—and then force myself to look away.

I go back to looking for my chart, wondering what really happened to James and Bella.

One of her desk drawers is locked, so I search through the pencil drawer for the key. It's in the back inside a fake worry stone—the same place Isabel would have kept it. I unlock the drawer and search through the hanging files until I find *Diego Crusoe (Nadales?)*

The top sheet in the file is handwritten and contains a list of questions. At the bottom are the words:

Suffers from grandiose hallucinations, persecution complex, and emotional instability.

Initial DX: delusional psychosis.

It's signed: S. Nadales, MD.

I shove the papers back in the file and push the drawer shut—and then notice the framed photo on her desk. It was taken in front of the Great Pyramid, and Soleil and Lucas look to be five or six years old. Soleil's face is a bit flushed—as if she'd been crying—but she's smiling in the photo. She's holding hands with Lucas—who is looking up at his mother—and leaning her head against me. Standing behind the twins, with his arm around Bella and his other hand on Soleil's shoulder, is Dave Kirk.

"Shit."

"What the hell are you doing in my office?" Soleil says. She's standing in the doorway with her hands on her hips.

"I..." I stare at her, my whole world crashing down around me. "I'm so..." I swallow. "I'm so sorry..." I wipe my face on my shoulder. "I'm so sorry I couldn't save—"

"Get out of my office," she says, her eyes like daggers.

I nod, feeling like a heel, and set the photo back down. "Sol, I'm sorry—"

"If you ever call me that again," she says, "I'll have my uncle lock you up. Do you hear me?"

"Yeah," I say and walk past her out the door—and then hesitate in front of the exam room.

"We're done," she says. "I'll send someone to collect more blood if and when I need it. In the meantime, I suggest you stay out of my sight."

CHAPTER 10

Lani: Don't Panic

After one cycle with the UV lamp, the *Virus Detected* light stops flashing. The inner door of the Bub airlock opens, and I step through.

Everyone is staring at me like I transformed from a black cat.

"How's Jack?" I ask.

Madders breaks the spell. "He's going to need some stitches, but Lucy says they have him stabilized."

I nod, relief flooding in. "Thank goodness."

"So you're immune," Madders says like he doesn't believe it.

I shrug, still having trouble believing it myself. "I guess so."

"What are the odds?" he says and lets out a soft whistle.

"Around one in a hundred million," Mindy says. "I just

checked. We've all seen that photo of a woman standing among hundreds of bodies, and everyone's heard rumors about people living in the ruined cities…"

"And there was a family in Japan—all five of them immune," someone says.

"So maybe the odds are better than that," Mindy says. "Only there's no way to know if you're immune—unless you're willing to risk your life to find out."

"Sort of like jumping out of an airplane to test a parachute," Madders says. "If you're wrong, you don't get a second chance."

"And everyone so far has been wrong," Mindy says. "Except Doc and Mr. C—and maybe Shannon."

Shannon might be immune!

Hope floods into me like sunlight breaking through storm clouds.

"Remember when she got that snakebite in her suit?" Mindy says, glancing between Madders and me. "And her panels went red? Maybe the virus *did* get inside."

"And the ultraviolet light destroyed it when she came through the airlock with Diego," I say.

"That was lucky," Mindy says. "If we hadn't needed the lights for Mr. C, Shannon could have killed us all when she took off her helmet."

"Okay, folks," Madders says. "Time to get back to work. I'll get on the horn to Kirk and let him know the patch on the outer wall failed—see if he has any other ideas. I imagine he'll want to know that Lani's immune, but as far as I'm concerned, it can wait—don't want him insisting we send her out to C-Bay for testing when folks here need a doctor."

There are murmurs of assent.

I almost add that being immune makes me the perfect candidate to rescue Shannon—but realize it also means I'm the best choice to help repair the biodome.

"Mindy, you do a headcount and let me know if any-one is missing," Madders says. "The rest of you split up into teams. We need to bury the dead, collect equipment and tools from the contaminated area, and set up a new radio room. Everyone pass along the message that the council will meet in the cafeteria after supper. We all need to do some serious thinking about an evacuation plan."

No one questions Matt Hudson's authority. He's a natural leader, and we're all grateful to have someone offer a plan of action.

What are we going to do when he's... gone?

Madders scans the worried faces. "Let's get to work." He waits for the crowd to disperse and then puts his unbandaged arm around my shoulder. "You okay?"

"Yeah, I'm fine," I say and stick my trembling hands in my pockets. "How's your arm?"

"Be good as new in a week or so."

We glance out the window at the distant mountains—and then both speak at once.

"Lani—"

"I—"

"Come on," he says. "Let's get you to the clinic. Once you have Jack and the others patched up, we can talk about Shannon."

That evening after the council meeting, I muster all my courage and corner Madders. "We're still leaving tomorrow to get Shannon, right?"

He winces. "I'm worried sick about her too, Lani, but we can't abandon the people here. If that patch on the wall had held, things would be different, but..." He puts his arm around me. "Let's go for a walk."

I let him lead me out of the cafeteria.

"I want to get her out of there too," he says as we're walking toward the park. "But it's too risky to leave the bio-dome now."

"Too risky? Surely someone can figure out how to fix the wall."

He exhales, watching a handful of kids on the play equipment. "I don't know, Doc. When that chunk of wall fell, it bent the outer frame. We'll have to see what Kirk says, but I suspect we're running out of options."

We sit down on a park bench as the lights in the park flicker on.

"I'm just another pair of hands, Lani, but you're the only doctor these people have. With the situation as precarious as it is, they need you here."

We sit in silence, the cheerful voices of the kids needling my pain.

"So what about Shannon?" I ask. "You know what those men are capable of. What sort of mother would I be if I didn't try to help her?"

He doesn't have a response.

I glance at my watch and then stand up. "I need to get back to work."

"I'm sorry," he says without meeting my gaze.

"The needs of the many outweigh the needs of the one," I say, fighting back tears. "Unless you're the one who's asked to make the sacrifice."

He stands and takes my arm, and we start walking toward the clinic. "The moment everyone is safe, I'll fly you to Catersville. We'll find Shannon and get her out of there. You have my word."

"That's not good enough." I stop walking—the thought of those perverts putting their hands all over Shannon making me sick to my stomach. "It will destroy her, Madders. Even if we eventually get her out, she'll never be the same again."

He doesn't respond.

I turn and look at him. "I'm going after Shannon whether you help me or not."

"Lani..." He shuts his eyes for a moment and runs his hand over the back of his neck. "The next storm that comes through is going to tear that damaged section to shreds," he says, glancing up at the roof. "And there's a good chance it could take the rest of the biodome down with it."

"So we send out a crew to cut away the loose wall," I say. "You can fly me out to Catersville while they're fixing it. We'll be back with Shannon in less than a week."

"You know it's not that simple, Lani." He pulls me back into a walk. "Getting to Catersville could take a week or more, and if we have problems finding gas or trouble with the plane..." He sighs. "Even if we manage to dodge this bullet, it's only a matter of time before another section of the Bub fails. This biodome was built as a prototype. It was never meant to last this long, and we're out of spare parts. She's been a good ship, but it's time to find a new home."

"What are you saying?"

"That we need to use the plane to locate Diego's underground city. Kirk thinks it's our best chance, and I agree."

I step around in front of him, forcing him to stop. "No, I'm not listening to this. Shannon was your responsibility. You told me she'd be safe—and I trusted you! Nadales may have talked me into letting her go, but she was in *your* plane. You have to help me get her back!"

He puts his hands on my shoulders. "I love Shannon like my own daughter, Doc. Knowing what she must be going through is tearing me up inside, but I can't walk away from my responsibilities here—and neither can you. Soon as the folks in the Bub are safe, I'll do everything in my power to get Shannon back."

I squeeze my eyes shut. "Then I'll go by myself. I'll take what I can carry and *hike* to Tennessee."

"Listen to yourself, Lani!" He shakes my shoulders. "It's over twelve hundred miles to Catersville, and it's winter out there. It would take you weeks, probably months, to walk that far—assuming you don't get sick or injured. And what are you going to do when you get there? Ring the doorbell?"

I look up into his tired eyes. "I won't abandon her," I say, shaking my head. "D-don't ask me to do that."

"I'm not. I'm asking you to wait for a week or two. Kirk said he'd get her back, and you've barely even given him a chance to try. Look around you. People are dying right here, right now."

I push him away, unable to listen to any more.

"What about Jack?" he says. "His leg is going to require multiple surgeries—you told me that yourself. And what about the others who are injured? Who's going to take care of them while you're gone?"

I don't meet his gaze. "Lucy and Becky can fill in while I'm away."

"Lani, they think the world of you," he says, "but we both know they'd be lost without you. You can't abandon all the people in the Bub."

I shake my head. "My daughter needs me."

"Right now, we need you more."

"After what you did to Shannon, you have no right to say that to me." The words come out like a curse.

He turns me around, looking old and worn down. "I know you, Lani. You couldn't live with yourself if you let something happen to all these people—and neither could I."

"And if something happens to Shannon, how am I going to live with that?" I pull away from him and hurry into the clinic, wishing for the first time in my life that I wasn't a doctor.

∞

A cold breeze bites into my exposed face as I watch Madders take off into the early dawn sky, Mindy in the co-pilot's seat. When I talk to David this morning, I plan to beg him to send out a plane to pick me up. In the twenty years since we were lovers, I've never asked him for anything, and I'm hopeful he'll say yes.

In the meantime, I'm doing whatever I can to help here at the Bub.

I turn toward the people dressed in black inside the bio-dome, and someone raises a hand in acknowledgment. I toss the bouquet of flowers from Lucy's garden on the mound of newly-turned earth and bow my head.

Goodbye, friends.

A minute later, I see the plane disappear over the snowy peaks to the west and get to work.

David asked for a look at the biodome damage from the exterior, and I was the obvious choice.

I trudge across the frosty ground toward the damaged sector, shivering in my thin jacket. I wonder how my life could have been different if I'd found out I was immune nineteen years ago, before everything fell apart. I stop and stare at the ridge where my brother was waiting for me the day he died—the day I got him killed.

Was he immune? Did he run into that flamethrower for nothing? Could the two of you have survived Outside for all these years? Would you have wanted to?

"The three of us," I say to the wind.

You were pregnant with Shannon.

I imagine giving birth as a seventeen-year-old, alone in a cold, dark warehouse, not knowing if my baby would die with her first contaminated breath. And if she does turn out to be immune, I envision raising her with no medical supplies, no schools, and no bed to sleep in on snowy winter nights.

The thought makes me shudder.

I couldn't save Sam, but so help me God, I'm going to save Shannon.

When I'm out of sight of the airlock, I stop walking and turn toward the rising sun, the rays touching my face for the first time in twenty years. Shannon is out there, fighting for her life, and I'm stuck here, letting the atrocities pile up.

I take one of her ribbons out of my pocket and bring it up to my nose, trying to remember what she smells like, the soft feel of her hair through my fingers as I braid it before bed, listening to her chatter about her day. The last few nights have been the worst of my life—even harder than the ones after I was burned—and it's all I can do to keep up my doctor facade during the days.

All the worry and fear and frustration overwhelms me. I drop down to my knees and let the tears flow, knowing it won't do any good but unable to fight the despair any longer.

I'm sorry, baby.

When I have no tears left, I force myself to stand and keep walking, silently praying to *Pele* that Shannon is alive—and unharmed.

The damaged area isn't visible from the ground, but the ribs of the biodome are numbered sequentially, and it doesn't take me long to find the one adjacent to the breach.

After I pull myself up on the lowest rung of the external access ladder, I switch on the radio. Mindy's sister, Allison, has taken over radio duties while their dad, Jack, recovers.

"Ally, this is Dr. Kai. I'm up on ladder forty-two now. Do you read me?"

"Loud and clear, Doc," she says. "How are things out there?"

"Cold and breezy. Hang on, I'll set up the camera." I take

off my gloves, take the camera headset out of my pocket, and fit it over my stocking cap. "Are you getting the live feed now?"

"Yep. Be careful out there!"

"Will do. I'm going to get closer to the hole."

"Roger that. I should have you patched through to Mr. Kirk in a jiffy."

"Thanks, Ally." I put my gloves back on and start climbing.

A minute or two later, David's warm and confident voice fills my ears. "Hey, babe. I hear you've been hiding super-powers from me. I always knew you were one of a kind."

I force a laugh. "Wish I would have known sooner, back before my brother—"

"Don't we all," he says. "What have you got for me?"

"I'm about halfway up. Are you getting the video feed?"

"Yeah. Looks good so far. How's the ladder holding up?"

"Fine. A little rust in spots, but not much." I keep climbing, being careful not to slip. "Any news on Shannon?"

"I expect to hear something today. And don't worry, Lani, I'll get her out of there."

I stop for a minute to catch my breath. "David, I know this is asking a lot, but can you send someone out here to pick me up? I'll donate tissue so C-Bay can investigate my immunity—and then I'll go with you to get Shannon."

"Sure I *can*, Wonder Woman, but it doesn't make any sense. The Catersville guys are trigger-happy as hell, and they'd just be itching for a reason to open fire. That hot temper of yours—and the fact you've got a pair of tits—could end up getting someone killed. Trust me, it's not a good idea."

"What about sneaking in?" I start climbing again, going over my plans in my head. "Madders says there are manual airlocks that can be operated from the exterior. I could go with you, sneak in at night, and take a look around. I'm small and quick—and I can survive Outside without a suit. It would be eas—"

"You're right about the airlocks, babe, but that biodome is huge. The chances that we could find Shannon without getting caught are negative zero percent—and the moment they know we're inside, they'll shoot first and ask questions later. I've been through all the options, princess, and the best way for you to help Shannon is to stay put."

"David—"

"Lani, you can't do anything to help Shannon right now. The moment that changes, you'll be the first to know. And as far as your immunity goes, we have your genome on file, so there's nothing more you can provide right now. I double checked. The Bub needs you—especially now that you can go Outside. Christ, you could be the one who ends up saving everyone."

"I don't want to be the hero, David. I want to get my daughter back before something horrible happens to her."

"Look, I know I can't stop you—she's your daughter—but I'm asking you to make the right decision."

"I can't abandon her—"

"Work with me on this, Lanikins. You know me well enough to know that when I say I'll get her out of there, I'll damn well do it."

I wipe my face on the back of my glove and continue climbing.

"You okay, babe?"

"Yeah."

"Good. You always were a fighter. Can you give me a shot of the wall to your right?"

I'm almost to the top now and climbing horizontally. I sit on a ladder rung and sweep my gaze across the top of the dome.

"A little slower. Yeah, that's good. From where you are, can you see any cracks or buckles?"

"No."

"Okay, good. Let me see the damaged area."

I shift my position and scan the other side.

"Shit."

"What is it, David?"

"Well, it's not fucking good."

There's a loud pop on the radio, and Ally's too-loud voice breaks in. "Dr. Kai, you have to get back to the clinic immediately! We think Miss Lucy's had a heart attack, and Mom is just sitting on the floor next to her crying."

"Go," David says. "Leave the camera pointed at the damaged area. I'll catch up with you tonight."

"Ally, I'm heading back in now," I say. "Is Lucy conscious? Is her heart beating?"

"Yes," she says, "but she's in a lot of pain—and she's having trouble breathing. What should we do?"

"Crush up an aspirin—there's a bottle in the desk drawer—and have her swallow it." I rip off the headset, disconnect the camera from the radio, and put it back on. "Then get her into a bed and put her on oxygen." I use a strip of Velcro to attach the camera to a rung of the ladder, do a quick check in the viewfinder, and start climbing down.

"But we don't know where anything is," Ally says, crying now. "Mom's gone all wonkers, and Miss Lucy is going to die!"

"Damn it, Ally, pull yourself together!" My foot slips on a metal rung, and I almost fall.

Slow down. You can't afford to get hurt.

I continue stepping down. "Nobody's going to die, Ally. Everything you need is in the storage cupboard. Who else is there with you?"

"All the D-1s are here. We were helping Mom and Miss

Lucy pack up medical supplies."

I force myself to slow down and pay attention to the ladder rungs. "You've all had a rotation at the clinic and know how to do CPR. So don't panic!"

"Okay, okay," she says between sobs. "We're giving her the aspirin now."

"Good. Put your mother on the radio. I want to speak to her."

"Here she is," Ally says, and then I hear her say, "Mom, Doc wants to talk to you…"

"Rebecca Lofgren Moynihan," I say in my sternest doctor voice, "you get your ass up off that floor and get an oxygen mask on Lucy. That's an order."

"It doesn't matter," Becky says, her voice flat. "We're all gonna die."

"Not if I can help it," I say. "Madders is going to find that underground city, and you're going to drive us right up to it in one of those big trucks you brought back from Dolce Base. Now get up, blow your nose, and help the kids with Lucy. I'll be there in ten minutes." I jump down off the ladder and run across the frozen ground, knowing what I have to do.

I need to help Madders find the Magic Kingdom and figure out a way to get everyone safely inside.

Forgive me, Shannon. I'll come after you as soon as I can.

CHAPTER II

Diego: Alone Again (Naturally)

A couple of days after Soleil tossed me out of her office, Kirk stops by my hospital room while I'm finishing breakfast. He tells me he's attempting to set up an exchange with Catersville: Shannon for a planeload of parts, medicine, and what he calls *bling*—coffee, liquor, chocolate and such.

"I've sent them the offer, but they're not jumping on it," he says. "They claim they're keeping Shannon for her own good—that you're mentally unstable and should be kept away from her." When I start to protest, he holds up his hands. "I'm not saying I believe them, I'm just stating what they told me."

We end up having a discussion about what happened on the tarmac at Catersville, and when I tell him about their request for me to "walk through Eden in the fashion that God intended," he takes out his phone and shows me the video they sent him.

It's quite eye-popping.

It's shot with a camera phone through a dirty windshield, and the image is shaky and small. I'm out on the tarmac, buck naked, apparently singing and dancing in the rain. There's no sound, but it's clearly me.

"It's been edited," he says. "I had one of my men take a look, and there are pieces missing and a section that repeats three or four times—to make it look like you're dancing."

I can't imagine what Lani would think if she saw this. "If you didn't know the truth," I say, "you'd think I was mad as a hatter."

He crosses his arms. "So you're sticking to your story? They took her unprovoked?"

"It's not a story, it's the truth." I fight to keep my temper under control. "She was hiding under a blanket in the backseat."

"And you didn't do *anything* to piss them off?"

I stare at him for a couple of seconds and then look away. "Besides landing on their runway, begging for fuel, and pleading with them not to shoot up the plane, no."

"But you realize that trying to trick them into thinking you were Jesus could be seen as provocation?"

"What are you saying?" I stand up. "That it's my fault they kidnapped Shannon?"

He scoots his chair back. "Of course not, but you do seem to have a talent for pissing people off."

"I didn't have a choice, Dave. If we wanted fuel, they insisted I take off my clothes and walk around in the goddamn Garden of Eden."

"Okay. That's what I thought, but I wanted to make sure I got the full story." He stands up and replaces the chair in the corner. "Anything else you've left out?"

I shake my head. "We did everything they asked,

cooperated to the fullest, right up until they forced Shannon out of the plane at gunpoint."

"Okay. Let me see what I can do—maybe turn the heat up a bit." He walks to the door. "I'll let you know as soon as I have more information."

"Thanks. Anything I can do to help?"

"Best thing would be to assist Soleil in unraveling the mystery in your blood. I heard she isolated the biotechs in your blood last night. It's a good start."

"She did?" I say, wishing Soleil would stop by and give me a chance to explain myself.

"Don't worry," Dave says and pats me on the shoulder. "I'll get Shannon back."

He strides out just as Nurse Ratched—whose real name turns out to be Nurse *Sweet*—peeks around the doorframe. Bella seems to have taken me off the torture list, and things have improved dramatically here in the hospital. Nurse Sweet has even taken to bringing me actual food and smiling at my jokes occasionally.

"Morning," I say. "What can I do for you?"

"Dr. Nadales needs more of your blood for analysis," she says as she collects my empty tray, "and an MRI for comparison purposes. I wasn't planning to go with you, if that's okay?"

"Yep. Just point me in the right direction."

After another stint at the Vampire Lounge—as Nurse Sweet calls the blood lab—I finish filling out Soleil's long set of questions on my genetic background and set off for the MRI lab. I end up sitting in an empty waiting room for two hours, twiddling my thumbs and wishing I had a cell phone to play games on.

I'm feeling exhausted and morose when I get back to my room.

At dinnertime, Nurse Sweet stops by, but her hands are

empty. "Dr. Nadales has requested that we get a spinal fluid sample," she says. "She wants to know if you're willing to undergo the procedure tomorrow, and she asked me to convey to you that it's important."

"Why doesn't she tell me herself?"

"She's been busy in the lab all day, Mr. Crusoe. I'm sure you're aware of how important her work is—to all of us."

"Yes, of course."

"I'll need you to sign this." The nurse hands me a consent form—which is the first of its kind I've seen since I got here. "And don't worry," she says, "the procedure can be painful, but it isn't dangerous."

"Sounds delightful. Could you ask Dr. Nadales to stop by and explain it to me, please?"

"I'll see what I can do," she says and then hesitates.

"What is it?" I ask, getting a bad feeling about this whole thing.

"Unfortunately, she wants to do it first thing in the morning. You won't be able to eat dinner tonight. But you should be done in time for lunch tomorrow." She places her hand on my arm. "I apologize for not bringing you something earlier, but I just now saw the orders."

"No worries," I say, trying not to look as hungry as I feel.

She squeezes my arm. "You're a trouper."

I pass the evening reading about spinal fluid taps and hoping Soleil will stop by to answer my questions—or even chide me for being a delusional psychotic—but she doesn't.

I wait up until midnight, my empty stomach getting steadily worse, and then give up and go to bed.

But I have trouble falling asleep.

I've been stuck in this universe for over a year, and my past life is starting to feel less solid, less real.

Am I crazy? Is this whole time travel nonsense a figment of my imagination?

When I finally nod off, I dream about rescuing Isabel from the hotel fire—only when I lift the rubble from her trapped body, she's a skeleton. Standing behind her body are Lani, Shannon, and Soleil in punctured biosuits, their panicked faces begging me to save them. I glance up and see the pod from the time machine falling down through the flames.

I jolt awake, covered in sweat.

Christ, maybe the operation will kill me, and I won't have to face the mess I've made of things.

"Good morning!" The light in my room comes on, and I blink back the affront.

A male doctor I've never met walks in wearing scrubs.

"I heard that you were a little worried about the procedure, and I want to assure you that it's perfectly safe."

"Okay," I say. "Where's Dr. Nadales?"

"She'll be meeting us in the OR."

I nod, still trying to clear the cobwebs from my tired brain.

Ten minutes later, I'm wheeled into an operating room, and the doctor puts a mask over my face.

I push the mask away. "What happened to Dr. Nadales?" I ask, feeling like a broken record.

"She couldn't be here this morning, but there's no reason to be worried, we'll take good care of you."

"Yeah."

"Haven't lost one yet," he says and places the mask back over my face.

Before I can say anything else, the world fades to black.

I wake up in some sort of recovery room, feeling sore and queasy.

A male nurse checks my vitals and asks if I need some anti-nausea medication. A moment after I shake my head no, I vomit yellow bile into the basin he's holding out.

"Sorry," I say, feeling disoriented.

"Happens all the time," he says. "Change your mind about the meds?"

I nod. "Thank you."

He adds something to my IV, and I fall gratefully back asleep.

Sometime later, I wake up with excruciating pain in my lower back, and the nurse gives me more pain meds. Between that and the anti-nausea stuff, I'm in the recovery room for the rest of the day, tripping in and out of painful consciousness.

Christ, this sucks.

When I finally come to—and realize the pain is mostly gone—it's after eight. Nurse Sweet meets me in the recovery room and insists that I use a wheelchair.

Not this again.

"I'm not going anywhere in that," I say. "I can walk just fine."

She gives me a disapproving look but doesn't argue. "Mr. Kirk wants you in the communications room as soon as possible. He said it's important. Would you like me to bring your dinner over there?"

"No, thanks. I'll eat when I get back."

She gives me a sympathetic smile. "I'll let Mr. Kirk know you're on your way." She hesitates. "I wanted to say I'm sorry about this whole thing—what with you missing dinner last night, and Dr. Nadales canceling, and all that nausea... "

"It's fine," I say and squeeze her arm. "All's well that ends well."

CHAPTER 12

Shannon: All the World's a Stage

When I startle awake, I can't remember where I am. The windowless room is dimly lit and the air smells stale. And then I remember. I'm stuck inside a broken-down biodome, force-married to a skinny acne farm with a wife-murderer for a father, and expected to pop out a soccer team before I'm twenty-five.

I pull the covers up to my chin and look around. A pillow and blanket are crumpled in one corner, but the covers next to me are untouched.

I'm so hungry I could eat a hen.

"Peter?" I say, afraid that he's here—and afraid that he's not.

The door to the bathroom opens a crack, and my pretend husband peers out.

"Hi," I say when he finally spies me hiding under the

covers.

"Hi." He inches around the door, his hair damp but combed. "They'll be coming for us soon. You might want to get ready—assuming you want breakfast."

"Yes," I say, my stomach growling.

"Okay," he says, relaxing a little. "I found some clothes for you in one of the drawers. They're probably not what you're used to but…"

"Thank you."

He nods. "I left them on the counter. While you're changing, I'll take care of the evidence."

"The evidence?"

"Yeah. We have to make them think we… you know, did *it* last night."

"Oh, right!" I wait for him to move away from the door. "Shut your eyes."

He does, and I hop out and scurry into the bathroom. I repeat my actions from the night before and then put on the clothes—a blue and silver outfit like the woman from *I Dream of Jeannie* wore. They're a bit baggy but a lot less revealing than the nightie. I rebraid my hair and step back into the dimly lit room.

Peter has put his pillow and blanket back on the bed, and he's in the process of messing up the covers.

"What are you doing?" I ask, wondering why he isn't *making up* the bed, and then I notice the blood on the sheets—and the cut on his arm. "Oh my God, what happened? Are you okay?"

"I'm fine. I'm making it look like…" He swallows. "If my father finds out I didn't actually force you to—"

"Thank you," I say, finally getting it. "Although bleeding after the first time is just an old wives' tale."

He gives me a funny look.

"That's what my friend Mindy says." I can feel my face

getting warm. "She considers herself an expert on sex and men because she reads a lot of books."

"We don't have any books here—'cept the Bible."

"Oh." I plop down on the end of the bed. "Thanks for fixing up the… evidence."

He sits down next to me, his eyes averted. "Shannon, when the others are around, you need to act like you're my wife, or they'll send you to Rehabilitation."

"Like I'm broken and need fixing?"

"Yeah." He glances up at me. "That's where they sent my mother after she refused to obey my father. I didn't see her again until I found her body hanging in the chapel."

"Oh God, that's horrible." His words bring up an image that I can't get out of my head.

Is that what's going to happen to me?

He exhales. "And we should act like, you know, we did it." He drops his gaze again. "So you should pretend to be really sore."

"Sore?"

"Yeah. Down *there*." He glances sideways at my lap.

"But Mindy says—"

He looks over at me, his eyes pleading.

"Ah. Okay."

"And you should act cross. Like you hate me for what I did to you."

I nod, feeling too embarrassed to speak.

He stands back up. "But not too… rebelling."

"Rebellious?"

"Yeah, like, you should keep your head down and not look any men in the eyes. And if I tell you to do something, you need to do it. But you can look mad about it—I mean, if you want to."

I don't respond.

"I know it's not how you treat someone you care about,"

he says, "ordering them around and stuff, but it's what I have to do to keep you safe."

"Okay," I whisper, fear stealing my breath.

"And the other women are going to be mean to you—say cruel things to you—but they won't hurt you as long as you belong to me. Pretend you don't hear them."

"Why would they be mean to me?" I ask, glancing over at him. "I haven't done anything to hurt them."

"I can't really explain it, Shannon. It's the way things are here. In any case, when we're alone, you can do whatever you want. You don't have to follow orders or anything, and I won't... do anything to you." He looks over at me, his eyes pleading. "But in front of the others, especially my father, you need to act like you're an obedient wife. Okay?"

Before I can answer, there's pounding on the door.

"Please?" he whispers, and I nod.

He unlocks the door and opens it.

A gaggle of men are standing outside, looking like they're ready to storm the castle.

Peter's father pushes through them and steps in, his gaze darting around the room before landing on me. I step backward, feeling awkward in the genie costume, but grateful it's not the nightie. He strides over to the bed, yanks back the blankets, and grunts. "Cover yourself," he says and tosses a folded red bundle at my feet.

It's some sort of tattered Red Riding Hood cloak—hood and all.

I put it on, wrapping the scratchy fabric around myself and pulling the hood up, all the while trying to act like I'm sore *down there*—which isn't hard considering how much my stomach hurts.

Peter steps in front of me, and I bow my head, avoiding his eyes. "After the Forty Days of Procreation," he says, his voice too loud, "you may wear women's clothing. Until that time, no one may look upon your flesh."

I nod, not meeting his eyes.

He grabs the front of my robe and pulls me closer. "Do you hear me, wife?"

I gasp and look up at him. "Yes," I say, not needing to fake my fear.

"When you address me, you will call me 'sire.' If you forget again, I will punish you."

"Yes, sire," I say and drop my gaze.

He releases me and walks out the door.

"Wouldn't have believed it if I hadn't seen it with my own eyes." Peter's father gives an approving grunt. "What do you know, boys? He just needed a ripe virgin to bring out the man in him."

"Do your legs not work?" Peter says from beside his father. "Or do you wish me to provide a horse and carriage?"

There's male laughter out in the hallway.

"That's more like it." The man gives his son a hearty pat on the back, and Peter walks away.

I scuttle after him, trying not to step on the hem of the long, red cloak.

When we round the corner, I smell food cooking, and my mouth waters. It's been a whole day since I last ate, and I'm so hungry I'm feeling weak. I follow Peter through a set of double doors and risk a quick glance up. The cafeteria is full of adult men.

"Slut."

I turn toward the sound—and lock eyes with a woman dressed as if she just stepped out of *Little House on the Prairie*, bonnet and all. There's a scar across her face, and one of her eyes doesn't focus right.

"You don't belong here," she says through clenched teeth, "and you'll bring nothing but evil upon us." She's carrying a tray of food, and her hands are red and chapped. She shuffles past me. "The whole world lieth in wickedness!"

I look away and hurry after Peter—who stops unexpectedly, causing me to crash into his back. "Sorry!" I blurt out.

I hear the collective taking in of breath and belatedly add, "Sir. I mean, sire, sir." I bow my head. "Sorry, sire."

There are mumbled comments that include the words *retard* and *halfwit*, and I hear someone say, "What did you expect from a dumb blond?"

Someone else adds, "Might be stupid, but I'll bet she's a good rut."

I'm not sure what *rut* means—and I don't think I want to know.

Peter turns around, and I risk a quick glance up, trying to apologize with my eyes for being so forgetful, but his face is blank.

"Have you not seen real food before?" Peter says. "Are the other places so wretched that they cannot afford to feed a clumsy girl?" He grabs me by the arm and yanks me around to face the back of the room.

"You're hurting me!" I say and pull away, frightened by his rough treatment.

A woman—the one with the bad eye—calls out, "Lock her up," and the others take up the chant.

I rub my arm and look around in horror at the leering faces. I can't do this.

Peter lifts his hand, silencing the room. "What did you say, wife?"

I drop to my knees, my head bowed. "Nothing, sire."

He walks away. "Women eat at the last table," he says over his shoulder. "But only after the men are sated."

I count the rows, realizing that there is one woman for every twenty men here.

They've lost ninety-five percent of the female population?

Peter sits down, leaving me kneeling there in the Red

Riding Hood getup. He glances over his shoulder, and our eyes meet. "Get my break"—his voice falters—"fast." He clears his throat. "And be quick about it."

I blink, his gaze still on me, and he motions with his head for me to get up.

But I can't stop thinking about how many women they've killed.

More than a hundred.

I stare at Peter, frozen by fear and my own rising panic.

"Please," he mouths and then turns away.

Pretend you're in a play, Shannon. Act the part. Find a way to stay alive.

I manage to get to my feet and stumble toward the kitchen, lurching out of the way every time a woman scurries past me carrying a tray of food and calling out under her breath.

"Halfwit."

"Demon."

"Whore."

CHAPTER 13

Diego: Flying Pigs

Fifteen minutes after leaving the recovery room, I shuffle into the communications building, feeling pretty shitty.
Should have used that damn wheelchair.

Ted, the radio operator, motions for me to sit down.

Dave is talking on the radio in the glass-walled room next to us, gesturing wildly and pacing around.

Ted finishes speaking with someone via headphones, writes down some notes, and turns to me.

"We're expecting a call from DC any moment."

"DC?" I ask. "What's up?"

Apparently, Kirk sent some men to Washington DC to see if they could find anything on the Magic Kingdom, and they discovered a room full of boxes marked *Top Secret*. One of those boxes had the word TARDIS on it.

Just as Ted finishes filling me in, the receive light comes

back on.

"That's probably DC now," Ted says and gestures at Dave—who acknowledges. Ted switches the radio over to the speakers. "Press the button on the mic to talk."

I nod.

"DC, this is C-Bay," Ted says. "We are standing by. Over."

"Armstrong here. Where is Mr. Kirk?"

"On the other line," Ted says. "He'll be here in a moment. What do you have for us?"

"We unpacked the box marked TARDIS," Custer says.

Dave walks into the room, looking like he's about to blow a gasket.

"It's full of status reports on something called…"—we hear papers shift—"a 'Trans-Temporal Viewing Device'."

Mierda. That's the Peeping Tom.

"We're taking photos of everything now," Custer says.

"Is that all you got, Armstrong?" Dave says.

"No, sir. There's something on a 'Hot Button' too."

Dave turns to me. "That mean anything to you?"

I nod. "It's a thumb drive."

"What about 'Single Genotype, Broad-Spectrum-Immunity Biotech Device'?" Custer says. "Some sort of scientific paper?"

I can't believe my ears. "Those are the instructions to build the biotech devices. Are they complete?"

"Stand by." We can hear him speak to someone away from the mic. "No. I repeat: The cover sheet is all we have. Looks like whoever collected this stuff didn't care much about the details."

"Anything else?" Dave asks.

There's some static on the line. "We do have the title page for a 'One-Way Temporal Computing Device.' The principal author's name is Phillip something—the ink is smeared. The second author is listed as…" There's a pause. "The second author is Matthew M. Hudson, PhD."

The plans to build the time machine.

"Are there any maps or other information on where the research was being done?" Dave asks. "Anything on the location of the project?"

"We're looking," Custer says. "I'm sending photos of everything now."

"We got 'em," Ted says and nods at Dave. "I'll print hard copies."

"What else do you have for me?" Dave asks.

"That's it, Mr. Kirk."

"Okay," Dave says. "I want that box in my office by tomorrow morning."

"Yes, sir," Custer says. "We're packing it up now."

"Safe travels," Ted says. "Over and out."

Bella, whom I haven't seen since dinner a week ago, arrives as the printer comes to life.

Dave fills her in on the news as the printer spits out paper.

Bella takes the first couple of sheets and starts reading. "This is definitely intriguing, and the summary states that the broad-spectrum immunity includes a wide variety of viruses, bacteria, and toxins." She picks up the next page from the printer, and then starts shuffling through the ones underneath it. "Where is the rest of this 'Biotech Device' research paper?"

"That's all they found," Ted says. "Just the title page."

"What? We need the rest of this. Where is it?"

"Probably inside a mountain somewhere in Colorado," I say. "It was part of a secret government project started before Doomsday. If we can figure out where that hollowed-out mountain is, we might be able to find the rest of those instructions."

"Excuse me, Mr. Kirk," Ted says. "There are other messages for you."

Kirk nods and runs his hand through his thinning hair. "Spit it out."

"The Bub wants to know when you'll have the repair parts out to them. And Kansas City called a half hour ago, asking for instructions. They have all the folks from the Lou, but they're over capacity, and some of the refugees are seriously injured."

"Tell the Bub I'm working on it," Dave says. "And tell KC I'll figure out a way to get the ones who need medical attention to C-Bay. We can spread the rest of them out across the other domes—have Population Control check on openings and requests. How many are injured?"

"Forty-three, give or take."

"We don't have enough hospital beds," Bella says. "Where are we going to put all of them?"

"We'll have to squeeze for now," Dave says. "Can you handle it?"

"Of course, I can," Bella says. "It's my hospital."

Everyone looks at Bella like she just said pigs can fly.

"Well," she says, stepping closer to Dave, "don't you think it's about time I started pulling my weight?"

Dave turns back to Ted, his eyebrows still raised. "Let KC know."

"Yes, sir. But there's more."

"Jesus fucking Christ," Dave says. "What is it now?"

Ted glances sideways at me, and I wonder what he doesn't want me to know. "The investigators are insisting we step up external examinations of all the biodomes. They suspect an outer seam failed, and if that's the case, whatever took down the Lou could take down other bubbles at any time. And I got a call from both San Francisco and MIT expressing concern. Those biodomes were built about the same time as the Lou, and if they fail, we'll lose access to their manufacturing facilities—which means no more batteries, metal tools, or computer parts in North A—"

"Alright, alright. Let's not jump to conclusions." Dave pushes past Bella and grabs the papers out of Ted's hand. "The Lou was built by different contractors using different suppliers. The failure could have been caused by a poorly manufactured part—or even a construction error. I won't know for sure until I get all the data back and have a chance to analyze it." He gives the radio operator a hard glare. "*I* sent out that inspection team, and they shouldn't have discussed their findings with anyone except me."

"They didn't, sir. They thought it was time-critical and asked me to relay the message."

"Well, let me suggest that you keep a lid on it," Dave says. "*Capisce?*"

Ted nods.

"And let Frisco and MIT know I'll have an update for them in the next couple of days."

"Yes, sir."

The printer stops, and we all stare at it, unnerved by the sudden silence.

Dave shuts his eyes, pinching his temples with one hand.

"What is it, David?" Bella asks. "Are you alright?"

"Yeah," he says and scoops up the papers. "C-Bay was built by the same contractor as the Lou—using the same damn plans."

Bella brings her hand up to her throat. "Are we in any danger?"

"I don't know." Dave turns back to Ted. "Get KC on the line and have them track down Shelly. Ask her if the Lou had any unusual air leaks in the days leading up to the failure."

Ted nods, looking worried.

"Do it now," Dave says. "Let me know as soon as you hear back from her. If I'm right, we may need to get a crew out first thing in the morning."

"Yes, sir." Ted puts on his headphones and gets to work.

Dave turns to me. "I may need your help—seeing that you can work Outside without a biosuit. You up to it?"

"Sure," I say. "If the lab needs more blood, I can work around their schedule."

"Good," Dave says. "I'll have someone get back to you with the specifics tonight." He exhales. "Shit, this is not what I needed right now." He hands the stack of papers to Bella. "Since you're back in the saddle, why don't you take a look at these, and we'll talk when I get home. Tell Soleil she needs to figure out how to make that damn vaccine work before it's too late." He strides out of the room.

I slump down in the chair, happy about the Magic Kingdom news, but almost hungry enough to eat Soylent Green.

"You gotta give it to the guy," I say to no one in particular. "He gets shit done."

Bella reads the title of the document before glancing at me, her eyes taking in my unshaven face and hospital scrubs. "What happened to you?"

"Me?" I say, unable to believe she's addressing me.

"No, your doppelganger from another universe, Mr. Crusoe. Yes, you."

I laugh uncomfortably. "Rough day. But I'm fine, thanks."

"Well, get some sleep. You look like hell."

"Yes, ma'am."

She rounds on Ted and he recoils, expecting to be reprimanded for listening in, I think.

"And don't worry, Theodore." She places her hand on his shoulder. "My husband can be a pompous ass, but he knows his shit when it comes to the biodomes."

"Yeah, I hope so," Ted says, staring at her like she's one of the Stepford wives. "Because I'm pretty sure the shit's about to hit the fan."

CHAPTER 14

Lani: Over and Out

I sign and date the list of medicines, slip the inventory sheet inside the box, and close up the flaps. After nearly twenty years inside this fish bowl, it's going to be hard to say goodbye.

It would be easier if I knew where we were going.

Even if we use all the fuel reserves, we don't have enough to get to Salt Lake, but David has assured us that as soon as he resettles the folks from the Lou, he'll figure out a way to get diesel out to us. KC is the closest, but they are already packed, and no one here wants to live in a converted airport terminal. There are other options, and now that we have rebreather masks, they aren't complete fantasy.

We haven't given up on repairing the biodome wall, but the council has decided to plan for the worst—and with a snowstorm brewing, no one is arguing. Everyone is packing up for a cross-country trek through the mountains in winter.

"Your attention, please!" Ally's voice booms over the intercom. "Dr. Hudson and my sister, Mindy the Magnificent, have located the underground city! I repeat: They have found the Magic Kingdom." She giggles. "And get this folks, it's only a hundred and thirty-four miles away as the crow flies."

The mood in the clinic improves substantially, and I suspect the rest of the folks in the Bub are just as relieved.

"They don't know how many people are inside," Ally adds, "and a rockslide took out their radio antenna a while ago. We have no way to contact them."

Murmurs break out around the room, and I raise my hand to curb the noise.

"But," she continues, "all the exterior access doors appear to be sealed—which is the good news. The bad news is: We'll have to send someone on foot to check if the power is still on, find the airlock, and figure out how to get inside. There will be a town hall meeting tonight to discuss the new options. Ally, out."

The mood at dinner that night is jubilant—despite all the unknowns—and when Mindy and Madders walk in, people are so busy cheering and slapping them on the back that the two of them barely have time to eat. When I mention that the celebration is a bit premature, Madders places his hand on my shoulder and gazes around the room.

"You're right, as usual," he says, "but the last couple of weeks have been pretty rough on folks, and hope is a good thing."

I drop my gaze and finish my dinner.

After the dishes are cleared, we get down to business.

We discuss sending a couple of people on foot. But even if they take the electric golf cart and don't run into any bad weather—which is doubtful at best—it could take weeks.

"We don't have that kind of time," Madders says.

Becky suggests that we could fly someone up to the mountain, and they could walk the rest of the way. But that idea doesn't prove to be any better.

"There's no place to land between here and the bloody mountain," Madders says. "I checked." He shakes his head. "I know time is of the essence, but unless someone's got a helicopter packed away in mothballs, it's gonna have to be on foot—and believe me, it won't be a walk in the park."

Mindy suggests we drop someone from the plane with a parachute, and after a bit of back and forth, people start taking the idea seriously. Unfortunately, there's only one parachute—in need of some patching—so it will have to be a solo mission.

"But I can drop supplies, including a radio," Madders says, "so we'll be able to get status updates and send out more equipment if needed." He glances around the room. "I think it could work."

Then comes the hard decision: Who to send?

Mindy volunteers right away, but I immediately veto the idea. "Anyone under thirty is out. We can't afford to lose you. Population Control would never approve it, and neither would I."

"Agreed," Madders says. "Whoever goes could be marooned for days or even weeks. If we can't figure out a way to get inside the mountain, he or she would have to hike back to the Bub—through mountainous terrain in winter, wearing a rebreather mask 24/7."

"One false step, one slip of the mask, and…" Ally slices her finger across her throat. "Just like those poor folks who died when the patch failed. Nobody's lived Outside for that long. Ever."

"They'd have to take an emergency bubble," Madders says, thinking out loud. "And set it up at night so they could eat, drink and sleep with the mask off. We'd have to rig up some way for them to haul it around and some way to power it over an extended period."

"Or I could go," I say.

There's nothing you can do for Shannon right now, but you can do this. For everyone.

I shrug. "I wouldn't need a mask or a portable bubble, I'm good with my hands, and I've survived Outside before. I'm pretty much the perfect choice."

There are protests from around the room, all of them centered on the fact that I'm the only doctor.

"I'll have the radio," I say. "Lucy will be back on her feet in a day or two, and Becky has surgical training..."

Everyone looks at Becky.

"I'm fine," she says, stroking her daughter's hair. "It won't happen again."

There's discussion for more than an hour, but the choice is obvious, and everyone eventually agrees.

Madders circles the plane around so we get a good look at the massive concrete ledge cut out of the mountainside. There's a short tunnel leading into the center of the rocky gash, with a door big enough to drive a semi through at the end.

"Wow," I say, apprehension filling me with the jitters.

"I told you it was awesome," Mindy says. "It must be eff-ing huge inside."

"How sure are you this is the place?" I ask Madders.

"Well, it's a bloody awful place to put a drive-in movie theater, don't you think?" He gives me an indulgent smile. "I'm certain it's the right place. Kirk says it matches the description exactly—right down to the access road on the south slope."

"Okay." I swallow and check the compass in my pocket

for the tenth time. "If you say so."

"Remember," he says, "when I give the signal, pop the door handle and push with your shoulder. You only need to open the door enough to get your feet on the landing gear strut—just like we practiced."

"Yes," I say, my heart leaping into my throat.

The copilot's seat has been removed from the plane, and I'm sitting on the floor facing backward, my feet wedged against the back seat.

I go over the actions one more time. "I open the door, put my feet on the strut, and roll out toward the tail, pivoting over the landing gear and letting gravity pull me down."

"Good," he says. "Don't push off, just fall, keeping your feet on the strut until you're well below the plane. You don't want to hit the landing gear."

"Okay."

He glances over at me. "Use your hands to protect the parachute handles until you're clear. Once your main chute has deployed, steer toward the ledge. You may pick up some wind coming down the mountain slope. So head into it when you brake and land."

"I got it, Madders," I say, flexing my fingers to dissipate the adrenaline.

"Once you give me the signal," he says, "I'll do another flyover, and Mindy will push out the backpack."

Mindy nods, her eyes wide behind the rebreather mask.

"Pay attention to where your gear lands," he says. "You're going to need that radio—and the supplies."

I swallow down the acid in the back of my throat. "Let's do it."

Madders brings the plane around and then reduces the airspeed, tips the wing down on my side, and cuts the engine power.

"Go!"

I shove the door open and fling my feet out, but my shoe snags on the door handle, twisting me around.

"Shit!"

I yank my foot free and the shoe disappears, but I'm facing the wrong way now.

For an instant I consider aborting the jump, but I'm already in the slipstream. I place my sock-covered foot on the strut, cover the release handles with my arms, and fall *backward* toward the tail.

The next few seconds are a blur, but I don't get hung up on the seat belt, don't release the chute prematurely, and don't hit the landing gear.

Once I'm in free fall, it's a lot noisier than I expected, and my stomach is in the wrong place. All I can see is blue sky and the plane moving away.

The disorientation makes it hard to think, and I close my eyes, trying to force my brain to work.

You're upside-down, Lani. Take it easy. Once you deploy the canopy, you'll be fine.

I release the pilot chute, and a slight jerk lifts my head and wrenches my stomach into place.

A few moments later, there's a bigger jolt, yanking me hard against the harness and causing the straps to cut into my skin. I let out the breath I've been holding and look up into a cloudless blue sky.

A bright orange canopy is fluttering above me.

"Well, that must have looked graceful," I say aloud.

I grab the toggles and turn the chute around, looking for the massive concrete ledge. When I see it, I steer in that direction, testing how much strength it takes to slow my descent: not much. I do a full 360, taking in the beautiful scenery—snow-capped mountains to the west, and rolling, golden plains spreading out to the east. The parachute is surprisingly easy to steer, and I let out a whoop of pure joy.

This is the most fun I've had in ages.

For a moment I wonder how that young, daring juvenile delinquent turned into stodgy old me.

Bad shit happened.

I force myself to focus.

There's a small lake on the other side of the ridge to the west, and I can see the old dirt road cutting into the eastern side of the mountain. There's a stiff breeze blowing toward the plains. I head for the far side of the concrete, giving myself room for error when I land.

Although the ground seems to be approaching way too fast, I wait until I'm close enough to see the cracks on the concrete and then turn and brake into the wind.

I manage to touch down on my one shoed foot—just like Tinker Bell.

The chute comes down behind me, and I jog across cracked, broken concrete and stand on the fabric while I take off the harness.

You did it!

I roll the parachute into a bundle so it won't blow away and scan the sky for the airplane. It's out over the prairie, heading back toward me.

I wave my arms, signaling that I'm okay.

Madders tips the wings and a minute later, I see something come out the door of the plane.

But the makeshift parachute snags on the landing gear, the heavy backpack dangling below it.

The airplane wobbles precariously.

Oka fefe.

I shade my eyes with my hand and stare up. Mindy is leaning out the side of the plane.

Mother of Pele, what is she trying to do?

As the plane flies over me, Mindy pushes and tugs at the stuck parachute, but it doesn't come loose. Madders pulls up over the next ridge and Mindy goes back inside. If the backpack falls off now, it'll take me days to find it. Madders flies back around, gaining altitude, and then he does a second pass, heading toward me again. But this time he tips the nose down into a shallow dive—and then rolls the plane over.

I hope Mindy has her seatbelt on tight.

When the plane is upside-down, the backpack swings around—and the parachute unhooks from the landing gear and falls away.

Yes!

Once the plane is righted, I wave my arms again and shout, "You're one hell of a pilot, Matthew Hudson!"

The handmade parachute catches the wind and the bundle floats down toward the massive gash where the ledge cuts into the mountain—a near-perfect drop.

Or at least that's what I think until all hell breaks loose.

Unbelievably loud gunfire erupts behind me, spraying the air with bullets.

My street-kid instincts kick in, and I drop to the ground. I can see flashes of muzzle fire coming from two turrets mounted in the overhang above the massive service entry doors. I look more carefully and see three other turrets, their weapons silent.

The guns don't seem to be swiveling properly, or maybe the targeting mechanism is broken, because the backpack falls through the hot zone without any visible damage. It lands heavily, ten meters from a turret. The machine gun fires more rounds as the parachute floats down next to the backpack.

A few seconds later, silence returns.

Good thing I didn't come down closer to the wall.

I sit up and then wave at the plane. Madders tips the wings again—oblivious to the gunfire—and then banks and heads back to the Bub.

I sit there in sun, the cool mountain breeze tousling my hair, feeling like there's nobody else in the world.

How am I going to get the backpack without getting shot?

"The most effective way to get something done... is to do it."

I toss my bundled up parachute toward the guns, keeping my foot on the harness so it stays put.

Nothing happens.

Okay then.

I crawl on my hands and knees toward the canopy and repeat the process.

The guns erupt, spraying the air with bullets.

I pull the parachute back and toss it *half* as far.

No guns.

I crawl closer.

For once, luck is on my side, and I manage to get less than a parachute's length away from the backpack without setting off the firing squad.

I pull up a large chunk of loose concrete, wrap it up in the canopy, and throw the bundle past the backpack.

Bang, bang, bang!

The chute unfurls and a suspension line snags on the backpack. The three closest turrets show no sign of running out of ammunition, and the racket is deafening.

I start reeling the chute back in, dragging the backpack with it, guns blazing the whole time.

The parachute comes loose.

"Damn it."

It takes four more tries, but I eventually manage to haul the backpack out of the hot zone.

I take a pencil out of a side pocket and scribble a heavy line on the concrete. I add the words "Danger! Guns!" and arrows pointing toward the three working rifles. After I get a drink of water, I crawl away from the guns, dragging the backpack behind me.

I find my shoe lying on the edge of the concrete and gratefully put it back on. Then I hike across the mountainside, heading for the trees and hoping to find a stream and a flat spot to pitch my tent. I haven't taken fifty steps when I see something bright red tucked behind some scrub oaks. I veer off course to investigate and discover a biosuit lying facedown in the rocky dirt.

The discovery gives me the creeps—but it also gives me hope.

That environment suit had to come from somewhere protected, and I'm betting that it originated inside the mountain. Which means, at the very least, there were people here after Doomsday.

I do a quick once-over, looking for a cut or hole, but don't see any.

Maybe he ran out of oxygen?

The CO_2 detector is electric, and the battery is long dead, so there's no way to know for sure. But the breach detector is probably mechanical, same as it is in our biosuits.

I use my foot to flip it over. It's too light to have a body inside, and I wonder how an empty biosuit got out here in the woods—until I realize it's not empty.

It's full of bones—human ones.

Yikes!

There's no nametag, no way to know who was inside, but the breach detector is fully red: contaminated.

"Whoever was in there was killed by Doomsday. But how?"

I check the front for damage.

The fabric is bright red where it was protected from the sun, and I don't see any obvious holes. The boots and gloves are on tight, and the faceplate is cloudy—probably from the moisture of the body decomposing inside—but intact.

Except the helmet looks... weird. When I poke it to see how loose it is, it falls off and a skull slips out, short brown hair still attached to one temple. The head rolls down the side of the mountain, bumping and tumbling over the thin ground cover until it disappears over a ledge.

I swallow and force myself to breathe.

He unsealed the biosuit on purpose?

I back away, trying to decide if it's a good thing or a bad thing that I found the biosuit.

Perhaps both.

An hour later, I finish setting up my campsite and then put in a radio call to the Bub.

Mindy's cheerful voice greets me. "Howdy-do, Doc. What did ya think of that loop-dee-loop we did to free the backpack? Fucking awesome, huh?"

Usually, I would scold Mindy for using language like that, but this time, I have to agree with her.

"Fucking awesome, indeed."

CHAPTER 15

Diego: Outside the Lines

It turns out that C-Bay suffers from the same problem that took down the Lou, and the next morning, I begin work Outside.

The weather is cool and fallish, and my heavy sweater and jeans feel odd given that the ground below me is crawling with red spacemen.

There was a training session this morning—how to make the repairs while wearing a biosuit—but most of it wasn't applicable to me. So, I left early. I managed to get through the airlock before anyone else, load everything into a handmade trailer attached to an old gas-powered scooter, and get started by myself.

That was a couple of hours ago. I'm only on my third repair now, but each one is going faster.

As I'm waiting for the sealant on the fourth repair to harden, I lean against the biodome wall, shut my eyes, and let the memories come flooding back...

I can almost see the outcropping of rock near the cabin, hear the stream rushing down below me, smell the mountain air. I visualize Isabel inside the cabin, working on her biome research or cooking dinner, both of us looking forward to an evening in each other's arms.

What the hell am I doing in this godforsaken place?

I take a deep breath and get back to work.

Still, after nearly a year of being an invalid—and a week of being a pincushion—I have to admit, it's good to be working outdoors again, good to be using my hands and doing something productive.

Mierda, what a mess you've made of things.

First, misleading Lani into thinking I was in love with her, and then turning Shannon over to those wackos, and now tearing open old wounds for Bella and Soleil.

Of course they all hate you. You've done nothing but fuck things up.

As ironic as it sounds, Dave is the only one who doesn't want me tarred and feathered, and as much as it pains me to say it, he seems like a decent—if arrogant—guy.

If you achieved half as much as he has, you'd be arrogant too.

By ten, I've finished a handful of repairs—but the suits have completed only a couple between them.

Each repair—of which there are 180—requires covering a seam with sealer goop and attaching two heavy metal plates welded together at an angle. It's not particularly difficult, but it's hard manual labor—and I neglected to bring leather gloves, so my hands are taking a beating.

I watch the suits lumber around for another minute and then get back to work. I check that my metal plates are secure and climb down the ladder. I'm stiff and sore, but for once, I feel like I'm actually doing something useful.

The day after we arrived in C-Bay, I gave Shannon's rebreather plans to Kirk, but it turns out no one believed a kid could come up with a fix for them. So no one bothered to investigate. This morning, I mentioned that Matt was involved in the project too, and Kirk promised he'd have someone follow up.

Better late than never, I guess.

Until they get some rebreathers fixed, the crews must climb forty-foot ladders, heft bulky metal plates, and apply quick-acting sealant while wearing stiff, clunky biosuits. Not even the knights on the fields of Agincourt had it that tough.

I heave a heavy plate over my shoulder and start hauling it up the ladder, shooing away the hoards of crows as I go. It takes me a few tries to wrestle the plate onto the pre-existing bolts, the muscles in my arms complaining. Once I manage to get it in place, I hurry down, mix up the sealant, and scramble back up to apply the goo before it sets. Then I screw on six bolts the size of donuts and tighten them down with a pneumatic drill.

By midday, my arms and back are protesting every movement, but I'm making steady progress.

The biosuits are assumed to have four hours of air, but with all the exertion required for the repair work, the first crew is forced to quit early. Thirty minutes later, the next crew appears, and I curse Dave and his minions for not listening to me about the masks.

No idea why the word of the most hated man in C-Bay didn't carry any weight.

Except for a short break to wolf down my lunch, I continue working through the day and into the evening. The crews appear and disappear around me until the sun gets low in the sky. In the fading twilight, I place the ladder flat on the ground, load all the tools back onto the trailer, and take everything back to a covered area in front of the airlock.

It's been nice to have an entire day to myself. No Bella to avoid. No Soleil scowling at me. No needles stuck in my arm. I've completed eleven repairs, and the crews have finished another seven. As long as we don't run out of parts or sealant—and the weather holds—we should have all the repairs done in a little over a week.

I hope that's soon enough.

I stand for a minute and look up into the dark sky, a brilliant array of stars popping out all over—way more than I've ever seen before. I look for the Big Dipper—and find it—but something about it looks... off.

Maybe it's all those extra stars you can't see in a world full of light pollution?

I draw an imaginary line through the last two stars in the cup and follow it to Polaris, the North Star. It's right where it should be. And Orion looks normal too, including the orangish glow of Betelgeuse and the bright shine of Rigel. I take a more careful look at the Big Dipper and realize what's wrong. One of the stars in the Dipper's handle is absent, a whole solar system moved or missing in this universe.

The realization casts a shadow over me, and I shiver.

What caused a whole star system to vanish?

I can't answer that question, but I do know that vast and powerful forces are at work, and my insignificant existence in this universe is tenuous at best.

I hurry back into the airlock, wait for the all-clear signal, and head back to my room without encountering a soul. I take a shower, eat the baked chicken dinner Nurse Sweet has left for me, and go to bed.

For the next eight days, my routine is broken only by a failed attempt to find leather gloves, two updates from Dave on Shannon ("I'm working on it, but the Catersville people are dragging their feet." and "We're hashing out the details now."), and three evening trips to the Vampire Lounge—sans Soleil.

As I'm walking across the lamp-lit park on the eighth night—heading back to my room for a cold dinner and an evening alone—I notice someone coming toward me.

In the unconscious instant it takes to recognize that walk, my heart leaps into my throat and sweat breaks out on my palms.

Isabel.

I don't realize I've made a mistake until she stops in front of me, her eyes glistening in the lamplight.

"Hi," she says, looking completely different. Her hair is no longer blond, and instead of a dress and high heels, she's wearing old jeans, a loose turtleneck sweater—and tennis shoes.

"Dr. Kirk?" I manage to croak out. "You've changed… your hair."

"Yes, I should have let it go gray years ago. What a relief it is to stop trying to be someone I'm not."

"Why the sudden switch?" I ask, not sure how to take the new Bella.

She glances around the park, not meeting my gaze. "At a certain age, a woman must decorate herself or lose her husband to a younger woman. Seeing you made me realize I'm past that age."

I laugh, finally seeing my Isabel underneath all the pretense. "As far as I'm concerned, age isn't important unless you're a cheese."

She pins her gaze on me, her eyes defiant. "I don't believe that for a moment," she says. "But I appreciate the sentiment. I was hoping I could buy you dinner—or even just a drink."

"*Mierda*, you have bars in here?" I say, still feeling off-balance. "Why didn't someone tell me that sooner?"

"Haven't you heard?" One corner of her mouth twitches.

"We all hate you."

I look more closely at her face, my heart still racing. She's not wearing any makeup either. "It's nice to have you back, hun."

She blows right by my words. "Well?"

"I'd love to have dinner," I say, "but I need to take a shower and change my clothes first."

"Right," she says, looking a bit off-balance herself. "Meet me at Milliways in an hour? It's a block west of the hospital. You can't miss it."

"Make it thirty minutes," I say. "I'll hurry."

She smiles for the first time, and it twists my heart into a knot. It's the closest I've been to Isabel in over a year, and it's sweet torture.

"I'll wait for you there," she says and turns away. "Table in the corner."

I watch her walk away, memories of Iz swirling in my brain.

Bella's a little older, a little warier, but she is, most definitely, the same woman I fell in love with.

I take one last look and then jog off into the night.

Twenty-seven minutes later, I walk into the bar at the end of the universe.

CHAPTER 16

Shannon: Ruby Red Slippers

At dinner, I set Peter's plate down in front of him, my back sore from scrubbing the cafeteria floor. He grunts, avoiding my eyes, and I hurry off to the women's table to wait for the men to finish eating.

The other women have been ordering me around all day, yanking my hair and scolding me when I make a mistake.

"Hasn't done a day of work in her life," the woman with a bad eye says when I sit down at the table.

"Too busy whoring," another says and shifts away from me. "Probably crawling with diseases too."

The others grumble and scowl—all except one.

I venture a glance in her direction, and she meets my gaze, nodding once, and then averts her eyes.

While the women sit and eat, I'm instructed to clear the men's tables. When I'm done, I sit down in front of the watery bowl of soup and dry cornbread they've left me.

There's no spoon or other utensils. I lift the bowl up to my mouth.

Someone shoves me from behind, spilling the soup across the table. "Hurry up, you lazy whore." The woman with the bad eye knocks my cornbread onto the floor. "And what a clumsy oaf you are. Go get something to clean up the mess you've made."

I grab the food off the floor and shove it into my mouth.

She snorts. "You're no better than a filthy animal."

I carry my dishes to the kitchen and come back with a dirty rag.

She stands over me, her hands on her hips. "You leave one crumb, and I'll have you beaten for disobedience."

For the rest of the evening, I'm forced to wash pots and pans—and then wipe the tables and mop the floor.

After I finish, the woman who nodded at me earlier escorts me back to the Room of Release.

She unlocks the door and bows slightly, holding the heavy wooden portal open for me.

"Thank you," I say, meeting her eyes. "You're very kind."

She offers me a sad smile.

"Why aren't you mean to me like the others?" I ask.

She shrugs.

"Have you lived here all your life?" The moment I say it, I realize it's a dumb question.

Of course she has.

But she shakes her head.

"Where are you from?" I ask. "Did they kidnap you too?"

She nods and then hesitates.

"What is it?"

She opens her mouth and shows me her stump of a tongue.

"Oh my God! They did that to you?"

She nods again.

"I'm so sorry!"

She takes my hand and squeezes it.

"How can you stand to live here?"

She puts her hand over her belly and forms it into a fist, pumping it open and shut like a beating heart. It takes me a minute to realize what she's telling me.

"You're pregnant?"

She smiles.

We hear footsteps in the hallway, and her eyes widen. She pushes me inside, shuts the door, and locks it.

I stand there in the half-lit room and cry.

When I run out of tears, I drop the cloak on the floor and crawl into the huge bed, exhausted.

But sleep won't come.

I lie there thinking about Mom, wondering when she—or Diego or Madders—will come rescue me.

What if the plane crashed? What if no one knows where you are?

The thought makes it hard to breathe.

What if you're stuck here? What will happen when forty days goes by and you're not pregnant?

I shudder and pull the covers up tighter.

You have to get out of here, Shannon. Before you run out of time.

"But how?" I say aloud. "You don't even know where the airlock is, and the only person who's nice to you can't speak."

I vow to keep my mouth shut so I don't end up like that poor woman—or Peter's mother.

So what are you going to do?

"Go to sleep," I tell myself. "Like Mom says, things are always better in the morning."

But first I have to pee.

I crawl out of bed, rubbing the sore spot on my arm

where Peter grabbed me this morning, and use the bathroom. When I'm done, I dive back under the covers and try to sleep.

Sometime later, there's a soft knock on the door.

Peter?

I hear the lock turn and the door open and shut.

"Shannon?"

I pull the covers up over my head.

He walks across the room and sits down beside me. "Are you okay? I'm sorry about this morning. I didn't know what else to do. I'm afraid they'll take you away from me if I'm not…"

I turn away from him, tears spilling down my cheeks onto the pillow. "Leave me alone."

He sets something down on the bed. "I got these for you. To help you escape."

Escape?

Curiosity wins out over indignity, and I glance down at what he's brought me.

"It's a map of the biodome," he says, holding up some blueprints. "And I stole a security card off Mikey. He'll just think he lost it—wouldn't be the first time."

I look at him, stifling a sob.

"I know you despise me," he says, "and I understand why, but I'm not really like that. I'm not hateful and cruel like you think."

"You hurt me today," I say, rubbing my bruised arm.

He bows his head. "I'm sorry. I didn't mean to. I just meant to… show you how important it is that you listen to me."

"Or they'll cut my tongue out?" I say, thinking of that poor woman.

"Yes," he says, sounding relieved.

I know he's right, but I can't help feeling cross at him.

"I'll be more careful," he says, taking a cautious look at me. "Please forgive me."

I swallow and then nod. "Okay." I pick up the access card and turn it over in my hands. "Thank you."

"You're welcome." He picks up the blueprints and points to a small, square room on one edge. "This is where we are now," he says. "And this is where we brought you in." He drags his finger to the other side of the drawing. "I don't know where they put your biosuit, but I've been looking for it."

"I appreciate that, Peter, really I do, but my suit is almost out of power—and the oxygen is low. Without batteries and a truckload of O_2 tanks, it's useless. What I really need is something light and self-contained like a rebreather mask."

He shakes his head. "We don't have any masks."

"Maybe there are some hidden in a box somewhere." I sit up, keeping the covers tucked under my arms, and take a look at the map.

The room is dimly lit, and it's hard to see details, but the round edge of the biodome is clearly visible on the blueprint—except the words are hard to read.

And then I realize he has the drawing upside-down.

I take the large sheet of paper out of his hands and turn it around. There are lots of rooms marked 'Storage Area.' "Wow. This is perfect. Where'd you get it?"

He half-smiles. "I took it from the old Control Room. No one goes in there anymore now that the power's off."

I nod, impressed. "Thank you. It's perfect. If we can find some masks—and the epoxy I need to repair them—I could leave right away."

He takes the blueprints and folds them up, his smile fading. "I'll look some more tomorrow, but it may take some time. I have to do all my regular work, and in the evenings we have to make them think we're… you know."

I take his hand and squeeze it. "Thank you."

He jerks away like I'm contaminated with all those diseases the women are afraid of and stands up. "It's late, and we should get some sleep."

"Yeah, sure." I take the comforter and a pillow off the bed and hold them out for him. "I don't hate you, Peter. I just want to go home."

He looks at me, his expression defeated, and takes the bedding. "I wish I had somewhere to go home to."

CHAPTER 17

Diego: Fish and Chips

Bella waves when she sees me, awakening some dormant longing in me.

Now that her hair's back to its natural color and all the pretense is gone, I realize I'd do anything for this woman.

I can't decide if that's good or bad.

Heads turn as I make my way across the crowded bar. A couple of guys from the repair crew wave—and then turn to see who's expecting me.

"Thanks for waiting," I say and plop down across from Bella—who's sitting with a half-empty cup of tea and a pile of papers in front of her.

She pushes the folders aside and smiles. "I took the liberty of ordering you a beer. It's not as good as a Guinness, but I think you'll like it."

I don't bother to ask how she knows what kind of beer I

like. "I'm sure I will," I say as the barkeep sets a glass of dark brown liquid in front of me.

"Finest Irish stout on the planet," he says, splashing a bit of foam over the rim. "I grow the barley on my allotment and brew it myself."

"Good head," I say and try the beer. "Wow." I can't remember the last time I had something that tasted this good, but it wasn't in this universe. "Spectacular," I say and mean it.

The man beams. "Were you wanting something to eat?" he asks. "I'm afraid it's late. So all I've got left is the fish and chips." He shrugs. "But I could have Hank do you up an omelette, if that suits you better."

"Actually, the fish and chips sounds great," I say, my mouth watering.

"Make that two," Bella says. "And a round of the beer for me, please."

The guy's eyebrows rise, but he recovers quickly. "Of course, Dr. Kirk. I'll have that right out."

When the man leaves, I turn back to Bella. "So, is beer incredibly expensive—or have you never ordered it before?"

"Both."

I spend a minute running my gaze across her face and hair, unable to keep the smile off my face.

She blinks but doesn't look away.

Finally, I clear my throat, my heart racing again. "What's up?"

She glances down at her teacup and then back up at me, her expression changed. "What do you know about Lucas?"

Her question catches me off guard, and I spill some beer in my lap. "Lucas?"

"Yes," she says, watching me dab at my jeans with a napkin. "I know you saw the biotech paper, and I'm sure you noticed the names on it."

"I did," I say. "But, unfortunately, I don't know anything

about Lucas."

I'm a terrible liar, and it's clear she's aware of that, because she glares at me until I drop my gaze.

I clear my throat. "Although I recognize the name, I've never met him."

She reaches across the table and puts her hand on my wrist. "Please. Tell me the truth."

The barkeep sets a beer in front of Bella and then places our dinners on the table. "Will there be anything else, Dr. Kirk?"

"No, thank you." Bella slips her hand back into her lap. "Put it on Mr. Kirk's tab, please."

"Yes, ma'am." He acknowledges me with a nod and leaves.

The meal is more poached fillet and hashbrowns than fish and chips, but I'm ravenous and it tastes fantastic.

"Thank you," I say to Bella.

"You're welcome."

We eat in silence for a minute, Bella watching me wolf down my food—but only picking at hers.

Finally she can't wait any longer. "So what's the truth? How did you recognize his name?"

I exhale. "In my universe, you and I chose the same names for our twins—Lucas and Soleil."

She raises her eyebrows. "In your universe?"

"Yeah," I say. "But I don't know what happened in this universe."

Her eyes get big. "This universe? What in heaven's name are you talking about?"

"I thought it was pretty clear."

She opens her mouth to speak, then closes it again. "Okay, for the sake of argument, let's say you are from another universe."

I smile, feeling right at home now.

"What the hell are you doing in my universe?"

I gasp. "Having dinner with you, of course."

She rolls her eyes. "*Why* are you here?"

"I came for my health," I say.

"Your health?" She gives a mirthless laugh. "This whole world is a mess."

"I was misinformed."

She stares at me.

And then the tiniest hint of a smile flits across her lips.

"Tell me about Lucas," I say.

"Soleil has always believed that he and James are alive," Bella says, biting her lip. "A few weeks after they were killed, she told her teacher at school that 'Daddy and Lucas are under the ground, but Daddy is mad at Uncle Dave.'"

"*Under the ground?*" I ask, my thoughts racing.

"Yes. The psychiatrist I took her to assumed she was coming to terms with their deaths—because they had been buried under the ground."

I raise one eyebrow.

"But they hadn't been. Their bodies were never found."

I wait for her to continue.

"Someone saw the car drive off the bridge and called 911, but by the time the divers got there, the bodies had been swept downstream by the current. Soleil refused to accept that they were dead."

"What happened that night, Bella?"

"It was dark, no moon, and there was snow on the ground. The car James was driving hit a patch of black ice on a bridge, and he lost control." Her eyes fill with tears. "We had been fighting that afternoon—about some trouble James was in with the Russian government. I had convinced him to go to the police that morning, but the cops didn't believe him—they thought he was some crackpot. When we got home, he told me he'd bought a gun—and that he wanted me to learn how to use it. I couldn't believe that he'd bring a gun into our home, and I... I just lost it. I started yelling at him for putting his family in danger. I said all sorts of horrible things." She looks away. "He insisted that I learn to protect myself and the kids, that he wouldn't always be there to take care of us. I asked him if he was planning to abandon us, and he didn't respond. Finally, I told him to get out, that I didn't want to fight about it anymore, and he just... gave up. He told me he was going to spend the night at David's—that he'd be back in the morning after we'd both cooled off—and I told him not to let the door hit him on the way out."

I shake my head, knowing exactly how that conversation probably went down.

"The kids were five, and they had seen us argue before—but never like this. I thought they were hiding in the bedroom, waiting for the yelling to stop—until I got the call from the police. Lucas had crept into the garage and climbed into the back of the car without either of us knowing."

"Oh, Christ in heaven, no." I reach out for her hand, but she withdraws it.

"It's possible James didn't know Lucas was in the back seat, that he had no idea his son was in the car with him when he lost control and plunged twenty feet into the icy river below."

I think about that for a moment, replaying in my head the panic he must have felt if he knew his son was going to die. "How did you know Lucas was in the car," I ask, "if they never found his body?"

"His Scooby-Doo backpack was missing from his room, and the divers found his slipper wedged in the door handle. Lucas took that backpack and a stuffed frog with him everywhere. Someone found the frog a few days later, six miles down from the bridge, lodged underneath a foot of ice."

"*Mierda.*"

She sighs. "Their deaths nearly killed Soleil too. She and Lucas were inseparable. They did everything together, from learning to play soccer to singing in the school play. After Lucas died, he became her imaginary friend. She told me that she talked to him in her dreams, and that he told her things. Things like—"

She glances around, making sure no one else is listening.

"—like he and James were building some sort of time machine, and that James was going to use it to fix everything."

She looks at me as if expecting a response, but all I can do is shake my head and stare at my empty glass.

She takes a drink, blinking back tears, and continues, "I knew it wasn't normal, but Soleil seemed happy, reasonably well-adjusted considering what had happened. But when she was sixteen—a year after we moved inside the biodomes—she started waking up screaming in the middle of the night, her sheets soaked with sweat. She insisted that James and Lucas needed help, that we had to find them. She said that Lucas was sick and needed a doctor—that he needed *me*."

I want to say something comforting, but I can't find the words.

"Then a year or so later, the nightmares stopped." She shrugs. "The doctor said she'd grown out of it." She's quiet for a moment. "But Soleil never returned to normal. She attended all her classes and did all her schoolwork, but something inside her had died."

"I'm sorry" I say. "I can't even imagine what both of you must have gone through."

"What happened in... your universe?" she says. "You obviously weren't killed in the car accident. Did Lucas survive too?"

I shake my head. "In my world, there wasn't a car accident. I knew Dave from college, but we had a falling out right around the time I met you."

Over you, actually—Dave showed his cards, but I wasn't smart enough to know what it meant.

"So things turned out differently," she says, looking as though she's responsible for her son's death and her daughter's mental illness. "Lucas and Soleil never... suffered?"

"No," I say, feeling a crushing pain in my heart. "They didn't suffer."

It takes me a minute to pull myself back together.

I look at her, wanting to reach across the table and take her hand. "Bella, what happened to you and the kids wasn't your fault. You need to stop blaming yourself."

She nudges the food around her plate for a minute, lost in thought, and then looks up. "Would you like the rest? I'm not very hungry, and I hate to see it go to waste." She's barely touched her food.

"Sure," I say, wondering about that opulent dinner I had at her mansion where she didn't eat anything either.

She scoots the plate over to my side of the table. "I don't know what I would have done if David hadn't been there when Lucas and James died." She sniffs her nose and then wipes her eyes on the back of her hand. "He helped pull the car out of the river, talked to the police, and arranged the funeral. He even offered to hire a private firm to search for the bodies."

"So Dave and James were still close then?"

She swallows, her lips pressed together. "Yes, but David and I were friends too. Up until the accident, we had always had James there between us, someone to smooth out the occasional disagreements and conflicting opinions. Then all of a sudden, James was gone. I had never really liked David as much as James did—we were friends by association, if you know what I mean—but I had no one else to turn to. So, I put up with his incessant bragging, and his teenage mistresses, and his thinly-veiled attempts to manipulate me because..."

She looks away. "Because I was afraid of the alternative. I can't say that's ever really changed."

"I'm sorry you had to go through that," I say and push a lock of hair back behind her ear, wishing I could do something more, wishing I could take all the pain away.

Her eyes get big—but she doesn't pull away. "Who are you really?"

"No one of consequence."

She plays along, reciting the lines, as I knew she would. "I must know."

"Get used to disappointment."

She laughs. "So you're sticking with the story that you're from another universe?"

"Would saying it again make you any more likely to believe me?"

Her smile fades. "To tell you the truth, I don't know what to believe. But I do know this much: You look like James and you sound like James, but you can't *be* James."

I glance back and forth between her eyes, falling in love with her all over again. "So how did you end up married to Dave?"

"Like I said, he and James were best friends, and when things started spinning out of control—and the biodome Soleil and I planned to move into was destroyed—David asked me to marry him. It was the only way he could get us in on such short notice." She covers her face with her hands. "And I said yes."

"There's no reason to be ashamed, Bella. In your shoes, I would have done the same."

She wipes away a tear. "And then you came back."

I reach across the table and take both of her hands in mine. "You're right, I'm not James. But that doesn't mean I don't... have feelings for you."

"It's too late for that," she says and pulls away. "It's too late for me."

"It's never too late for us," I say. "At least, I hope it's not."

She drops her gaze to her lap.

"So how do you know I'm not James?" I ask. "The simplest explanation is that I am—and the biotechs have kept me from aging."

She looks up, her eyes defiant. "Because James would have known better than to show up twenty years younger sporting the latest biotech gadgets and claiming to be Robinson Crusoe." She exhales. "That and I verified your biological age. You're forty, not sixty. Unless they had you in the deep freeze for two decades, you aren't James."

I smile.

She wipes her face on her napkin and then blows her nose on it. "What?" she says, looking annoyed. "Why are you smiling?"

"Because you remind me of someone—someone I miss more than I could possibly say." I let my gaze run over her face and hair, taking it all in. "And I like the new look. A lot."

She glances down, taking a vial of pills out of her purse. "You're just saying that to flatter me—keep me off-balance."

"Is it working?"

She blushes and dumps three tablets into her hand.

"What are the pills for?" I ask, trying to read the label.

"Stress, of course." She shoves the bottle back in her purse and then washes the tablets down with the last of her beer. "Do you have any idea how many things can go wrong in this place? How many people I have begging me to give them drugs or treatments that no longer exist?"

I shake my head.

"Trust me," she says. "If you were in my shoes, you'd be popping a few pills now and then too."

I reach across the table and take both her hands in mine. "I'm sure I would."

She's quiet a moment, her gaze moving from my hands up to my shoulders and finally to my face. "So you don't know anything about James?"

"No," I say. "I'm sorry." I peer into her turbulent green eyes, trying to get the words right. "But I can tell you this: James loved you more than life itself, and if there was a way—*any* way— he could have gotten back to you, he would have done it. I'm absolutely certain about that."

She nods, fighting back tears.

"Come on," I say, not letting go of her hand. "Let me walk you home."

CHAPTER 18

Lani: Breaking and Entering

The following morning, I eat a granola bar and check in with the Bub without getting out of my sleeping bag. Ally, who's still filling in for her father, tells me that Mr. Kirk is planning to send some men to get inside the Magic Kingdom, but at the moment, none of his aircraft are available. As it is, he's going to have to pull a plane off the Lou rescue efforts in order to get Shannon out of Catersville. He wants to know how badly I need them.

"Not that badly," I tell her. "Have him get Shannon out first and worry about me later. How's everyone at the Bub?"

"Fine," Ally says. "Dad's hanging in there, Lucy is insisting she doesn't need to be in bed, and Mom's back to normal and won't let Lucy get up."

I laugh and promise to give them an update as soon as I know more. "Over and out." I turn off the radio and get dressed.

Outside, the air is frosty, but the sun is out, and there's no sign of the snowstorm Seattle was predicting. Yesterday afternoon, I set up camp in a glade near a stream. So, I grab my things and hike back up to the concrete ledge, going over the options in my head.

Just as I suspected, the two turrets on the east side of the wall seem to be broken or out of ammo. I consider crawling up from the west side, but I have no way of knowing if or when those guns might start firing. So, using the parachute again, I work my way closer on hands and knees, marking a safe zone with the pencil as I go. After an hour of tossing, crawling, and scribbling, I press my gloved hands against the fortress wall and stand up.

A stone's throw to my right, there's a U-shaped tunnel cutting back into the mountain, and according to my scouting yesterday, ten or twelve meters inside that opening there's a huge blast door. As far as I can determine, there's no other entrance on this side of the mountain.

What are you going to do if the blast door is sealed shut and there's no way to open it?

"Try something else," I say aloud, unnerved by the silence.

I drink from my canteen and take out my binoculars, getting a better look at the angle of the machine gun turrets. It looks as though I should be safe if I stay up against the wall. If I'm wrong, I won't get a second chance.

What are you going to do if there are machine guns inside the tunnel?

"Worry about the things you can control, and let the rest go."

I continue tossing the parachute ahead of me and sliding my body along the wall toward the mouth of the tunnel. When I get there, I roll up the parachute and stick the end out into the tunnel opening, trying to keep my hands behind the wall.

Nothing happens.

I take a small mirror out of the first aid kit in my pack and hold it out in front of me, moving it sideways until I can see into the tunnel. I scan the ceiling and walls, checking for holes or vents or anywhere bullets could shoot out. There isn't anything except smooth concrete all the way back to five or six piles of threadbare fabric.

I take a closer look and let out a yelp. The entrance to the mountain fortress is littered with decomposed bodies, bones sticking out from the disintegrating clothing.

I lean back against the wall and wait for my heart to stop pounding.

They died twenty years ago, Lani. They aren't going to hurt you now.

I wait for my pulse to settle and then stick the mirror back out. The blast door is definitely shut tight. I stick the mirror in my pocket and unwrap the parachute. Then I take a deep breath and toss the fabric into the center of the tunnel. There's a faint buzzing sound, but nothing else. I use the mirror to take a look.

Recessed lights in the ceiling have come on, and a panel next to the blast door flashes red.

I let out a whoop. "There's power!"

I drag the parachute canopy back and toss it one more time, letting it catch the air and drift slowly down to the ground.

No gunfire.

I consider going back to my camp and letting the Bub know what I've discovered, but curiosity gets the best of me. I slink into the tunnel, keeping my back against the wall, and edge my way up to the blast door, trying not to look at the desiccated bodies.

Once I get up to the flashing panel, I take a virus test strip out of the vial in my bag and break the sealed plastic wrapper. The pale yellow paper turns bright red almost immediately.

"Contaminated."

I take a deep breath and stick the trash back in my pocket, wondering for the hundredth time why Doomsday doesn't kill me.

"Bad luck," I say aloud.

The blast door is five meters high and about the same in width. I run my fingers along the side edge, checking if I can feel any air leaking in or out.

I can't. It looks to be sealed up tight.

The painted metal door is cold to the touch, and by the amount of detritus wedged up against the bottom, hasn't been opened in a long time. I don't know whether that's good or bad.

"Probably bad."

I walk over to the other side of the door and look at the red control panel. The writing above the display panel reads, "Place palm of hand on reader and wait for instructions." I tap the display.

"Welcome to the Warm Springs Complex," says a disembodied female voice.

I pull my hand away and step back.

"Place your hand on the biometric panel," says the computer, "and state your full name."

"Uh…" I rest my palm on the panel. "Ka'iulani Kalakaua Kai," I say, not having spoken my full name in decades.

"Working…"

I look more carefully at the access panel. There's a camera lens above the screen and a tiny circle of holes in the metal panel for a speaker or microphone.

"Biometrics not recognized," says the computer. "Please

stand by. Security has been alerted."

I drop my hand to my side and stare at the flashing panel. "How long is that going to take?"

"Please stand by. Security has been alerted," the computer repeats.

"Great," I say, wondering how long it's been since security was last alerted. "Is there anyone inside the mountain?"

"Please stand by. Security has been alerted," the computer says for the third time.

"I got that part," I say. "Can you open the blast door?"

"Authorization is required to enter. Please authorize."

I try twice more to no avail.

Now what?

I sit down on the floor of the tunnel, away from the erstwhile mosh pit, and nibble on a handful of dried fruit.

"Who's there?"

The voice is deep and fearful, and it takes me a minute to realize where it's coming from.

The access panel.

"I am!" I shout and scramble to my feet. I step in front of the camera lens. "My name is Dr. Lani Kai, and I'm from the Kirkland Biodome." The panel continues flashing red. "I'm looking for an underground city, a government installation sealed off from the Doomsday virus."

I wait a few seconds, but there's no reply.

"Hello?" I say. "Are you there?"

"Give me a second to put something on," the male voice says. "Christ, I wasn't expecting visitors." There's some noise in the background. "You got any cuttlefish bones?" he asks, his voice barely audible.

"Fish bones?" I say, wondering what the hell he's talking about. "Um, no. But I do have some dried apples with me. Will that do?"

"How come you don't have a suit on?" he says, sounding

worried.

"I'm immune," I say. "I found out a few days ago."

"Oh. What happened to your face?"

The guy is not a master of subtlety.

I run my fingertips across one of the disfiguring scars on my cheek, scars that cover nearly a quarter of my body. "I was burned in an accident," I say. "It happened a long time ago, when I was seventeen. The day they sealed the biodome."

The display goes dark and then a man's face appears in black and white. He looks to be in his sixties, with a scruffy beard—and hair that would put Einstein to shame.

"Benny likes apples," he says and then runs his hands through the mop of hair on his head. "Sorry, I must look like some crazy dude. Guess I haven't cut my hair or shaved in, well... decades. Ran out of razors early on, and it didn't seem worth the effort to keep it trimmed. Been stuck inside this godforsaken mountain for twenty-eight years, seven months, and"—he glances down—"thirteen days. And you're the first visitor I've had."

I smile, my heart still pounding in my throat. "I don't blame you one bit."

He narrows one eye. "How come you're immune?"

"Dumb luck," I say. "How come you're not dead?"

He laughs. "Well it ain't for lack of trying." He moves closer to the camera. "What'd you say your name was?"

"Lani. I'm a medical doctor."

"What are you doing outside my mountain?"

"I need help," I say. "Can you please let me in?"

"Nope. If I open the door, all the good air'll get out, and Benny'll die."

"Benny?"

"Yeah." He glances off screen. "The indicator says the exterior air is still bad. I can't open the door."

"Are you Benny?" I ask.

"Of course not. You think I'm crazy or something?"

I shake my head, but I'm not so sure.

"Benny's my chinchilla. We've been together for going on twenty years. He's all I have left."

This guy has been locked up inside the mountain—all by himself—for two decades?

The man moves out of the image and comes back with a small furry creature on his shoulder. "Benny, this is Lani. She's a doctor. That means she gives people shots and takes out their tonsils and stuff."

"Nice to meet you, Benny," I say, unsure how I feel about his description of me.

"He's pleased to meet you too, doc." He scratches the rabbit-sized creature between the ears. "He's named after Ben Gunn. You know, 'Yo-ho-ho, and a bottle of rum!'" He laughs. "He likes cheese."

The guy's nutty as a fruitcake.

"Ah… hi, Benny," I say. "What's your friend's name?"

The man's eyes get big. "You sound a little cuckoo, doc. Everyone knows chinchilla's can't talk."

I laugh. "So what is your name?"

"Oh, I'm…" He thinks for a moment. "Jimbo. Haven't said that word in ages."

"Don't you have an airlock inside the blast door, Jimbo? A sealed room that protects you from the Outside air?"

"Sure we do, but the thing's busted. Won't work without the main power, and that's been off longer than I can remember."

"Surely it can be operated by hand in an emergency?"

"Don't call me Shirley," he says and then grins. "That was a little movie joke."

I force a smile. "What about the airlock, Jimbo? If you let me in, you can have my dried apples or anything else you want."

"To be honest," he says, "I don't know how to operate it. Never had the need, you see. Sorry about that."

"Is there anyone else in there—besides you and Benny?"

He shakes his head. "My son died a few years ago…" He wipes his eyes on his bathrobe sleeve. "Could have used a doctor back then—but it's no use now."

"I'm sorry to hear that," I say. "It must have been hard on you."

"Well, it's been nice talking to you, doc. I hope you find that underground city, seein' as the one in here is ruined."

"Wait!" I say. "Don't go!"

He laughs. "Couldn't go anywhere if I wanted to."

"Do you think you could figure out how to operate the emergency airlock? I mean if it was really important?"

"Probably, but it would take me a while. I'd have to look through all these manuals." He lifts up a stack of what looks like old phone books. It's over a foot high. "See what I'm talking about?"

"Yes, that does look challenging. But, this is important, Jimbo. Lots of my friends are stuck inside a biodome that's failing, and they need a new place to live. Do you think you could help me find a safe place for them?"

"There's not enough room in here," he says, looking alarmed. "And I told you, the Magic Kingdom is contaminated. I haven't been down there in years."

Oh my God, this is it!

"So," I say, forcing my brain to slow down, "the Doomsday virus is inside the Magic Kingdom?"

"No, of course not—if it was, I'd be dead. The cave is full of CO_2. Has been since the main power went off. Without the air exchangers, the place is a death trap."

"Okay," I say, hope flooding into me. "What if we figured out a way to turn the power back on? Would there be room for my friends inside the Magic Kingdom?"

He raises one eyebrow, and something about the gesture seems familiar.

"Depends," he says. "How many friends do you have?"

"Around fifty."

He's quiet for a minute, rubbing his hand across his bearded face. "I didn't think there were that many people left in the whole wide world," he finally says. "There's space for five hundred people down there—and food and medicine for them too."

I can barely contain my excitement. "Oh that's wonderful news!"

"But you'd have to find a way to turn the main power back on—and then wait for the air to clear."

"I think we can do that, Jimbo. Mr. Kirk can figure out a way to turn the power back on, and we'll get the carbon dioxide cleared out. Do you know where the generator is located?"

"Mr. Kirk?" He leans right up to the camera, his eyes narrowed. "You mean, Dave Kirk?"

"Yes! Do you know him? He's the man who invented the biodomes."

"Yeah. I know him. He's the one who fucking locked me up in here. Friend of yours, huh?" He moves off camera. "I have to go now. Benny needs his lunch and his exercise, and then he takes a nap."

"Wait!" I slap my hand against the control pad. "Don't leave me out here! I need your help. Please."

His face reappears, and then he glances at his wrist—which has nothing on it. "Come back at two. I'll take a look at the manuals. We can chat while Benny's napping—but we'll have to keep our voices down so we don't wake him."

"Yes, of course."

"And if you have any cuttlefish bones, you could bring

those. I let him chew on plastic, but it's bad for his health—all that BPA, you know."

"Yes it is. I'll see what I can do. Anything else you need, Jimbo?"

"Some real coffee would be great. I haven't had a cup in ages. *Tres Ríos* is my favorite, but I don't imagine there's any of it left now." He raises one hand. "Bye."

The display goes blank.

"Wait!" I jab at the access panel. "Jimbo?"

The display starts flashing red again.

I press my palm against it. "Come on, come on. Answer."

"Welcome to the Warm Springs Complex," the computer says. "Place your hand on the biometric panel and state your full name."

CHAPTER 19

Diego: Time Bomb

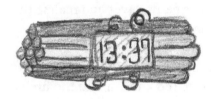

By sundown on the ninth day, we've finished repairing all but two of the seams Outside. As the last crew heads inside, I tell the foreman I'm going to stay out and see if I can finish the work. The night is mild, and there's a quarter moon. Between that and a flashlight, I manage to complete all the repairs.

"Woo-hoo," I say after I tighten the last bolt.

I climb down, put the tools on the trailer—balancing the ladder on top—and head back toward the airlock.

The night is still and dark, and the biodome is glowing. It's a beautiful sight, but it makes me sad. And lonely. And miserable.

Just as I start refilling the scooter's gas tank, the sky lights up behind me, and an instant later, there's a supersonic boom loud enough to shake the biodome walls.

"Holy shit, what was that?"

I turn in time to see something bright streak across the sky. It screams through the treetops and crashes into the swamp on the other side of the airport, setting a good portion of the woods on fire.

A meteor?

Smoke rises along the line of burning trees, marking the passage of the projectile.

A meteor that sets everything in its path on fire?

Something about that is familiar. Really familiar.

The Einstein Sphere!

I feel my socks getting wet and realize the scooter's tank is overflowing onto my shoes.

"*Mierda.*"

I put down the gas can, screw the lid on the tank, and use the intercom to let Ted know about the fireball.

Custer comes on as I'm starting up the scooter. "Do not approach the bogey, Mr. Crusoe. I'm sending out armed men to investigate. Over."

The scooter coughs and sputters to life.

"Do you read me, Crusoe. I said stay where you are. Do not approach the meteor. That's an order."

I laugh and open the throttle, heading toward the burning trees. "What are you going to do, put me in jail?"

Luckily, the sphere landed inside the double security fence surrounding C-Bay, or I wouldn't be able to get to it without opening the gates.

It occurs to me that the Einstein Sphere destroyed half of downtown Denver, and if this one had come down a few hundred meters to the west, it would have drilled a hole right through the biodome.

And killed everyone inside.

"Shit, that was close. Whoever is sending these things is a complete nutter."

I head down the runway at a blistering twenty miles per hour, the trailer bumping and banging along behind me. Once I get into the swampy area, I throttle back.

You don't want to hit any alligators, and you definitely don't want to drive into a sinkhole.

Turns out, the "meteor" is easy to find.

Just follow the yellow blazed road.

When I get to the end of the burning trees, I park the scooter with the lights trained in the direction the projectile was heading and get off to take a closer look.

About thirty meters farther on, I spy a ghostly apparition. I push the scooter closer and realize it's vapor rising from the ground. The steam is coming from a hole in the swampy earth that's barely wider than my hand and oozing boiling, muddy water like some mud pot in Yellowstone.

"That's one hot potato."

I take a shovel off the trailer and stick the handle into the newly created geyser. The hole goes down at a sharp angle, but the shovel isn't long enough to touch the bottom.

"Damn."

I pull down a sapling that's three or four meters tall and shove the trunk down into the muck, jabbing it around until I hit something solid.

Something hard and smooth.

Something about the size of *un balón de fútbol.*

I grin. "You've got mail."

Come on, McFly. Tell me how to get back to Isabel.

I do a quick guesstimate and start digging.

Thirty minutes later, I'm joined by three camo biosuits. One of them shines a flashlight into the pit I'm digging and then points the beam up into my eyes, blinding me.

It's Custer, of course. "What are you doing, Crusoe?"

I tap the shovel tip against the tungsten ball, steam still rising off the hot metal sphere. "Retrieving my mail."

"Your mail, my ass," he says and turns to the other two. "Load that thing onto the trailer and get it back to the dome." Custer motions for me to step away.

I just spent the last ten minutes trying to pry up the sphere—and couldn't get it to budge even a millimeter. There's no way three guys in biosuits are going to have any better luck.

"Be my guest," I say and sit down on the ground.

This is going to be good.

I watch them flail around in the muck for fifteen minutes and then suggest we open the sphere where it lies.

"Open it?" Custer asks. "What if it's a bomb?"

"I could be mistaken," I say, "but I think it's a message. For me."

He drops the broken shovel he's been waving around. "Let me check with the boss."

"Take your time."

He turns away, and I lie back in the weeds, staring up at the stars and hoping that the message inside that sphere really is for me.

After a couple of minutes, Custer walks over. "Boss wants to know how you're planning to get it open?"

"Good question," I say. "Last time one of these showed up, we crushed it in a vise, but it took an awful lot of pressure."

He conveys that information to the boss.

"Mr. Kirk suggests we shoot it," he says, "see if it'll shatter. You got an opinion on that?"

I shrug. "Good a plan as any." With the sphere still stuck at the bottom of the pit, I figure the bullet will ricochet off into the muddy ground—but it's hard to say how far the shards might fly when the metal shatters.

Custer takes his handgun out of its holster and points it down into the hole.

"Assuming it's not a bomb," I add.

He lowers the gun and takes a step back.

"It's going to explode into a million pieces," I say. "I don't think I'd want to be standing next to it in a biosuit when all of those shards come flying out. You?"

I reach out for the gun.

Custer considers it for a moment and then hands it over.

"Try not to shoot your foot off," he says.

I wait for all of them to move a safe distance away and then lie on my stomach, keeping my head down, and fire a bullet into the hole.

Nothing happens.

I try again, lifting my head up high enough to aim. The sphere shatters on the third shot. I lean over the pit and use the broken shovel to lift out the white contents.

It's a sock—muddy now—with something stuffed inside it.

Custer tries to snatch it out of my hand, but I step away. "I'm pretty sure this is for me."

"Give me the gun," Custer says.

I ignore him and step around to the other side of the hole.

"Grab him," Custer says, and the suits lumber toward me like redshirts in some bad sci-fi flick.

It's been a long day, and the whole scene strikes me as absurd.

I laugh and point the gun at Custer. "Tell them to stay where they are. All I want to do is see what's inside."

He hesitates—talking on his radio, I think—and a second later, the men stand down.

Custer inclines his helmeted head. "My apologies, Mr. Crusoe. Mr. Kirk says to be our guest."

"Tell him I said thank you." I turn so the sock is in my shadow, keeping the gun trained on Custer, and reach inside.

There's a folded piece of paper—and a seashell.

I discretely stick the shell in my pocket and then hold the note up in the headlights and read the typed message:

```
Locate the Mountain. Use the machine.
Find her.
```

Below it, handwritten in a hurried script I recognize as my own, are the words:

You have 15 days until it's too late.

CHAPTER 20

Shannon: Release the Kraken

With Peter looking on, I press the curved plastic faceplate into the black bead of sealant around the edge of the mask. I hold it tight, my hands resting on a small table Peter nabbed from the unused choir room.

"Will these masks work to keep out smoke?" he asks.

"I'm not certain," I say, "but I think so. Can you bring over the bar clamps, please?"

He glances up at me, his eyebrows squished together. "The what?"

Over the past two weeks, Peter's father has mostly left us alone, and Peter and I have fallen into a routine. During the day, I follow him around with my head bowed and my eyes averted, careful to act the part of the dutiful wife. Every morning I'm given a job, and he's supposed to make sure I do it properly. After I finish, he can order me to do whatever he wants, but instead of making me do his laundry or clean his apartment, he's been using it as an excuse to show me around the biodome.

At first I hated the long, bulky robe I had to wear in public, but it turned out to be perfect for hiding tools and supplies—including six old rebreather masks and two tubes of sealant. If other people are around when we need to take something back to our workshop, Peter announces that it's time for me to submit. I stifle a frightened cry and give him a fearful look, and then he orders me back to the Room of Release.

So far, it's been working like a charm.

The second night in the Room, I noticed that if you shut the bathroom door, it's nearly impossible to see it, and I asked Peter if he knew about any other concealed doors—besides the bathroom and the cabinet with water. He shook his head, and we spent the evening tapping on walls, examining cracks, and checking behind all the paintings. We managed to find three other hidden doors, two concealing drawers full of strange things: impractical women's underwear, weird rubber body parts that wiggle and vibrate, and creepy stuff you'd expect to find in a torture chamber—handcuffs, blindfolds, and whips. Neither of us had any idea what they were for so we just put everything back. But behind the third door, we found a secret passageway to another room, and that's where we are now: in our private workshop.

Peter says they'll give us forty days and nights together—a sort of honeymoon before they force me to live and work in the Women's Quarter. We've been taking full advantage of what little time we have.

"The bar clamps." I say again, motioning with my head. "The long metal things with the orange handles. You're going to need both of them."

He gets the clamps and stands across from me, holding

them out.

"Good," I say and suppress a yawn. I had to scrub pans in the kitchen after dinner tonight and didn't get back to the Room until late. "Squeeze the handle to adjust the plates," I say. "We're going to need them both about ten centimeters apart."

He gives me the squishy eyebrows again, and I remember that he uses some ancient system of measurement based on a king's body parts.

"Ten centimeters is about the width of your hand."

"Right." He takes a moment to adjust them. "Now what?"

"Make sure you're holding them so that gravity causes the plates to *close* when you pull the release, and then come stand behind me, one in each hand."

He tests to make sure they are in the correct orientation and then resets them to the proper width. "Ready," he says and moves behind me, our bodies almost touching.

"Put your arms around me and position the clamps across from each other, the lower pads resting on the bottom edge of the mask. When I give the word, tighten them up—firm but gentle."

He nods. "Firm but gentle."

"Yep. Try to keep the pressure the same on both sides. When you're ready, go ahead."

He leans his chest lightly against my back and reaches around me, his chin against my temple. "O-kay," he says, his voice cracking. It's the first time we've been this close, and I can feel his heart pounding.

"You're doing fine, Peter," I say and watch a smile flit across his lips. "Go ahead and tighten the clamps, but don't let go until I say so."

When he's done, I slide my hands on top of his, checking that the vises are on properly. "They look good," I say and verify that the mask is still balanced on the stool. "Tomorrow night, we can make another one for you."

He pulls his hands out from underneath mine and backs away. "You don't have to do that, you know. Pretend that you like me."

I turn and look at him. "What do you mean 'pretend'?"

He looks down at his hands. "I mean, you don't have to act like you want to be with me or anything..."

"But I do like to be with you, Peter." I start cleaning up our makeshift tools. "Especially here in the lab where we can both be ourselves."

"You do?" His voice cracks.

"Sure. You're kind and helpful—and smart too." I twist the cap on the sealant and then shut off the makeup lamp we borrowed from the bathroom.

He follows me back into the Room of Release. "You're not just saying that to be nice?" He reseals the door and moves the footstool back in front of it.

"Nope." I plop down on the bed, exhausted. "You tracked down the box of rebreather masks, you managed to get in *and* out of the Chemical Room without being noticed, and you helped me get all our tools here without raising any suspicions." I look over at him standing there next to a naked woman riding a centaur. "And on top of that, you're a good listener. My mom says those are all great things to look for in a man."

His eyes get big.

"I know it's not your fault I'm stuck here, Peter. And I don't blame you for what's happened." I fall back into the pillows, too tired to take a hot shower—even though they're the one good thing in this horrible biodome. "As soon as we finish with the masks—one for each and four spares—we'll put together a plan and bust this Popsicle box." I roll over on my side, facing him. "And if you want, we'll go to C-Bay together. Both of us, okay?"

He nods and then turns away.

"What's wrong, Peter? Don't you want to leave this awful place?"

He shrugs.

"Well?"

"I don't know how to read and write as good as you do," he says. "They'll make fun of me there. Tease me for being stupid." He slumps down onto the footstool.

"You don't know how to read and write?" I say like some half-wit lolo.

He crosses his arms and drops his gaze. "Not very well."

"I mean, I didn't know. I just assumed…"

"When you asked me to look for the box of masks, I had you write down all the letters, remember? That way I could compare your words to the writing on the boxes until I found the one that matched."

"Oh my God, that must have taken hours!"

"And in order to get the tubes of sealant you needed, I had to go through hundreds tonight—while you were working in the kitchen. If you hadn't told me what color the tubes are, I never would have found them."

"Oh, Peter, I'm sorry! You must think I'm some sort of show Venice pig."

"No, I don't." He looks up at me, his eyebrows scrunched. "What's a Venice pig, anyway? All the pigs we have around here are plain ones—and most of them are pretty smart."

I laugh. "To tell you the truth, I'm not sure. I heard my mom say it once, and it sounded bad."

He cracks a smile for the first time, and something in my chest is set to fluttering in a way I've never felt before.

The feeling is wonderful—and a little scary.

Peter is not all mature and confident like Diego, and he's not like any of the buff guys in Mindy's magazines or the men in the movies, but he's...

Honest and trustworthy and real.

I stare at his face, more grateful than I could ever say for his kindness and decency—and for the risks he's taking to help me. Ever since the first night, he's been sleeping on blankets in the corner and letting me have the huge bed to myself. And every morning when I'm in the bathroom, he messes up the bed to make it look like he's slept with me. But the only time he's gotten that close to me was tonight—when he put his arms around me to fix the mask—and it made me feel all warm and squishy inside.

"I like it when I make you laugh," he says, breaking my train of thought. "I wish I could figure out how to make you do it more often."

And then I get this great idea.

"I'll teach you to read and write, Peter. So when we get to C-Bay you won't have to be embarrassed, and everyone will be able to see how smart you are. Mindy and I help the D-2s with their reading all the time. It's not hard if you have someone to teach you the alphabet and show you how to sound out the difficult letters. But you would have to practice—at least a little."

He looks a bit skeptical—which is surprising given what a great idea it is.

"Well, what do you say?" I ask.

"I don't know, Shannon. We don't have many books here, and..." He swallows. "And I'd get in a lot of trouble if someone finds out I'm practicing evil habits."

"Evil habits?" I say, unable to keep the disbelief out of my voice. "Good grief, Peter, we're supposed to be making babies at night, not masks, and you're worried about a few words in a book?"

He doesn't respond.

"Wait a sec. What about the Bible? Aren't you allowed to

read it?"

"Yeah, sure. But lots of the words don't make sense—and it's full of men getting smited and fathers killing their sons and people being turned to pillars of salt."

"Really?" I say, grimacing. "I didn't know that."

He smiles again. "Yeah."

"Well then, we'll just read the nice parts."

"Okay. But I think I have something better. I got it while you were working in the kitchen tonight, but I wasn't sure when to give it to you." He gets up and takes a book out of the bottom drawer of the red chest. "It's only a book of poems."

"That sounds wonderful, Peter. Thank you." I scoot up on the bed, leaning my back against the headboard. "We'll sit here where the light is good and practice every night." I pat the spot next to me.

He hesitates.

"Just while we're reading, I mean. So we can both see the words."

He sits on the other side of the huge bed and then pushes the collection of poetry over to me.

I give him an incredulous look. "If you want to learn to read, Peter, you're going to have to come closer. I promise not to call you a Venice pig, no matter what."

He looks unconvinced, but he scoots over until our shoulders are almost touching.

I open the book and set it on his lap, turning the pages until I come to "The Road Not Taken." I pick up his hand and touch his fingertip to the first line.

"*Two roads diverged*," I read, moving his hand along with the words, "*in a yellow wood...*"

When I finish the second stanza, I stop reading and let go of his hand. "Did you follow along with that?"

He nods—and then reads the next few lines by himself,

stumbling on some of the bigger words, but not many.

"So you *can* read."

"Yeah," he says, not taking his hand out from underneath mine. "And write a little too. Grizzly taught me after my mother died. But I haven't read a whole book in years, and I can't remember big words—like the name of the masks and the ingredients in the sealant."

He's quiet for a moment, his hand perfectly still beneath mine.

"But I like reading with you," he says. "So maybe we can keep practicing?"

"Sure." I glance down at my hand on top of his. "You can sleep here on the bed, Peter—if you want. It was selfish of me not to offer sooner." I bite my lip. "I'm sure the floor must be cold and hard—and you'd sleep much better up here on the bed. I mean if you want to..."

He shakes his head, his eyes downcast. "No."

"Oh." I can't keep the disappointment out of my voice. "We could both stay on our own sides, of course. It wouldn't be difficult in a bed this big."

He shakes his head again.

"Is it because you don't really want to, you know, be close to me?"

His head jerks up. "No, of course not. What makes you say that?"

"Well, um... you." I shrug. "Every time I suggest you come closer, you act like it's something horrible."

He stares at me, one of his eyes twitching. "It's not you that's horrible, it's me. There's a monster inside me that takes over after I fall asleep. When I wake up in the morning, I remember what it wants to do to you—what it *did* do with my body while I was asleep." He looks away. "And I don't know if I can control it."

"A monster?" I ask, somewhat shocked by his revelation.

"What does it want to do to me?"

He exhales. "I'm not my father."

"I know you're not, Peter. You're nothing like him, nothing. You're the gentlest, kindest, sweetest boy I've ever known—and I love the book of poems."

He gets up, takes a pillow and blanket off the bed, and drops them in the corner.

"Peter?"

He crosses the room and shuts off the lights. I hear his footsteps in the dark, a minute or two of rustling in the corner, and then silence.

"Good night, Peter," I say, but there's no response.

CHAPTER 21

Diego: Lock Him Up

The minute I step through the inner portal, I see Bella pushing through the crowd.

"Diego!" she calls out. "Are you okay?"

"I'm fine," I say, still not used to seeing Bella with gray, curly hair.

"Easy there, kitten." Dave grabs her by the elbow. "He's got a gun."

I laugh and hold the pistol out to him butt first. "Come on, Dave. We both know I'd never shoot anyone."

He takes the gun out of my hand and then lets go of Bella. "Right."

"Did you hear the news?" she says and takes my arm. "They found the Magic Kingdom, and there's someone inside. He's been stuck in there for decades!"

"Mom!" Soleil calls out.

We turn and watch her jog across the atrium. It's the first time I've seen her since she threw me out of her office. Her eyes have dark circles under them.

"What's happening?" she says, breathing hard. "I heard there was some sort of bomb outside!"

"Not a bomb," Dave says, "a meteor. Caused a bit of excitement when it hit the ground, but it's all quiet out there now."

She eyes my muddy clothes—and her mother's hand on my arm—but doesn't comment. "And I heard they found that underground Disneyland—"

"—the Magic Kingdom," I say.

"Yes," she continues, "the place that's rumored to have the state-of-the-art genetics lab."

Dave shuts his eyes and pinches his nose. "Looks like Ted blabbed to pretty much everyone."

"And did you hear?" Bella says to Soleil. "There's a man inside!"

Soleil nods, her eyes wide. "Some old man named Jimbo. They say he's delusional."

"Well, if you'd been locked up inside a cave for twenty years," Bella says, sounding annoyed, "you'd be a little nutty too."

"Easy there, princess," Dave says. "We're all on the same team."

Bella holds tighter to my arm, but doesn't respond.

"So is it true?" Soleil asks, glancing at Dave and then me.

"Yeah," Dave says and puts his arm around Bella, pulling her away from me. "Jimbo spends his time babysitting some sort of weasel he's trying to teach ballet. He refused to let Dr. Kai inside because she didn't have any fish bones, told her to come back later—after the weasel finished his nap."

"Well, at least we know there's air inside," I say. "Plus electricity, food and water."

"I agree, it's a start," Dave says and lets go of Bella. He empties the bullets out of the handgun I gave him, drops the ammunition into his pocket, and hands the pistol back to one of his men. "Tell Armstrong I want to see him in my office, first thing in the morning. That moron is going to be cleaning toilets from now on."

Looks like Custer just had his Last Stand.

"Yes, sir," the uniform says.

"And get all these people out of here. Fun's over."

"Yes, sir. Right away, sir." The man starts shooing people away from the airlock.

Dave turns back to me. "What's up with the cannonball? Armstrong said you broke it open, grabbed the contents, and hightailed it out of there."

I hand him the note.

Dave reads it and then tucks the paper into his pocket. "May I?"

"Yeah," I say. "I don't need it anymore. I got the message."

Soleil glances at me and then her adoptive father. "What's going on here? What are you talking about? Who sent the message?"

"I did," I say. "To myself."

Bella gives me a curious look. "What does it say?"

"That it's time for me to go home."

Dave and Soleil exchange looks, and Soleil gives a slight shake of her head.

"Go home?" Dave says, looking annoyed. "What does that mean? You need to go back to the Bub?"

"No," I say. "I need to get to the mountain, Dave, and I'm going to need your help."

He rubs his forehead, not meeting my gaze. "You can't go running off on a wild goose chase with so much at stake here. Soleil tells me she's close to a breakthrough." He glances at her for confirmation. "Until that happens, we need you here."

"So freeze my blood," I say. "I'll give you as much as I can spare."

"I wish it were that simple," Soleil says. "Cold temperatures destroy the biotechs—I can't even refrigerate samples—so freezing your blood isn't feasible."

"Christ," I say, trying to come up with a compelling plan. "Dr. Nadales can come with me to the Magic Kingdom." I nod at Soleil. "I know it'll have everything you need to recreate the biotechs—because that's where mine were made."

"Most of it is contaminated," Bella says. "Jimbo claims you can't go down to the underground city or labs anymore. He says it's been sealed off for more than a decade."

"*Mierda*," I say, desperate to come up with a reason to get back there. "Maybe I can figure out a way to clear out the virus? You have to let me try!"

"Except it's contaminated with CO_2 not Doomsday," Dave says. "And that'll kill even you, Superman. Plus the main power is off and the radio doesn't work. Until I can fix those issues, it would be a waste of time." He shrugs. "We don't even know if Willy Wonka can find the front door."

"I need to get back there," I say, glancing at Bella and then Dave. "Please."

"What about Shannon?" Dave says. "You want me to strand her in that cesspool while you take a plane to go gallivanting in the wilderness? Do I look like I have planes coming out my ass?"

"No," I say. "But—"

"And what about all the people here in C-Bay—and KC and the Bub and the biodomes all over the world? Don't those lives matter to you?"

"Yes, of course, but—"

"Until we figure out that magic shit in your blood," Dave says, "our days are numbered, and right now, that number isn't looking very big. I can keep patching seams and moving people around until I'm blue in the face, but the bio-domes—and even that Magic Kingdom of yours—are eventually going to fail, every single one of them. And when the last one goes down, mankind will be functionally extinct." He looks at Soleil.

"Maybe you and Dr. Kai could last another fifty years," Soleil says.

"Assuming you can fight off the gators and the crows," Dave adds.

"But it's inevitable," Bella says. "Unless we can find a vaccine."

"You'd risk all that, sacrifice all those people for this?" Dave yanks the note out of his pocket and holds it up. "For this one woman?"

I glance at Bella, knowing the answer but unable to confirm it out loud.

"I've told you," I say, unwilling to give up, "we don't need to sacrifice anything. I guarantee the facilities inside the mountain will be more than sufficient to create the biotech devices. Hell, there may even be a file on how to make the vaccine from scratch in there."

"You can't guarantee any such thing," Soleil says, not bothering to control the anger in her voice. "From what Dr. Kai says, you've never been inside this one—you didn't even know where it was! It could take months to pump out all the carbon dioxide—months in which thousands of people could die—and at the end of it all, we could discover that the lab was destroyed by a fire, or the cave ceiling collapsed and there's nothing left down there, or any of a hundred other possibilities." She exhales, her face lined with stress. "All we're asking for is a little more time."

"Think about it, Diego. I got one cargo plane here at C-Bay and a shitload of problems. I need to ferry supplies to trade for Shannon, rescue the injured folks stranded at KC, and help three other biodomes with the same flaw that took down the Lou. Or," he says, his voice steadily rising, "I can fly you out to a remote mountain fortress locked up tighter than a clam's ass at high tide so you can sit on your butt in the snow?"

I glance down at my hands. "Of course not, but—"

"Well then give me a break, buddy. I'm doing the best I can, and you're sure as hell not helping."

"What about Matt?" I say. "He could come pick me up in the Cessna and fly me out there."

"Where is he going to stop for fuel, Einstein, in Catersville?" He gives a mirthless laugh. "Believe me, I've looked at all the possibilities, and your best option is to stay put. Once Soleil gets the Doomsday vaccine sorted out, I'll get you to where you need to go."

I swallow, unable to get the words *Time is running out* to stop banging around inside my skull. "*Mierda.*"

Dave puts his hand on my shoulder, and I resist the urge to shove it off.

"Work with me here," he says in that condescending voice of his. "Once we figure out how to get inside, I'll send people out there to check on the power generator and get the radio working. Then we can pump the CO_2 out and get the place up and running again. That'll give the Bub folks someplace to go and us a chance to see what's inside."

Fifteen fucking days and Isabel dies.

"In the meantime," he says, "Soleil needs you, and I need time to ferry all the KC people here, get Shannon back, figure out what to do with the Bub folks, and get repair parts to the other biodomes. Until all of that's taken care of, I'd have to be an idiot to let you risk your life—and the lives of others—on a lark."

"Then I'll get there on my own," I say. "I'll take my

backpack and walk to Colorado."

"Where's your brain, Domingo?" Dave's voice is full of contempt. "It'll take weeks to get there. Soleil would have to stop the research on your biotechs, and if something does go wrong with the biodomes, hundreds of people could die because of your selfish obsession."

"I'm going to the Magic Kingdom, Dave, whether you like it or not." I glance at Bella, but she won't meet my gaze. "I've done all I can here. I need to get back to my own… life."

"Mr. Crusoe, please," Soleil says. "I've made good progress on the vaccine, but I can't finish it without you. I know we got off to a bad start, but this is about more than just the two of us. It'll only be a few more weeks, a month or two at most. Please. I need you here."

"You can come with me," I say, turning to her. "The lab is *under the ground*, Dr. Nadales. The Magic Kingdom is a cave. It's inside the mountain."

Her eyes get big.

"I was locked up in there," I say, "back when you had those dreams about your father and your brother." I glance at Bella and then our daughter. "There are secrets in there, Sol. And answers."

The color drains out of her face, and she walks across the space between us and slaps me hard on the face. "How dare you!"

"You are one sick bastard," Dave says. "There's nothing in that mountain except carbon dioxide and rat shit. I'm not letting you do something stupid, and I'm definitely not letting you risk the lives of thousands of people. You're staying right here until we have the vaccine."

I step away from him. "You can't keep me here."

"Well, actually," he says and snaps his fingers, "I can."

A couple of uniforms appear out of nowhere, shoving Bella aside and grabbing onto my arms.

I try to break free, but Bella steps in front of me and puts her hands on my shoulders. "You can't win this one, Diego. Please."

"I'm sorry it's come to this," Dave says, "but I can't risk you doing something stupid while I'm gone."

I look at Bella, begging her with my eyes to intervene.

She shakes her head. "David's right. We need you here."

Dave hands the note to Soleil and then takes her arm. "I'm leaving you in charge. So keep your eyes open." He glares at me. "And I know you need his blood, but I wouldn't trust Tarzan as far as I could throw him."

I turn my head toward Dave, feeling the old animosity flooding into my chest. "Let me go, you two-faced prick."

He nods at his men. "Lock him up."

CHAPTER 22

Lani: Jimbo

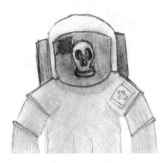

"The guy's a loony," I say, rubbing my hands together to keep them warm. "He and his pet badger have been locked inside that mountain for ages. For all I know, he couldn't get the blast door open if he wanted to."

"He has a badger in there?" Madders says over the radio. "Those things are mean as hell."

"I don't know what it is, Madders. Benny was having luncheon when I rang the doorbell and I didn't ask." I wrap my sleeping bag tighter around my shoulders. "I'm supposed to come back after his afternoon nap and bring coffee and fish bones."

I hear him sigh. "Okay," he says. "Do the best you can. Kirk says he'll get some men out to you in the next week or so. Will you be okay until then?"

"Yeah, sure. It's a bit on the brisk side, but I have plenty of food and water. If worse comes to worst, I can hole up inside the tunnel. It'll be protected from the wind and snow, and maybe I can play tiddlywinks with Benny."

"Whatever it takes. Tell Jimbo you'll give him coffee and fish bones once he lets you inside."

"You mean, lie to him?"

He's quiet for a moment. "We need to find out what's in there, Lani—and soon."

"Yeah, I know."

"And I wouldn't be surprised if Kirk can come up with the goods. So it wouldn't be a lie—at least not yet."

"Okay," I say and pull my sweater tighter around my neck. "How are things there? Any news on repairing the damaged wall?"

"No, Kirk's all out of ideas, and folks here are scared."

"I'm scared for them too," I say.

"We all know winter is coming," Madders says. "And unless the Almanac's wrong—which it never is—it's going to be a stonker. We need to evacuate soon, Lani. Before the snow is too deep for the trucks to get through."

I stare at the radio receiver, listening to the wind whip through the trees around the tent.

"Lani—"

"Yeah, I know. I'm working on it." I start putting my shoes back on. "I'll give you a call when I get back from afternoon tea with the Jimbo and Benjamin. Lani out."

By the time I get back up to the concrete ledge, the wind has died down, but the sky is dark and heavy with snow clouds.

I crouch down, follow the pathway through the hot zone, and then slide along the concrete wall until I get to the tunnel. This time, I only set the guns off once. I wave my jacket in the tunnel to make sure nothing's changed, then walk up to the flashing red panel and place my hand against it.

After a brief interaction with the computer, it tells me that security has been notified, and I wait for Jimbo to come on.

But he doesn't. I wait for the panel to reset and then try again. No Jimbo.

"Damn it, where is he?"

I check my watch and try again in five minutes.

Nothing.

For the next four hours, I sit on the cold, hard concrete shivering and going over our initial conversation in my head, getting up every ten to fifteen minutes to try again.

Okay, so he's not just a loony—he's a jerk.

Over and over I press my hand to the pad and wait while the computer tells me security has been alerted.

Is he afraid the virus will kill him if he lets me in? Or did I scare him off when I mentioned David? Or is he stark, raving mad, and at this very moment, he's off teaching that badger how to do ballet?

When it starts to get dark, I decide to head back to the campsite to get some dinner and warm up, planning to come back later with a flashlight for another try.

But as I shuffle back against the concrete wall, I realize my mistake.

Snow is falling, and the concrete ledge is covered in pristine white—six inches of it. There's no way to see the pencil scribbles that mark the safe pathway out.

"Oka fefe."

When I get close to where I think the pathway ends, I get down on my hands and knees and start sweeping the deep snow away, frantically looking for the pencil markings. After only a few minutes, my gloves and pants are a soggy, frozen mess, and my knees are burning from the cold, but I can't seem to find anything.

You stupid, lolo girl. You should have known this would

happen.

I pack a handful of snow into a ball and toss it out. The report of the guns in the still night air is so loud, it makes my teeth hurt. But when they stop, I can see their firing pattern in the snow right in front of me.

You haven't gone far enough!

I walk ten or twelve feet farther down the wall, scraping at the edge of the snow with my shoe, looking for the markings.

It's almost dark now, but there's a moon rising in the east—and the pencil scribbles are visible beneath my frozen shoe. I get back on my hands and knees, pushing the snow out of the way with my forearms to reveal the parallel lines.

If there hadn't been a moon tonight, you'd be dead.

"But there was. And I'm not."

Progress crawling across the huge expanse of frozen concrete is painstakingly slow, and twice the clouds of snow I toss out set off the guns—but somehow I manage to avoid getting shot in the back or frozen to death.

It's after midnight when I finally stumble up to my tent. Not only did I have trouble getting through the hot zone, I had trouble finding my campsite in all the snow.

Good thing you chose a location next to a stream or you never would have made it back.

"Stupid, stupid, stupid."

I unzip the tent fly and collapse into the darkness.

"And lucky."

When my heart stops pounding, I manage to find a flashlight, pull off my snowy, half-frozen clothes, and put on some dry ones. My fingers and toes are so cold, I can barely feel them, and when I attempt to make hot tea, I'm shaking so badly I can't get the tiny camp stove to light.

After using up nearly half my supply of matches, I give up, crawl into my sleeping bag, and shiver.

The following day dawns cold and still.

After a hot breakfast and a quick call to the Bub, I put plastic bags over my socks and stick my feet back into the damp shoes, making a mental note to ask David to send out some boots. Then I gather up my things and get to work.

As I hike up the mountain, I use a small hand ax to notch the sides of the trees, marking the trail back to camp. When I get up to the ledge, I cut down a pine bough and use it to sweep the dusting of snow off my pathway—the parallel lines of snow I crawled through last night still visible. Then I start lining the pathway back to the wall with rocks.

By the time I reach the end, the sun is overhead and I'm sweating hard.

"Beats freezing to death."

I shimmy along the wall and peek around the corner of the tunnel. When I wave my jacket in the open space, nothing happens.

"Good."

As I approach the blast door, the tunnel lights come on and the panel flashes red.

"Come on," I say as I place my palm against the pad. "I need you to be here today."

The computer barely has time to tell me "Security has been alerted." before Jimbo's smiling face fills the screen.

"Thank goodness," I say, incredibly happy to see him. "I was worried about you. What happened? I waited for you all afternoon yesterday."

He's dancing around so much that the screen keeps getting blurry. "I figured out how to get you in, doc! How to work the airlock!"

"You did? That's great news. How soon can I come inside?"

"Well," he says, plopping down in the chair, "I have to cycle the lock by hand. It may take a while to get the inner door to open, but if you use the viracide gun, I think we can do it—even if it costs me some clean air."

"The viracide gun?" I say, wondering how crazy he really is. "What is that?"

"Something my son and I cooked up while we were sitting on our butts in here."

"You and your son invented a gun?"

"Well, mostly him. I just soldered the wires. We used it to kill the Doomsday virus back when this whole section was contaminated."

"The Doomsday virus was inside?"

"Yeah, but we killed 'em all with the Ray Gun. Wasn't hard. We just had to find the right frequencies—and believe me, we had plenty of time to figure it out."

I nod, but I'm getting a bad feeling about this. "How does the Ray Gun work?"

"It's ultrasonic. It uses high-pitched sound waves to vibrate the—what is the word?—the outer shell of the virus…"

"Capsid?" I say, surprised by his knowledge of genetics.

"Yeah, capsid. That's the word. The viracide vibrates the capsid at resonant frequency until it tears the virus apart, rendering it harmless." He looks up at me. "But it doesn't hurt anything else. You can't even feel it killing the little buggers. Works every time—at least it did the last time we tested it."

"When was that?"

"Oh ten, twelve years ago, but the concept is sound." He smiles. "Get it? The *concept* is *sound*."

I force a laugh. "Good one."

His face falls. "It wasn't that funny, was it?"

For once in my life, I wish I were better at lying. "I'm sorry. Maybe when all my friends are safe, you can try it out on me again?"

"Yeah, sure. I understand." He shrugs. "Do you still want to come inside?"

"Yes, I do."

He gets an uncomfortable look on his face.

"Is everything okay in there? You didn't... lose Benny or anything?"

"No, Benny's fine." He turns the camera so I can see Benny running on a wheel. "He's exercising now—which is what I should be doing. I mean if I wasn't talking to you."

"Thanks for helping me, Jimbo. I can't tell you how much I appreciate it."

He half smiles and then looks down at his hands.

"What is it? Is there something wrong?"

"My name's not Jimbo." The corner of his mouth twitches. "In fact, the only person who ever called me Jimbo was Agent Dick, and he just did it to annoy me." He glances away from the camera. "He was one of the first ones to go loco. Put on a space suit and walked out the front door. No one tried to stop him, least of all me. We thought he'd be back when his O_2 ran low, but we never saw him again." He exhales. "That was back before the power went off."

"I see." I shift my weight, imagining that skull tumbling down the mountainside. "How soon can you let me in?"

"Well, I could start right now if you're ready? Did you bring me any coffee?"

I shake my head. "I'm sorry, but I'll do my best to get you some if you help save me and my friends."

"Okay," he says. "That's a fair trade. Are you ready? Once I open the blast door, you'll only have a few seconds to get inside."

I consider going back to the tent to let the Bub know what's happened, but I decide it's not worth the risk of losing Jimbo or whatever his real name is—or having him change his mind.

"I'm ready," I say. "What do I need to do?"

"Just come in once the door opens and bring your stuff.

There isn't a video screen in the airlock, but there's an intercom so we'll be able to talk."

"Okay," I say. "What happens if we can't get the inner door to open? Would I be trapped in the airlock?"

He thinks about that for a minute, his nose scrunched up. Then he rubs his hand across his beard. "I'm not sure," he says. "It's possible you could be stuck forever."

"There's no other way out?"

"Not that I know of."

The prospect of dying in there is not very appealing, but what other option do I have? "Are you sure you can get the inner door open?"

"Pretty positive," he says. "But I won't know for certain until I try."

I hesitate.

"My wife always said a ship in the harbor is safe, but that's not what ships are built for."

"Smart woman, your wife. What happened to her?"

"I don't know," he says, his voice a whisper.

"I'm sorry."

He shrugs. "She probably died when the virus mutated, same as everyone else."

I take a deep breath and exhale, trying to decide what to do.

"Don't worry," he says. "I'll get you through the airlock one way or another."

"Okay," I say, making up my mind. "I'm ready."

"I'm starting the sequence now."

I can hear gears turning, and a moment later, the huge door starts to pivot open. "It's working!" I say. "The door's opening!"

"Knew it would," he says. "This place is built to last for centuries. If we can get the power back on, there's even a bowling alley."

I laugh.

"And doc?"

"Yes?" I pick up my stuff and move toward the gap that's opening behind the blast door.

"My real name is James," he says, sounding far away. "James Nadales."

His words stab me like a katana. "Oh my God. It's… you."

"I guess you were hoping for someone else?"

I don't know what to say.

"You still want to come in?"

"Yes, of course, James."

"Okay. See you on the other side."

CHAPTER 23

Diego: Cross That Bridge

I sit on my ass in the C-Bay equivalent of jail for two days, my only contact with humanity the guy who drops off my food tray twice a day.

So far, our conversations have been pretty deep: me begging him to let me talk to Kirk and him saying "Breakfast." or "Dinner."

On the morning of the third day, Soleil walks up carrying my breakfast tray, Mr. Blabbermouth on her heels.

"You gonna behave?" the guard asks me.

"Yeah," I say and rub my hand across my scruffy chin. "Right up until King Claudius has me murdered."

The guard doesn't look amused. "Give a holler when you're done, Dr. Nadales." He lets her in and then locks the door behind her.

"Thanks," she says, holding on to the tray like it's a life

preserver on the Titanic.

We both watch the guard walk away.

There's a jangle of keys and a clank as he locks the outer door.

"Thanks for coming," I say to fill the silence.

She stands, her back to the steel bars and her gaze on my breakfast. "I apologize for striking you in the face. It was... unprofessional. I shouldn't have let my emotions get the better of me."

"I'm sorry for snooping in your office," I say and take the tray she's holding. "I shouldn't have let my emotions get the better of me."

She presses her lips together and nods, looking like her mother.

"What do you say we call it even," I say, "and start again?"

She looks up at me, her eyebrows knitted together. "If you don't mind, I would prefer to skip the part where you show up unexpectedly at dinner impersonating my dead brother and scare the shit out of me."

I suppress a smile. "Okay." There aren't any chairs, so I use one hand to tidy the blanket on my bunk. "Please. Sit down."

She stands there, looking ill at ease.

"I promise I won't bite."

She sits down on the edge, her hands in her lap. "Why did you say all that stuff about the Magic Kingdom being *under the ground?*"

"Your mother told me about Lucas," I say and sit down next to her. "She also told me you had... unusual dreams."

"Did she also tell you she put me on antipsychotic drugs that turned me into a zombie?"

"No, she didn't," I say, wanting to put my arm around her, but afraid she'll push me away. "She told me how worried she was about you."

She takes a deep breath and lets it out.

"Do you still have the dreams?"

She shakes her head, her eyes downcast. "Not since Lucas died."

I give her a confused look. "So you had the dreams before the car accident too?"

"No," she says. "Lucas survived the crash. And so did Dad."

I stare at her, all sorts of thoughts racing through my head. A lot of the details are altered—from the twins' birth, to the car accident, to the arrival of the sphere—but in all the universes, the theme is the same: Someone wants me to disappear. "Tell me what happened after the car accident."

"I started having dreams," she says. "Maybe more like visions. Lucas and I always had some sort of... connection, and sometimes I could see what he was seeing, hear what he was hearing. At five years old, I thought it was perfectly normal—until I realized that no one else had those sorts of dreams."

She hides it well, but I can still see the pain. "That must have been rough," I say.

"Mom started taking me to a psychiatrist. The woman listened to my stories, decided I suffered from trauma-induced hallucinations, and tried to convince me I was imagining everything. I told Mom I didn't want to talk to that lady anymore, that she made me say things that were untrue—like 'Lucas and Daddy are dead.' But Mom just cried and then sent me back to her."

"She probably didn't know what else to do," I say.

"I trusted Mom," Soleil says, her lips pressed together. "I assumed she was trying to help me..."

"I expect she was."

She turns, her eyes flashing. "But she never listened to what I said. She insisted I was sick and that the drugs would help." She exhales, the emotion draining out of her face. "Eventually I learned to keep my mouth shut, but by then it was too late."

"Too late for what?"

"To save Lucas." She drops her gaze. "I thought I was going crazy, that Mom and Uncle Dave and the psychiatrist might be right. But I knew things that were impossible to know."

"Like what?"

"Like Lucas and Dad were trapped inside an underground city. And later, that Lucas was sick and needed help. No one believed me, but I *knew* it was true."

"I believe you," I say. "That city inside a cave is the Magic Kingdom."

She stares at me for a moment. "Are you sure? Or is this your way of getting me to take you there?"

"It's the truth. I was kidnapped and locked inside that mountain too—although it was years later. There are apartments, a hotel, laboratories, and offices—even a bowling alley and a rec room with a ping-pong table and some old video games. The buildings are spread around a big—"

"—lake," she says, her face going pale. "But you weren't allowed to drink the water."

I nod, my chest tight.

She closes her eyes, her lips pressed together. "So I'm not crazy."

"No. Not even close." I rest my hand on her arm, and she doesn't pull away. "How certain are you that Lucas and your father survived the crash?"

She shrugs. "I'm psychotic, remember?"

I laugh. "Join the club."

A smile flits across her face but is quickly replaced by something darker. "So who are you?"

"Your father from another universe, one where things

played out differently."

One of her eyebrows rises precipitously.

"Trust me, you don't have the market cornered on crazy. There have been plenty of times when I've doubted my own sanity. But just like you, I know things I shouldn't."

"So what happened to Lucas?"

I hesitate, struggling to say the words aloud. "In my world, you and your brother were stillborn."

She nods, but I can see the disappointment.

I give an uncomfortable laugh. "You know that first day we talked—and I couldn't stop staring at you? It's because I couldn't come to grips with the fact that it was actually you." I try to clear the lump in my throat. "Christ, I'd held your tiny body in my hands, buried you in the dirt, and hated myself for letting it happen. And yet there you were." I look over at her. "And here you are."

She reaches over and takes my hand.

"The loss nearly killed your mother," I say, fighting back my emotions. "And I still dream about that night—still wish there was something I could have done to save you and Lucas."

I spend a minute looking at her, memorizing the way my daughter would have looked had she been given the chance to grow up.

She blinks, her lips pressed together.

"As far as I'm concerned," I say, "the best thing about this universe is that you're in it."

She gives a self-conscious laugh and then pulls her hand away. "Do you know what happened to Lucas and my father—I mean in this universe?"

"If it's anything like what happened to me, they were probably taken to the Magic Kingdom—just as you dreamed. But beyond that, I don't know."

We sit in silence for a bit, lost in our own worlds.

"How is the vaccine coming along?" I ask. "Have you made any progress?"

"Some. You'll be happy to know that you were right: The biotechs only work on one person, and your DNA footprint is encoded in their little brains."

"It sounds like you're making headway."

She nods. "I have the biotechs isolated in saline solution now—which makes it much easier to tinker with them." She hesitates.

"What is it?"

"I've come up with a way to replace their target genome."

"You have?" I can barely contain my excitement. "That's awesome, Soleil. You're almost there!"

"Not really," she says, wincing. "The host's immune system starts destroying the biotechs the moment they're introduced into the bloodstream. I just started tests with the live virus, and the immunity only lasts for a few minutes."

"But still, that sounds like great progress, " I say, feeling a little deflated but still hopeful.

"I guess it is—except there's no way to create new biotechs. All I can do is take the ones already in your blood and trick them into protecting someone else—and twenty minutes later, I have to start all over again."

"You need to go to the Magic Kingdom, to the lab where the biotech was engineered."

"Once it's safe." She glances at me and then drops her gaze. "Right now, I need more of your blood."

"And you're welcome to it."

She gives me the eyebrow. "As long as you don't do something stupid like getting yourself killed."

"I need to get back to the Magic Kingdom, Soleil. The sooner, the better."

She sighs. "I can't let you out, Diego. Uncle Dave would be furious."

I rub my face with my hands. "You saw the note. My world is on the line. I *have* to get back before it's too late."

"Why?" She looks up at me, her eyebrows furrowed. "Why do you need to go there?"

I exhale and then sit down next to her again. "There's a time machine inside. The same one that brought me here. I'm convinced it can transport me home."

"Even if I believed that," she says, "it makes no sense to go there until the power is back on."

"For all we know, it could be as simple as throwing a breaker. If you fly me out there, it could take ten minutes."

"Or it could take ten months."

"If it's anything like the one in my world, it was designed to last decades—centuries even. I bet all I need to do is switch the power back on. If you'll help me get there, I'm sure I can figure out what's wrong. I've been there before. I know it like the back of my hand. Please."

"I'm sorry, Diego. I really am, but I'm on the brink of a breakthrough that could mean life or death for thousands of people. If you leave now, you would be condemning what's left of mankind to a short and grim future. Uncle Dave doesn't want it to get out, but he thinks the Bub will collapse in as little as a month, and Catersville is unlikely to survive the year. Even C-Bay is degrading faster than anyone expected. I know you feel I'm being unfair to you, but try to see if from our side."

"Come with me! There's bound to be a treasure trove of information inside, maybe even the complete instructions on how to build the bionano from scratch."

"Or there could be nothing," she says, looking over at me and frowning. "And we'll have wasted weeks or even months trying to get into the place. From what you've told me, your world played out very differently from this one, and that means you don't know what's inside the mountain any more than I do."

"But whoever is sending those goddamn spheres knows!"

"And who is sending you messages inside fireballs?"

"I don't know for sure. Me from another timeline, I think. But that doesn't matter right now. What matters is the time machine is in that mountain. I'm sure of it. And if my future self tells me I need to go now, then I need to go. Now."

She looks unconvinced.

"The lab to build the biotech devices is in there too," I say. "You don't have to take my word for it. The papers they found in DC say as much."

"*If* the power can be restored, and *if* we can get the radio working, and *if* we can clear out the CO_2 and get the Bub folks resettled—"

"Christ, Soleil, that could take weeks, maybe months! I don't have that kind of t—"

"—and *if* the genetics lab is as good as you claim, I'll ask Uncle Dave to fly us out. Until then, you stay here. I know that's not what you want to hear, but it's the best I can do."

I let my head fall into my hands, too frustrated to reply.

She places her hand on my back. "I came here this morning to ask for your help, Diego. I need more of your blood to continue my research, and rather than sedate you as Uncle Dave suggested, I'm asking for your cooperation."

I don't respond, and she eventually pulls her hand away.

We sit in silence for a minute, and then she stands up. "I should go."

I watch her walk over to the door. "I'll cooperate," I say. "The sooner you get the biotech figured out, the sooner I can go home."

"Thank you." She turns back to me. "The 'her' in your message, is that my mother? I mean in your universe?"

"Yes."

"That's what Mom thought. She said it was Dad's

handwriting—your handwriting."

"Yeah. The only woman I've ever loved is dying, and I'm sitting here on my ass counting ceiling tiles."

She drops her gaze. "When Mom read the note, she did something she hasn't done in years."

I shut my eyes, not sure I want to hear this.

"She started crying," Soleil says. "She's locked herself in her room, and she won't come out. She says it's her fault Dad and Lucas are dead."

"*Mierda.*" I turn away from her, feeling adrift in turbulent seas.

"I'm ready now," Soleil calls out, and after a few seconds, I hear the outer door clang open.

She turns back to me, looking exhausted. "If I can't figure out how to build the biotechs, Mom's going to die right along with the rest of us—along with what's left of the human race."

"Yeah," I say, hating myself six ways to Sunday. "I know."

CHAPTER 24

Shannon: Now I Know What Love Is

The door of our room bursts open and Peter's father stumbles through, struggling to keep his balance.

I watch him fumble for the light switch and stifle a scream.

"Get up! I need your help finding another box of bourbon." The light comes on, and he freezes. "What the fuck?"

He must have had a lot of ethanol because I can see him struggle to make sense of the scene: I'm alone in the huge bed, and Peter is cowering in the corner underneath a pile of blankets.

And then what few neurons the man has left kick in and he staggers toward his son. "You chicken shit, limp dick, faggot."

"This is my room," Peter says, backing away from his father, "and you're not allowed—"

The man backhands his son across the face, sending Peter sprawling onto the floor. "You lying son of a bitch. You ain't a man, you're a—"

I scream and kick off the covers, scrambling over the bed toward Peter.

The drunken man grabs my ankle and drags me back across the sheets. "Not so fast, blondie."

I shriek and try to kick him away, but he pins me flat on my stomach, yanks down a bed curtain, and wraps it around my ankle.

"Don't fight," Peter says from the floor, his nose bloody. "He'll only hurt you worse."

"That's the smartest thing out of your mouth since you told your whore of a mother the exact same thing." The man loops the thin fabric around a bedpost and secures it to my ankle, tying me down to the bed.

"Alright," Peter says, getting to his feet. "Just don't hurt her. I'm begging you."

I stare at him, unable to believe he's giving his father permission to rape me.

"I'll do as I damn well please." His father lifts my hips and flips me over onto my back. I scream and try to kick free, but he grabs my throat, cutting off my breath. "Shut it, blondie, or I'll cut your tongue out."

I twist my head toward Peter, pleading with my eyes for his help, but he turns away.

"You ain't even got the balls to fight for her," his father says as he climbs on the bed. "You disgust me."

The man looks down at me, his scarred face twisting into a grin. "Even if she's dumber than a box of marbles, she's a might pretty." He squeezes one of my breasts and then kisses me hard on the mouth, his saliva getting all over my lips and chin.

I try to push him away, but he's too strong.

"I usually like to do a bitch from behind," he says, grabbing my wrists. "But with you, I wanna see that satisfied look on your face when you finally get what that faggot here ain't been giving you." His breath smells horrible, and I shut my eyes and turn away.

He laughs and pins my wrists above my head. "Listen up, Petey. The spunky ones like it hard and rough." He rips down another curtain and ties my wrists together. "They like a man who can show 'em who's boss, give 'em something to scream about. Don't you, blondie?" He yanks on the fabric, dragging me across the sheets.

I let out a surprised shriek and try to break free.

"Please, Shannon," Peter says, almost crying. "Let him have what he wants."

The man loops the end around another bedpost and cinches my arms up so tight that it cuts off the circulation to my hands.

"Stop it!" I say. "You're hurting me!"

He laughs. "The boy's right. It's high time you was introduced to the staff of a *real* man."

A tear runs down my cheek, and I look over at Peter, begging him to help me.

He sits there on the floor, cowering.

"He ain't gonna do nothin' but watch," Peter's father says and slides his hands up my thighs. "And wish he was man enough to do it himself."

He squeezes my breasts hard enough that it makes my eyes water, but I don't cry out.

"See, Petey? It's just like I told ya. For women, sex is pain, and the sooner they learn to tolerate it, the better." He slides his hand down between my legs, grabs on to my crotch, and rips off my underwear.

"Please, Peter! Don't let him—"

The man clamps his hand over my mouth. "You make

another peep, and I'll beat all that pretty out of you, you hear me?" He stares down at me, spit dripping from the corner of his mouth. "Well? What's it gonna be?" He raises his eyebrows. "Don't matter to me either way."

I shake my head.

"Suit yourself." He takes his hand away and starts undoing his pants. "And if you think what I done so far hurts, wait till you take all my meat inside that tight pussy of yours." He grins. "Now that's gonna be some real good hurtin'."

Behind him, I see Peter raise the footstool above his head.

I stifle a scream, but the man's eyes get big and he turns quickly, ramming his elbow into his son's face. Peter staggers back, but manages to swing the heavy piece of wood down, bashing the sharp corner of it into his father's skull.

There's a dull crunching sound, and the huge man collapses on me, his blood spurting across my face and chest.

I try to shove him off me, shrieking and kicking and crying, but he's too heavy.

Finally, Peter drags his father away, shoving the man's lifeless body onto the floor.

I try to wipe the blood off my face, but my hands and feet are still tied to the bedposts, and all I can do is lie there on the damp bedding and sob.

"Are you okay?" Peter asks, his face white and his hands bloody.

I stare at him, unable to speak.

He covers me with the sheet and then unties my hands and feet. "I shouldn't have let it come to this. I thought we'd have more time."

I close my eyes, my whole body trembling.

Gentle hands slip beneath my shoulders and knees, and then Peter picks me up in his arms and carries me into the bathroom.

He sets me down on my feet, but I'm too weak to stand.

I grab onto his shoulders, and he wraps his arms around me, holding me against his chest. "I'm sorry, Shannon. I was trying to protect you from that, and all I did was make it worse."

I sob into his shoulder until I have no more tears inside.

"Hey," he finally says, looking down at me. "I'm sorry."

I press my lips together, trying not to cry.

"Did he hurt you?"

I shake my head.

He holds on to me with one arm, grabs a washcloth off the towel rack, and wets it in the sink. I can feel his hands trembling as he wipes the blood and tears off my face.

"You killed him," I finally say, my voice sounding disembodied. "What are we going to do?"

He drops the soiled cloth and reaches into the shower. "Well, to start, I need to get you washed up and into clean clothes." He turns on the water, waits for it to get hot, and then starts unbuttoning my blood-stained dress. He eases the soiled material up over my shoulders and then pulls it off me.

I lean against him, shivering in my thin slip.

"I'm taking you into the Wilds," he says, "the abandoned part of the biodome. It's dark and cold, especially at night, but it has oxygen—at least it did the last time I was there." He lifts me up and carries me into the warm stream of water. "You'll be safe there—at least for now." He sets me on my feet again, but when he tries to step away, I cling to him, refusing to let go.

"Don't leave me," I say, my voice trembling.

He puts one arm around my waist, steadying me. "I won't."

And then he washes the blood off me, starting with my hair and moving down to my shoulders and chest.

"Is he really dead, Peter?"

He nods, sliding his hands over my hips, legs and feet, his touch gentle and sure.

I wait until he's done, and then look up into his eyes. "You saved me."

He doesn't respond.

"Thank you."

He turns off the water and wraps a towel around me. "We'll stop by the kitchen and take as much food as we can carry. And we'll bring the rebreather masks with us, just in case."

"But we haven't tested them," I say, and use my towel to wipe dried blood off his face. "If the seal isn't perfect, we'll die the second we're exposed to the virus."

"I trust you, Shannon. If you say they'll work, then they'll work."

I stare at him, not recognizing the man looking back at me.

Finally, he turns away.

I bite my lip. "You don't have to come with me, Peter. Everyone knows about your father, how he killed your mother and abused you. They won't blame you for this—most of them will be happy he's gone."

He's quiet for a bit, and there's a part of me that's terrified he'll agree.

Finally, he meets my gaze. "If you don't want me to come, then I won't."

I reach up and wipe more blood off his lips. "Oh, Peter," I say, glancing at his mouth. "I *want* you to come with me."

"Okay, then," he says, still holding on to me. "But we have to go now. It won't take them long to miss my father."

I nod.

"Can you manage getting dressed by yourself? While I pack our things?"

I nod again but don't let go of him.

Even though I'm standing there in a torn, damp, see-through slip—no part of me hidden from him—I don't feel embarrassed or afraid anymore.

I trust him.

He helps me back to the room and I sit down on the unstained side of the bed, unsure what to put on. Besides a handful of underwear and the bulky woolen robe, the ruined dress is all I have.

He opens one of the hidden cabinets. "I got you some clothes. They're more... practical than a dress." He takes something out of a drawer. "I know they're not as nice as what you had at the Bub, but they're clean—and they'll keep you warm in the Wilds." He sets them on the bed next to me and walks back toward the bathroom.

"Why are you helping me, Peter?" I run my fingers across the clothes he's saved for me. "And why didn't you force me to sleep with you that first night—or any other night? There was nothing I could have done..." I look up at him. "But you didn't. Why is that?"

"Because I"—he exhales—"Because it wouldn't be right."

"Oh."

He closes the door.

I put on the clothes, some pants like the woman in *I Dream of Jeannie* wears but made of heavier cotton, and a man's button-down shirt that is thick, soft and warm. I collect our meager belongings and then knock on the bathroom door.

"Okay," I say. "I'm ready."

He comes out, the blood gone, but his lip fat and a bruise forming around his left eye. He opens the door to our workshop. "I'll get the masks. Can you fold up a couple of blankets?"

"Yes, of course."

He disappears, and I pull his clean blankets out of the

corner, roll them up into a tight bundle, and look for something to tie them together. I consider using the bloody bed curtains, but end up pulling the belt out of the man's pants and wrapping it around the bundle.

Peter comes back a minute later and puts my toiletries and underclothes into his backpack.

"Good thinking," he says when he sees the rolled up bedding. "First I need to get my bow, and then we'll go to the kitchens."

"Your bow?"

"For protection," he says and rolls his father's body over. "We need to get through the Barrier before they discover what's happened." He takes a set of keys out of the man's pocket. "And these will help."

"What about water?" I ask. "Should I bring the glass bottle in the cabinet?"

He shakes his head. "I know how to collect condensation off the biodome walls. We should be okay as long as we have something to store it in."

"Should I take the empty bottle?" I ask and pick up the bundle of blankets.

"No. The abandoned side is full of garbage, Shaz." He swings the pack up onto his shoulders and then takes the bundle out of my hands. "We'll find something."

It's the first time he's called me by my nickname—although he's heard me call myself it tons of times—and I realize that something between us has shifted.

More like tipped over.

"I can carry the blankets," I say, reaching out for them.

He half-smiles. "I've got them for now."

"Really," I say. "I want to help."

"I'm glad to hear that. And, again, I'm sorry I let things go this far. I've been planning to leave for a while, but I was afraid you..." He glances down at his hands. "That you wouldn't want me to come with you."

"I like you and all, Peter," I say. "I like you a lot, actu-ally—but sometimes you say the dumbest things." Without really thinking about it, I kiss him softly on the lips.

He closes his eyes—and kisses me back.

Time stands still, our lips touching and my heart pounding.

And then he pulls away. "We need to go."

"Just a sec." I get the book of poems he gave me and zip it into the side of his backpack.

"Anything else?" he asks.

"No," I say. "I'm ready."

He takes my hand and leads me out of the room.

"Thank you for saving me, Peter."

"*Nunc scio, quid sit Amor,*" he says and shuts the door.

"Is that French?" I ask, looking up at him.

"No, it's Latin." He guides me down the dark hallway. "My mother taught it to me."

"What does it mean?"

"You're welcome."

CHAPTER 25

Diego: Alternate Facts

I'm awakened by a noise, but by the time I'm fully conscious, it's stopped.

It's pitch black—the only lights are a dim LED above the toilet and the flashing red beacon of the smoke detector in the empty cell across the hall.

I hold my breath and listen, my heart rate quickening.

There's the faintest scratching sound—and it's getting closer. Someone switches on a flashlight, the beam flickering across the floor and ceiling out in the hallway.

"Mr. Crusoe?" The voice is a whisper. "Where are you?"

"Over here." I feel around for my jeans and then shove my legs into them. "Last cell on the right."

I hear footsteps, and then the flashlight beam jumps into my cell, bouncing off the metal sink and toilet until it finds me.

"Diego?"

I put my hand up to shield my eyes. "Yes. Who's there?"

"Ingrid."

I can't recall anyone with that name—in this universe or my own. "Ingrid?"

"Yes," she says. "Nurse Sweet."

"Nurse Sweet?" I squint into the beam of light. "What are you doing here?"

"I have something for you," she says. "From Dr. Kirk."

I still can't get used to the fact that Bella uses Dave's last name, and before I can stop myself I say, "You mean Isabella Kirk?"

"Yes, of course," she says. "She asked me if I could deliver this to you. Mr. Kirk is not letting anyone in to see you, and Dr. Kirk said it was important."

She drops the beam to her feet, and I hear rummaging in a paper bag.

I get up and walk over to the bars, the concrete floor cold on my bare feet. "How did you manage to get in?"

"Oh, it wasn't that difficult. The man who's been delivering your meals is my husband. I waited until he fell asleep—and then borrowed his keys." She pushes something through the metal bars. "Here."

I take a thin, heavy object out of her hands. "Thank you. What is it?"

"A tablet computer. Dr. Kirk said you'd know what to do with it. I have to get back now, Mr. Crusoe, before he realizes I'm gone."

"Yes, of course. Please tell Dr. Kirk I said thank you."

"I will," she says. "Oh, and there's one more thing. Dr. Kirk said the password is her favorite villain."

"Her favorite what?" I ask, not understanding.

"Villain. You know, bad guy. She said you'd know who that is."

"Ah, okay. Thank you, Ingrid. I owe you one."

"I'm hoping we'll all be in your debt soon," she says. "The whole human race." She reaches through the bars and squeezes my arm. "Good night, Diego."

I listen for the soft *clang* of the outer door and the turn of the deadlock, my pulse still racing.

What could Bella possibly want me to know—or see?

I take off my jeans and get back in bed, pulling the blanket up over my head to block the light. In the twenty-four hours since Dave locked me up, I haven't been able to find a camera in the cell, but that doesn't mean there isn't one.

After making sure the blanket is covering me, I slide my fingers over the glass surface of the iPad and press the home button. The display blinks soundlessly to life, a photo filling the screen. It's James and Bella with two young kids standing in front of a huge, crumbling step pyramid.

I stare at the photograph and then run my fingertips over the family I never had.

At my touch, a transparent keypad appears, the words "Enter Password" hovering above it.

I think for a minute and then type in *Strasser*—he's the Nazi bad guy in *Casablanca*—and push *Send*.

The keypad shakes and then resets.

Shit. Maybe you're not that similar to James.

And then, like Harry Potter's patronus, it comes to me in a bright surge of light. I type in *Umbridge*, and the device unlocks.

The photo of Zoser's Pyramid is still there, but in the foreground, there are three icons, one labeled *David*, a second named *Diego*, and a third entitled *James*.

I tap the first icon.

A file containing photos of official-looking documents appears. The first one is entitled Police Report and the name listed at the top as the offender is *Nadales, James F.*

I scroll through the pages, reading the other titles. After the Police Report, there's a Psychiatric Report, an Accident Report, and a Death Certificate.

Mierda.

I go back to the Police Report and start reading. The complaint is dated nearly thirty years ago with the offense listed as "Threatening an officer of the peace."

The details section contains a description of James arriving at a Denver police station mid-afternoon, asking to report suspicious behavior, and stating, "You need to contact the CIA."

The report details his claims, including that *The Russians are attempting to kidnap me due to a meteorite from space* and *The object came down in Siberia and contained my name—along with plans to build a time machine.*

James insisted that he and his family were in danger—and wanted the police department to contact the NSA. After the duty officer refused to make the call, James threatened to "stalk the reporting officer until he called in the Feds." James was subsequently taken into custody for making criminal threats against a police officer, but the charges were dropped at the request of the district attorney. Mr. Nadales was later released to his wife, a medical doctor.

The Psychiatric Evaluation is dated the same day and must have been performed after James was locked up. The psychiatrist who examined him stated that he "suffers from acute paranoid schizophrenia" and recommended that James "seek professional psychiatric help."

The next document is an Accident Report. It's dated later that same evening. I begin to read, my whole body tense with dread:

A witness called 911 at 8:17 pm to report
seeing a car swerve and plunge over the
north railing of the Aspen Street Bridge
into the Platte River. Emergency vehicles
responded, arriving within four minutes,
but found no witness. (The caller ID was
later traced to a prepaid, disposable
cell phone.) Emergency responders were
able to see the submerged vehicle through
the hole it made in the ice, and at 8:48
pm, divers entered the water through that
same gap to search for bodies. They found
both doors on the vehicle's driver's side
open, but no bodies inside.

Divers recovered:

• a child's slipper lodged in the rear
door handle. (See attached photo.)

• an adult's down vest caught on the
handbrake. (Subsequently identified by his
wife as belonging to James F. Nadales).

The air temperature was recorded at 46° F
and the water temperature at 34° F. Skies
were clear and the road surface of the
bridge was determined to be dry and free
of hazards.

Due to the 8-9 inches of ice covering the
river, the freezing water temperature,
and the swift current, no further attempt

was made to recover the bodies at that time.

A search and rescue team was alerted. Personnel started at dawn and spent the next forty-eight hours searching down river for the bodies. On the second day after the accident, a child's stuffed animal (see attached photo) was recovered. It was found lodged beneath river ice approximately six miles downstream from the accident. The mother positively identified the item as belonging to the missing child (name withheld due to age).

The vehicle was recovered the morning after the accident, and subsequent examination revealed:

• No mechanical problems (brakes, steering, and headlamps checked).

• The right, front tire had lost air pressure due to a rupture on the rim near the valve stem. Probable cause: blunt force sustained when the falling vehicle struck the river ice.

• Both windows (front and back) on the driver's side doors were down 1-2 inches.

• In the back seat on the driver's side there was a 5-point, forward-facing child car seat (properly installed). The double shoulder restraints on the car seat were found unlatched.

• A 9mm Glock 43 handgun (unloaded) was found in the passenger seat.

• A 70cl bottle labeled Laphroaig Scotch Single Malt 32 Year whiskey was found on the floorboards of the passenger seat. No cap was recovered. The bottle contained river water.

The wife (Isabella Sanborn-Nadales, MD) of the driver (James F. Nadales) states that she and Mr. Nadales had an argument that day, and he had stormed out of the house in a rage, intending to spend the night with his best friend (name redacted). The accident was reported seven minutes after a neighbor saw Mr. Nadales driving away from his house. After the wife was notified by the police, her five-year-old son was discovered to be missing from the home and was subsequently presumed to be in the car when the accident occurred. (See list of items above.)

Driver: James F. Nadales, male, 30. Body not recovered.

Passenger: (name withheld due to age), male, 5 (son of James F. Nadales and Isabella Sanborn-Nadales, MD). Body not recovered.

Cause of Accident: Inconclusive. Possible
alcohol-related. Possible driver error.
Possible suicide.

There's an addendum, dated six months later:

Search for victims' bodies suspended at
the request of the family. The court has
ruled there is sufficient evidence to
declare death in absentia.

Case closed.

CHAPTER 26

Lani: Journey to the Center of the Earth

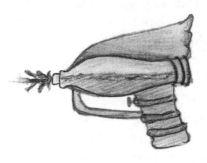

"James Nadales?" I say out loud, still unable to believe it's him.

So everything Diego told me must be true?

I watch the blast door close and then feel my ears pop. There's a computer screen with a keypad on the wall, but it remains dark despite my attempts to summon the silicon genie inside. I stand in the large space for ten minutes, waiting for something else to happen, and when nothing does, I sit down on the floor next to my backpack, take a drink of water, and await my fate.

There are worse ways to die.

After forty-seven minutes, I hear gears turning, and then my ears pop again. The inner blast door, which looks to be identical to the outer one, begins to open.

Pele, *help me, I hope this isn't a mistake.*

Inside the second blast door is a familiar-looking airlock, albeit a lot bigger than the one in the Bub. In the middle of the floor is a tripod with an orange and blue plastic rifle mounted on top. It looks like a big, pump-action squirt gun—except it has a cable coming out the bottom. Sitting next to it is a car battery.

"That's the supersonic annihilator."

I let out a gasp, almost tripping over the battery in my haste to locate the source. "James?"

"Yeah. I can see you, but you can't see me. Sorry."

"No worries." I spot the camera in the corner. "You scared the sh-shit out of me."

"I guess that makes us even."

I laugh. "I imagine so. What do I need to do with the… squirt gun thingy."

It's his turn to laugh. "That was my son's idea—putting the components inside the water cannon—but it works pretty well. Makes it easy to know which way to aim the nozzle."

"Your son must have been a smart kid, just like his dad."

"More like his mom, I think, but thanks. You need to turn on the gun and kinda spray it around the room. See that round sensor by the inner door? Once it stays green for a while, I can let you in."

"So you're not going to cycle the airlock?"

"No. The Ray Gun will kill all the Doomsday bugs so I don't have to waste any air."

"Waste it?"

"Yeah. The back-up filtration system is on the blink, and if I dump any clean air, the CO_2 level will rise. Benny and I try to avoid that."

"Oh my goodness," I say. "Of course you do."

"Connect the red cable to the red battery terminal to turn it on."

"Okay." I check out the Ray Gun, trying to decide if I

should trust a man who's been locked up inside a mountain for thirty years all by himself. If he turns out to be wrong, it'll kill him—and contaminate the whole inside. "How sure are you this squirt gun will make the air safe for you and Benny?"

"Willing to bet my life on it, I guess. But you seem like a nice person. I want to help you—and your friends too, if I can. Plus, it's been pretty lonely inside here all these years…"

"I can't even imagine what you must have gone through," I say. "And what you're risking to help me." I swallow and wipe my eyes, wondering if I would have survived as long as he did.

Probably not.

"Thank you, James. You're very brave."

"Wait till we get the power back on before you go all gushy on me, okay?"

I smile. "Deal."

"Like I said, just hook up the battery and start spraying it around. You'll need to squirt everything in your backpack—and then stand in front of the gun and, you know, turn around, so it sprays you too."

"Okay. Do I need to take my clothes off?" The thought makes me cringe.

With all your scars, he'll think you're some sort of hideous demon.

He hesitates. "Well, I certainly don't want to discourage you, but I don't think it's necessary."

I can feel my face flush.

"No need to be embarrassed, doc," he says, a hint of amusement in his tone. "It was a good question. The ultrasound goes right through fabric, but it doesn't penetrate past the epidermis. You won't feel a thing. But you might take off your shoes and coat, just to be safe."

I nod and remove them, along with the plastic bags around my socks. I pull off my sweater and drop it on the floor.

"Damn it," he says. "I should have said yes."

I stifle a smile and start taking things out of my backpack.

"It's, uh," he says, "been a long time since I was with a…" He clears his throat. "Well, since I had any company besides Benny—and I should have said, 'yeah, you need to take your clothes off.' Except if you found out it wasn't required, you would have thought I was a dirty, old man—which I'm not, at least I didn't used to be, dirty, that is, not old. Obviously I wasn't always old—but, Christ, it's been so lonely in here for all these years, and then a young woman rings the doorbell, asking me for help and offering to take her clothes off, and I…" He stops. "I'm rambling, aren't I?"

I laugh. "Yes, but I don't mind."

"Sorry. It's just so nice to have someone to talk to. I miss that more than anything."

"Well, don't worry, I'm not going anywhere—at least not until all the Bub folks are safe." I tip my backpack upside down to make sure it's empty.

"What's the Bub?"

"My biodome," I say, wondering if David has figured out a way to fix the collapsed wall. "The one that's failing."

"Are there more?"

I nod and take the last few things out of my pack. "Somewhere around forty, spread all around the globe."

He makes a hoot of delight. "Did you hear that Benny? Maybe there are some girl chinchillas out there waiting for you."

I smile. "It's certainly possible."

"Is it okay if I call you Lani?" he asks.

"Mm-hm." I make sure all the pockets in the pack are unzipped.

"Thanks for finding me, Lani. I don't know how much longer I could have…"

I set down the pack. "James?"

"Yeah?"

"What was your wife's name?"

He sniffs his nose, and I realize he's been crying. "Isabella. God, I miss her."

I swallow, trying to decide if I should tell him the truth.

If it were you, you'd want to know.

"She's alive," I say. "And so is your daughter."

He's quiet for nearly a minute. "Where are they?" His voice is a whisper. "With your friends?"

"No. They're in a biodome on the east coast, one of the biggest and best ever built. It's on Chesapeake Bay in Virginia. C-Bay, they call it."

"Dave Kirk married her, didn't he."

I look up at the camera. "Yes."

"That bastard. He tricked me into faking my own death and then stole my wife and daughter."

"Mr. Kirk arranged for them to move inside a biodome, James. He saved their lives."

"Yeah, just like he saved me and Lucas? Got us locked up inside this underground tomb so he could be the hero and marry Isa. Made me stand by and watch my own son die..." I hear him take a shaky breath. "Fuck. I'm going to kill him."

I stand there, staring at my hands, unsure what to believe about David. "I'm sorry, James. It must have been terrible for you."

"*Mierda*, how could I have been so stupid?" I hear him blow his nose a couple of times. "Are you married?"

I shake my head. "But I have a daughter, and I can't imagine being forced to stand by while she suffers and dies."

"Yeah."

I wipe my face on my sleeve, hoping with all my heart that Shannon is okay.

"Well, we'd better get to work, hadn't we?" He exhales.

"Why don't you fire up the Ray Gun so we can open the damn door."

I connect the wire to the battery and pick up the plastic gun. "Here goes nothing." An LED light blinks on, and a thin cloud of dust falls off the squirt gun. I can feel a slight buzzing in my hands, but the sonic annihilator is otherwise silent. It appears to be a plastic toy with a couple of wires taped to it.

"When was the last time you used this thing?" I ask.

"A couple years ago. You can tell it's working, right? The light is on?"

I nod, but I'm not getting a warm and fuzzy feeling about the whole thing.

What if he is crazy and the alleged viracide cannon is just a broken water pistol? What if he opens the inner door and the virus attacks him?

You'll be responsible for his death—and the contamination of the whole Inside.

James must read the look on my face because he laughs.

"Point it at the virus detector. You'll see. It works—at least it used to."

I do as he suggests.

When the nozzle of the gun is aimed at the sensor, it turns orange and then green. When I point it away, the indicator goes back to orange, then red.

"It works!"

"You sound surprised," he says.

"Maybe a little."

"What are the chances I could have survived in here for thirty years if I was mad as a hatter, doc?"

"You do have a point," I say, spraying the invisible ultrasound around the room. "You know, you can do the same thing with an ultraviolet light—kill all the viruses, I mean—and it takes only a minute, two at the most."

"Well, when FedEx delivers the replacement bulb I ordered, I'll be sure to give it a try."

I smile. "You sound like Diego."

"Wedge the gun barrel so it's pointing straight out and then stand in front of it and turn around, hands over your head."

I do as he says, feeling self-conscious whirling around in front of a plastic squirt gun with my arms raised.

Thank Pele, *you're not naked.*

"The stream is pretty wide," he says, "so you don't need to bend down or anything."

"'Kay."

"Who's Diego?"

I hold my breath for a second.

Go big or go home.

"He's your parallel from another universe—only he's from the past. So he's twenty years younger than you are. He came here in a time machine, but it was by accident. The targeting was broken or something."

He's doesn't respond.

I stop moving for a second. "You *do* know about the time machine, right?"

"*Mierda.*" He coughs. "It's downstairs next to the bowling alley—but we never got it to work."

"Well, in Diego's universe, they did." I lift up my braid, letting the Ray Gun get underneath. "And he has the biotech devices in his blood too. The ones that protect him from Doomsday. The instructions were inside a mysterious metal sphere, sound familiar?"

"Yes."

"And Diego's the guy who told us about you, about the Magic Kingdom, that is. If it weren't for him, we wouldn't have known that there was a government installation here."

He's quiet for nearly a minute, and I continue bathing in

the invisible ultrasonic stream.

"James?" I say, at last. "Are you still there?"

"Yes. Is Lucas alive in Diego's universe?"

I lower my arms. "I'm sorry, but I don't think Lucas ever existed in his world."

"And Isa? Is she married to him, or did Dave fuck Diego over like he did me?"

"I don't know, James." I hold up my backpack and point the beam inside. "You'll have to ask Diego when he gets here."

Something bumps his microphone, and there's a bit of feedback. "He's coming here?"

"When Diego finds out you have a time machine, I don't think the devil himself could keep him away. He wants to get back to his universe. He wants to go home."

I glance at the Doomsday sensor.

It's green.

"Just a couple more minutes now," he says, "and it should be safe to let you in."

I start putting everything back into my pack. "Are you immune, James? Did you get an injection of the biotech devices like Diego did?"

"As far as I know, they never deciphered the plans. They were destroyed in the explosion."

"Damn. I was hoping you had the instructions in here."

"Well, there *is* a state-of-the-art genetics lab downstairs—and, believe me, they tried to come up with a vaccine—but even the best geneticists in the world couldn't make heads or tails of the melted bits they recovered from the Bomb."

"The Bomb?"

"That's what we called the metal sphere. It took out a good chunk of Moscow when it came down. People thought it was a nuke, because it ignited gas lines all across the city.

Blew up everything."

"I remember that—the bombings in Russia."

"Took the Ruskies months to determine it wasn't a terrorist attack, but they never told the public the truth."

We're both quiet for a bit.

"Anything else I need to decontaminate?"

"No. The sensor's been green for a while." He blows his nose again. "Ready to open the door?"

"Are you sure it's safe, James? Once it's open, there'll be no going back."

"Pretty sure," he says. "Lucas and I used the Ray Gun to clear out the space we're living in now, and it's much bigger than the airlock."

"Clear out?"

"Yeah, someone overrode the computer and opened the blast doors back when things started to get dicey. Because Lucas and I were kept locked downstairs, we survived. But all of this area was contaminated. When we realized what had happened—that we were alone—we built the Ray Gun and took turns wearing the one biosuit we recovered to shut the blast doors, seal the airlock, and decontaminate this whole upper level."

"Wow."

"We had plenty of time to do it," he says. "Years, in fact."

"I imagine so."

"Okay," he says. "I think it's probably safe to enter, but if you wouldn't mind breathing right on the sensor to check? We've never had to decontaminate anything living, and I want to make sure we killed all the Doomsday virus in your lungs."

"Of course," I say and walk over to the sensor. I breathe right on it, filling my lungs with air and exhaling five or six times.

It stays green.

"Good. I'm opening the airlock now."

One whole wall of the room starts sliding sideways, and on the other side is a huge cavern, the walls and ceiling rough-cut rock.

Walking across the large, empty space is a man in a knee-length, plaid bathrobe and fuzzy slippers.

He's cut his hair and shaved, and the resemblance to Diego is striking now. He's a very fit—and quite attractive for his age. There's a gray furry animal with big round ears sitting on his shoulder.

James walks up to me and stops, his eyes widening when he gets close enough to see the scar tissue.

We stand there in awkward silence, and I resist the urge to touch the mangled skin on my face.

"Nice to finally meet you," I say and offer him my hand. "And I like your new haircut."

"You do?" He stares at my hand for a second and then shakes it. "At first I hated the short hair, but now it's growing on me."

I laugh. "*That* was a good one."

He frowns. "You think so?"

I nod, but I don't think he believes me.

"Benny," he says, glancing sideways at the creature on his shoulder, "this is Lani. She's a doctor, and she's going to be staying with us for a bit. We'll have to make up the guest suite."

"Nice to meet you, Benny. James tells me you're looking for a new girlfriend."

James smiles.

It's uncanny how much he sounds like—and even moves like—Diego.

He picks up my backpack. "Welcome to the Magic Kingdom."

Chapter 27

Diego: Betrayal

The final document is a Presumptive Death Certificate for James F. Nadales.

It's dated six months after the accident but gives the time of death as the night of the crash. The cause of death is listed as "Drowning (South Platte River below Aspen Street Bridge) due to automobile accident of same date. Suicide suspected. No body recovered from beneath the ice, but the state has granted legal Presumption of Death due to overwhelming evidence."

I close the file and stare at the smiling photo of a man who looks to be my twin, wondering what could have possibly gone wrong in the short time between when this photo was taken and his presumed death.

Presumed.

There are things a man learns about himself as he grows

older, but I can say with unwavering certainty that I would never kill myself to escape my problems, not as an outcast stranded in another universe—and definitely not with a wife and family.

Never.

Something else happened that night on the bridge. Something that cost me my life—and cost Isabella her husband, her son, and her future.

I close the file and tap on my name, a dark shroud of dread falling over me.

A photo of a handwritten note appears.

Diego

Thank you for giving me the courage to uncover the truth.

What I found out tonight can't bring James back, but it does give me some comfort. At the very least, I know that he didn't abandon us—abandon me. David never delivered the enclosed letter from James. I didn't know the truth about what happened until now.

David has been lying to me for the past thirty years, Diego, and I believe he lied to James too. Why David would do something like that—and if he actually killed James and thereby Lucas—I don't know. But if he did it once, he could do it again.

If and when Soleil unravels the biotech vaccine, I fear for your life. David suspects you know something. Something you shouldn't. And now you most definitely do.

-Isabella

I place my finger over the last file, the one labeled *James*, and then freeze.

Do I want to know what really happened?

I tap the icon and read the first three words of a letter.

My dearest Isa-

It's dated three days before the car accident, and it's in my handwriting.

If you are reading this letter, then the "accident" has happened, and I am presumed dead.

But let me assure you, if all went as planned, I am not.

I apologize for deceiving you. I saw no other way to keep you and the kids safe—and that has always been my highest priority.

Even if you can't forgive me—and I certainly understand it if you can't—at least let me explain:

All that crazy stuff I told the police about the meteorite and the Russians chasing me was true, Isa. Every word. The FSB had been following me for weeks and finally confronted me on the way to Dave's poker game—the night I came home with blood on my shirt, remember?

The Russians told me about the time machine and offered me a lot of money to "disappear" with them. After I refused, they threatened to hurt

Lucas and Soleil—and to kill you if I mentioned a word of it to anyone.

They gave me three days to think about it—as if I had any choice.

That night, David and I came up with a plan that would allow me to "die"—while keeping all of you safe. To that end, I gave the police reason to believe that I had gone over the edge—and that things had gotten bad enough between the two of us that I might consider killing myself.

It was all a ruse, hun, and I'll never forgive myself for the pain and suffering my actions must have caused you. I'm sure you're furious with me—and I deserve it—but I needed you to believe I was gone. So everyone else would believe it too.

Please try to understand.

So what happens now?

If my deception went as planned, then the police believe I lost control of the car on an icy bridge, plunged into the river below, and drowned. My body was never recovered, but that is not unusual in cases like these—given the dark night, freezing water, and swift current—so I assume no suspicions were raised.

I imagine the funeral was held a week or so after the crash, and since then you have been picking up the pieces of your life and trying to go on alone. David has assured me he will do everything in his power to protect you, and I have asked him to give you this letter when he feels it's safe.

Please don't hate me.

It shouldn't take much to have the state declare me dead in absentia. If you haven't done that already, please let David help. (He's friends with the district attorney.) This will allow you to collect on my life insurance. That money should be enough to live on indefinitely, including college for the twins.

I can't tell you where I am, Isa, but once I'm sure it's safe, you'll hear from me. I beg you to come find me—but if you choose not to, I'll understand.

I hope someday you and the kids can forgive me.

I love you more than life itself, Isabella.

Forever yours,

James

I stare at the letter Dave never delivered until the low power warning appears.

Christ, I'm going to kill him.

I shut off the computer, hide it under the foot of the mattress, and imagine myself choking that fat neck of his.

If I have to murder him to get out of here, I sure as hell will.

CHAPTER 28

Shannon: Where the Wild Things Are

In the fading light streaming through the airlock window, I mark day twenty-nine on the calendar—nineteen days in the Room of Release plus ten days in the Wilds—and then sit down on my improvised bed and towel dry my hair. So much has happened, that it feels like I've been away from home for months. I miss Mom and Mindy a lot, but things are getting better now that Peter and I have escaped to the Wilds.

Still, the first few nights here were scary.

We used the keys Peter took from his father to get what we needed from the Compound and then used the stolen access card to unlock the door through the Barrier. It's a massive steel wall that separates the part of the biodome with power from the part that's busted. After Peter got the door open, he squeezed a whole tube of epoxy into the lock mechanism and resealed the door.

By that time, it was after midnight, and I was so exhausted I could barely stand. Peter didn't think they'd find his father until morning, and he figured it'd take them a couple days to pry the Barrier door open, but he wasn't willing to bet our lives on it. So, he insisted that we hike across what's left of the old biodome—which is unbelievably huge and a lot like the Outside, with dirt and plants everywhere—to a maintenance tower on the far side.

Then he made me climb what seemed like a million steps before he put our stuff down. I tried to sleep while Peter kept watch, but there were lots of strange noises, and I finally gave up and sat next to him in the dark, wishing I was at home in my room with Mom asleep in the bedroom next to mine.

When Peter asked me what I was thinking, I didn't want to tell him how scared I was. So, I told him about my pet rat, Wilson, and how he helped me test the rebreathers—and that he was loyal, smart and gentle.

Even though Peter didn't say anything, I could tell that he didn't think keeping a rat as a pet was such a great idea. But I think he would change his mind if he met Wilson. He was much more impressed when I told him about Bearhart—and that Madders had flown all the way to San Francisco to get him for me—and about how I had taught the puppy tricks and stuff.

Peter had never seen a real dog, and he started asking questions about Bearhart. But talking about home always makes me sad, so I didn't want to talk about him anymore.

We sat there staring out into the dark biodome for a long time.

It got really cold, and I started shivering. So Peter put his arms around me to keep me warm. I snuggled against him, feeling safe for the first time since they forced me out of the airplane at gunpoint, and fell asleep.

But I had nightmares about being crushed to death by a

rotting corpse, and I woke up screaming. Peter pulled me to his chest and stroked my hair until my heart stopped pounding, and at some point, I must have fallen back asleep because when I woke up in the morning, there were two blankets over me and Peter's sweater under my head.

He was making breakfast, including hot oatmeal and a steaming mug of tea.

When I asked where he'd gotten the water and the cups, he just smiled.

That was the day we found my biosuit still lying on the floor where they had taken it off me.

The map I drew up in the airplane was still in the pocket—along with the seashell Mr. C gave me. If I ever have to make a run for it, it will be good to have the biosuit and map. Still, I haven't given up hope that Mom or Madders will figure out a way to get me out of here—get *us* out of here—but every day that passes makes it seem less likely.

Peter says we might be able to live in the Wilds indefinitely, but I don't want to stay in Catersville. I don't want to live in fear of Peter's clan, forced to scavenge for food in the half-darkness that passes for day here, and worried that the biodome could fail at any moment.

The second day, Peter showed me his stash of camping supplies, including a shortwave radio and a portable environment bubble that works like a tent. He spent the afternoon showing me how to put it up and take it down and then demonstrated how to use a compass. Madders taught me how to navigate using the North Star—which is great in a plane but not much help inside a biodome—but it turns out I'm pretty good with a compass too. I now have my own backpack, a wind-up flashlight, a whistle—which I showed Peter how to use for an SOS signal—and a Swiss army knife with a can opener and scissors. I grabbed an extra pocket-knife to give to Mindy when I get home.

On the third day, we went back to the Barrier to see if they'd tried to get the door open.

They hadn't.

Peter said there were men who hated his father, and they were probably fighting over who would be the new leader. But he was sure they'd eventually figure out a way to get through the Barrier and come after us—especially if the men loyal to his father won.

I asked why the men didn't just go around the Barrier—out the airlock on their side and in the one on our side. It turns out that no one at Catersville knows how to operate the main airlocks without the computer—which is why the men brought me in through that emergency airlock on the abandoned side, and why Peter was so surprised when I told him I knew how to open and shut the main airlock by hand.

Thank goodness for the emergency training everyone at the Bub gets.

Manually opening the airlock requires a bit of muscle power, but we do it at least twice a day now, and I think I could do it blindfolded. Peter is faster than I am, but if I really focus, I can do it in less than a minute.

Like a walk in the picnic, as Mindy would say.

Because no one else knows how to do it, Peter says we're safe in here. So for the past week we've been sleeping on separate piles of blankets inside the west airlock. With a foam pad on the bottom, a blanket in the middle, and a sleeping bag on top, it's warm and safe.

We haven't tried the external door of the airlock, but if need be, I'm pretty sure we could get out that way. We do have my biosuit and the rebreathers—I just wish we could come up with a way to test the masks before we have to use them.

I guess we'll burn that bridge when we get to it.

Peter says they used to have a zoo here, sort of like Noah's Ark with two of every animal, but when the power failed, people started eating them. Still, a lot of the creatures must have escaped because the biodome is full of weird noises at night. When I asked Peter what kind of animals are out there, he just shrugged—but he won't let me go exploring by myself.

To be perfectly honest, I don't really mind.

The Wilds are creepy even in the daytime, but after the sun goes down, they're downright terrifying. When I was little, I was afraid of the dark, but I've never lived anywhere it was actually dangerous at night. Even though I told Peter if I wasn't rescued, I was going to walk back to the Bub, I can't imagine being Outside after dark. The whole idea gives me the creeps.

I take a deep breath and continue drying my hair.

You're safe for now, Shaz.

The air in the Wilds doesn't seem much worse than it was in the Compound. The fire that was burning when I first arrived has gone out, and the smoke has dissipated—filtered out by whatever environmental controls are still working, I assume. I asked Peter if he knows how the fire got started in here, but he just shook his head. He's hard to read sometimes, and I couldn't decide if he was telling me the truth—or hiding something from me.

Peter says there are more people living here in the Wilds—the Others, he calls them—but I haven't seen anyone. He showed me some trash that hadn't been there the day before—which, as he was quick to point out, could have been left by the wild things.

Very clever wild things, if you ask me.

One of the wrappers we found was folded into a perfect isosceles triangle. When I showed it to Peter, I had to explain who Isosceles was and what his triangles are, but we both knew it wasn't made by a rat—or any zoo animal.

It's funny how Peter knows so much about living in the Wilds, but almost nothing about the past.

Sometimes, he asks me about how things used to be. About how we ended up in biodomes, and what the world was like before Doomsday killed almost everyone.

I tell him about the movies I've seen and the books I've read, but I don't think I've done a very good job of explaining things, because all he says when I'm done is, "That doesn't sound so smart."

I know Peter is worried about something—especially at night—and I think it's the vigilantes looking to avenge his father's death. But every time I ask him about it, he just shrugs.

I want to get out of this failed biodome more than anything, but if I leave here now, Mom—or whoever shows up to rescue me—won't be able to find me. I told Peter that, and all he said was, "They better hurry."

We spend our days exploring what he calls the ghost town—the area with old buildings and houses with broken-in windows. When we find food, tools, or other valuables, we haul them back inside the airlock for safekeeping. I've been making a map using a pencil and a piece of cardboard. I mark all the buildings where we find boxes of food, clothing, tools, and such so that we can go back if we need more.

I've also started marking the map with the places where we find signs of the Others. Today we found cans opened with a jackknife, so I know it wasn't the zoo animals eating the baked beans. There are definitely other people hiding out here—and probably watching our every move.

Peter never mentioned it again, but I can tell it worries him too.

Now that we're on our own, he's teaching me how to make traps to catch vermin—whatever those are. Once we actually catch one, he's going to show me how to skin it and roast it. It sounds kind of gross, but useful.

Even without power, the taps are still working, and we've been taking hot showers in the changing room next to the airlock. Peter says the water comes from underground wells and is heated by solar panels, but all I know is, it's divine. He's also teaching me how to shoot using his compound bow, and that's totally awesome.

Just the thought of it makes me all tingly inside. Not because I'm Pocahontas or anything, but because of... other stuff.

I'm not very strong yet. So Peter has to help me get the bowstring started. He stands with his arms around me, and I lean against his chest, listening to his heartbeat as I watch the muscles in his arms flex. Sometimes I close my eyes and imagine kissing him again—but he never seems to notice.

We've been practicing every afternoon, and it's my favorite part of the day.

Well, that and the hot showers in the evening.

Water at the Bub was always rationed, and showers there were tepid, short, and rare. Mindy would be so jealous—of Peter *and* the hot showers.

That's the one thing I'm going to miss when I finally get out of here.

Peter brought the tubes of sealant with the masks, and the same day we found the camping supplies we also found a huge box of rebreathers. We've set up another workshop in a room full of broken-down machines and are fixing more masks. I assumed we'd add the new masks to our store of things for Outside, but Peter said we should give them to the Others. I asked him what they were going to do with rebreather masks if they never go Outside, and he shrugged—and then insisted that we already had three each and could always make more for ourselves later. So, every morning we fix two new ones, leave them in a vise to cure overnight, and then set them out when we find signs of the Others. They're always gone the next day, and in their place are carrots and potatoes. I think that's a good sign.

So far, no one's tried to hurt us or steal our things, and as long as the men don't come after Peter and me, I think we'll be okay for a while.

I hope Mom gets me out of here soon...

Peter steps through the airlock door, bringing me back to the present.

He watches me run a brush through my hair—another of our daily scavenging finds—and then turns away. "Anything else you need before I seal the door?"

"No," I say. "I'm good."

"Is your mask in your backpack?" he asks, same as he does every night.

"Yes," I say, just like I do every night, and then add, "I know we've been handing them out to the Others, Peter, but we really should test one sooner rather than later. That sealant we're using is different from what I used at home, and it could be totally useless against the virus."

"It's not." He finishes closing the airlock and starts arranging his pile of blankets on the other side of the room.

"You don't know that," I say, a little annoyed that he's not more concerned.

"Yes, I do." He looks up, watching me divide my hair so I can braid it.

I'm a bit surprised when, this time, he doesn't turn away.

"Would you like me to do that for you?" he asks. "Braid your hair, I mean?"

"Um, sure. My mom used to do it before... you know." I clear my throat. "Anyway, it's much easier if someone else braids it for me."

He sits behind me on my bed and runs his fingers through my hair, gathering it into his hand.

"Have you ever braided hair before?" I ask.

"No, but I've been watching you for almost a month, and I think I can do it." He picks up my brush and runs it lightly over the long strands. "And anyway, if it's bad, you can always undo it."

I laugh. "You're the one who has to look at it, Peter. If *you* don't like it, you can always try again."

"I'll keep that in mind."

I shut my eyes, enjoying his touch. "So how do you know the masks work?"

"After you told me about using Wilson to test them at the Bub, I glued two of them together—with a mouse inside."

"Oh my God! What happened?"

"They worked fine."

I turn and look back at him, pulling the hair out of his hands. "I mean to the mouse?"

He smiles. "It was fine too. I let it go once I got it back inside." He stares at me for a moment. "Because I knew that would make you happy."

I let my gaze move across his face, coming to rest on his mouth. "Why didn't you tell me?"

He takes my hair in his hands again and pulls my head back around so I'm facing away. "You never asked."

I try to turn back around, but he doesn't let go of my hair. Instead, I cross my arms. "So you only tell me things if I ask?"

He laughs. "Of course not. I told you about my mother, didn't I? And the Wilds. I tell you a lot of things I never told anyone else."

"So why didn't you tell me about the masks?"

"I don't know, Shannon. Sometimes I just don't, okay?" He starts braiding my hair, tugging on my head a little as he works the separate strands together.

The mood is spoiled, and I chastise myself for always

asking so many stupid questions.

Why do you always have to know everything?

We sit in silence until he finishes—which is very quickly.

I hand him the rubber band, and he wraps it around the end of my braid and releases my hair, done with me.

"Thank you," I say, wanting to be closer to him—to stay close to him—but not knowing how.

"I was afraid you'd leave if you knew the rebreathers worked," he says. "That's why I didn't tell you."

I turn around to face him.

Peter is a weird combination of strength and humility, and when I'm with him, he makes me feel both powerful *and* protected—often at the same time.

No one has ever made me feel that way before.

"Oh, Peter," I say. "Just the *thought* of being without you is enough to make me miserable. In fact the whole time you were braiding my hair, I was trying to figure out a way to keep you from ever being done."

He blinks at me, looking totally surprised by my revelation.

I shake my head. "I'm not going to leave you."

"You're not?"

"Of course not, silly." I use my hand to check the braid—and just like everything Peter sets his mind to, it's perfect. "When we leave," I say, "we'll go together." I take his hand and form his little finger around my own. "Pinkie promise."

He gets a goofy look on his face, but I can tell he likes it.

"You have to say it out loud, or it doesn't count." I wait for him to speak.

"I love you, Shannon."

I stare at him, my heart stuck in my throat. "You do?"

He nods and then rummages around in his backpack. "I have something for you." He places a small box in my hand.

"What is it?" I ask, half-smiling.

"Just open it."

Inside is an exquisite silver arrow mounted on a hairpin.

"Oh my God, Peter, it's beautiful!" I swallow, my eyes filling with tears. "Where did you get it?" I take it out and hold it up in the last rays of sunlight coming through the west-facing window.

"It was my mother's," he says.

"Oh, Peter, I can't…"

He takes the arrow out of my hand and kneels down next to me. He wraps the braid around my head like a crown and pins it with the silver treasure.

I turn toward the gangly, muscled, secretive boy who makes my heart race.

"You look beautiful," he says, his jaw twitching but not looking away. "But then you always look beautiful."

I throw my arms around him, pushing him over onto the blankets—and then I kiss him right on the lips.

CHAPTER 29

Diego: See You on the Other Side

After lunch the following morning, they let me out of jail—except now I have a 24/7 shadow.

More like a lunar eclipse.

Dave's goon, aka The Hulk, outweighs me by fifty pounds, all of it muscle. The superhero escorts me back to the hospital and lets me know that I'm not allowed out of the building without Kirk's approval—no exceptions.

He wordlessly accompanies me to the Vampire Lounge, not looking happy about the assignment.

Later that afternoon, when they take the needle out of my arm and give me grapefruit juice that tastes like it's been in a metal can for twenty years, Soleil walks in. It's the first time she's made an appearance, and the staff is clearly surprised to see her.

And so am I.

She acknowledges my shadow with a nod.

"Dr. Nadales," he says and gives a crisp salute—which Soleil awkwardly returns.

She sits down on the chair next to mine. "Good to see you back in the thick of things, Mr. Crusoe. Thank you for agreeing—"

"Dr. Nadales!" Nurse Sweet hurries into the room. "You're needed in the radio room immediately."

"Can't it wait until I've finished my rounds?"

"No. The Bub has collapsed, and they're evacuating now. Ted says once they leave, they won't have radio contact—and he asked me to bring Dr. Kirk and Mr. Crusoe too. The Bub is standing by to speak to all of you."

"Oh, shit," I say and start putting on my shoes. "Did they lose anyone?"

"They're checking now," Nurse Sweet says. She turns to Soleil. "I've sent someone to round up your mother, but she's…"

"Yes, I know." Soleil stands and hands her clipboard to a tech. "Has Mr. Kirk been informed?"

Nurse Sweet shakes her head. "Ted's been trying to contact him all day, but he isn't responding."

"Damn it." She nods at me. "Let's go."

The Hulk steps in front of us. "I'm sorry, Dr. Nadales, but Mr. Kirk gave me strict orders not to let Crusoe leave the building."

Soleil doesn't bat an eyelash. "Who's in charge when Mr. Kirk is away, Mr. Erikson?"

The Hulk looks confused.

"Well?"

"You are, ma'am."

"That is correct. Mr. Crusoe will be accompanying me to the comm building. Is that understood?"

You can almost see the smoke coming out of the guy's

ears, but he doesn't protest further. "Yes, ma'am."

We hurry out of the room and down the hall into the elevator, the Hulk right behind us.

"Where can they possibly go?" Soleil asks as the doors close, her face ashen.

The Hulk jabs his hand between the doors and then squeezes in beside me. The elevator groans as we all crowd into the tiny space.

"There's no room for them at KC," Soleil says, bringing her hand up to her throat. "And no way to get them to Salt Lake." She looks at me. "What am I going to tell them?"

"According to Ted, they got inside the Magic Kingdom." Nurse Sweet eyeballs the Hulk, her forehead wrinkled. "The Bub folks are going there."

"I thought the place was full of carbon dioxide." Soleil says. "Is it safe?"

"A small section is on emergency backup," Nurse Sweet says, "and the air in that part is okay—at least for now."

"If they get the main power back on," I say, "it's simple to restart the filtration system. Christ, if you'd just—"

Soleil raises her hand and shakes her head.

"Okay, right," I say. "Now is not the time."

The elevator doors open, and we exit the hospital and hurry across Central Park.

When we get to the door of the radio room, Soleil stops and turns to my shadow. "As soon as I'm done with Mr. Crusoe's services, I will return him to you. In the meantime, I suggest you get a cup of coffee."

He glances over his shoulder, like she's talking to someone else, and then hesitates, the cogs turning. "Yes, ma'am," he says. "I'll wait right here."

She nods and I follow her through the door.

The moment Ted sees us, he hails the Bub. "Kirk Biodome, this is C-Bay. Madders, are you there?"

We wait for three or four seconds, and then Ted repeats his call out.

"I'm here," Matt says, sounding out of breath. "Ignore the background noise. I'm packing up as I talk. Are the others there?"

"Diego here," I say and sit down in front of the microphone. "And Dr. Nadales is with me. What's up, Matt? Is everybody okay?"

"We don't know yet," he says, "but we have our fingers crossed. We all knew it might come to this, and everyone was carrying a mask, just in case."

"Good," I say. "What do you need from me?"

A red light starts flashing in the glassed-in radio room next to ours.

"That must be Mr. Kirk," Ted says and gets up. "I'll be right back." He walks through a door into a separate sound-proof booth, and we watch him put on a headset.

There's some noise on the radio, and then Matt comes back on. "Damn piece of shite. The bolts are rusted on." He exhales. "Sorry. Things are a bit topsy-turvy at the moment, but I think we're okay. It's going to be a bit dark and cramped in the trucks, but we should have enough diesel to get to the mountain—assuming the trucks can make it through the snow."

"When do you expect to have the power back on?" I ask.

"Kirk assures me he's working on it," Matt says. "In the meantime, Lani thinks there's enough air for the short term—but adding all those warm bodies isn't going to help the air quality any...."

Ted steps back into the room. "Tell him that Mr. Kirk will be out as soon as he's done at Catersville. He estimates it may take him a day or two to get to the mountain, but he'll bring men and supplies."

"That's what I wanted to hear," Madders says after I relay

the message. "Tell him thanks."

Ted nods and then returns to the other room.

"Can you stand by?" Matt says. "Lani wants to talk to you. I'm going to patch her through now."

"Yes, of course," I say, wondering what the hell she wants to say to me. The last time I spoke to her she nearly ate my face off.

We hear a couple of clicks and then a bit of static.

"Hello?" Lani says, her voice sounding far away. "Are you there, C-Bay?"

"Yes," I say, shifting in my seat. "How are you, Dr. Kai?"

"I'm doing well, Diego. It's good to hear your voice."

I don't know what to say to that.

She clears her throat. "I wanted to apologize for being so hard on you about Shannon. Madders told me what happened at Catersville, how you tried to fight back..."

"I'm just glad Kirk's brought them to their senses," I say. "And that Shannon will be home soon."

"Yes, me too," she says. "But that's not why I wanted to talk to you."

I glance at Soleil, but she shrugs.

I turn back to the microphone. "What's up, Lani?"

"The, uh, *machine* is here," she says. "The one that deposits people in trees. It's in the contaminated area."

"*Mierda*," I say, my heart jumping into my throat.

Soleil gives me an inquisitive look but doesn't comment.

"I know it's a bit late for this," Lani says, "but I believe you."

I swallow. "Where are you now? Inside the mountain?"

"No," Lani says. "I'm just outside the blast door. My signal isn't powerful enough to get through all that rock. I'm going to hike up to the old radio tower as soon as I sign off. See if it's still connected."

"Have you tried resetting the circuit breaker in the

machine room? It might just be stuck."

"Yes, that was the first thing we tried."

"Okay, right."

"David Kirk will be out in a day or two to help," Lani says. "And he's bringing Shannon."

"Yes, I heard," I say, wrestling with my own annoyance that Dave gets to be the hero again. "That's great news."

"Is Soleil Nadales there with you?"

"Uh, yeah." I scoot the mic over to Soleil.

"Hello, Dr. Kai," Soleil says. "Congratulations on getting inside the mountain. I hear it was quite a feat."

"Thank you, Dr. Nadales. Is your mother there as well?"

"I'm afraid not."

"Would you be able to send for her?"

"We did," Soleil says. "But she's… indisposed. Was there something you needed from her?"

"There's someone who wants to talk to her," Lani says. "Hang on…"

"We're standing by," Soleil says, asking with her eyes if I know what's going on.

I shake my head.

The door behind us bursts open, and Bella stumbles in, her eyes red and swollen—and a bottle of whiskey in her hand.

"What is it?" she says, looking unsteady on her feet. "The nurse said it was an emergency!" She sees me and lets out a sob. "Why did you do it, James? Why did you abandon me? Didn't you love me?"

Mierda.

I get up and help her over to the couch. "I loved her more than anything," I say. "I still do."

She's so drunk, she can barely hold her own head up.

I'd never seen Isabel even a little bit tipsy—so I'm caught off guard when she throws her arms around my neck and says, "You should have told me. I would have gone with you."

"Are you okay?" I finally manage.

She is clearly not okay, Captain America. She's shit-faced drunk.

I put my arms around her, trying to think of something comforting to say. "Dr. Kirk... Bella, I..."

She turns to me, her mascara smeared and her nose running. "Oh, James." She falls against me, kissing me on the mouth.

I take her shoulders, steadying her. "Bella, I'm not—"

"Mom, please!" Soleil says, wincing. "You're embarrassing yourself."

Before I can say anything, the radio crackles back to life.

"Hello?" a male voice says. "Soleil? This is Daddy. I can't tell you how much I've missed you and Mommy."

I hear Soleil's audible intake of breath.

"Dad?" She scrambles for the microphone, but knocks it onto the floor and then dives to pick it up. "Daddy? Is that you?"

"Yes, it is, baby," James says. "Boy, oh boy, is it good to hear your voice!"

"You're alive," Soleil whispers, her voice trembling with emotion. "Oh my God, you're alive!"

"Yes, sweetie. I'm sorry, but I need to go," he says. "As soon as we get the big radio inside working, I want to hear about everything that's happened since I left. Everything. Okay, sunshine?"

"James?" Bella says, pushing me away. She attempts to stand, and when that doesn't work, she collapses against me, sobbing and hiccupping.

"Okay," Soleil says, tears running down her cheeks. "Daddy, is Lucas there with you?"

There's a pause. "No, sweetie, he's not."

She wipes her face on her shoulder. "Where is he,

Daddy?"

He sighs. "He's gone, Sol. He wanted me to tell you and mommy that he loves you. I'm sorry."

It takes her a moment to respond. "I'm sorry too, Daddy."

"Is your mother there, Soleil?"

Soleil glances over at Bella who's crumpled on the couch, unconscious. "No."

"Okay." We hear something bump the mic, and a few seconds later James says, "Is Diego around?"

"Yes," Soleil says.

I untangle myself from Bella and step back to the microphone. "I'm here, James."

"Take good care of them for me," he says.

I put my hand on Soleil's shoulder and lean over. "You got it, buddy."

"And don't trust a word that comes out of Kirk's mouth," James adds. "Not a fucking word."

Soleil gasps.

"Yeah," I say, meeting her startled gaze. "I already figured that out."

"Good." He clears his throat. "I have to go, Sol. Tell your mother I love her—and that I hope to talk to both of you again soon. I love you, sweetie, more than you could possibly know."

"I love you too, Dad."

The radio signal drops.

A few seconds later, Matt comes back on. "I gotta go, mates. See you on the other side. Kirk Biodome, over and out."

CHAPTER 30

Lani: Tell Him to Hurry

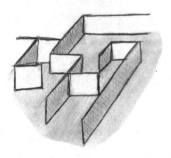

It turns out, James and Benny have been living in a labyrinth of hallways and conference rooms for over a decade.

James takes me into a giant storage area full of rail-car-sized shipping containers. The ones in the front are open, and I can see cardboard boxes stacked inside.

"Those three are full of food," James says, pointing to the shipping containers on the left. "And that one is full of bathrobes, pantyhose, and athletic socks."

I walk over and take a quick look at the shipping containers. They're nearly full of boxes the size of refrigerators. "Wow."

"Those other two are full of coffee filters, toilet brushes, and other useless crap—although there is a fifty-pound bin of aspirin and some other over-the-counter meds too."

"Do you have any prescription drugs or other hospital

supplies?"

He shakes his head. "No idea. I've tried to get into the shipping containers behind these, but they're stacked together like bricks, and even that empty one over there is too heavy for me to budge. And there are more crates and boxes downstairs… lots more, actually. But I haven't been down there since before Lucas got sick."

"What's in the food containers? Is most of it still good?"

"Almost none of it is spoiled, if that's what you mean. But I wouldn't call it gourmet dining. That first one's full of Cheez Whiz and tuna fish. Second one's mostly canned fruit cocktail and instant mashed potatoes. The third one's got brownie mix and oatmeal, although I did find a couple barrels of corn flakes, and one of Lucky Charms."

"Nice," I say and laugh. "Haven't had those in years."

He rubs his chin. "Benny loved those marshmallows, but I ended up eating most of them myself. At one point I weighed nearly three hundred pounds." He shifts his weight. "Come on, let me show you his playroom. It's my masterpiece."

We step into a conference room that's packed full of PVC pipes at odd angles, all of them duct taped together. "Where'd you find all the tubes?"

"Took them out of the crawl spaces in all the rooms. They used to be full of phone cables and the like, but I figured we didn't need them anymore."

He sets Benny in one of the tubes, and the creature takes off running, obviously happy to be in his playroom.

I chuckle. "You clearly know how to make the little guy happy."

He nods, not meeting my gaze, and then turns to leave. "Let me show you the rest. Benny'll be fine in here for a while."

I follow him out the door and close it behind me.

He takes me to an exercise room with hand weights and a stationary bicycle, a sleeping room with two metal couches pushed together, bathrobes tucked around the cushions, and a room full of board games.

There's an elaborate card game on one table, a Scrabble game on another, and a chess game on a third.

"As you can see, I mostly play chess," he says, "but I also like Yahtzee and Backgammon. My son loved Pokémon. We made cards and a game to go with them. I couldn't bring myself to put them away."

I walk over to the table of cards and pick up a handmade drawing of Pikachu, wondering how terrible it must have been to be alone inside here for so long.

"I always win," he says with a straight face, and when I don't respond, he frowns. "That was a joke."

I nod, still lost in thought.

We stand there for a moment, staring at each other.

"I'm sorry," I finally say. "It's just that I can't imagine what you've been through. How you could go on living for so long with no one to talk to and no one to be with…"

He swallows, his hands opening and closing at his sides.

"I'm glad it was you inside here, James. Really glad." I walk over to him, looking up into his dark brown eyes, and then I put my hands on his chest and lean in on my tippy-toes to kiss him on the cheek. "Thanks for being here for me."

He puts his arms around me, awkwardly at first, and then he pulls me against his chest—and I realize he's crying.

He sniffs his nose and then takes my hand. "Come on, I need to show you the Control Room. If we have any chance of saving your friends, we're gonna need to figure out how to get it working again."

The Control Room looks like something out of a science fiction movie set in the 1970s, complete with reel-to-reel tapes, a computer the size of a refrigerator with only a handful of lights and toggle switches on the front, and a huge printer with green and white striped paper in it.

"Wow. This is right out of the dark ages."

"This place was built in the fifties. Hard to believe it lasted this long, no?" He presses a button and one of the tiny screens comes to life. "That's the inside of the airlock." He turns a dial. "And that's the view outside the blast door. Most of the other stuff in here I've never used." He taps a button on a desk set into the wall, and a large, round dial lights up behind it. "That's the radio, but it hasn't worked since I got up here. I think maybe the antenna is broken."

"But it has power," I say.

"Yeah. That's the backup system. Everything up on this level still has electricity, but the main generator that runs all the stuff downstairs has been off for years. I tried to figure out where the generator is located, and why it's not working down there, but eventually gave up."

"Any idea what's in all those locked rooms we passed?" I ask.

"Mostly offices, I think, but to be honest, I don't really know. I don't have any passkeys, and I can't cut the power to the doors without turning off the whole mountain."

"Yikes. Where do you get water to drink?"

"From the taps in the bathrooms. I don't have any idea where it comes from, but the toilets still flush, and there's a shower in one of the bathrooms too." He looks at me. "Did you need to use the bathroom? I'm sorry, I should have asked you sooner."

I smile and shake my head. "I'm fine. What about cooking? Do you have a kitchen?"

"No, but there's a break room with a coffee maker. I use it to heat water. Each coffee maker lasts about three years, and then I open a new one. Luckily, the cabinet is stocked full of them."

"You do all your cooking on a coffee maker?"

"Yep. Tried a campfire once, but it made too much smoke. I got soaked."

I laugh.

"I used to have a small microwave, but it gave out years ago. There's also a Betamax VCR in the break room, but there weren't many movies for it, and they're all broken now. I kept trying to glue the tapes back together, but eventually I was putting patches on the patches."

"Can you show me the underground city? Where all the labs and sleeping quarters are located?"

"Yeah, but you'd need a biosuit to go down there now. There's a three-story hotel with beds for three hundred, plus staff quarters with rooms for a couple hundred more. And there's an infirmary, a cafeteria, a gym, a barbershop, lots of labs and storage areas, and even a lake."

"So it *is* an underground city."

"Yep, complete with golf carts, fake stars, and a bowling alley. I can show you the access door and the elevator that takes you down, but like I said, the whole area is full of CO_2. When the power went off, the air exchangers quit working, and within a year, the place was a death trap. That's why Lucas and I had to move up here."

I nod. "Do you still have any biosuits?"

"You wouldn't be able to get through the access portal alone, and there's only one suit. Believe me, Lucas and I looked for more."

The image of the skull rolling down the mountainside fills my head. "I think I know where I can get another biosuit, although it'll need new batteries, and we'll have to come up with some way to test it."

"You've come to the right place for that," he says. "There's a changing room right next to the airlock, and there are plenty of batteries and patches in there."

"Okay then. I think we can save that part of the tour for later," I say, "but I could sure use that cup of tea now."

He smiles. "Coming right up. After that, I can prepare a room for you. It won't be the Ritz, but it'll be all yours." He glances over at me. "You are going to stay, right?"

"My radio isn't powerful enough to work in here. I need to go back Outside to let the Bub know what I've found."

"But you'll come back?"

"Of course I will." I steal a peek at my watch. "It's going to be getting dark soon, and with all the automatic guns out there, I may sleep in my tent tonight. But I'll definitely be back in the morning when it's light."

"The automatic guns?"

"Yes, there's some sort of defense system out on the concrete ledge—automatic rifles or something. Nearly got myself killed when I first got here."

"Shit, I'm sorry. I didn't know what they did." He walks over to a panel full of switches. "It says External Weapons System, but I didn't want to turn it off for fear it would disable the blast doors or something." He moves the toggle switch to OFF.

"External Weapons System disabled," says the disembodied computer voice. "Maintenance on the External Weapons System is overdue by seven thousand, four hundred and thirteen days. Shall I add External Weapons System maintenance to the duty roster?"

"Yes," James says and shrugs. "How many items are on the duty roster?"

"Sixteen thousand, three hundred and thirty one. Would you like me to list them?"

I laugh.

"No," he says.

We spend the next thirty minutes in the break room drinking hot tea and eating dried apples from my pack. He saves a few for Benny, and I promise to bring more. He asks me about the Bub, and everything that's happened since it was sealed. I end up telling him about Shannon and how she was kidnapped on her way to C-Bay—and how I intend to go after her once all the folks from the Bub are safe.

"There's a jeep in the storage area," he says. "I don't know if it still runs—or how you'll find gas for it—but you're welcome to take it. Might get you back to the Bub quicker than walking."

I get up and hug him again. "Thank you, James."

"I'm looking forward to meeting your daughter."

After I use the bathroom, I go back out through the airlock and then the blast doors. There's still enough light to see, but it's freezing cold and there's a slight breeze. I hurry back out the tunnel, along the wall, and through the safe passage across the ledge. When I get out of range of the guns, I find a tree branch and toss it back into the hot area, testing the automatic guns.

Nothing happens.

"Hallelujah."

I follow my own footprints back to the tent and fire up the radio, anxious to share the good news.

The moment Madders says hello, I know something is wrong. His voice sounds a bit muffled.

"What is it?" I ask. "What's happened?"

"Another section failed last night, and we couldn't get the bulkhead sealed in time. We're evacuating."

"Is everyone okay?" I ask. "Did they get their masks on in time?"

"Yes, everyone is fine. We're loading the last boxes into the trucks now."

I tell him what I learned this afternoon.

"Well, mutt's nuts, Lani, that's the best news we've had in years," he says, sounding downright giddy.

"Like I said, there's room for everyone inside the mountain, but there's some sort of problem with the ventilation system, and the CO_2 is building up. We need to get the generator up and running to clear the air."

"Could just need a new breaker or something," he says.

"Have you talked to David?"

"Yep," Madders says. "He's planning to fly out to the Magic Kingdom with men and supplies right after he picks up Shannon. He'll erect environment tents for everyone. It'll be tight quarters for a while, but manageable."

"Tell him there's a radio in there, but it doesn't have any reception. James thinks the antenna's broken."

"James? I thought the guy's name was Jimbo."

"It's James Nadales, Madders." I exhale, still uncomfortable saying the rest aloud. "He's Diego's parallel."

"Blimey. Poor bloke got the short end of the stick in this universe, stuck inside that underground mausoleum. That'd make anyone daft."

"What about your plane?" I ask. "Are you going to leave it at the Bub?"

"No. Once I see the trucks off, I'll fly her to the army base that's east of you—same place Kirk plans to land. Won't take me more than an hour, and the map says you're about twenty miles from there. I promised Kirk I'd find some sort of vehicle to ferry supplies up to you. I plan to look into that tomorrow morning. If all goes well, I should be on your doorstep in time for dinner."

"Send up a flare if you get into trouble? I plan to hike up to the radio tower to get some photos of the damage, but I'll keep an eye out for you."

"Roger that. Is there anything else you want me to tell Kirk before I shut down for good?"

"Tell him to hurry."

CHAPTER 31

Diego: Don't Call Me Shirley

When I get back to my room, the Hulk holds the door open and lets me pass. "I'll be back at seven," he says. "Don't go anywhere." He laughs and then shuts the door, locking it from the exterior.

I listen to his footsteps fade down the hallway, write down the GPS coordinates James gave me, and zip them into my pack. I know it's a long shot, but I'm convinced it's my *only* shot.

A stab of guilt cuts into my gut like a switchblade, but I ignore it. I gave enough blood this afternoon to last Soleil for a month, and I tell myself it'll be enough.

I gulp down my cold dinner and get to work.

Although my plan is not exactly the Colditz Escape, I figure if I can make it Outside, it'll be nearly impossible to stop me. All I have to do is make it to the Magic Kingdom, figure out a way to get inside without getting locked up, and use the time machine before Dave can stop me.

Easy peasy, mae.

I take Shannon's jaguarundi drawing down off my wall, roll it up, and put it in my backpack with the rest of my modest belongings. By now, she should be safely back with her mother—at least I can thank Dave for that.

I stuff the pack under the blanket on my bed—in case someone peeks in to check on me—and then use the tools I 'borrowed' from the Vampire Lounge and start picking the lock.

When I first found out that Soleil had ordered that I be put back in my hospital room instead of the jail, I was ecstatic.

How hard can it be to break out of a hospital?

I try for an hour with no success.

"*Mierda*, this place is like a penitentiary. Why would they put such expensive locks on the doors?"

I look around for something to use as a screwdriver, figuring I might be able to get the hinges off, but it's slim pickings.

I try to turn a screw with some forceps and nearly stab myself in the thigh.

"Shit."

There's a soft rap. I jump to my feet, switch off the light, and stand behind the door, my heart pounding in my throat.

A key turns in the lock, and the door opens a crack.

A slat of light cascades in from the hallway, and then Bella peeks through, her finger pressed against her lips and her gaze pinned on my bed.

I step out from behind the door.

She squawks with surprise—but recovers quickly.

"Hi." I give her a tepid wave.

She shuts the door, turns on the light, and sets a bulky canvas bag down in front of me.

I raise an eyebrow. "What—"

She slaps her hand over my mouth and brings her finger back up to her lips, not looking the least bit tipsy.

I nod and she releases me.

She glances at the pile of medical instruments on the floor, takes my arm, and leads me into the bathroom.

"What the hell's going on, Bella?"

She turns the sink *and* the shower on full blast, pulls me into the tiny bathroom, and shuts the door.

"Don't call me that," she says. "David started calling me that years ago, and I've always hated it."

I stare at her, not having any idea what to say to this baffling, but hauntingly-familiar woman.

"I'm leaving as soon as it gets light," she says, "and you're coming with me."

"But—"

"Sit."

I push down the lid on the toilet and follow orders—with Isabel, that's generally the best thing to do.

Bella leans back against the sink and crosses her arms. "Here's the deal: I break you out. You get me to James. James gets you to the time machine. We all get to live happily ever after."

I laugh. "You're breaking me out?"

"Yes," she says. "Assuming I don't strangle you first."

"So you can go with me?"

She narrows her eyes. "Didn't I just say that?"

If looks could kill, I'd be bleeding to death.

I shake my head. "You can't be serious."

"Oh, I'm dead serious."

I stare at her, trying to absorb what she's proposing.

She taps her foot. "Yes or no?"

"How are you going to survive Outside, Dr. Kirk?"

"Damn it, don't call me that either!"

"Well?"

She pins me with those beautiful green eyes. "I'm going to help myself to the universal biotechs Soleil is stockpiling. I won't need many, and whatever I don't use, I'll give back."

I raise my eyebrow.

"And I've taken the liberty of putting together food and camping supplies, along with a map, a compass, and a portable GPS." She puts her hands on her hips. "Are you in or out?"

"It's eighteen hundred miles, Bella. It could take days, weeks even."

She glares at me. "Don't call me—"

"Yeah, sorry. How long will the biotech injections protect you?"

"A couple of weeks. But we're going to take an SUV—so that should be more than enough time to get to the mountain."

"Christ, Dr. Sanborn, how are we going to find gas for it? And even if we do, the fuel will have been sitting in a rusty tank for twenty years. There's no telling if it'll do anything other than ruin the engine."

"It's been decades since someone called me that," she says and laughs.

I stare at her, not following.

"You called me Dr. Sanborn."

"I'm running out of options."

"That old gas works fine," she says. "David's been scavenging it out of tanker trucks and gas stations for years—you just have to strain it through a sock." She crosses her arms. "But if we run out, we'll find bicycles. And if that doesn't work, we'll walk, goddamn it. You were always good at winging it. So improvise!"

"Across eighteen hundred miles?" I can't keep the disbelief out of my voice. "No offense, but you're over sixty. It's winter out there, and the whole world is crawling with giant reptiles—and God only knows what else. Alone, I'd have a decent chance, but with two of us..."

"The pioneers did it two hundred years ago, and they didn't have paved roads. I'm a medical doctor who knows the flora and fauna. I may not be as young as you, but I'm just as determined—and twice as smart. We'll stay on the old freeway and sleep in empty buildings and scavenge for food when we run out."

I don't know what to say.

"At least," she says, "we don't have to worry about lions and tigers and bears."

"Oh, my." I stare at her. "That's a shit plan, doctor."

"Yeah, I know. You got a better one?"

I glance back and forth between her eyes. "Yeah," I say. "I go by myself."

"How were you planning to get out of your room, Mr. Crusoe?"

"Don't call me that," I say. "And for your information, I was picking the lock when you barged in with that shit plan of yours."

She rolls her eyes, and I almost laugh.

"I was doing just fine until you showed up, doctor."

"For God's sake, James, even if you did manage to pick the lock, you'd never make it out of the hospital. There's an alarm on the front exit, and David's wolves will be all over you the minute it goes off."

"I'll go out the back way," I say and then add, "And stop calling me James."

She ignores me. "You're a prisoner here, with an armed goon following you around, and I'm offering you a way out."

"Thank you for unlocking my door, doctor. I'll just be leaving now."

She puts her arm in front of me, blocking my exit. "You

walk out on me, Nadales, and I'll sound the alarm. I'll tell them I caught you trying to escape. David will lock you up and throw away the key, and in the meantime, I'll leave without you."

"You wouldn't."

She narrows one eye. "Try me."

"How do you know I won't put a gag in your mouth and leave you tied up in here?"

"I don't," she says. "So, I didn't disarm the front door."

I let out an annoyed huff. "I should have guessed you'd do something like that. You always were one step ahead of me."

"No, I wasn't," she says. "I was just a bit more pessimistic."

This time, I do laugh. "Once we get to the Magic Kingdom, how are we going to get inside without getting arrested?"

"So you'll do it," she says. "I knew you'd see reason."

"It doesn't look like I have any choice."

"Give me your word you'll take me to James, and I'll tell you everything."

"I give you my word that I'll *try*, Isabella." It's the first time I've called her by her first name, and it feels like poetry on my tongue.

She looks away, her eyes tearing up, and it makes my heart hurt.

"James will be expecting us," she says and wipes her face on her sleeve. "I'm sure of it."

I nod, knowing she's right.

"And," she says, shutting off the water in the sink. "I'm betting he'll figure out a way to keep David out too." She takes a bottle of pills out of her pocket, dry swallows four, and puts it away.

I turn off the shower. "You've got a lot of faith in a guy who fucked things up thirty years ago."

A smile sneaks across her lips for the first time. "Yeah," she says. "Funny how he reminds me of you—or is it you who reminds me of him?" She shrugs. "We're pretty good together, aren't we?"

I nod. "You should have believed James when he said he'd find you."

"Yes." A tear runs down her cheek. "I hope she waits for you—your Isabella, I mean."

"Me too," I say, unable to meet her gaze. "I only have eight days left before it's too late..."

We stand there in silence for a moment.

"Okay," she says and opens the bathroom door. "There are clothes and a wig in the bag. I'll be back when they unlock the front doors at seven."

"Why don't we leave now?"

"I need to get the vaccine and make the other arrangements."

"But—"

"Trust me." She puts her hand on my arm. "Okay?"

"I always do."

She opens the door and checks that no one is in the hallway. "Good night, Mr. Nadales." She gazes up into my face, her lips slightly parted. "And thank you."

"Good night, Mrs. Nadales," I say and wait for her eyes to get big—and then wink and kiss her on the cheek. "See you at dawn."

Chapter 32

Shannon: Making the Braid

When we exit the airlock the following morning, we find a stack of arrows—thirty or forty of them—next to a smaller compound bow.

On top of the arrows is a handwritten note: *8 mor masks plez. 6 adalt. 2 kidz.*

I do the math. There are eighteen Others hiding in the Wilds.

We spend the morning walking across the biodome to get more masks from the box I have marked on my map. We manage to find some child-sized ones, and spend an hour stripping and fixing two of those when we get back. Those plus the ones we made a day ago means we're still short four. In two more days, we'll be able to deliver all the masks and then start making some extra ones.

After lunch, Peter and I spend an hour testing out the

new bow and arrows. Peter insists on trying each of the new arrows in his own bow first. I stand to the side, arms crossed, and watch him notch an arrow, pull the bowstring, and aim. He exhales, keeping his body still, and then lets the arrow fly.

One after the other, the arrows bury their tips in the bull-seye of our improvised target.

As I watch him aim and shoot, I wonder why he insisted that I learn to use a bow. Up until now, I thought he just enjoyed practicing with me—which is pretty much why I liked it. But now, I'm not so sure. What or who does he intend to shoot?

"Wow," he says as he collects the last set of arrows. "These are better than any of the ones I have. I wonder where they found them?"

I turn the new bow over in my hands. "And why would they give us all this valuable stuff?"

"They're bartering," he says. "They may not be educated like you, but they're proud folk. They won't accept charity. We give them something, they give us something back. That's how it works here."

I nod.

"And I don't think we need to be afraid of them anymore," he says. "If they wanted to kill us, they would have done it by now."

I find the thought unsettling, but Peter doesn't seem to notice.

He holds out one of the new arrows. "Why don't you try the bow?"

"Okay." I move closer to him, adjust my stance, and notch the arrow. But instead of putting his arms around me, he stands there with his arms crossed.

And then he calls off the practice after I make only a handful of shots.

"You don't need my help anymore," he says. "That's

good, Shannon."

I'm not so sure.

After I collect my arrows—all of which are in the target, though not as close to the center as Peter's were—he insists that we take more food from the huge storage area back to our airlock hideout.

After our third trip hauling boxes of canned goods and sacks of grain using a wheelbarrow and a pallet jack, I'm exhausted.

It's been a long day, and I didn't sleep well last night—after I kissed Peter, he abruptly got up and went back to his own bed. I could hear him lying there, breathing fast, like he was angry at me.

I lay awake wondering, if he loves me, why doesn't he want to kiss me?

And then today, he refused to put his arms around me when we practiced archery.

I slump down on the floor outside the airlock, refusing to go back for another load. "Mookers, Peter! We already have enough food for a month. Why do we have to get more?"

For the first time since we escaped, he raises his voice to me. "Because I said so, Shannon. Sometimes you should listen to me and just do what I ask."

"If you stopped ordering me around like some sort of... house elf, maybe I would." I pinch myself so I don't start crying.

"I'm going back for another load," he says. "Stay here until I get back."

I look away, angry that he's ordering me around again.

"Do you have your whistle on?" He sounds like Mom checking if I finished my homework.

I pull mine out of my shirt and hold it up for him, not meeting his gaze. Ever since we found the whistles, we take them everywhere—although we've never actually used them for anything except practice.

He grunts and turns away.

When he returns with another load of supplies, the sun is low in the sky—which usually means it's shower time. But instead of leaving everything stacked outside our door, Peter insists on hauling it all into the airlock.

I wordlessly get up to help.

"You can rest," he says, slinging a bag of rice over his shoulder. "I can get it."

"And let you have all the fun?" I say under my breath. "I'd have to be crazy."

When we're done, I take a long, hot shower, put on my pajamas. Then I go back to the airlock to dry my hair and get ready for our nightly reading and writing lesson.

There are twenty huge jugs of water lined up in the middle of the room, and I realize Peter must have hauled them all in here while I was taking a shower. We usually keep a few small bottles of drinking water in here, but never this much. It's like he's preparing for some sort of... siege.

I've only just sat down on my bed when Peter steps through the airlock, his hair dripping wet.

"What's going on, Peter?"

He sets the masks we made today outside the door and starts the sequence to shut the airlock. "Is your rebreather mask in your backpack?"

"Yes," I say, watching him work the heavy handle. "Why are you so angry at me?"

He freezes for a moment, his back still turned to me—and then he finishes sealing the door.

When he's done, he gets up and moves the heavy jugs of water to the back of the room, then rearranges some bags of food so they're not blocking the outer door.

I sit there on my bed, staring at him. "Peter?"

He takes the towel out of my limp hands and sits down

next to me.

"They're going to come tonight," he says, and starts drying the tips of my hair. "But you'll be safe in here."

"Who's coming?" I say and turn to face him. "What are you talking about?"

"The men from the Compound." He glances back and forth between my eyes. "Twice a year they come here to… round up the Others."

I stare at him, not understanding. "Why would they do that?"

"Because the Others are all women," he says and then continues drying my hair. "The men capture them and make them… do things. If they refuse, they're killed. The ones who submit are taken back."

The horror I'm feeling must show on my face because he drops the towel and puts his hands on my shoulders. "Shannon, I won't let them touch you—or take you back. I promise."

"Tell me the truth about the Others," I say, my voice icy cold. "Start at the beginning, and tell me all of it."

He glances down at his hands. "Turn around, and I'll braid your hair."

I hesitate.

He pulls the rubber band off my wrist and puts it on his own. "Please."

I follow his request.

He takes my hair into his hands and begins.

"When I was five, there were rumors of an uprising—mostly by the women, but some of the men too. My grandmother was one of the leaders, but my mother wasn't involved—my father always treated her special, and she had me to take care of—his only son and the next king. But my father found out about the rebellion and had all of the suspects put in jail. There was a trial, of course—what Grizzly called a kangaroo court—and all of the accused were convicted of high treason and sentenced to death. My father planned to kill one person a day until all the guilty had been punished."

I sit in silence as Peter runs the brush over my hair, his voice almost a whisper.

"The following morning," he continues, "my father started executing the traitors. The first man was brought out, stripped naked, and forced into the airlock. The Outside door was opened, and people cheered and hooted as the poisoned air choked him to death. It became a daily ritual—a public spectacle. People brought out lawn chairs and argued over who got the best view and made bets over how long the next one would last."

"So they're true," I say in a shaky voice. "The rumors that you killed all those women."

"Yes." He drops his hands to his lap.

It's nearly dark now, and Peter gets up to light a candle.

When he sits back down, I ask, "What happened next?"

"On the day before my grandmother was to die, my mother begged my father to spare Gran's life. I was in the room when she pleaded with him to have mercy—if not for her sake, then for his son's. He got angry and started hitting her. I'd seen him slap and push her before, but this time it was worse. I tried to stop him, but I was only five, and he struck me hard enough that I blacked out."

He sets the hairbrush down and starts dividing my hair into sections.

I wait for him to continue, and eventually he does.

"I think Mother knew he would refuse, and that night, she poisoned him. Once he had collapsed, she stole his keys, got the women out of jail—by then, all the men were dead—and helped them escape through the Barrier."

I turn and look at him over my shoulder. "Why didn't your mother go with them?"

"Because of me. Grizzly was watching over me that night—I was still recovering from the beating my father had given me—and my mother refused to leave without me. After the other women were free, she came back for me, planning to take me out of my bed and escape with me that same night."

He stops braiding my hair, but I can hear his soft breathing behind me.

"But the poison didn't kill my father," he says. "I found my mother hanging from a rafter in the sanctuary the next morning."

"Oh my God, Peter. I'm so sorry." I try to turn around, but he won't let me.

He holds on to my hair, pulling my head back so I can't look at him.

When he's certain I won't try again, he continues with the story.

"My father assumed the women would all die once they crossed the barrier. There were stories about devil creatures that lived in the Wilds, and they would slaughter anyone brash enough to cross over. But the women managed to survive. My father would step through the Barrier every evening and see their cooking fires—and that made him angry. A few months after they escaped, he ordered the men to round them up and kill them all." He clears his throat. "He made me go along with them so I could see what evil my mother and grandmother had brought down on his kingdom."

He's quiet for a bit, his hands still.

"It didn't take long for us to find the women, and once they were rounded up, the men decided to take a few liberties before killing them. The women fought back, especially after they realized they were to be killed afterward, but it didn't help. When my father saw what was happening, he decided to show mercy. He told the women that if they cooperated, they wouldn't be killed—and most of them agreed."

He runs his hands over my braid—and then undoes it and starts over.

"The raid proved popular, especially with the men who could never expect to marry and were not allowed to touch what few women remained in the Compound. So twice a year there's a Culling. The Others are rounded up, and any man who captures one is allowed to keep her for three days and nights. When the Culling is over, the youngest captives are brought back to the Compound and beaten until they cooperate. The children—sometimes there are boys—are turned over to the Giver of the Law, and the girls who have experienced first sin are added to the Breeders."

"First sin?" I ask, not understanding.

"The blood," Peter says, "that God sends to punish women for tempting Adam."

Maybe it's because I'm so tired, but I still don't get it. "Why would God send people blood?"

"It comes once a month unless a woman is with child." He hesitates, and I feel my face get hot. "Do you not know of it?"

Sometimes you're a real lolo, Shaz.

"You've been here over a month," he says, tying off my braid, "and I've seen no blood." He exhales, still holding on to my hair. "Are you carrying someone else's child?"

I shake my head and then turn around so I can see his face. "In my biodome, girls aren't allowed to get pregnant until they're twenty-one, and they're discouraged from having children until they're twenty-five."

He nods, still looking skeptical.

"But we're allowed to start practicing—both the boys and the girls—once we turn eighteen."

His eyes get big, so I know he understands what I'm talking about.

"And to keep from getting pregnant, all the girls have a small device inserted under our skin—one that is simple to remove when we decide to have children." I show him the tiny scar on the inside of my arm. "It keeps me from getting pregnant—and also keeps me from having a period. The scientific word for it is menstruation, and it's not God's punishment or anything."

"So..." he says, his eyebrows rising. "Have you, uh, practiced?"

I shake my head. "Have you?"

He drops his gaze. "No."

"Peter," I say and take his hand. "I like it when you braid my hair. I like it a lot. And I wish you would have kissed me last night instead of running away."

He swallows, running his fingers across my palm. "Shannon, I—"

There's a loud clanging sound outside in the Wilds, and we both turn toward the airlock door.

"How sure are you that the men don't know how to open it?" I ask, knowing he won't lie to me if I ask a direct question.

He looks at me. "The biodome is a big place, and they don't know we're in here."

"So you're positive they can't open our door, even if they find us?"

"No one but you—and now me—knows how to open it, Shannon. I'm sure of that." He lifts my hand to his lips and kisses it. "But there'll be fires out in the Wilds—that's how the Others fight back—and it may take days, even weeks, for the smoke to clear."

"That's why you insisted we move the food inside? And why you hauled in all that water? So we'd be safe inside here?"

He shrugs. "Remember all the smoke when we first brought you in here? The Others must have seen us come through the Barrier and assumed it was time for the Culling."

"Why didn't you use the airlocks on the side with electricity?"

"Because they're befouled. It's forbidden to use them for anything except the Cleansing." He drops his gaze, and I don't have to ask what 'the Cleansing' is to know it's something bad—and probably involves doing mean things to women.

"When will the men come?" I ask.

He looks up. "At dawn."

"And if they *do* discover us inside here, will they be able to break down the door?"

"No. They'll have knives and rope, but nothing heavy enough to break the glass. I tested that on one of the other airlocks—the morning I got up early."

"I'm sorry I wasn't more help," I say, feeling embarrassed by all the work he's been doing to protect us—protect me. "I'm glad I met you, Peter. And I'm glad you came with me to the Wilds."

He runs his fingertip across my bare ankle. "Does that mean you still want to kiss me?"

I lean sideways and blow out the candle.

Chapter 33

Diego: Who Let the Dogs Out?

After Bella leaves my hospital room, I try to get some sleep—but eventually give up.

I lie there in the dark, thinking about Isabel and imagining her in my arms again.

Wait for me, Iz. I'm coming home.

At 6 a.m., I get up, take a quick shower, and shave. Then I take the women's clothing out of the bag Bella brought and pull them on over my own. There's a blond wig and some thick glasses in the bottom. I set them on the bed and then fill up the empty sack with everything I can find.

A little before seven, there's a knock on the door.

"It's me," Bella says and peeks in. "Are you ready?"

"Yes."

She switches on the light and backs a wheelchair in through the doorway.

Why is it always wheelchairs?

"What did you do with my shadow?" I ask as I put on the wig and glasses.

"Nurse Sweet told him you didn't get up until eight and suggested he get a cup of coffee in the cafeteria. He'll be back in a few minutes. We need to hurry."

I grab my backpack and the sack full of toiletries—and then hesitate.

"Have a seat."

"I hate wheelchairs," I say, knowing it sounds lame.

"You want to go home or not?" She puts her hands on her hips.

I sit down in the goddamn thing.

She takes my backpack and hangs it behind the seat. "Put the bag in your lap and keep your head down. With all the new people who arrived from the Lou today, no one's going to look twice."

"Okay. Thanks."

She adjusts the wig, gives me a once-over, and pushes me out the door.

"Good morning, Mrs. Katz," Nurse Sweet says as we come down the hallway.

I wave at her, unsure if I can do an old woman's voice.

The elevator bongs—and then I hear the nurse's sudden intake of breath.

The Hulk is just stepping out of the elevator.

Mierda.

Bella pushes me past the nurses station. "Tell proctology I'm bringing Mrs. Katz down now."

"Of course, doctor."

The big man strides past us, not even glancing at the old woman in a wheelchair.

Bella dives for the elevator door and then swings the chair around and backs me into the elevator.

She stabs at the lobby button as The Hulk disappears around the corner.

Nurse Sweet winks.

Just as the door starts to close, another doctor slips in with us.

"Morning, Dr. Kirk. Good to see you back on rounds."

"Thank you, doctor. It's good to be back."

The man nods at me. "Are you one of the refugees from the Lou, ma'am?"

I clear my throat and then answer in falsetto, "Yes, sir. It's very kind of you to take all of us in, and the hospital food's been absolutely wonderful."

"I'm… glad to hear that," the doctor says, sounding surprised, and then nods at Bella. "Thanks to Dr. Kirk, I'm sure."

Bella places her hand on my shoulder and gives it a painful squeeze. "Mrs. Katz has been having trouble controlling her bowels, but I'm sure we'll get it sorted out soon enough."

"I'm sure you will." The elevator door opens, and the man gets off. "Good luck to you, Mrs. Katz."

"Thank you, doctor. I'm hoping everything comes out okay."

When the door shuts, Bella steps in front of me, her eyes like slits. "What in God's name do you think you're doing, Nadales?"

"Just being friendly, doctor."

The door opens before she can respond.

She steps back around behind me, shoves the chair hard out of the elevator, and wheels me toward the exit—leaning over me and pretending to adjust my flowered blouse. "You do that again, buddy boy, and I'll strangle you myself."

"Promises, promises."

She nods at one of the nurses coming in—who looks shocked to see her—and continues wheeling me toward the reception desk.

The young man sitting behind the counter jumps up when he sees us. "I've, uh, been given orders not to let anyone—"

Bella doesn't even slow down. "I'm taking Mrs. Katz out to see what lovely… marigolds we have here at C-Bay. Please inform proctology that I'll have her back in time for her exam."

"Yes, of course, Dr. Kirk." The youth sits back down. "Enjoy your, um, walk."

"Marigolds?" I say when we're out the front doors. "I hate marigolds. Can't we look at the tulips?"

"You always were a pain in the ass when you were sick."

I laugh. "That's a low blow for someone on their way to proctology."

She snorts. "Men."

When we approach the main airlock, she stops the wheelchair and turns it to face the windows. "Shit," she says under her breath. "Now what?"

There's a group of Dave's men standing in front of the airlock access doors—and one of them has a gun.

"Here goes nothing." She wheels me closer.

All the chatting and laughter stops.

Bella pats me on the arm. "I told you, Mrs. Katz, everything is perfectly fine with the air pressure in our biodome. There's no need to be worried about any failures. As you can see, these nice young men are working hard to make sure our seams are nice and tight, aren't you boys?"

They shuffle their feet, and then one of them says, "Yes, Dr. Kirk."

It's Custer. I recognize the dandy boots.

Bella stops the wheelchair and turns toward them. "So why are you all standing around?" She glances at them, one by one. "I'm sure Mr. Kirk isn't paying you to watch the grass grow." She puts her hands on her hips. "Well, Mr.

Armstrong?"

"No, Dr. Kirk," he says. "We've been assigned to, uh, keep an eye on things."

"I'm so glad to hear that because there's a whole group of refugees back at the hospital waiting for someone to show them to their temporary quarters. You five would be perfect."

They look at each other.

"Tut, tut," Bella says in her doctor voice. "Go make yourselves useful before I tell Mr. Kirk he should transfer you to Sewage and Reclamation."

"Yes, ma'am," Custer says, looking like he'd rather die than shovel shit for the rest of his life. He hurries off in the direction we just came—and the others follow.

"I've a bit of a reputation for being a bitch," she says.

I laugh. "God, I've missed you."

Bella keys in the code to the door, waits for it to slide open, and wheels me through.

"We need to hurry," she says. "As soon as those goons get to the hospital, they'll know something's up."

I take off the women's clothes and wig and toss them into the seat of the wheelchair.

Bella takes off her white doctor's coat and bumps a box with her foot. "All this needs to go."

"Okay." I start stuffing freeze-dried food into my pack while she changes her shoes and puts on a heavy sweater.

"David always leaves his Humvee parked in the loading dock," Bella says. "You know where that is?"

"Yes," I say. "You can see it from the airlock."

"The gas tank should be full, and the keys should be in the cup holder—and they keep a twenty-gallon gas can in the back." Bella holds up a long rubber tube. "For when that runs out."

"Good thinking," I say. "How are we going to get through

the security fences?"

Bella hands me a garage door opener. "With this. Push and hold the button until the gate starts opening—it can be finicky. So don't give up until you see the barrier start to move."

"Okay—push and hold, don't give up," I repeat and then look up at her. "Why are you telling me?"

"Because I'm going to be driving," she says. "My reflexes are better than yours."

"But you don't know where the hell we're going."

She crosses her arms. "Are you accusing me of not being able to read a map?"

"No. I'm just saying that I know how to drive a car, doctor."

"Well, bully for you, Mr. Andretti." She unzips the pack and rummages inside. "I'm driving."

I know better than to argue with her when she starts calling me names.

"We follow the road around the lake going west," she says and drops a compass around my neck. "You know how to find west, right? If not, give it back to me."

"Yes, I know how to use a compass, Isabella. I'm the one who taught you how to use one, remember?"

She rolls her eyes. "We should be able to see the raised freeway after we pass the second fence. It'll take us north and then northwest. Last I heard, the bridge over the James was still standing, but if it's gone, there's another one ten miles to the west. Either one will get us where we need to go."

"Maybe this isn't such a shit plan."

"Thank you. It's a straight shot on the old interstate to Warm Springs, Colorado, and the mountain is a half hour drive further. I have the GPS coordinates that James gave me."

Gave me.

"Are you ready?" she asks and puts on her backpack.

"What about your vaccine?" I ask.

"I took an injection this morning, and they're good for twelve hours. I won't need another one until tonight at six." She pats the side pocket of her backpack. "Everything's in here."

I stare at her for a moment and then nod. "Let's blow this popsicle st—"

There's a dog bark, and a moment later, the door slides open.

Bearhart comes racing through the crack, dragging his leash and heading straight for Bella.

And then Soleil steps in—holding a Glock.

"Morning, Dr. Nadales," I say. "I heard your vaccine works for twelve hours now. Congratulations."

She points the gun at me. "What are you doing here?"

"Going home," Bella says, ruffling the dog's ears and then standing up. "What are you doing with Bearhart?"

"I just gave him the latest vaccine. I was going to test it Outside," Soleil says, glancing between me and her mother. "I brought the gun for self-defense."

She glances at the wheelchair with the wig and flowery clothes, putting two and two together. "David said you might try something like this, but I didn't believe him."

Bella puts her hands on her hips. "If you want to stop me, you'll have to shoot me."

"Don't be so melodramatic, Mom." Soleil walks over to the control panel. "I'll just override the airlock controls until security gets here."

"No, you won't." Bella walks over to her daughter, stopping when the muzzle of the Glock touches her chest. "Because that would be the same as killing me, sweetie. Take the dog and get in the airlock, Diego. We're taking Bearhart with us."

"But—"

"Do it."

I pick up his leash. "Come on, boy. We're going for a ride."

Soleil lowers the gun. "Mom, I need Diego to finish work on the vaccine."

"No you don't, Soleil—and we both know it."

They stand there staring at each other, both of them strong-willed, whip-smart, and leaking tears.

To my surprise, Soleil nods. "I may still need him if there are unforeseen complications."

"He'll be in Colorado with me—at least for a little while. I suggest you pack up your lab and get out there as soon as possible."

Soleil smiles at her mother. "It feels like going home, doesn't it?"

Bella nods. "I did the best I could raising you, sweetheart." She pushes a lock of hair back from her daughter's face. "I'm sorry it wasn't... what it could have been."

"Oh, Mom," Soleil says and puts her arms around her mother. "I don't blame you for what happened."

We hear shouting out in the park.

Soleil takes a syringe out of her coat pocket and offers it to her mother. "Here's the rest of the dose for Bearhart. He only needs half a cc."

Bella nods, too choked-up to reply.

"Go," Soleil says and steps away from her mother. "Once the cycle starts they'll have to wait until it finishes."

Bella takes the syringe and follows me into the airlock—and then turns back to her daughter. "Thank you, Soleil. I love you more than you could ever know."

"I love you, too, Mom." She presses the *Cycle Out* button and turns to me. "Take good care of her, okay?"

I nod and put my arm around Bella. "She turned out

pretty damn well, if you ask me."

We watch the door slide shut and then lock. There's a hissing sound as the positive pressure increases and the numbers on the status screen count down from thirty. I walk over to the door and gaze out into a beautiful, cloudless morning.

Only Dave's Humvee isn't parked where it should be.

I press my forehead against the thick glass and scan the area around the biodome. "Shit."

"What is it?" Bella says, still looking through the small window at Soleil.

The supplies for repairing the biodome are stacked on the trailer of the old Vespa scooter, but Dave's SUV is nowhere to be seen.

"Where the hell is it?" I say.

"What are you talking about?" Bella comes over to me, pulling something out of her pack.

"Kirk's car is gone." I glance at the Glock she's holding. It's the same model as Soleil's. "Where'd you get that?"

"David keeps a drawer full of them in the bedroom, but I insisted they be unloaded. It took me a while to remember where I'd hidden the bullets."

I give her the eyebrow.

"In a cereal box in the storage closet—Corn Pops."

"Hah."

She tries to hand the gun to me, but I refuse to take it.

"Do you know how to aim and fire it?" I ask. "As I recall, you refused to let me teach you."

She shortens the puppy's leash a bit. "David insisted I learn back when everything was falling apart."

"Remind me to thank him." I take Bella's other hand as the outer door slides open. "How do you feel about motorbikes?"

"I've never ridden one," she says. "Why?"

"Looks like I get to drive after all."

CHAPTER 34

Lani: Call the Shots

The late fall air is nippy, but the sun is warm on my back as I sit on an outcropping of rocks and eat my lunch. I'm just below the summit of the mountain that encloses the Magic Kingdom, and I have a digital camera full of radio tower images in my pack.

I gaze out over the eastern plains and sip my water, so happy I could sing.

David should have Shannon back today.

Just thinking about hearing her voice makes me want to sit by the radio all day—and I wish I could have. James offered to climb up here in that old environment suit I found, but it didn't make sense. It would have been nearly impossible for him to clamber over the huge boulders and up the steep scree in that bulky thing.

David needs information on what's up here, and I'm the

one to give it to him.

The rockslide that took out the radio looks to have happened years ago, but as far as I can tell, the tower is undamaged. Only the underground cable connecting it to the Magic Kingdom has been severed. I took lots of photos of the damage. I'm no electrician, but I think reconnecting it will be straightforward.

Once David gets here with the proper tools, we should have the power back on in no time.

As I'm packing up to head back down, I spy a wisp of orange smoke coming from below me on the mountain. I shift my position to get a better look and realize it's a signal flare—one of the sort Madders keeps in his plane.

He was planning to fly in last night and drive up today, but he must have run into a problem. I tell myself it's just a flat tire or a washed out road, but some part of me knows it's worse than that. Madders would know how to handle either of those.

I stuff everything back into my pack and scramble down the rocky slope, dread spilling into my chest with every footstep.

It takes me ten minutes to get back to the concrete ledge and another ten to follow the road down to Madders.

He's sitting in a military-issued jeep loaded to the gills with supplies—but it's parked precariously on the edge of the road, one of the back wheels up in the air.

He waves when he sees me but doesn't get out of the vehicle.

Uh-oh.

"Are you okay?" I ask when I get there, out of breath from jogging. There's blood on the inside of his faceplate, but his suit looks undamaged.

He forces a smile. "I'm fine, Lani. Just a little disoriented."

"Disoriented?" I check the readout on his display. His

pulse is fast, but everything else is within the high-normal range. "What happened, Madders?"

"I lost the vision in one eye, and my right arm quit working. But before I could pull over, I got dizzy, and the next thing I knew, I was in this ditch."

I put my hands on the sides of his helmet and study his pupils. He looks exhausted and scared, but his eyes appear normal. "Any headache?" I ask.

"No."

"It sounds like you had a stroke, Madders."

Now that I think about it, it's not surprising given his age and the amount of stress he's under. He's been hauling equipment, loading trucks, flying the plane, and worrying about the safety of all those people for months.

You should have seen it coming.

"Can you lift your hands above your head?" I ask "And hold them up there?"

"I think so." He tries.

Neither arm drifts down.

"Good. You can relax now. Smile for me?" I say and take a closer look at his face. As far as I can tell, there's no muscle atrophy, and his speech is fine. "I'm guessing it was a TIA, transient ischemic attack or mini-stroke. It's serious—we should get you inside the Magic Kingdom so I can take a closer look—but they don't usually cause permanent damage."

He nods, looking relieved. "That's good to hear."

"How about the crash?" I ask. "I can see you hit your forehead. Is there anything else that hurts?"

"No. I was nearly stopped by the time I lost control. So it's just a bump. But if I get out of the driver's seat, I think the jeep might just tip over the edge."

I walk around the back and take a look. He's right. The jeep is high-center on some rocks, and his weight is preventing the vehicle from flipping over.

"There's a winch in the boot," he says. "If you hook it up to one of those trees, you could pull me back up on the road."

It's not quite as simple as he makes it sound, but thirty minutes later, we have the jeep back on all four wheels and all the supplies reloaded.

Ten minutes later, Madders backs it into the access tunnel in front of the blast door. I hop out, press my palm to the panel, and wait for James to get to the Control Room.

"How'd the photo shoot go?" James asks, and it takes me a moment to remember what he's talking about.

"Fine," I say. "I don't think it'll be difficult to reconnect the radio. The main cable was cut by the rockslide, but the tower looks fine."

"Wish I had known that twenty years ago when Doomsday hit. Could have used the company."

I motion for Madders to come stand next to me.

"By the way," James says. "I figured out a way to lower the CO_2. I spent the morning testing ideas, and I think I have something that works."

"I knew you'd figure it out," I say. "I can't wait to see what you've got."

"We can celebrate tonight. I've been saving some chocolate for a special occasion."

"James," I say. "There's someone I want you to meet…"

I put my arm around Madders and introduce the two men—only to discover they already know each other.

James did some freelance work for Madders when he was a university professor, and the two of them lived on the same block back before things went south.

"Small world," I say, and then wonder how unlikely that is.

What are the chances that two random men in the country have met before? Pretty damn near zero.

"Don't know if you've heard," Madders says, "but the Bub folks should be here in the morning. No need to worry about taking care of them right now. They have environment tents and plenty of food—and should be good to set up on that concrete ledge until Kirk gets here."

"Oh, we can start bringing them in right away," James says. "I opened up twenty more rooms, and as long as my air freshener works, the water supply holds out, and we don't drive each other crazy, there's room for everyone Inside."

"They're gonna be mighty happy to hear that," Madders says, looking like he's back to himself.

I give his arm a squeeze, glad that his stroke wasn't any worse.

"Okay, boys," I say. "Why don't we haul all this stuff in, have something to eat, and then I can set up the shortwave for the evening chat? I'll check up on the trucks first and then contact Kirk. I can relay the news on the radio tower, update him on the Bub folks, and finally say hello to my daughter."

An hour later—after a full checkup for Madders that turns up absolutely nothing of concern—the three of us sit down to an early dinner, including fresh carrots for Benny, canned salmon for us, and warm apple crisp for all.

When Madders sees the spread, he laughs. "Have you been eating like Henry VIII all this time?"

James nods. "I got a greenhouse, a Deepfreeze, and a boxcar full of canned fish—but I would have traded them all for a crate of MREs and one radio that worked."

At five on the dot, I sit at a card table in the mouth of the access tunnel, flip on the shortwave, and call up the Bub folks. I let them know we're ready for them tomorrow, answer a couple doctor questions, and then sign off to set up the connection to David in Catersville. I'm so excited to hear Shannon's voice that I can't stop smiling, and I have to keep telling myself not to get my hopes up. It could be a week or more until I see her again.

David's going to bring her back to me. He promised, and he never breaks his promises.

But the moment I lock on to his signal, I know something's gone terribly wrong.

"Lani," David says over the staccato sound of what can only be gunfire, "I can't talk long. We're up shit's creek here, and we need to get the hell out before these fuckheads kill someone else."

My heart feels like it's going to explode in my chest. "W-what's happening, David? Where's Shannon?"

"She's been accused of some sort of crime. Some crazy woman who calls herself 'the Giver of the Law' claims Shannon's an accessory to homicide—"

"They think my d-daughter is a murderer?"

"—which we all know is bullshit, but the old witch won't listen to reason. Seems Shannon was present when the head honcho got his skull bashed in by his sex-starved teenage son. After the kid killed his father, he forced Shannon to go to the crippled side of the bio—"

"Oh my God, David!"

"There's air and some battery power in there, Lani, but the whole biodome is teetering on environmental collapse. I couldn't touch a thing without tipping it over the edge."

"Why didn't you tell me this before, David? I thought you said the negotiations were going well, that you'd have Shannon back today!"

"They were going well. I'd made a deal with the guy who runs the place—even sealed it with a case of my best bourbon—and then he went and got himself killed. With the old man pushing up daisies and the crown prince on the lam, the political situation went into free fall. I thought once things settled down, they'd see reason—I've got a fucking planeload of luxury items sitting on their doorstep—but I was wrong.

The batshit old witch took over and claims Shannon is a dangerous fugitive and has to stand tri—"

"My daughter is a dangerous fugitive?"

"Logic and reason are not a part of her vocabulary, babe. She'd happily see the whole biodome burn rather than give a single inch."

I pound my fist so hard against the table that the radio almost bounces off it. "David, you have to go in there and get her out. Now."

"Yeah," he says, his voice droll. "I tried. That would be why they're shooting at us. Some numbnuts with a high-powered rifle put a hole in the dome a couple days ago, and the autonomic system sealed all the bulkheads. Even if I did get past those idiots with the M16—and believe me, I brought enough firepower to do it—there's no way to open the bulkheads without killing everyone."

"But there has to be some way! You can't just leave her. You built that biod—"

There are more gunshots, and then the sound of metal scraping on metal.

"David?" I shout at the microphone. "David, please!"

"I gotta go, babe. As soon as I get back to C-Bay, I'll look into other options. Kirk out."

I sit there in the dark night and stare at the red light on the radio until my hands and face are numb from the cold.

If Madders won't fly me out to Catersville, I'm going to take the jeep and start driving at first light. I'm going to get my daughter back, if it kills me.

I pack up the radio and head back inside to say goodbye.

CHAPTER 35

Diego: Duck and Cover

As the airlock portal closes, I grab a hammer and toss it in between the door and the wall. The mechanism makes a couple of failed attempts to shut and then gives up, causing an alarm to sound.

"That should keep them busy for a while," I say.

I shove all the stuff off the trailer and toss my pack and the extra bag onto it.

Bella sets her pack next to mine and secures them with a bungee cord from the pile of tools. She picks up an ax and wedges it under her pack.

She leads Bearhart over and pats the trailer. "Hup!"

The dog jumps on between our backpacks, his tail wagging a mile a minute.

"Sit."

He does.

"Settle." He looks a bit iffy about it, but he lies down. "Good boy."

"You think he'll stay in there?" I ask.

"Yep. Trained him myself." She ruffles the fur on his head and then picks up a couple of empty plastic jugs and hooks the handles on to the bungees.

"For gas," she says, picking up a metal bucket and securing it to the trailer as well. "And water."

"Smart woman." I give the scooter a quick shake to make sure the tank is full—it is—and then climb on and start it up. It coughs, chuffs out a cloud of black smoke, and sputters to life. Bearhart barks, but doesn't jump off.

I swing my leg over the scooter and rev the engine.

Bella hops on behind me and wraps her arms around my chest. It's not an unpleasant experience.

"Let's go!" she says.

I notice that she's still holding the gun—and that it's pointed right at my crotch.

That is not going to end well.

I ease the Glock out of her fingers, checking that the safety is on, and stick it in my jacket. I turn my head to make sure she hears me. "If you need it, it's in my pocket."

She nods and loosens her hold a little, her head resting against my shoulder.

I release the kickstand. *"Hasta la vista,* baby."

The dog barks, and I gun the engine.

The scooter lurches forward, weaving and sputtering like a drunken sailor.

Bella lifts her head, looking back at the biodome—which is not getting smaller as quickly as I'd hoped. "I found David's Humvee," she says.

I steal a glance back.

The massive black SUV is parked by the west loading dock, and camo biosuits are pouring out of the airlock all around it.

"Shit."

I spot the security gate on the other side of a huge percolation pond. The road leading up to it curves around the lake like a big U. I head in that direction.

"Can't this thing go any faster?" Bella asks.

"Not unless you want to jettison the trailer," I say and then get an idea. "Hold on! I'm going to take a shortcut!"

I make a hard right off the road, Bearhart barking as we crash through the weeds.

"I knew I should have driven," Bella says.

I gun the engine and we shoot up onto the raised levee that surrounds the pond. It's made of hard-packed gravel and it doesn't look like anyone's been on it in years because the place is crawling with snakes.

"Oh, God," Bella says, lifting up her feet.

I lay on the horn, and hope to hell the big ones aren't poisonous.

"We're not going to make it," she says, glancing back at the SUV.

"Don't be a spoilsport."

I do the calculation in my head: If we're doing 20 mph, and they have to drive three times as far... it's going to be close.

"Can you shoot out their tires?" I ask.

"Are you serious?" She leans sideways, staring at me. "I couldn't hit the broadside of a dirigible from this distance, let alone a tire. People only do that sort of thing in James Bond movies."

"Well, you could at least try," I say.

She holds up her fingers like a pistol, aims them at the SUV, and says, "Pow. Pow."

"Very funny."

She puts her arm back around me. "At least this way I

don't have to worry about killing someone by accident."

"You do have a point," I say. "You got any better ideas?"

She lets out a squeal as I run over a particularly large snake.

"Sorry, buddy." I hit the horn and then shout, "Get your asses out of the way, will you?"

"Snakes lack the anatomical equivalent of an ass, Mr. Crusoe. Perhaps that's why they're ignoring you."

"Hah. And will you stop calling me that?"

"*This* is a shit plan, Diego."

I laugh. "Can you get the gate opener out of my pocket, please?"

"Which pocket?" she says.

"Jeans. Front, right."

She holds on with her left arm and slides her other hand down my chest, searching with her fingers for the pocket. I swerve to avoid some sort of huge toad, and she grabs on to my crotch.

"That costs extra, madam."

"Sorry!" she says. "Why didn't you put it somewhere easier to get?"

I stand up a little on the running board of the scooter, and she manages to slip her hand into my jeans and retrieve the opener.

"Press and hold!" I shout, hoping the signal will reach from this far away.

Nothing happens.

"Did you press and hold?" I ask.

"Yes," she says, her voice testy. "Despite my excessive age, oppressive personality, and lack of a Y chromosome, I am not an idiot."

The SUV is coming around the far side of the lake, going way too fast for the curve.

"That's not going to end well," we both say at the same

time.

We watch the driver slam on the brakes and then struggle to keep the massive thing on the dirt road. It fishtails and then disappears over the embankment.

We both cheer.

I head down the embankment at the end of the lake, across a dry concrete culvert, and back up onto the road, the trailer bumping and groaning behind us.

I glance in my rearview mirror—and don't see the damn dog. "Where's Bearhart?"

"Stop the bike!" Bella says, pounding on my back with one hand.

"But we're almost—"

"Stop the damn bike!"

"Okay, okay." I brake to a stop, and we scan the raised embankment behind us.

No dog.

"There!" Bella points at the lake.

Bearhart is paddling his little heart out across the lake, scaring up ducks as he splashes toward us.

"Beats running through all those snakes," I say.

Bella bends over and claps her hands together, encouraging the pooch. "That's it, boy. You can do it!"

On the far side of the lake, I see the SUV scramble back onto the road.

"You might want to pick up the pace there, hun. We've got company."

Bella glances at the car and then the closed gate up ahead. "Shit. We're not going to make it."

"Come on, buddy. Paddle faster," I say, watching the SUV pick up speed.

Bearhart is almost to the shore.

I grab a handful of the rocks and start tossing them out into the water, aiming for the ducks.

The dog looks like he's going to turn around and chase the splashes, but Bella shouts, "Bearhart, come!" and he continues swimming.

I throw more rocks, aiming at the huge flock of birds in the middle. A few take off, and then few more, and a second later, the sky is filled with honking, panicked ducks heading right toward the SUV.

Bearhart wades out of the water and shakes off.

"Nothing like a little fowl play to liven things up," Bella says.

We hear the car horn blaring and more tires skidding.

"I was just winging it."

"Hah." Bella tells Bearhart to get on the trailer. "And stay there this time."

The dog barks and jumps right back on, his tail still wagging.

"He's a keeper," she says, and I have to agree.

"Hold on!" I wait for her to comply—and then gun the engine.

The scooter lurches forward.

She holds the gate opener in front of me, her cheek nestled against mine, and presses the button.

The twelve-foot barbed-wire gate starts rolling open.

"Woo-hoo!" she says and kisses me.

I turn my head, our lips almost touching, and stare at her for a moment, feeling that... pull we have.

Bearhart barks and I turn back to my driving, my heart still in my throat.

She wraps her arms around my chest and kisses my shoulder. "Thank you. Even if we don't make it."

I let go of the handlebars and squeeze her hand. "You're welcome. We're gonna make it."

When we're almost to the gate, I glance over my shoulder at her. "See if you can get the gate to shut."

The gate starts closing, and I lean forward, trying to make the scooter go faster.

"Oh, shit," she says. "We're not gonna make it."

"Have a little faith, woman." I manage to get the scooter and trailer through with a couple of feet to spare, Bearhart barking the whole time.

I put on the brakes and turn the scooter around.

The SUV is bearing down on us, but it's not going very fast.

"One of their tires is flat!" Bella says.

"And you said you couldn't hit a dirigible."

She rolls her eyes, and I laugh.

I hop off the scooter, wrench the shovel out from under the backpacks and start wedging it into the wire mesh of the fence so that it'll jam when the SUV tries to open the gate.

Bella walks up behind me, takes the gun out of my pocket, and aims it up at the motor housing.

"Cover your ears," she says, pointing at the plugs in hers. I do.

She fires three shots, all of which hit their mark.

"Remind me not to piss you off," I say.

She pulls her earplugs out. "What did you say?"

"Nice shot."

"Thanks." She presses the button on the opener.

Nothing happens.

She tosses the opener over the fence, sticks the gun back in my pocket, and dusts off her hands. "Let's go."

We hop back on the scooter and head for the second gate.

It turns out to be manually operated, but there's a chain with a padlock holding it shut.

"Ax," Bella says and hops off the scooter. She pulls it out from under the backpack.

"May I?" I ask.

"Be my guest."

I take it out of her hands and swing it down on a rusted link.

It takes only a couple of tries before the chain slithers off the gate.

I push the gate open while she returns the ax to the trailer.

"How'd you know we'd need an ax?" I ask her.

"Read it in a book."

The SUV pulls up to the first gate, and we hear the doors slam as five or six biosuits pile out.

And then I hear a gunshot.

"Get down!" I shout and drop to the pavement. "Bearhart, come!"

The dog jumps off the trailer, lopes over, and licks my face. He's still dripping wet and smells like stale pond water. "Down!" I say, and he flops over next to me, soaking my shirt.

I hear a couple more shots and see Bella still standing by the trailer.

"What are you doing?" I shout. "Get down!"

She walks back to the scooter, completely unconcerned about those goons firing at us.

"Well?" she says. "Are you coming?"

I zigzag over to the bike, keeping low and trying to be unpredictable, Bearhart on my heels.

Bella watches me, an amused look on her face. "No need to panic, Mr. Nadales. They're firing blanks."

"What?" I get on the scooter. "How do you know that?"

Bella convinces Bearhart to get back on the trailer. "David never gives out live ammo—doesn't want some trigger-happy noob shooting holes in the biodome. Besides, do you actually think they'd try to shoot us? You're Miracle Man, and I'm the boss's wife."

"Now you tell me."

She laughs and gets back on the scooter. "I haven't had this much fun in ages."

Me neither.

I ease the scooter into high, Bella waving back at the lads and singing "On the Road Again" as we follow a double yellow line into the future.

Chapter 36

Shannon: Heart of Darkness

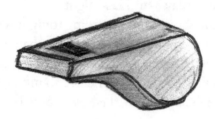

When I awaken, the warm memory of kissing Peter floods back into me, filling me with a sublime sense of contentment.

You have Peter now. Everything's going to be okay.

I lie there in the half-light, thinking about falling asleep with his arm wrapped around my waist, the soft tickle of his breath against my cheek.

And then I remember what he told me last night about the Culling, and an icy fear pushes out my euphoria.

Where is he?

I blink, trying to clear my head.

My internal clock says it's morning, but the room is still shrouded in gloom. I roll over, panic starting to rise, and force my eyes to focus.

Both the inner and outer airlock doors are closed—and

Peter's in his bed right next to me.

Thank goodness.

One glance out the window tells me why it's so dark in here: It's raining Outside.

I imagine snuggling close to Peter and putting my head against his chest. I listen for the soft rhythm of his breathing, but the rain is too loud. The drops hitting the biodome fill the airlock with a deep thrumming. I lie there, listening to the soft hum, trying to decide if I should wake Peter. He's always up before I am, so I know he must be exhausted from all the work yesterday—and last night.

I smile at the thought of spending tonight with him, kissing him and touching him and having his hands on my skin. I sit up and stretch, finally understanding what Mindy means when she says you can want someone so much, it hurts.

Like the whole universe is there just so he can put his arms around you.

And then I see the note by my pillow.

Shannon-

I went to help the others.

STAY HERE!

I'll be back as soon as I can.

Peter

"No!" I grab the blanket off his bed.

His backpack is underneath, but his clothes and shoes—and his bow—are gone.

I rush to the inner door and press my face against the glass, looking out into the Wilds.

The air is heavy with smoke. The whole southern part

of the Wilds—the area containing our archery range and our workshop—is lost in the gray haze.

Oh, my God, Peter is out there!

I dress, put on my shoes, slip my whistle around my neck, and look for my bow.

But it's not hanging on the wall where I left it.

Peter's hidden it somewhere—so I don't try to come after him.

I search behind the jugs of water and sacks of grain until I find it tucked behind stacked boxes of pasta and mashed potatoes. I wrench it out, put the quiver of old arrows over my shoulder, and grab a rebreather from my pack. For a moment, I stare at the two others still in there—and then pull them out and hook the straps around the quiver.

How many more did we need? I do the calculation: Eighteen minus the twelve masks we already gave them and the two smaller masks we made yesterday, leaves four. With my two extras and Peter's two, we'll have enough.

I check Peter's backpack. All three of his masks are gone.

He probably went to the workshop to get the two for the kids.

It takes forever to get the inner airlock door open, and when I finally manage to slip through, the smoke is terrible. I put on my mask, trying to decide if it would be better to leave the airlock door open or shut it.

I decide to close it but not seal it. That should keep out most of the smoke—but only require a minute to get it open again.

Once I finish, I move as fast as I can toward the workshop, keeping to the cover and staying away from the main areas. I hear gunfire and shouting from the Barrier, but don't stop moving until I'm inside the building with our workshop.

I rush into the room, hoping to find Peter, but he's not there—and neither are any of the repaired masks. I spend a second looking around. The vises and sealant are gone too!

He must have taken the ones that were ready, along with

the supplies to make more, and gone… where?

To find the Others.

Yeah, but where the hell are they?

I hurry toward the maintenance tower—the one we spent our first night in—keeping an arrow notched in my bow. The smoke is getting thicker, but my mask seems to be working. Even though I can't see far, I'm not coughing. When I get to the tower, I climb up six flights of stairs, but by the time I get to the top, I realize it's a mistake. The cloud of smoke is so thick I can barely see my feet—let alone Peter.

I race back down the steps and out the door and almost crash into Grizzly. He's got some sort of rag over his nose and mouth, but it's definitely him.

His eyes get big when he sees me.

"Sorry!" I try to step backward, but he grabs my arm.

He smiles. "I've missed those nice manners of yours." He has a large knife on his belt, but he doesn't take it out. "Where's Peter?"

I shake my head and pull away. "Let me go!"

"Don't worry, missy. I ain't gonna hurt you—but I can't speak for the rest of 'em, if you get what I mean?"

I stop struggling, and he lets go of me.

"You tell him they convicted him of murder and sentenced him to burn at the stake, now, will you?"

"Burn at the stake?" I can barely breathe. "Like they used to do to witches?"

He glances at the bow in my hand. "The Giver has brainwashed folks into believing Peter's father was weak—and that God has punished him for it. She has ordered the Garden of Eden to be cleansed of those who desecrate it. The men aren't here today for amorous congress; they're driven by bloodlust. Those who refuse to submit will be killed—and everything on this side of the wall burned."

The magnitude of what he's saying leaves me cold.

He inclines his head. "You best find that hero of yours and skedaddle while you can."

"Peter *is* a hero," I say, my voice wavering. "He saved my life."

"I didn't mean to imply otherwise." He turns and walks away. "Tell him I said good luck."

"I will," I say. "Thank you."

He doesn't look back but raises his hand in acknowledgment. A minute later, he disappears into the smoky half-light.

I walk around the tower, trying to think. And then I remember the whistle around my neck. I know it'll alert the men that I'm here, but I don't know what else to do. The smoke is pretty thick, and I decide as soon as I blow it, I'll move so they won't be able to find me.

At least I hope they won't.

I take a deep breath, pull off my mask, and blow three short whistles. I put the mask back over my face and exhale to clear the smoke.

Before I have a chance to blow the three long blasts, I hear Peter's reply.

That sound is sweeter than anything I've ever heard.

He's alive.

I start running toward him, taking twenty breaths and then pulling off the mask to blow the whistle again. I listen for his reply and then repeat the process two more times.

The smoke is becoming so thick that we nearly run into each other.

I throw my arms around his neck—almost knocking off both our masks—before I realize he's not alone.

There's a group of women and children crowded around him, carrying backpacks and dragging large sacks, one of them pulling a child's red wagon full of pots and pans.

"We have to get out of the open," Peter says. "The men will have heard our whistles."

Peter takes my hand and leads me through a door into a large room. It must have been a toddler's play area because the floor is littered with soft mats, and you can still see elephants and giraffes painted on the walls.

The smoke is a little better in here.

"I saw Grizzly," I say, keeping my voice low. "He says you were convicted of murder and sentenced to be... burned at the stake."

"For blasphemy. It's been a while since they had one of those." He looks spooked. "Was he alone?"

"Yes," I say. "I ran into him at the base of the tower."

"He used to take me there when I was little," Peter says. "To see the world."

"He also said the Giver is in a rage. The men have been ordered to kill anyone who resists and burn everything in the Wilds. He told me we should get out while we can—and he wished you good luck."

Peter stares at me, a far-off look in his eyes. "That's why they brought guns today. They're not planning to let anyone escape."

"We have to get back to the airlock, Peter. I left it open so that we could get inside quickly, but if the men find it—"

"We'll figure out something else," Peter says and puts his arm around me, waiting for the Others to come inside. "The important thing is you're safe."

"Sorry I didn't stay put, but I couldn't let you go off and..."

"Have all the fun?" He smiles. "I should have known you wouldn't listen to me."

The last of the group pulls the red wagon through the door and then shuts it. All but two of the Others are wearing our masks—and the ones without are wearing swim goggles with strips of cloth covering their faces.

They look like the sand people from Star Wars.

The thought gives me the creeps, and I edge closer to Peter, my heart still racing.

All of them look tired and scared—and all of them are women.

There are two D-2s and a handful of D-1s, but most of them are the same age as Mom, and one of them is as old as Lucy.

Peter pulls the mask away from his face. "This is Shannon," he says, turning toward the crowd. "She's the one who made the masks."

I hear a murmur, and a few of them nod.

"The masks were made to be worn Outside," Peter says. "They'll protect you from the poisoned air if something happens to the biodome."

There are more murmurs, and everyone looks at the two people without masks.

I take the spare rebreathers off my quiver and offer them to the sand people.

I hope they're all sealed properly.

The women remove their headgear and slip the masks on.

"Thank you, Shannon," the older woman says. "You're a gift from God."

"You're welcome." I slide my gaze across the motley crew. "Thank you for the bow and arrows."

"We have more," the old woman says. "But we don't know how to get the string on the bow. Perhaps someday you will show us?"

"Of course," I say, wondering what sort of future that might be. "Peter knows all about archery, and he's a good teacher."

"We don't need bows," one of the women says, her left eye not tracking properly. "We need guns. How are we going to fight them if we don't have guns?"

"We're not," Peter says. "We're going to outsmart them. But we need to get back to the airlock before they find us. Once we're inside, we can seal off the door and talk."

"They've been setting fires," the old woman says. "I think they mean to burn everything in the Wilds and force us back to the Barrier."

"Why would they do that?" I say, glancing from the old woman to Peter, unable to believe that someone would destroy a whole biodome on purpose. "If they burn a hole in the outer wall, this side would be contaminated in a matter of minutes. Anyone without a rebreather would die—including all of them."

"It wouldn't be the first time that heartless bitch was willing to sacrifice lives to gain power," the old woman says. "But I imagine she's expecting us to surrender before things get too bad."

"I ain't going back to that hellhole on the other side," the woman who walks with a limp says. "They can shoot me first."

Some of the others nod in agreement.

A voice booms out from hidden speakers all around us. "When the Lord thy God brings thee into the land and drives out before thee many nations, thou must destroy them totally. Make no treaty with them. Show them no mercy!"

"It's the Giver," Peter says, the muscles in his jaw tight.

"Thou shalt not suffer a witch to live!" The Giver's voice is frenzied and loud, and some of the Others cover their ears. "Submit to thine husband, as to the Lord!" We hear whooping and wolf whistles. "He who curses his father must be put to death!"

"Come on," Peter says and takes my hand. "Out the back door."

He pulls me into a jog, the band of outcasts following along behind us.

"Do you know how to get back to the airlock from here?" he asks as we move between abandoned buildings, keeping to the smoky shadows.

"Yes," I say, visualizing the map I drew.

"I want you to lead the group. Stay next to the buildings until you get to the other side of the park. Once you pass the guard station, head straight for the airlock. I'll make sure everyone stays together."

"Peter, I don't want you to leave me—"

"I won't let you out of my sight, Shaz. You have my word. Just remember everything I taught you."

I nod, wondering what happened to the shy, fearful boy who was afraid to shake my hand. "Okay," I say, trying not to cry.

"And if you fire an arrow, shoot to kill—then keep running."

I stare at him, fear taking my breath away.

"Once you get back to the airlock," he says, "start the cycle. I'll be there before you're done." He kisses me, and all I want to do is bury my face in his chest and make the rest of the universe disappear.

"Be careful," he says, holding me by my shoulders.

"I love you, Peter." I throw my arms around his neck, and this time he has to push me away.

"Go!" he says.

And I do.

I—and the eighteen others carrying everything they own—sneak across a smoky biodome in the half-lit darkness, trusting Peter to keep us all safe.

Twice I look back to see if Peter is there, but the haze is too thick, and I finally give up.

I say a prayer to Peter's God, asking Him to keep everyone safe—but especially Peter.

We manage to make it all the way to the far edge of the

park before we're seen.

Just as I step out of the cover of the guard station, I hear an arrow fly, and a man only a few meters ahead of me lets out a scream and falls to the pavement. Another arrow flies, and there's another shout. And then I see more men up ahead. They're carrying knives and one has an ax, but I don't see any guns.

A woman behind me cries out, and I turn to see a man with a knife grab her around the waist and start dragging her away. The other women try to fight him off, but he cuts at them with his blade.

"Get away so I can shoot!" I yell, and the moment they do, I fire an arrow, aiming between his shoulder blades.

It hits him in the arm, and he releases the woman, stumbling back and trying to pull the arrow out. Then he turns and sees me. "You fucking bitch, you shot me!" He staggers toward me, and I fumble with my bow, notch an arrow, and let it fly point blank.

It embeds itself deep into his shoulder, almost going all the way through. He falls to his knees and then collapses on the ground.

I stand there, staring at the blood pooling around him, unable to move.

You killed him, Shannon. You killed another person.

And then I hear more arrows whiz past.

Peter.

A man who was closing in on me goes down, two arrows in his chest.

I look away.

Oh, God, this is horrible.

I get everyone back behind the small guard station and take aim around the corner, hoping that Peter is protecting us from behind.

Shoot to kill and then run like hell.

My first arrow goes high because my hands are shaking, but the next two get closer to their marks. Both men drop their knives and start sprinting in the other direction.

The man with the ax shouts at them, calling them cowards—and then he sees me. He raises the ax over his head and starts rushing toward me.

An arrow hits him in the chest—and then a second lands a hand's width away from the first. The huge man drops the ax right in front of me and crumples to the ground.

I swallow, trying to get my legs to move.

And then we hear gunfire coming from the other side of the park—and all hell breaks loose.

The breach alarm goes off, and the red lights mounted on the roof of the biodome start flashing, making the smoky half-darkness look like some weird version of Dante's *Inferno*.

I fire more arrows, aiming at the men between me and the airlock. When they fall back, I move forward toward safety. One of the women rushes past me and starts grabbing dropped weapons.

And then I would swear the ground starts shaking. Loud grating noises fill the air, metal scraping against metal, coming from... everywhere.

The bulkheads must have some sort of backup power because the massive doors are closing all around me.

You should have marked them on the map!

And then I realize if the one between here and our airlock closes, we'll be trapped.

"Run!" Peter shouts, and I realize he's up on the roof of the guard station behind me.

I drop the arrow I have notched and race toward the airlock, the Others on my heels. I pass a huge metal wall creeping across an ancient rail set in the concrete. And somewhere in the back of my mind, I estimate it's going to take half a minute for the bulkhead to shut.

God, I hope that's long enough for Peter to get through.

I hear arrows whiz past me, but I don't stop running until I reach the airlock door.

I pump the handle, counting down as I go.

Hurry, hurry, hurry!

Once it's open wide enough, a young girl slips through, and then the rest of the women follow, one by one. I count them... ten, eleven, twelve. More are coming, but I can see three men chasing after them.

One of the men falters—and then another.

Peter must still be up on the guard station?

Through the narrowing gap of the bulkhead, I see him drop down onto the ground and run toward me.

He's going to make it. Oh, God, please let him make it.

And then he slows down, pulling another arrow out of his quiver to shoot at the man between us.

"No!" I shout. "Run!"

Peter glances at me—and keeps moving.

I notch an arrow, step away from the airlock so if I miss I won't hit Peter, and shoot at the last man. The arrow flies wide, clattering into the closing bulkhead—just as Peter slips through ahead of it.

I draw another arrow, take a breath, and let it fly. This time, the shaft buries itself in the man's thigh, and he rolls to the ground, howling with pain. Peter jumps over him, barreling toward me, as the last of the women enter the airlock.

"Shannon!" Peter shouts. "Watch out!"

Someone grabs me from behind, choking me with his arm.

"Stop right there, lover boy," the man says, "or I'll send your girl up to heaven."

The guy licks the side of my face, and I let out a surprised shriek.

He laughs. "Or down to the other place."

Peter stops running, his bow in one hand and an arrow in the other. "Mikey."

"Got it in one," Mikey says. "With your pops outta the way, you ain't such a big dog anymore, now are ya?"

"Let her go," Peter says. "It's me you want, not her."

"Oh, I want her somethin' fierce," Mikey says, his breath hot on my neck. "But I won't kill her if you do as I say."

Peter takes a step closer. "What do you want?"

"Put down your weapon and kick it over here," Mikey says, jerking my head back when Peter doesn't immediately comply.

"Okay," Peter says, bending over to place the bow on the ground. "Don't hurt—"

The bulkhead wall clangs shut, and some sort of pump engages, the noise louder than the airplane engine.

Mikey turns toward the sound, loosening his grip for an instant.

I twist around and knee him in the groin as hard as I can—which is difficult because he's a lot taller than I am.

"You, bitch." He throws me down on the floor.

A second later, an arrow whizzes over my head, and Mikey falls backward against the wall. "You bastard!"

Two more arrows follow in quick succession, one of them hitting Mikey in the throat.

I close my eyes, unable to look anymore.

Peter takes hold of my shoulders and lifts me up. "Are you alright?"

I nod, too terrified to speak.

"Inside," he says and helps me through the airlock.

He does a quick headcount and then starts sealing the door.

I stare at eighteen terrified faces, knowing mine must look the same.

We're going to be okay.

I say it again, out loud this time.

"Yes," Peter says and puts his arm around me, facing the crowded room. "We're gonna be alright."

My eyes come to rest on the elderly woman. She's the one who collected all the weapons. Even in old age, she's tall and full-figured.

Her skin is darker than Peter's, but her hair is the same shade of copper.

His grandmother.

Peter realizes who I'm staring at. "Shannon, this is my Gran. Before today, I hadn't seen her since I was five."

"Nice to meet you, Shannon," she says. "Peter tells me you're a most amazing young woman, and I can tell that he's right."

I don't know who blushes more, me or Peter.

Before I can respond, there's some sort of banging outside the airlock.

All of us turn to see a group of men pounding on the other side.

They look really angry—but they don't look like they know how to get in.

"What are we going to do?" asks a girl peeking out from behind Gran. She looks to be five or six.

"We'll head to Texas," Gran says. "They have two big biodomes in Dallas. Probably take us four or five months to walk there—a lot fewer if we can find some vehicles that still run."

"How long will the masks keep working?" the woman with the bad eye asks.

"I don't know for sure," I say. "The filters were designed to last eight months, and they haven't been used before today—but they're also twenty years old."

"How will we eat and drink with the masks on?" someone else asks, a raven-haired girl who looks to be a few years older than Peter and me.

"The masks have a built-in drinking straw, but you have to be careful using it." I show her. "We'd have to set up environment tents to eat."

"Which we have," Peter adds.

The men swing the blade of an ax into the glass, making lots of little cracks in the outer layer—and that makes up everyone's mind.

"If we don't leave before they manage to break in, they'll kill us all anyway," the woman with the limp says.

"Are there any opposed?" Gran asks.

No one speaks, but we can hear the men pounding on the door.

"Well, then, open the damn exit," the woman with the bad eye says.

We put our masks back on, and while I start the sequence to unlock the Outside door, Peter has everyone run through the checklist to make sure their rebreathers are properly sealed.

"Ready?" I ask.

"Yes," Peter says and helps me spin the valve wheel to open the heavy outer door.

We stare out into the downpour.

He takes my hand as the others crowd around, all of us scared and anxious.

But alive.

CHAPTER 37

Diego: The Long and Winding Road

With the sun low in a sky full of snow clouds, we get off the freeway and roll into a small town just inside the border of Colorado.

Five days ago, when we broke out of C-Bay, we didn't slow down until the low-fuel light came on 171 miles later. The whole time, we were expecting to see that black SUV on our tail. We decided to stay off the main freeways, but we both still got sore necks from looking over our shoulders. But either Dave told his men not to come after us, or they guessed wrong about which route we'd take because they never caught up.

Once we passed the 250-mile mark, Bella relaxed a little. She said Dave's militia wouldn't risk running out of gas that far away from C-Bay and would turn back.

It would seem she was right.

The morning of the second day, we ditched everything we didn't absolutely need, and I pumped up the trailer's tires using a canister of air we nabbed from a car parts store. Then we hit the main highway west and put the pedal to the metal, blistering along at a whopping 42 mph.

Despite our mediocre pace, we've made good progress, blowing past the halfway mark the day before yesterday.

Last night, I was thinking I'd get to the mountain with a week to spare.

Unfortunately, things didn't go as well today.

A few days ago, when we passed through St. Louis and Kansas City—places where people have been living in biodomes for the past twenty years—the area for miles around the freeway was picked clean.

No food, no gas, no nothing.

We saw piles of trash and old campfires everywhere, but Bella said scavengers sent out from the biodomes made them. I had no reason to doubt her.

Until we got to Topeka.

We planned to stop there for food and gas, but we kept coming across graffiti drawn on the freeway walls—skeletons and mass graves and bodies being dragged down to hell. Some of the drawings had warnings about "jujment day" and the "end of the wurld." We tried to toss it off as twenty-year-old Black Death Art, but we both knew it was more recent than that. To be honest, it spooked us. We felt like people were watching us, people who didn't need biosuits or rebreather masks or vaccine shots.

We didn't even slow down.

Two days of hard traveling later, we're in the middle of what Thomas Jefferson called the Great American Desert: miles and miles of rolling hills covered in cactus and tumbleweeds with nary a stream, pond, or puddle in sight. We had to use our fuel reserves to get this far, and we have less than a gallon of drinking water left. The last four hundred miles have been through arid terrain with small towns scattered few and far between. We ended up spending more time searching for supplies than driving.

As we bump down the rutty main street of an old cattle town—not a car or truck in sight—I keep my fingers crossed that we'll find both food and gas—and that the river south of here is still running. It looks like there was a fire here recently, and most of the buildings on the east side of the street are black skeletons.

Bearhart barks from the trailer, and I stop in front of the burned-out library and let him do his business.

"Who do you think started the fire?" Bella asks, sounding worried.

"Lightning," I say, pretty sure I'm right. "With all the wood construction and desert climate, this place is a tinderbox."

I let Bearhart stretch his legs for a bit, and he trots along next to us as we look for a place to settle for the night.

We manage to find a brick building surrounded by trees and a park. The sign out front says it's Eisenhower's Presidential Library, Museum & Boyhood Home, and it reminds me of Shannon and her comment about dead white guys. I give the bronze statue a salute before driving up the handicap ramp and parking the scooter and trailer behind massive stone pillars.

The double entrance doors are locked, but the ax makes short work of that problem.

While Bearhart chases birds out front, I unload the trailer, and Bella sets up camp inside the lobby. She's been keeping an inventory of our supplies, and when I finish unloading, I ask her how the food situation looks.

She hands me a sheet of paper and goes back to setting up our beds.

"Could be better," I say, "but it still beats your Soylent Green."

She doesn't reply.

I tuck the paper back in her pack. "Hey?"

She's been keeping to herself all day, and I can tell that the journey is wearing on her. She never complains, but I know it's been years since she hefted a backpack or carried heavy jugs of water or walked for miles in search of food. Even if she were twenty years younger, this would be a challenge for her, and I make a mental note to let her sleep in tomorrow morning.

"Are you feeling okay?" I ask.

"Yep," she says.

Despite her response, I know Isabel well enough to be worried by the look in her eyes.

And things are going to get worse before they get better.

I glance at her handwritten numbers.

After tonight, we'll be down to instant mashed potatoes, mushroom flavored ramen noodles, and twenty-year-old Cheez Whiz—which is Bearhart's favorite but not so much ours.

Once we finish setting up camp, Bella says she's going to rest for a bit.

"Will you be okay for an hour?" I ask. "I want to check out the river water, take a peek into a few houses, and look for cars that might still have gas in them."

She nods, looking exhausted, and then lies down on her sleeping bag.

"Want me to leave Bearhart with you?" I ask, wondering if I should give the gun to her too.

She shakes her head. "I'm just going to sleep, and I'm sure he'd rather go exploring with you."

"Okay. I'll be back in an hour or less. If something happens and you need me, set off a flare."

She rolls away from me and waves her hand. "Be careful."

"Always am." I load up the empty jugs, wait for Bearhart to jump on the trailer, and head south.

I stop and search three different houses, but I can't find any canned goods. One of the houses has a pantry full of pickle and jam jars, but I don't want to take a chance on botulism. You can't see it or taste it, and even boiling the food won't kill it.

Better safe than sorry.

I do nab a plastic-wrapped box of black tea, thirty feet of nylon rope, and a huge bag of Purina Pig Chow—which Bearhart assures me is tail-wagging good. The third house has a pickup parked in the garage, and it's full of gas.

"Yes!"

Bearhart nearly bowls me over in his attempt to see what's so exciting.

I fill up the scooter and top off our reserves while he goes back to sniffing around for food. As I'm screwing on the gas can lid, he barks.

It turns out to be a family-size box of Twinkies—all of which are desiccated and covered in dark green mold.

"So much for the old adage that those things have a twenty-year shelf life," I say and rub his ears. "But good work finding them, buddy!"

He barks again.

There's an unopened jar of honey on the top shelf of the pantry. Honey is one of the few things that lasts pretty much forever. I pull it down, grab a couple of coffee mugs from a rack in the kitchen, and take the stuff back to the scooter.

We get back on and drive over to what the sign says is the Ute Hill River. Where I come from, it would barely qualify as a drip from a leaky pipe.

There's enough water to fill the jugs, but not much hope for any fish bigger than guppies.

Thirty minutes after leaving Eisenhower's hangout, I come back with a full tank of gas, four gallons of fresh water, tea, honey, and a wet mutt.

I'm thinking that tomorrow I'll let Bella rest for the day while I scavenge for food.

When I suggest that to her, she doesn't protest—which surprises me. Up until today, she's been pressing me to keep moving, insisting that we get up early and ride until sundown.

Now I'm wondering if I should have listened to my own instincts and taken things a bit slower.

I sit down next to her, resting my hand on her shoulder. "Is everything okay, Isabella?"

She looks over at me, her eyes hiding something, and I resist the urge to put my arms around her.

"I'm fine," she says, and looks away. "Thanks for getting the water. If you get a fire started, I'll put together something to eat."

I nod and get up, letting it go.

Maybe she is just tired. Hell, I'm pretty damn tired myself.

Out in the park, I collect wood and start a fire next to Eisenhower's statue. There's a stone bench facing the monument, and I figure it's as good a place as any to sit and eat.

Bearhart manages to catch a bird and make a huge mess of it while I'm heating up dinner.

By the time he's down to something edible, he's got feathers all over himself—including a few stuck on his nose and eyelashes—and I have to laugh.

But as the light fades and the snow clouds settle in, silence descends, and a morbid melancholy falls over me.

It feels as though Isabella and I are the last woman and man alive.

How the hell did it come to this? How did the human race fuck up this bad?

Only an hour ago, things seemed almost normal. There

were birds in the trees and a dog running around on the lawn. It was like we weren't barreling headlong toward the end of mankind.

If you run out on these people before they find the vaccine, where does that leave them?

Dead.

Mierda.

Bella brings me a sweater, and we sit down in front of the fire to enjoy our last cans of chicken, applesauce, and baked beans—Bearhart with his paws around a big bowl of Pig Chow.

We eat in silence, wintery darkness descending around us, safe—for now—inside the warm circle of firelight.

Precisely at seven, I give Bella her evening shot of bio-techs. Her thigh is covered in red welts from the previous shots, and I try to be as gentle as I can—but I can still see her grimace with pain when the needle breaks her skin. I give her a minute to make sure she's okay, and then she helps me give a shot to Bearhart. He doesn't like being held still, but he doesn't seem to mind them as much as she does.

At least I don't have to worry about them dying from Doomsday. Even if we continue traveling at the paltry rate we managed today, there's plenty of vaccine to last until we reach the Magic Kingdom.

As long as nothing goes wrong.

"More tea?" I ask.

"Please."

I get up, put more wood on the fire, and set water to boil.

"Tell me about her," Bella says as we watch Bearhart lick our dishes. "My parallel in your world."

It's still above freezing but getting cold now that the sun's down. "Okay," I say and grab a blanket from inside, sit back down next to her, and wrap it around both of us.

She snuggles against me, her face reflecting the firelight.

"What would you like to know?" I ask.

"Why you're here with me—instead of there with her?" She turns to me, her eyes taking in my face and hair and chest. It's a very intimate look, and it makes my heart beat a little faster.

"It's complicated," I say and kick an ember back into the fire.

"I have all night."

I smile, not looking at her. "If I didn't know better, I'd say that was a proposition, Dr. Sanborn."

"Perhaps you're right."

She's an older, more fragile version of Isabel, and in that moment, I realize that I love her too. Not in a rip your clothes off sort of way, but something much deeper and enduring. I want her to be happy. I want her to find James and believe that everything is going to turn out fine.

"He's just like you," she says. "James. I know that sounds cliché, but it's true."

I stare into her eyes for a moment. "I know *exactly* what you mean."

She lifts my palm, stroking the back of my hand with her fingertips. "It was easier to be around you back when I was still angry at you—although to be honest, that was no picnic either."

"Love is telling someone to go to hell..." I say, wondering if she's struggling with her emotions as much as I am, "and worrying if they'll get there safely."

She laughs for the first time in days.

"Let me get the tea," I say and pull my hand gently out of hers.

"Why don't you like to talk about her?" she asks, watching me work. "Or does that only happen when you're around me?"

I use a potholder to pull the boiling water off the fire

and then pour it into our cups. Bearhart, who's been chewing on a stick, gets up and lies down by Bella's feet, bringing nature's chew toy with him. I put the old teabags back into the mugs and offer one to her.

"Thank you," she says and reaches down to pet Bearhart. "You don't have to answer that." She shrugs, still stroking the dog. "I don't doubt that both you and James did everything in your power to stay with... us. I guess it's hard to let go of the possibilities, all the what-ifs that spring up when things don't turn out the way you had hoped."

I sit down next to her, our breath visible in the frosty air. She scoots closer to me, pulling the blanket back around my shoulders. "Does she know where you are?"

I shake my head. "It's been two years since I kissed her, held her in my arms."

"It's been twenty-eight years for James and me."

I rub my eyes with my hand. "Not a day goes by, I don't wonder what I could have done differently, Isabella—done better. And when I first peered into another world, it made me question if I'd ever get it right. In any universe."

"You mean *we*," she says, placing her hand on my thigh. "Made you question if *we* ever get it right."

I pick up her hand and kiss it, taking strength from the connection between us, a connection that defies both space and time.

"When we're together," I say, "there's this feeling that things are as they should be—that the vast and indifferent universes spinning uncontrollably around us are somehow... good."

"Yes."

We sit in silence, watching the fire.

"I want you to tell him something," she says.

"Tell who?" I ask, turning toward her.

"James, of course." She tips her head to the side, resting

it on my shoulder. "In case I don't make it."

"What are you talking about, Isabella? I know we had some issues today, but we should be there in a couple of days."

She looks up at me, her eyes glossy. "I have cancer, Diego. I've known about it for months, but I thought I had... more time."

"That can't be!" I say, my throat tight. "That red-haired kid looked in all the timelines, and he didn't say anything about—"

"I'm dying," she says like she has a headache and needs an aspirin. "A few years ago, it might have been treatable, but no one has a working linac machine anymore." She pulls a bottle of pills out of her coat pocket. "I've been taking these for the pain, but soon they won't be enough. Perhaps they aren't already."

I stare at her, unable to speak.

"I need you to tell James that I—"

"No!" I say, anger giving me strength. "You tell him yourself, Isabella. There are medical facilities inside that mountain. The best this world has to offer. You can bet they have whatever machine you need for treatment. But if three days is too long for you to wait, then I'll get you there tomorrow."

She narrows her eyes. "What are you talking about? We still have two hundred miles to go."

"I'll rig up the trailer so that you and Bearhart can ride on it, and I'll drive straight through to Warm Springs tomorrow. We have enough gas and water, and I'll give you a spoon to use in that honey. Hell, I can eat when we get there."

She starts to protest, but I don't give her a chance to get started.

"This time, hun, I'm going to save you."

CHAPTER 38

Lani: Gator Aid

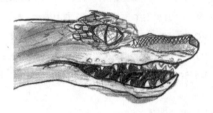

At first light, I crawl out of my sleeping bag, put on my shoes, and make my way out of the truck-stop convenience store. Madders is snoring in the environment tent we put up last night, and I do my best not to wake him. Between the Bub's evacuation, the work inside the Magic Kingdom, and now the hard traveling, he's looking a bit worse for wear—but now I'm keeping a closer watch on him.

Despite his brush with death, he has insisted on keeping his promise to me, and I'm grateful for that.

The day after they restored the power in the Magic Kingdom, Madders and I climbed into a jeep, drove down the mountainside, and flew off to rescue Shannon.

Surviving Outside is tough at the best of times, let alone during winter—which is why we flew south to start. It's our fourth day of travel, and we're somewhere northwest of the

Ozarks—about halfway to Catersville. This whole area is swampy and crawling with alligators—which makes takeoffs and landings dicey—but so far, they seem to be afraid of the engine noise.

Our progress has been slower than I'd hoped due to the difficulty finding fuel—and because Madders insists that we err on the side of caution. We've been stopping for the night while there's still half a tank of fuel—in case we need to get out in a hurry.

Madders says there's an old military base in Memphis with plenty of fuel. We're headed there next. From Memphis it should take less than an hour to fly to Catersville.

That's when the fun starts.

We've fallen into a routine. At night, I erect the environment tent inside whatever closed-off building we can find—hopefully close to food and gas. During the day, I go in search of gasoline and whatever other supplies I can find. Then we fly until we reach half full, find a safe place to set down, and pitch camp.

Slowly but surely we've been making our way toward Shannon, flying a few hundred miles a day.

The first night, Madders insisted on going with me on the foraging trip, but with his medical concerns and advanced age, it quickly became apparent that it would be better for me to go alone. He keeps telling me he's fine, but I see him struggling to climb over wreckage and breathing hard when we have to go up stairs. I told him he was too valuable to risk having another stroke and insisted that he stay with the plane and our gear. Now he spends his downtime charting our course, inventorying the items I bring back, and keeping the plane in top condition.

Before I head out for the morning's fuel run, I make some hot tea, grab a stale granola bar from a box in the back of the plane, and power up the ham radio. Madders insists that Shannon knows how to use a shortwave radio—and that she'll figure out a way to find one and use it.

With the sun coming up in the east, I put on the headset and start scanning the bands.

"Shannon," I say, "if you're out there, this is Mom. I'm on my way to get you. Are you there, baby?"

I wait for a few minutes and then try the hail again on a different band. After the fifth attempt, I shut off the power, finish my tea, and put everything back in the plane.

When I go back inside to get my scavenging gear, Madders is just getting up.

I wave good morning and make sure he has enough food inside for breakfast. Then I grab my things and start wheeling the fuel container down the highway toward an overpass covered with abandoned cars. The bridge looks golden in the first rays of light.

A hawk calls from the thick woods to my left, but I don't see anything move. The swampy lake on my right is still and silent in the early morning chill.

I climb up the embankment of the overpass, happy to be on higher ground and out of the shadows, and start checking cars. I pry open the fuel tank cover on a white sedan and unscrew the gas cap.

The odor of gasoline fills my nose.

Bingo.

I set down the crowbar and pick up the stick, glancing through the window as I stand back up—and let out a gasp.

There's a skull staring up at me—its straight, white teeth smiling even in death.

"Oka fefe!"

The back seat of the car is littered with disintegrated clothing and child-sized bones.

Images of frightened people trapped outside the Bub flood in, and I wrestle down panic.

They've been dead for decades, Lani. Let it go.

I take a deep breath and return to the task at hand.

I feed the stick into the dark opening, jiggling it around so that it will make a noise when it hits the gas. I keep pushing until the stake won't go any farther and then pull it back out.

The wood is bone-dry.

"Damn it." I kick the bumper and then grab my toe in pain, hoping I didn't break anything.

There's a loud hiss—almost a snarl—on the other side of the car. I vault up onto the car's trunk and crawl onto the roof, my heart pounding in my throat.

The hiss turns into a low-pitched growl, and although I've never heard that animal noise before, it fills me with primal fear.

Whatever is making that sound killed a lot of your ancestors.

From up here I can see the east-facing slope of the overpass, brilliant gold in the first rays of sunlight.

Every inch of it is covered with sleeping alligators.

And one of the largest reptilian monsters I've ever seen is on the overpass next to the car. He's a good three feet longer than the sedan and does not seem to have received the memo about running away from people.

He's probably never seen a human before, you lolo.

I bang the stick against the side of the car, trying to scare him away, and the growl turns into a roar. Scores of alligators bolt toward the murky water, but the huge one next to me stands his ground, thrashing his tail and bellowing.

I poke him hard in the back with the stick, and he wheels around, grabbing it with his jaws and ripping it out of my hands.

Oka fefe. Getting killed won't help Shannon. Just get back to the plane.

I vault onto the hood of the sedan and jump over to the

next car, thinking I'll lead him away from my stuff, and then circle back around to grab it.

It sort of works.

He follows along next to me, roaring and snapping his jaws and trying to get up on the cars.

You should have brought the gun.

I continue jumping across the sea of automobiles until I get to a full-size truck with sandbags stacked in the back. The alligator stays with me, growling and biting into the already-flat truck tires when I stop moving. I attempt to pick up one of the heavy sacks to drop on the gator, but the cloth bag disintegrates in my hands, spilling sand all over me and the truck bed. I pick up a second bag with similar results, and then grab a handful of sand and pelt the monster in frustration.

The gator roars and throws himself up against the side of the truck, pushing the huge vehicle up on two tires and knocking me back against the side wall.

I scream as the reptile tries to grab on with his front claws, scraping the paint off as he attempts to find purchase, his huge jaws swinging back and forth a couple feet away from me. If he manages to pull himself up into the truck bed, he'll kill me.

I consider trying to make a run for it, but I don't have any idea how fast giant, angry alligators can move.

And I don't think I want to find out.

I try the driver's door and when it opens in my hand, I dive into the cab and then slam the door shut.

Thank Pele *there aren't any bones in here.*

I look out the passenger window just as the gator falls sideways across the glass, his white, scaly belly leaving a swath of muck on the window. I sit there in the front cab, trying not to hyperventilate, his low growl coming through the rusted floorboards a foot away from me.

Find something heavy to throw at him.

I check, and the glove compartment is locked. I search under the seat—forcing out images of coiled snakes and hairy spiders.

Nothing.

I slide the passenger seat forward and spy a large jack behind it. I drag it out, guessing that it weighs twenty-five pounds easy.

I slide over and peer out. The gator is resting next to the door, keeping up a low growl. I consider rolling down the window and dropping the jack on him, but the windows are electric and the truck battery is long gone. I don't think opening the passenger door would be a particularly good idea. I hoist the jack under one arm and climb back out of the driver's side into the truck bed, struggling to hang on to the unwieldy tool.

The gator doesn't move.

I set the jack on the roof of the cab and slide up next to it on my belly. I peek down at the alligator, feeling a pang of guilt as I hoist the heavy steel jack over his head and drop it.

It hits him on the head and then bounces loudly onto the concrete.

He lets out a thunderous roar and then runs faster than any human down the embankment toward the water. A moment later, he dives into the lake and disappears, the ripples splashing against the bank the only sound.

I go back to look for my rubber hose, checking to make sure I'm alone before climbing down onto the pavement. There are no alligators in sight.

I try ten more cars, each filled with bones, each with the same result: no gas. Either the cars were still idling when the people in them died, or it's been too long for the tank to hold a seal.

I check again for gators and then lean against the side of

a small truck. The back is full of junk: camping gear, a bicycle with flat tires, a case of water bottles that have all burst, a rusted ax, and four small canisters of propane—which are all empty.

Then it hits me, and I smile. "A gas can."

If I were trying to escape by car, I'd fill up my tank and take as much as I could carry in a can. I check the truck bed and then go back through the cars, looking carefully into each. After twenty-odd attempts, I hit pay dirt: There's a huge, black SUV with four large gas cans in the back.

Good thing this guy didn't get rear-ended.

I try to open the hatch, but it's locked. I check the other doors. All locked. I try to pry the back door open with my crowbar, but it's impossible to get any leverage between the door and the bumper. I jab the window as hard as I can, but my small crowbar just bounces off.

"Damn it."

I kick one of the flat tires, and then jog back to the pickup and grab the ax out of the back. I weave back through the cars to the SUV, checking for gators twice, and then swing the ax as hard as I can against the back window. The glass cracks, and after a couple more whacks, it falls as a sheet into the back.

The gas cans look like military surplus—dark green metal canisters with heavy duty handles. I pick up the first one and curse.

It's empty, but on closer inspection, I can see that the cap isn't sealed properly.

I pick up the next can, and then let out a whoop.

It's too heavy to lift. And so are the other two.

Still unable to believe my luck, I snap open the lid and take a sniff, afraid it might be water.

Twenty-year-old gasoline fumes fill my nostrils, and I laugh—and then cough.

I stick my rubber hose in and start siphoning the gas into my 25-gallon tank with wheels. It takes me two trips to unload all the gas.

While Madders filters the gasoline using an old tube sock, I try to raise Shannon on the radio again to no avail. Then I help him pour the fuel into the wing, load everything into the plane, and we take off into a cloudless blue sky.

That evening, we make camp less than a hundred miles west of Catersville.

Prior to bed, I make one last attempt to raise Shannon. There's a lot of static interference tonight. I sit for twenty minutes and wait for the sun to go down before trying again.

In the purple and orange twilight, I put the headset back on and power up the radio.

"Shannon," I say, "if you're out there, this is Mom. I'm on my way to find you. Please come in, baby. Are you there?"

I wait for ten minutes and then try again.

"Lord in heaven," an old woman says over the radio, and I wonder if I've somehow managed to reach Catersville. Before I have a chance to ask, a voice I have been longing to hear for weeks comes on.

"Mom? Oh my God, Mom is that you?"

"Yes, baby!" I say, pressing the headphones to my ears, unable to believe what I'm hearing. "Are you okay? Where are you, Shannon?"

"I'm fine, Mom. We're near Memphis—on our way to a biodome in Texas. Everyone is using my rebreathers, Mom! They work great."

"You walked out of Catersville on foot?"

"Yeah," she says. "Those wankers were being cruel to us—so we had to leg it out of there fast."

"*Pele*, help me. How many people are with you?"

"Twenty total. And Mom?"

"Yes, baby? It's so good to hear your voice!"

"I want you to meet someone. His name is Peter, and he's my husband."

CHAPTER 39

Diego: We Don't Need Forever

It's dark by the time I drive through the open security gate and start up the road to the Magic Kingdom, the scooter managing only twenty-five on the steep mountain incline. The air is brittle, and I can see my breath as the headlight illuminates a sliver of road up ahead.

Bearhart is tucked in next to Isabella on the trailer, both of them under a pile of blankets. I'm hoping it's enough to keep her warm for a bit longer.

With the lousy roads and blowing snow, it's been a long and grueling day. We left Eisenhower's Library this morning at dawn, and after twelve exhausting hours of driving, I'm ten clicks past spent.

Thank God, we're almost home.

I flex my hands and feet, trying to keep the cramping at bay, and glance up at the brilliant display of stars.

Are you out there, mi amor, *looking up at the night sky and wondering where I am?*

I only have three days left to get back to my own world, and I don't even know if there's a working time machine inside the mountain—or the power to run it.

If someone went to the trouble to send you that note, there has to be a way to get back to her. There has to be.

Although the rational part of me knows it's nearly impossible, I cling to that thought—and drive on into the cold, dark night.

When I come around the last, steep curve and see lights along a huge gash in the mountainside, my heart beats a little faster.

The Magic Kingdom.

There's a dim glow coming from an opening in the middle of the wall. I drive across the ledge, swerving around potholes, chunks of concrete, and scattered garbage probably left by the Bub folks. I head for the illuminated tunnel, trying not to bump or disturb Isabella while praying that James comes through for us.

There's some sort of access panel flashing red at the end of the passage, but the blast door is open. I park in front of it and turn the scooter off. I spend a moment getting the circulation back in my arms and legs and then wrap a blanket around Isabella and lift her out of the trailer.

She's as light as a hummingbird, but her pulse is strong.

"Hang on, hun, we're almost home."

She smiles weakly and squeezes my hand.

Bearhart follows me into the airlock, his toenails clicking on the concrete.

I use my elbow to push the *Start* button and then collapse on a wooden chair, cradling Isabella in my lap. I'm so exhausted, I can barely keep my eyes open.

There's a soft musical bong, and the computer says,

"Welcome to the Warm Springs Complex. Commencing airlock cycle in thirty seconds. Stand by for decontamination."

I watch the huge blast door close, grateful that it's out of my hands now.

Isabella rests her head against my shoulder, her breath soft as snowflakes on my cheek. I kiss her on the forehead. "Not much longer now, Isabella."

Bearhart lies down next to us and lets out a soft whine. I glance down at him. "I'm worried about her too, buddy."

A pump starts up somewhere, and Isabella squeezes my arm. "Thank you."

I stroke the hair back from Isabella's face, hoping it's not too late to save her. In my world, the medical center had every possible machine and gadget. I can only hope it's the same here.

A male voice says, "Thank you for bringing her back to me…"

The sound startles me until I realize it's coming from a speaker in the ceiling.

"James?" Isabella says, turning her head toward his voice.

"At your service, hun. I'll have you safely inside in eight minutes."

She smiles, her eyes bright. "Oh, James. It's so good to hear your voice."

"And yours, *mi amor*. Christ, you don't know how much I've missed you."

A tear rolls down her cheek, and I wipe it away with my thumb.

"I'm sorry, Isa," James says, his words laced with torment. "I'm so sorry about everything."

"It's not your fault, James. I should have trusted you when you said we were in danger. God, I was such an idiot to believe you would kill yourself. I knew you would never do something like that." Her voice is trembling, but I don't know if it's with anger at Dave or regret for the years lost—perhaps both. "I should never have let David talk me into it."

"He didn't give you the letter, did he?" He sniffs.

"No," Isabella says letting out great heaving gasps. "But I found it last week, hidden in his safe." She shakes her head, her jaw clenched. "I hate him, James. I hate him!"

"I'm the one you should hate." He lets out a sob. "*Mierda*. All those years, you had to live believing that I killed Lucas and abandoned you and Soleil."

"I was like a selfish child, James, too angry and hurt to ask the hard questions. Even after Soleil insisted that you and Lucas were alive, I never wondered why things didn't add up. All I could think about was how you had abandoned us—but I should have known better." She presses her lips together, fighting back tears. "I should have known."

James fights to breathe, and it's like listening to a wild animal struggling to get out of a trap. I can almost hear his heart breaking. "No, Isa. No."

"David wanted me to think you had betrayed us, that you were some sort of coward. How could I have been so stupid?"

James lets out a roar of frustration. "That fucking bastard."

Isabella squeezes her eyes shut and takes a labored breath. "You should rest, *mi amor*."

"No." She sits up a little, her eyes defiant, and I recognize that look.

There's no way she's going quietly into the night.

She sighs. "I need you to know the truth."

"I do, hun."

She wipes her face. "He talked me into marrying him, James. God, he even adopted Soleil so she wouldn't have to suffer the stigma of having a father who committed suicide."

There's a loud bang, like a fist hitting a wall. "I'm going

to kill him."

"Yeah?" Isabella says. "Well, take a number."

James laughs. "I love you, Isa."

"Not as much," she says through sobs, "as I love you."

Some sort of hidden fan turns on, moving the cold air around the room, and Isabella shivers. I tuck the blanket in around her and then hold her tighter, trying to use my body to keep her warm. She lays her head on my shoulder again, snuggling against me, and I stroke her back. "We're almost through, hun, and it'll be better inside."

"Yes," James says. "It's not the Ritz Carlton, but it's warm and safe in here. I'm so glad you came."

"Me too," she says.

"I wish Lucas was here," he says, his voice trembling. "I tried to find a way to save him, Isa. Really, I did." He takes a ragged breath. "He was strong and brave to the bitter end, stronger than I was." He exhales. "Christ, I miss him."

"I miss him too," Bella says and dries her cheek on my shoulder.

"I should have found another way to keep you safe without lying to you," James says like he can't get past it. "Some other way to protect you and the kids."

"It's not important now," Bella says. "The only thing that matters is that you're alive. That you waited for me."

"I love you, hun... More than... life itself." He's sobbing so much that it's difficult to understand him. "The only thing that kept me alive all those years... was the hope that you and Soleil... were out there somewhere."

"Oh, James," Bella says. "Your daughter's a most amazing woman—smart, vivacious, caring. Every time I look at her, she reminds me of you. And even when I made things difficult for her, she held fast to her faith in you."

"I'm so grateful you both made it Inside," James says. "But I can't think about it without getting angry—not being able to watch her grow up, meet her first boyfriend, see her graduate from college."

"You'd have been so proud of her, James. I know I was."

We hear him blow his nose. "*Mierda*, I've been a basket case since I found out you're alive."

"Ditto," she says, crying and smiling at the same time.

There's a harsh beep, like the sound of a smoke detector triggering, and a few seconds later it stops.

"There's a goddamn helicopter out there," James says.

"A helicopter?" I say. "Dave?"

"Well, he's not in here," James says. "After I let him chat with the access computer for an hour, he gave up and took the trucks back to the Bub. To be honest, I don't think he wanted to be around when the two of you arrived."

"Smartest decision he's ever made," I say.

"*Mierda*," James says. "It's landing right out front."

"Who's flying it?" Bella asks.

"Some guy without a suit or mask."

"Maybe he's using the temporary vaccine?" I say, trying to fit the pieces together.

"He's the spitting image of that Civil War idiot, what's-his-name…"

"Custer," I say.

"Yeah. Zow-wee, that's some mustache he's sporting."

"Custer's one of Dave's minions," I say. "I wouldn't trust him as far as I can throw him."

"Gotcha. There's a woman with him too—also without protective gear."

"It would seem this mountain is a very popular tourist destination," I say. "Maybe you should sell tickets."

"And ruin the solitude?" James says. "I'd have to be nuts."

We hear the computer announcement out in the tunnel, followed by "Place your hand on the biometric panel and state your full name."

"Daddy?" a woman says. "Are you in there?"

We hears James's sharp intake of breath. "Soleil? *Mierda*, it's good to see you! Give me a minute, and I'll let you in."

"Have you heard from Mom?" she says. "I'm so worried about her. She left C-Bay—"

"She's in the airlock, sunshine," James says, a smile in his voice. "She and Diego just arrived. They rode all the way out here on a scooter—the one right beside you—but she's fine now. In another minute or two, she'll be inside."

"Dad," Soleil says, "she's not fine. She has cancer. I found out yesterday."

The flashing *Virus Detected* light goes from red to orange.

"Cancer?" James clears his throat. "Isa? Is that right?"

She looks up at me, her eyes pleading, and I nod.

"Yes," she says and shuts her eyes, "but we don't need forever."

"Not now," James says, his voice breaking down again. "Not after all this time. Just... fuck."

"I found your medical records, Mom," Soleil says. "You should have told me."

"What purpose would it have served, Sol? There was nothing to be done."

"Oh, Mom!" Soleil sounds like she's crying too.

There's a click, and the LED light on the speaker goes off.

We sit in silence, the virus detector green, and watch the timer count down from thirty. There's another melodic bong and the inside door slides open.

My sixty-year-old twin walks in breathing hard, his eyes red and swollen.

"James," Bella says and tries to stand.

He rushes over and takes her in his arms.

And something in this universe is right again.

∞

I give them a few minutes together, and then James calls me into the Control Room.

Bella is asleep in his arms, and I can see Soleil and Custer standing in the airlock, waiting for the all clear.

Lucy knocks softly and steps in.

I put my finger to my lips and then give her a big hug.

"Lordy, Lordy," she says, straightening the Air Force cap she's wearing. "It's good to see you, Mr. C—but you sure could use a shower."

I smile. "I'm looking forward to it."

She turns to James. "There's a gurney in the hallway, James. If you want to put her on it, I'll take her down to the hospital and get an IV started. Dr. Nadales is one of the best doctors in the world, and the facilities here are unbelievable. Don't you fret, now. It's in God's hands."

James lifts Isabella up, sets her gently on the bed, and then covers her with another blanket. "I'll be down as soon as Soleil comes in, Lucy."

She squeezes his arm and then wheels Isabella away from him.

He stands there, staring into the empty hallway for half a minute.

"So all the Bub folks are here?" I ask.

"Yep," he says. "Once we got the CO_2 cleared out, everyone moved downstairs."

"And Shannon?" I say. "Did Dave get her out of Catersville?"

"No," James says. "That overconfident prick pissed off their new head honcho, and Catersville sent out the big guns to show him who's boss. According to Ted—he's the radio operator at C-Bay—Dave skedaddled out of there with his tail between his legs faster than you can say bait and switch."

"*Mierda.*"

"And when he got back to C-Bay," James says, "he tried to blame the whole thing on Shannon. Said she got into some sort of trouble with the law—so it's not his fault."

"Shannon? *Mierda*, she's as close to an angel as it gets. He probably just fucked it up and—"

"—needed someone to blame it on," James finishes for me.

I clap him on the shoulder. "Goddamn, it's nice to find someone else who thinks Kirk is a prick."

He laughs, but I can feel the rage behind it.

"Do you know anything about a time machine?" I say. "A computer with wires attached to a barrel-sized capacitor and a big metal coffin. Might be in the bowling alley?"

"Game room, actually. Lucas and I tried to use it hundreds of times before the carbon dioxide forced us out of there. We could never get past the lock screen."

I raise an eyebrow.

"It's some sort of riddle about a man who's able to see the future but surrounded by cretins who don't believe him."

"Woman," I say. "Cassandra. She worked on the project—insisted that the targeting was off, but no one ever listened to her."

"I'll show you how to power it up first thing in the morning," he says. "Right now, let's go meet my daughter."

CHAPTER 40

Shannon: Smoke and Mirrors

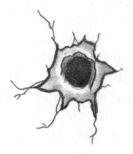

I set down my backpack and watch Peter light a small campfire of dry tree branches and some paper scraps from his pack. There's a breeze blowing out of the east. So he's arranged the wood next to a large boulder, using it as a windbreak.

Now that we've stopped hiking, I'm getting cold. I pull my sweater up around my neck and rub my hands together. The sun is low in the sky and, with the rain last night, the air is cold and damp.

I glance at the long, straight line of asphalt running next to us and then scan the treetops to the west.

There's no sign of the plane.

"Grab me ten or twelve of those big leaves?" he says, pointing to a huge tree. "Just the green ones, please."

I do as he asks, water droplets raining down on me as

I tear the wet leaves off the low-hanging branches. When I bring them back, the fire is blazing. I drop the leaves next to the boulder and move closer to the flames, warming my hands and face.

He tosses two or three leaves on the fire, turning the heat into useless smoke.

"What are you doing?" I ask, now cold *and* wet.

"Making smoke."

I give him a funny look.

"So the plane can find us." He stands up. "As soon as they spot it, I'll put it out."

Peter may not have read many books, but he knows a lot about how to survive—way more than I do.

"Aren't you worried someone else might see the smoke?" I ask, wrapping my arms around myself to stay warm.

"Of course I am." He walks over, stands behind me, and puts his arms around me. "But we're six days out from Catersville, and I figure even if the men did manage to open the bulkheads, retrieve their biosuits, and get out through an airlock, they won't know which way we went."

I lean back against his chest, basking in his warmth.

"But I could be wrong about the men following us," Peter says, his cheek touching my temple. "That's why I made you hike for an hour this morning—so we'd be away from the campsite."

Last night, Peter told me he wanted to leave camp early, so I said my goodbyes before bed. I told Gran that I'd talk to Mr. Kirk and ask him to send help—and that I'd tell him about the terrible conditions at Catersville and see if he would offer asylum to the women and children still imprisoned there.

When Peter woke me up before dawn, I thought it was so we'd have plenty of time to find a makeshift runway. But just like always, he's one step ahead of me.

I shade my eyes and search the sky again.

It's full of scattered, high clouds and, with the breeze out of the east, it's perfect flying weather. There's still no sign of the plane, only bazillions of blackbirds flitting above the trees—like in that creepy old horror movie where the birds take over the world.

I shiver and snuggle against Peter.

We stand there in silence for a few minutes, watching the smoke rise.

Then he lets go of me and puts more wood on the fire.

After it catches, he tosses on even more leaves.

I wait for him to come put his arms back around me, but he doesn't. He just stands there with his hands in his pockets, staring at the smoke.

"What are you thinking?" I finally ask.

He shakes his head.

"Peter?"

He was super quiet last night, and when I asked him what was wrong, he got this agitated look in his eyes and said he didn't want to talk about it.

Even now, his dismissal makes my chest tight.

"I know you thought we had more time," I say, "but I told you my mom would come get me."

He nods, keeping his eyes on the fire.

"You have to understand that Mr. Kirk needs the plane back, Peter. It would be selfish to expect them to wait around while you… decide."

I watch him stir up the coals with a stick.

"Are you coming with me, Peter?"

He gets that look in his eyes again. "I can't abandon Gran and the other women."

I keep my gaze on the fire. "She's the one who knows which berries to eat and where to dig for potatoes. And I know she can't use a bow, but some of the other women are already better than I am."

"Yeah," he says, kicking one of the burnt logs so it collapses into the coals.

"And like you said, it's been almost a week, and we haven't seen any signs of the men—or anyone else."

He rubs his hand across the back of his neck but doesn't respond.

"And I know there are tons of birds to worry about, but the mammals are all dead, Peter. All the bears and mountain lions and wolves were killed by Doomsday. I'm not saying it's safe, but don't you think if the Others could survive for years in the Wilds without you, they could last for a couple more weeks Outside? Gran says we're nearly halfway to Texas already… and they have the van to carry the heavy stuff… and plenty of batteries… and even if they ran out, they all know how to pump the tents up by hand."

"I don't want to talk about it, Shannon, okay?"

I stamp my foot and groan. "I hate it when you get like this." I pick up a stick and hurl it into the fire. "It's like you're angry inside, and instead of talking to me, you push me away. So why don't you just say it?" I force myself to look at him. "You don't want to be with me anymore."

"Of course I want to be with you." He looks up at me, the muscles in his neck standing out. "Why would you say something like that?"

"Because it's true."

He shakes his head, his eyes downcast.

"What are you scared of?"

He kicks a rock into the fire.

"What is it, Peter?"

"I'm afraid of losing you."

I stare at him, at a loss for words.

He tosses another leaf on the fire. "I'm not coming with you."

I feel like the bottom just fell out of my world. "That doesn't make any sense, Peter. I'm going back with Mom and Madders, and if you decide to stay here, you'll be choosing to lose me."

"I'll lose you either way, Shannon." He meets my gaze. "But if I stay here, I won't have to watch it happen. I won't have to see you fall in love with some other boy who's whip-smart and has read lots of books and knows how to make you laugh—and doesn't keep getting angry inside."

"I didn't mean it like that, Peter. I meant it like I... I want to know what you're thinking. I want you to trust me."

"Yeah, well, I do trust you, but sometimes I need to be alone. That's just the way I am."

I stand there, staring at the leaf-choked fire, feeling all the happiness drain out of me.

A month ago, I would have given anything to be rescued, but now I'm not so sure I want to go back to my old life—especially if it means being stuck somewhere with Mom treating me like a child.

Peter takes something out of his back pocket and offers it to me. "I thought maybe you'd want to take this with you. To remember me."

I glance at the book of poems and then up into his eyes. "So you're going to let me go?"

He nods, still holding out the book.

"Fine." I jerk it out of his hand and stick it inside my sweater.

He motions with his head. "Plane's here."

I whirl around and watch the Cessna flare, bounce down the old asphalt road, and roll to a stop fifty meters past us.

Peter is already dumping water on the smoky mess behind me.

Someone jumps out of the plane and starts running toward me—someone without a biosuit *or* a mask.

"Mom?" I whisper.

"Your mother's... immune?" Peter says, sounding spooked. "Mookers, Shaz, why didn't you tell me?"

"Because I didn't know," I say and start running toward her. "Mom!"

"Oh, Shannon!" She goes to hug me and then stops. "I don't want to knock your mask off, baby." She grabs my hands and squeezes them, tears streaming down her face. "It's so good to see you. I've missed you so much!"

"Me, too, Mom. I knew you'd come for me."

"Of course, I would. Are you okay, baby? Did they do anything to hurt you?"

"I'm fine, Mom. Really."

Madders turns the plane around and taxis over to us. He waves, shuts down the engine, and a minute later, hops out.

He's wearing one of our masks.

I jog over to meet him. The rebreathers seal onto your face, so it would be pretty hard to accidentally knock one off, but I'm careful anyway.

He gives me a bear hug and then holds me by my shoulders, looking me over. "Your mother told me how you escaped that sodding place. I'm mighty proud of you, Shenanigans."

I give him a thumbs up, feeling almost silly about it now. "Identify the problem, engineer a fix, and Bob's your uncle."

"That's my girl!"

"It was mostly Peter's doing," I say, "but I did show him how to make the masks." I give him another hug. "Thanks for coming back."

He nods, looking a little choked up.

"Come on," I say and take his hand. "I want you to meet him."

Mom is helping Peter put out the fire.

After I introduce Madders, the two guys shake hands,

and then Madders puts his arm around me.

"Thanks for taking care of Shannon for us," he says to Peter. He glances at the bow Peter always has slung over his shoulder. "I hear you put Robin Hood to shame."

Peter nods, half-smiling, and turns to me, his eyes dark. *He doesn't know who Robin Hood is.*

Out of the corner of my eye, I see Mom give me a knowing nod.

"Excuse me for a minute," Madders says. "I'm going to top off the fuel and check on the flaps. They didn't want to come down when we landed, and I want to make sure it's not something serious." He gives me another squeeze and then turns to Peter. "Nice to meet you, son. I'm looking forward to hearing more about your adventures on the way home."

"He's not coming with us," Mom says like it's the best thing since sandwich bread.

Madders glances at me and I nod, my lips pressed together so I don't cry.

"Well," he says and shrugs. "I guess it's up to Shannon—and Peter." He releases me. "Go ahead and load your stuff into the plane. I should have her ready to take off in a few minutes."

I watch Madders walk away and then give Peter a fierce look, angry that he told Mom—and even angrier that Mom's so happy about it...

I'm crushed that Peter doesn't want to come with me.

"I'll help you load your stuff," Peter says and turns away.

"I can do it myself." I hurry over and pick up my pack.

"I know it's hard right now, Shannon," Mom calls after me. "But it's for the best. You're too young—both of you—and even though you can't see it right now, it won't end well. Soon enough you'll have a crush on some other boy, and Peter will be left high and dry. He didn't grow up in the same world you did, Shannon, and now that the two of you have gone and upset Catersville—Mr. Kirk says Peter's wanted for murder—we can't just drop him off on their front step when you get bored with him."

I stop and turn around, facing down my mother. "Is that what happened between you and my father? You got bored with him? But instead of crushing on 'some other boy,' you made the mistake of getting pregnant, and that ruined your life!"

She takes a step back, looking horrified. "Of course not!"

"Well it sure sounds that way, Mom." I lift up my backpack and sling it over one shoulder.

"No, Shannon. I never regretted having you, not for one moment." She takes a step toward me, holding out her arms. "I love you more than anything in the world, baby. I just wish things had... turned out differently between your father and me."

I walk back to her, standing up for myself for the first time in my life. "So that's why you won't tell me who he is? And why you never got married? And why you won't admit that you still love him? Were *you* too young to fall in love, Mom?"

She shuts her eyes and then covers her face with her hands.

"If you had it all over," I ask, "wouldn't you try a little harder to make it work with my father?"

She swallows. "Shannon, I..."

I shake my head. "I love you, Mom, and I love Madders too." I take a deep breath, steeling my courage, and look at the man who's captured my heart. "But I love Peter more."

He stands there with his mouth stuck open.

"He always expects the best of me," I say. "When I'm with him, I feel strong and happy, more like the person I *want* to be. I know we don't come from the same background, but that's a strength, not a weakness. He doesn't need to know about ancient history and all the classics because... well, because I already do. Every day I spend with him, I learn something new, something more important than the name of that dead white guy who lived in Sherwood Forest."

Mom's eyes get really big.

"Peter's the best thing that's ever happened to me, Mom. If he's not going, then I'm not going either." I set down my pack. "Period. End of conversation."

Mom crosses her arms—and then uncrosses them again.

"Holy shit," Peter says, swearing for the first time, in like, forever.

Mom turns on her heel and addresses him in her sternest doctor voice. "I suggest you hurry and get your things packed, young man—assuming you feel the same way about my daughter?"

He gulps and turns to me. "Do you really mean that, Shannon? The part about me making you strong and happy?"

I nod. "Sometimes you can be infuriating, Peter, but I'd rather die than live without you."

"No need to overdo it," Mom says. "We get the point. Peter?"

"I packed everything last night, ma'am." He glances at me, looking sheepish. "Just in case."

"Well..." Mom says, still recovering. "Good. Put it in the plane."

Peter takes off his bow and ties it onto his backpack and then looks over at me. "Once we get settled, Shannon, maybe we could invite Gran and all the women..." He lets go of his pack, leaning it against the boulder, and gets up. He walks in front of Mom, over to me, and takes my hand.

I glance back and forth between his eyes, wondering what's going on.

And then he gets down on one knee.

"Oh, my God, Peter, what are you doing?" I can feel my

face getting hot.

"Will you marry me, Shannon?"

I stare at him—my heart stuck in my throat.

"I mean properly this time."

I pull him up to his feet and throw my arms around his neck and kiss him right there in front of Mom. "Yes!"

"Flee fornication! He that committeth fornication sinneth against his own body!"

Peter jerks around as someone in a battered biosuit walks out of the woods, a rifle aimed at us.

"I will not have mercy upon her children, for they be the children of whoredoms."

"The Giver," Peter whispers and runs for his bow.

The woman fires the rifle, knocking Peter's backpack down into the dirt. "You touch that bow, boy, and I'll show you God's wrath. They told me what you done to the Righteous, and I intend to see you pay for it."

Madders comes out from behind the airplane, hands in the air, another biosuit holding a gun to his back.

"All we want is the boy," the man says, shoving Madders up next to me. "That girl's more trouble than she's worth. You let us take Peter, and the rest of you can hop in that fancy airplane of yours and fly back to wherever you came from."

Peter turns. "Grizzly?"

"He's to be tried for murder," the Giver of the Law says. "And stoned to death for his sins."

"No!" I rush toward Peter, but Madders grabs my arm and pulls me back, holding me so I can't get away.

"Stoned to death?" Mom says. "Is this some sort of joke?"

The Giver points the rifle at Mom. "Let your women keep silence in the presence of God's messenger."

"Take the boy and go," Madders says, "but the girl belongs to us."

"I don't belong to anyone!" I twist out of his grip and

rush over to Peter, holding on to him as tightly as I can.

"Shannon, no." He tries to push me away. "Go with your mother."

I shake my head, refusing to let go.

"On the wicked," the Giver says, aiming the rifle at Peter and me, "He shall rain fire and brimstone. This shall be *their* lot."

Grizzly moves closer to us, keeping his gun trained on Madders, and turns his head toward the Giver. "You said we'd leave the girl."

"Changed my mind," the woman says, speaking in her regular voice now. "Besides, she's the one who started this whole mess." She motions with her gun. "Let's go, you two." She glances over at Mom. "And just so's you know, if I see anyone following us, I'll shoot the girl first."

Madders brings his hands up to his head, his eyelids fluttering, and then collapses onto his knees.

And then everything happens at once.

"Run!" Peter shouts and lunges for Grizzly's gun. The old man looks up at him, his eyes wide, but he doesn't pull the trigger. Peter yanks the gun out of his hand and pushes him out of the way.

The Giver's rifle discharges, and Peter shoves me sideways and drops to the ground.

I dive behind the rock and scramble toward his pack. I try to wrench his bow off, but my hands are like flippers, and it won't come loose.

A moment later, Mom is beside me. She grabs an arrow out of Peter's pack and jabs it into Grizzly's suit, poking a hole in the leg.

Grizzly's breach alarm goes off as Peter rolls away from him and fires the handgun at the Giver—and I realize that Peter's shirt is covered in blood.

"No!" I scramble across the dirt toward him.

The Giver starts lumbering back into the woods, but her biosuit is big and bulky, and it's like she's moving in slow motion.

There's another gunshot, but this time it comes from Madders.

He's still on his knees in the dirt, one hand clutching his head and the other holding his gun. The Giver falls to the ground, and a few seconds later, we hear her breach alarm sound.

Mom rushes over and takes the gun, holding it on Grizzly. "Put a patch on your suit."

He shakes his head. "Don't have no more." He kneels down next to Peter. "I wasn't going to let them hurt you, son. I wasn't."

"There's a spare rebreather in the plane!" Mom says, her eyes wild. "And bring my medical bag!"

Peter looks up at Grizzly, the anger gone from his face. "Guess we found a way outta that collapsed coal mine after all."

The old man nods.

"Shannon!" Mom shouts—and I finally realize she's talking to me. "Get the rebreather mask and my medical bag!"

I nod.

"Hurry!"

I run faster than I've ever run before.

Chapter 41

Lani: For Pete's Sake

Grizzly waves from the ground, his helmet held uselessly at his side, as Shannon accelerates past him and takes the plane up into the hazy sky.

Good thing for Shannon's masks or that old man would be dead—and it would be your fault.

My stomach lurches as the plane banks hard and struggles to gain altitude.

Madders suggested Shannon avoid flying low over the woods, and now I can see why. Hundreds of birds are taking to the air above the trees, filling the sky with a black fog.

I peek around the seat and watch Shannon fly the plane, her knuckles white from gripping the controls so hard. Her lips are a thin line of determination, and her eyes are narrowed in concentration. She's changed so much during our weeks apart that I barely recognize her.

She's a grown woman now, and it's high time you started treating her like one.

I resist the urge to ask if everything's okay.

She glances at Madders, then me, and then the boy. Her jaw seems to set even more firmly in place.

When we reach cruising altitude, Shannon locks in the GPS coordinates I gave her and sits back in the seat—but I can see that her hands are still trembling.

"Lordy!" as Lucy would say. Treating a gunshot wound and a stroke victim while bouncing around in a single-engine Cessna piloted by a teenager who's never flown a plane before and happens to be your daughter.

What next?

Shannon let's out a shaky breath. "How's he doing, Mom?"

I rest my hand on her shoulder. "As well as can be expected, baby." I see her cringe at the last word, and make a mental note to find a different pet name.

I lean forward so I can see Madders. "You hanging in there?"

He nods from the copilot's seat but doesn't open his eyes. His breathing is labored but steady.

I need to get him back inside the mountain within four hours, or it'll be too late for the tPA to help him.

We're going to be cutting it close.

I check the pressure bandage on Peter's shoulder and then adjust the pillow behind his head. I'm worried about shock, but there's not much I can do besides keep him warm and comfortable. His pulse is slow, but steady, and I thank *Pele* that the low caliber bullet didn't do any more damage.

"Shannon," I say, "when you get a chance, can you turn up the cabin heat, please? I want to make sure we don't let Peter's temperature drop too much."

"You got it, Mom." She adjusts something, and I feel the

warm air on my face. "Better?"

"Yes, baby." I chastise myself for calling her that and then redouble my efforts to make sure it doesn't happen again. "You get us safely to Colorado, Shannon, and I'll patch him up good as new."

She bites her lip, and I know she's trying not to cry. "We should be there in about three hours," she says. "How far is it from the airport to the mountain?"

"If someone meets us at the Air Force base, the drive is about forty minutes. How soon will you be able to contact the Magic Kingdom?"

"Not until we can see the mountain," she says. "Maybe twenty minutes out."

I do the math. If the Magic Kingdom has to send down a jeep, we'll have to wait for them to arrive. Add that to the ride back up the mountain, and it may be too late to give Madders the anticoagulant—assuming they even have it in the pharmacy. And a bumpy car ride isn't going to help Peter either. He's going to need blood—so we'll have to do a blood type first—and morphine so I can remove the bullet and sew him back up.

I go over the steps in my head, wishing I had another doctor to help.

"Is there any way to cut down our flight time?" I ask Shannon. "Even twenty minutes would help."

She makes an adjustment and I hear the whine of the engine change.

"I can't push the engine any harder," she says, "or we won't have enough fuel. And if I take us up higher, we'll save a little fuel, but it'll cost us time."

"Okay," I say. "Whatever you think is best. But the sooner we can raise them on the radio, the better."

The next few hours drag by, Peter's pulse weakening and Madders looking the worse for wear.

When we spot the first hint of mountains rising in the west, Shannon tries the radio, and ten minutes later, Jack's voice floods into my ears.

"They must have one whopper of an antenna," Shannon says as we wait for Dr. Nadales.

"They do," I say, remembering the hike up to the summit and the massive tower. "At least something's going our way today."

Dr. Nadales says she'll send down a military helicopter to pick us up and will have the OR ready for Peter when we arrive. In the meantime, she'll find a donor with O negative blood—a universal donor.

"No one from the Bub is O negative," I say.

"Except Diego," we say together.

"And James," she says. "I'll have someone find him."

Jack comes back on and gives Shannon a weather report. She nods, taking in the temperature and wind speed, but I can tell she's worried about landing the plane.

"What's your fuel situation, Shannon?" Jack asks.

"The gauge is on empty," she says, "but I think we still have enough to land." She swallows. "And if not, I'm right above a freeway, following it all the way in now."

I resist the urge to swear out loud, and instead check the guys' seatbelts and then my own.

When we finally see the air force base, Shannon takes the plane lower, and by the time we're lined up with the runway, we're flying just above the treetops.

When we're over the runway, Shannon struggles with a lever on the dashboard.

"Mookers! I can't get the flaps down!"

Before I have a chance to respond, the plane hits the runway hard—and then bounces back up into the air.

"Damn it!" She gives up on the flaps and wrestles the plane back down. It hits hard again and skids around to the left, sliding toward the edge of the huge runway.

"Rudder," Shannon says and manages to straighten it out, but we're still going really fast.

I hold my breath as we bounce and skid down the runway.

But Shannon doesn't give up, and one long minute later, we're taxiing over to the helicopter.

The pilot gives Shannon a crisp salute—which she returns—and then he powers up the blades.

Hurry, hurry, hurry!

Shannon helps Madders into the chopper and then the two of us get Peter in. Seven minutes later, we help them onto gurneys and into the Magic Kingdom's airlock.

I check my watch. It's been just over three hours since Madders collapsed and Peter was shot—not ideal, but much better than anything I could have hoped for.

"Welcome back," a woman says over the speakers. "This is Soleil Nadales. We have the OR ready, and Lucy is scrubbed and standing by."

"Do we have blood?"

"Yes, *two* units of O negative. Your nurse says you have experience with bullet wounds, Dr. Kai. Is that correct?"

"Yes. I did rounds in the ER."

"Good. I'll take care of Professor Hudson if you'll stay with Peter."

"Yes," I say. "It's good to have you on board, Dr. Nadales."

"My pleasure. Becky is here as well. Is there anything else you need right now?"

"A quick blood type on Peter—so we can get another donor lined up."

"You got it, Doc," Becky says. "I'll be ready the moment the door opens."

"And the pharmacy has tPA," Dr. Nadales says, "Dr. Hudson is within the time window, so I'll give it to him as soon as the airlock clears."

"So who flew the plane?" Becky asks, her voice rising.

"I did," Shannon says, her hand on Peter's good shoulder. "It was a piece of pie right up until the fuel got low and the flaps wouldn't go down."

"Couldn't have d-done it better m-myself," Madders says from the office chair he's sitting in.

We wait ten seconds for the inner door to open, and then an attractive woman about my age rushes toward Madders. She swabs his arm with alcohol and gives him the anticoagulant injection.

Mindy comes in right behind her, and she gives Shannon a quick hug. "Oh my God, you have to tell me everything!"

We hear barking, and a moment later, Bearhart comes zooming into the airlock. Shannon scoops him up into a hug and lets him lick her face.

Diego steps in, looking older and thinner than the last time I saw him. He smiles when he sees Shannon with the dog and then pins his gaze on me.

"Thank you," he mouths and then bows his head.

I nod and return his smile.

Shannon puts Bearhart down, and Diego gives her a hug. "It's good to have you back, Shannon." He rests his hand on Peter's shoulder. "Thanks for taking care of her, *mae*."

Becky hustles in, pushing a portable IV with oxygen attached and carrying latex gloves.

Diego takes hold of the chair Madders is in and nods at me. "We'll talk later?"

"Wouldn't miss it for the world," I say and then address Shannon. "Keep pressure on this for me."

She moves around to Peter's other side, holding the blood-soaked bandage against the gunshot wound.

"Get that mask on him, Becky."

She follows orders, her eyes wide.

Becky puts the gloves on me, starts the oxygen, and then

does a quick blood draw while I insert the IV.

She hands me a syringe. "Morphine. I had to guess his weight."

I nod and add the painkiller to Peter's IV. "Everything's going to be okay, Peter. Hang in there for a little bit longer."

He blinks his acknowledgment.

"Follow the red line on the floor," Becky says. "Mindy will take you to the OR. I'll be there with another blood donor in ten minutes." She rushes off with the blood sample.

I check that the IV is dripping and the oxygen is flowing. "Let's go."

As we wheel Peter down a long hallway, his eyelids flutter shut and then his hand falls limp on the gurney. For the first time since he was shot, I see tears trickle down Shannon's cheeks.

She bites her lip and turns to me. "Can you save him, Mom?"

I nod, blinking back my own tears. "Peter's going to be fine, baby. We're all going to be just fine."

CHAPTER 42

Diego: Out of Time

I type on the keyboard attached to the time machine, Matt sitting next to me on his relocated hospital bed and kibitzing. We've been at it for the better part of two days—Matt making suggestions while I try things out. But for all our combined efforts, we haven't managed to get so much as a single status light to blink.

And my time runs out at midnight—which is four short hours away.

The lock on the game room door clicks, and we both glance up.

Lani comes in, clipboard in hand. "Making any headway?"

"We've got all the hardware configured," I say. "And the status checks all pass—"

"That sounds like progress," she says and walks over to Matt's bedside.

"—but the targeting is giving us fits." I look up at Matt. "Figuratively speaking."

"Do you have any idea where it's going to send you?" she asks and starts checking Matt's vitals.

"No," I say. "But I'm hoping somewhere close to the cabin—and Isabel."

"But you expect to arrive before Doomsday mutates," she says. "Is that right?"

"Yes," I say, still typing on the computer. "Last I heard, my version of Dave was planning to build a biodome—the Bub, probably—and I'm hoping he succeeded."

She checks Matt's eyes and then rests her hand on his shoulder. "You still feeling fine? No headaches, numbness, or dizzy spells?"

"Not a one," he says. "Now that everyone is safe and sound, I feel better than I have in months."

"Don't we all," she says and picks up her clipboard. "Uh, D-Diego?"

I stop typing and turn to her. "What is it, Lani?"

"My brother, Sam." She touches the burn scars on her face. "If you get back before the virus spreads, do you think you could... try to warn him?"

I remember her telling me about the day they sealed the Bub. She had persuaded Dave to get Sam a ticket to join her Inside. But when she went to collect her brother, the two of them got caught up in a panicked mob. Lani was severely burned by a flamethrower in the ensuing melee—and Sam was killed.

"Of course," I say. "I'll do everything in my power to help him."

And you, I silently add.

"Thank you." She forces a smile and then walks to the door. "I'll be back in an hour to check on both of you. Let me know if you need anything."

She checks that the coast is clear and exits.

A while later, Custer presses his nose against the small window, trying to see what we're up to. He's been checking up on us every hour, but he doesn't have an access card for the door, and James took away his gun. When he determines that we're not doing anything new, he disappears—probably reporting back to his boss.

So far, Dave hasn't shown his face inside the Magic Kingdom.

Given that both James and Isabella would just as soon strangle him as give him the time of day, I don't imagine he's too anxious to ring the doorbell.

At least I don't have to worry about him—just the damn targeting software.

"Damn it." I bang my fist against the desk. "The program keeps asking me to *present the targeting object.*"

Now that Lani's gone, Matt sits up on the edge of the bed. "Are you sure you can't remember anything about that?"

"No," I say. "But we had trouble with the targeting too. I think that's why I ended up in this universe instead of the one I was expecting."

He takes off his reading glasses and rubs his eyes. "Was there something you had to put in the coffin before you got in?"

"Not that I know of." I rack my brain, trying to remember. "We did have the inner capsule to protect against sudden decompression—that translucent thing I told you about—but I know for a fact that they sent mice back in time without it, and a few of them survived."

"At least that part makes sense," he says. "If the trip through the black hole is instantaneous, then there wouldn't be time for your cells to react—the same way fighter pilots can take very high g-forces for a few milliseconds. That protective shell would make it more comfortable, but it wouldn't be requi—"

"The shell!" I smack myself in the forehead. "It's the seashell, Matt. That's the targeting object."

"You could be onto something, mate." He sits up straighter. "Remember that seashell I found in my fridge the night the Bub was sealed? It was with that Kirk*land* Enterprises letter that warned me about the bomb—and contained the note for you."

"Yeah," I say, my hopes falling. "Unfortunately, that shell's at C-Bay. Dave confiscated it when he threw me in jail." I think for a moment. "But I had a shell with me in the time machine too."

"Where is that one?"

"I gave it to Shannon as a birthday gift—back at the Bub."

"Bloody hell. It's probably still there."

I walk over to the door and check that Custer is gone. "I'll go ask Shannon. Maybe she remembers where it is."

"And what? You're gonna pop over to the Bub, find it in all that wreckage, and be back before midnight?" He rubs his hand across his face, looking tired.

"You got any better ideas?"

He shrugs. "Hand me the keyboard. I'll see if I can make any progress while you're gone."

"Don't let Lani catch you doing that," I say, turning the computer display so it's fully facing him.

"Right-o."

I give him the keyboard and hurry out the door.

I jog over to the hospital and head to Peter's room—or rather Shannon and Peter's room, as it looks like she's set up shop in there too. She's sitting on the bed with her pet rat, Wilson, in her lap, teaching Peter how to play poker. He looks to be a quick learner if his pile of plastic chips is any indication. Bearhart is sprawled at her feet, and he thumps his tail when I enter.

"Mr. C!" Shannon gives Wilson to Peter—who looks a little iffy about holding the rat—and hops up to give me a hug.

"It's good to have you back, Shannon," I say, keeping one arm around her. "I'm so sorry I left you at that—"

"Going to Catersville was the best thing that ever happened to me, Mr. C," she says and looks at Peter. "The absolute best."

"Can't argue with that," I say and wink at Peter. "Welcome to the Magic Kingdom." I shake his hand. "And thanks, again, for all you've done for Shannon."

"She's worth it," he says, basking in the glow of her smile. "I'm grateful you brought her to me."

I laugh. "My pleasure."

"Are you going to make it home in time?" Shannon asks. "Mom says you have to leave today."

"I'm hoping you can help me," I say. "I need that shell I gave you for your birthday. You wouldn't have any idea where it might be?"

She laughs. "I keep it in my backpack for good luck." She crosses the room, gets it out, and hands it to me. "I hope it works as well for you as it did for me." She beams at Peter.

"Thank you," I say. "I hope so too."

Ten minutes later, I unlock the game room door and start resetting all the hardware. When I'm done, I place the seashell in the coffin, and Matt runs the program.

"Bollocks," he says. "It's not working."

We try three more times.

"It's stuck at the same damn place—asking me to present the targeting object." He shuts his eyes, his hand on his forehead. "It's the one that brought you here." He opens his eyes. "Therefore it must be from *this* universe."

"So it wasn't an accident." The realization is unsettling.

"It would seem not." He rubs his beard stubble. "But if

we're going to get you home, we need something that came from *your* universe."

"I was wearing a towel in the time machine. Would that work?"

His face brightens. "Any idea what happened to it?"

I shake my head. "It's probably still stuck in the tree."

"Wait a sec," he says. "If your time machine didn't prompt you for a targeting object, why did you take the seashell?"

"It was stuffed inside a dirty sock along with another cryptic note," I say, my heart banging in my chest. "And I have another shell *exactly* like it, one that I found on the beach as a teenager."

He shakes his head. "That doesn't make sense. If the one in the sock was used for targeting, it must be from your universe. It wouldn't have brought you here."

"What if I mixed them up? It's possible I brought the wrong shell—the one I found on the beach."

"Bingo," he says, pointing at the coffin. "The one you found on the beach must be from this universe. It brought you *here*." He thinks for a moment. "And I'm betting the shell at C-Bay is also from here. In fact, the two shells could be the same Jinn object stuck in some sort of time-travel loop."

I nod, trying to follow his logic. "So maybe there's a shell from *my* world in this universe—the one on the beach."

"James." We both say it at the same time.

I grab the shell and race back over to the hospital.

James is sitting next to Isabella's empty bed reading a book, Benny sitting on his shoulder.

"How is she?" I ask.

"She's in surgery," he says. "But Soleil is confident this will be the last time." He looks tired but in good spirits. "I'm hopeful, and Isabella's a fighter."

"That she is." I show him my seashell. "Have you ever

seen a shell like this?"

His face lights up "Yeah, found it on the beach as a kid. Isa showed the twins how to listen to the sound of the sea with it, and after that, Lucas took it with him everywhere. He had it in his Scooby-Doo backpack the night of the accident." He swallows, his eyes getting damp. "After we got locked up in here, he told me he could hear Soleil in it too."

"It was his connection to her."

"Yeah," James says and gives me a sad smile. "He used to talk into it and tell me what Soleil answered." He sighs. "The shell is on my desk in the Control Room."

"I think that seashell is my ticket home," I say, euphoria filling my chest.

"Really? How so?"

"It may have come from my universe."

He raises an eyebrow. "Strange how the impossible can link up with reality now and then. You're welcome to it."

"Thank you," I say. "For everything."

"I didn't do anything except stay alive," he says.

I jog toward the door. "Exactly."

Custer is in the Control Room arguing with Jack when I rush in, but I don't waste any time finding out why. I grab the shell and run all the way back to the time machine.

I swap the shells and then lean over with my hands on my thighs to catch my breath.

Matt is sitting at the desk—which he's not supposed to be doing. He ignores my order to get back in bed, resets the software, and leans back against the chair. "Here goes nothing."

The computer makes a beep, and all the equipment in the room comes to life, clicking and blinking and humming.

"Target acquired," a female voice says. "Enter number of seconds for countdown and press enter. Hit escape to cancel."

I look up at Matt, who's grinning. "Better go say your

goodbyes, mate."

An hour and a lot of hugs later, I change into a cotton T-shirt and sweatpants—organics that will pass through the time portal—and swap one sock for the timey-wimey one. I grab Shannon's charcoal drawing of the jaguarundi, stuff the note on Kirkland Enterprises letterhead into my pocket, and hurry over to the game room.

Lani and Shannon are pushing Peter's wheelchair through the door when I arrive.

Matt is back in bed, but he starts assigning jobs the moment the door closes. He has Shannon sit at the computer and run some tests while Lani reads out the instructions for her. Peter parks in front of the circuit panel and lets us know when the status lights change. I start resetting the hardware and checking that all the cables are tight.

When I'm done, all the control panel lights are green.

"Okay," Matt says. "What's the next test?"

"It's called Load Capacitor," Lani says, "and it's the last one."

"Shall I run it?" Shannon asks.

"No time like the present," I say, and Shannon starts it up.

There's a knock on the door, and Lani opens it for Soleil and James.

They come in, Lucy and Mindy—and half the folks from the Bub—right behind them. Everyone crowds in around the time machine, talking in hushed voices.

A second before the door clicks shut, Custer grabs it and wrenches it open.

Mierda.

Dave walks in, a Glock in his hand.

"David?" Lani looks like she's seen a ghost.

He stares at her, his face unreadable, and then sweeps his gaze around the room. "What the fuck is going on in here?"

"We're sending Mr. C back to where he belongs,"

Shannon says and stands up. "Who are you?"

Dave points the gun at her. "Get away from that computer."

"Please, David," Lani says. "Lower the gun."

To my surprise, he listens to her.

The room erupts in chatter.

Dave waits for the room to quiet. "Nadales isn't going anywhere until the vaccine works."

Soleil shifts her weight, and then clears her throat. "I'm very close."

"So you've figured out how to stop them from self-destructing?" Dave asks.

"No," she says. "But I'm confident I can do it."

"Confident isn't fucking good enough, Soleil." He glances at the other faces in the room. "The biodomes are failing—you've all seen it—and this place will eventually go down too. If I let Nadales leave, and we run out of the biotech devices from his blood, it will be the end, folks."

He waits for the whispering to stop.

"I need one-hundred percent certainty, Soleil—or Nadales stays. End of discussion."

There's a lot of shifting of weight, and one or two people nod in agreement.

"Inject me with his blood," James says. "We have the same DNA. I shouldn't have an immune reaction."

Dave rounds on Soleil. "I thought you told me a transfusion would kill him."

"Their epigenetics are different," Soleil says. "I don't know enough about the biotech to predict what will happen. It could be lethal."

"I'll take that risk," James says. "Draw some of his blood and inject me with it."

"Back in the hospital," Soleil says. "That way I can treat any—"

"No," James says. "There's no time. Do it here and then let Diego go." He sits down in a chair next to the coffin and nods at Soleil. "You have a syringe in your pocket. I saw you put it in there."

Everyone looks at Dave.

"Okay," he says. "If you can transfer the immunity, then he can go."

She walks over to me, rubs alcohol on my arm, and withdraws a tiny amount of blood.

"Are you sure?" she asks James.

"Yes." He meets my gaze. "Diego's the reason I got to see my wife again. I want to be the reason he gets to see his."

Soleil slips the needle into his arm, pulls a bit of his blood into the syringe, and then injects all of it back into his vein.

He exhales, his breathing slow and controlled.

Soleil puts her fingers on his wrist, keeping her eyes on his. "Are you okay?"

"It stings a lot," he says and gives her a forced smile, "but I'm fine."

We wait for more than a minute.

Considering that he gave two units of blood yesterday and is worried sick about Isabella, he looks pretty good.

"Any pain?" Soleil asks. "Is your heart racing?"

He shakes his head. "I feel a little—" He slumps over in the chair, looking like he might throw up.

"Okay," Dave says. "Show's over. Let's get him back to the hospital. If he makes it twenty-four hours, we'll re-evalu—"

"I don't have time to wait and see," I say and stand up. "The last guy who was injected with the biotechs was showing signs of anaphylactic shock in a less than a minute. If the biotechs were going to kill James, we'd know by now."

"Diego's right," Soleil says. "There aren't any signs of shock. It's probably just the stress on his immune system." She hands me a folded sheet of paper from her pocket.

"Probably?" Dave says. "You want me to risk humanity's future on a 'probably'?"

I glance at Soleil's instructions on how to filter the bio-techs in my blood and then slip the paper into my pocket. "Thanks."

She nods.

I open the coffin lid and climb in.

"Don't fucking mess with me," Dave says, pointing the gun at me. "We give him twenty-four hours."

"I need to leave now," I say and glance at the clock. "So if you're going to shoot me, get it the fuck over with."

Nervous whispers fill the room.

James lifts his head and raises his hand to silence the noise. "I'm okay." With an effort, he turns to meet Dave's gaze. "You ruined my life once, Kirk. Don't you think that's enough?"

"I did what I had to do to save you and your family," Dave says. "If you had checked to make sure your car was empty the night of the accident, things would have gone as planned."

"Why didn't you give Isa the letter?" James asks, barely containing his rage.

"What was she supposed to do?" Dave says. "Waste her life trying to find you and Lucas? The plan was to do some plastic surgery and give you a new identity, but that flew out the window when you got Lucas involved. By the time I could get things sorted out, the whole world was busy screwing itself over."

"You should have told her the truth," James says. "You were my best friend, and you fucking stole my wife."

The blood leaves Dave's face. "Use your brain, Nadales, will you? I had my hands full trying to save as many people as I could. When they told me you and Lucas were safe, I let it go. After I lost the biodomes in California, I had to sacrifice everything to save your wife and daughter." He glances at Lani. "Everything."

"Yeah," James says. "You're a real hero."

"Let him go," Lani says. "He's done enough."

Shannon sits back down at the computer.

Dave swings the Glock around, pointing it at Shannon. "Don't even think about it, young lady."

"That's enough!" Lani says, stepping right in front of the gun. "You can't blame Diego for what happened to us."

Dave pulls her against his chest, still pointing the handgun at Shannon. "There are thousands of lives at stake here, babe. If I let him leave, everything I've done—all that I've worked for—could be lost."

Lani looks up at him, her voice calm. "You saved the world once, David. Now it's someone else's turn. If Soleil says she can do it, then I believe her—and you should too."

Dave hesitates, his eyes moving from Soleil... to James... to me.

"You're the one who has to rebuild the world," Lani says. "Assuming you don't spend all your time playing with the grandkids."

"Grandkids?" Dave says, looking like he's never heard the word before.

"Yes," Lani says. "Shannon and Peter are getting married as soon as Peter's grandmother arrives, and I'm hoping we'll have grandkids."

"Shannon?" He lowers the gun.

Lani smiles and rests her hands on his chest. "Yes. Shannon's your daughter, David."

"Mr. Kirk is my dad?" Shannon says, her eyes wide.

Dave clears his throat and then looks at Shannon—who's sizing him up like he's an iffy contestant on the *Pick Your Father* game show.

Dave turns back to Lani, his eyebrows knitted together.

"Why didn't you tell me, babe?"

She reaches up and strokes his face. "I tried to, but I didn't want to... take away your dreams."

"Holy fuck. I have a daughter?"

Lani nods, tears in her eyes—and then looks over at Shannon. "Isn't she just perfect?"

Shannon rolls her eyes, taps a key on the keyboard, and waves to me. "Good luck, Mr. C. Have fun storming the castle!"

"Ten seconds to activation," the computer says. "Nine..."

I lie down in the coffin and pull the lid shut.

"Eight..."

Someone seals it from the outside.

My heart is pounding so loudly, I can't hear the countdown anymore.

I close my eyes and take a deep breath, wondering where I'll go back to... and hoping it's not that damn tree. At least I'm not naked this time.

There's no place like home. There's no place like ho—

And the time machine engages.

Chapter 43

Diego: Arrival

It's cold and dark when I come to, and for a moment I wonder if the time machine has failed.

Something sharp is poking me in the back—not the smooth, hard metal of the coffin—and it smells like… a pine forest.

Christ, I hope I'm in the right universe.

I force my eyelids to open.

Stars swim behind a watery film.

I try to sit up, but my body is still numb, and the muscles don't respond. I lie there for another minute, letting the cool night air move in and out of my lungs.

Not in the Magic Kingdom and not on a tropical beach.

And not in that damn pine tree.

I close my fingers around the seashell. If Matt is right, and it has brought me home, Isabel is alive and well.

Either at the cabin or safely inside Dave's biodome.

There's a rustling sound next to my shoulder, and I turn my head. An arm's-length away, two glowing orbs are floating in the darkness, eyes reflecting the light coming from behind me.

"Shoo!" I say, but the sound comes out as more of a cough.

The raccoon—an animal extinct in the place and time I just left—turns and lumbers back into the forest.

Wherever—and whenever—I am, the virus hasn't mutated yet.

I blink a couple of times and look around.

I'm lying on a forest floor, looking up into a starry night sky, a half moon hanging above the treetops. I look for the Big Dipper, afraid it will be distorted—or even gone.

It's right where it should be—and all the stars are twinkling in their correct locations. I check the North Star and then the Orion constellation. All is as it should be—which leaves me ninety-nine percent sure I'm home.

Some heavy weight I didn't realize I was carrying evaporates into the night.

I can hear water cascading over rocks, and in the distance, the periodic whine of a heavy-duty drill—and music coming from somewhere nearby.

You're at the cabin?

I push myself up into a sitting position and check that my clothes made the trip—

Hallelujah.

—and then flex the muscles in my arms and legs to get the blood flowing.

My eyes still sting and my throat is dry, but at least I'm not at the top of a tree.

The Bub is down the hill from me, its circular dome glowing in the still mountain night.

I glance down at the seashell in my hand.

Whoever programed the shell targeting knew his shit.

There is scaffolding on one side and workmen near the apex of the dome, their huge spotlights pushing back the darkness. The man-made fishpond next to the biodome is only half-full of water—that's the waterfall I can hear, a long fire hose dumping water into it—and the apple trees lining the raised embankment are all saplings. A handful of guards are walking along a security fence that encloses the biodome—and a warm tongue of light is streaming out the main airlock door.

Dave hasn't sealed it yet.

All around me are tents of every shape and size, their outlines flickering in the light of campfires for as far as I can see. It's like Woodstock in the Rockies.

I need to find a phone.

"You okay, mister? I heard a loud bang."

I turn toward the voice.

"Y-y…" I clear my throat, looking up at a young boy. "Yes. But I seem to have hit my head on a branch and knocked myself out. I'm afraid I'm a bit disoriented. What is today's date?"

He tells me, and I do the calculation. I've been gone for the same amount of time I was in the bubble universe.

I'm home.

"You don't have it, do you?" he says and takes a step back. "That disease that makes you puke your guts until you die?"

"Nope," I say. "No puking here. What are you doing out so late?"

"Had to pee," he says and flicks on a flashlight he's holding under his chin. It casts ghostly shadows across his face. "Only *I* remembered to bring my flashlight so I wouldn't run into any trees." He looks to be seven or eight.

"Well, that definitely makes you smarter than me."

"Yeah." He flicks the flashlight off. "But my sister told me not to use it unless I really needed it because there are no such things as monsters and we don't have any more batteries."

I smile. "I wish I was as certain as your sister about the monsters."

"Who are you talking to, Sam?" a soft female voice calls from behind the boy. Sam turns to watch a flashlight bobbing through the trees toward us.

I'd recognize the lilting Hawaiian accent anywhere.

Lani!

Whatever forces are at play in the fabric of space-time, there seems to be some sort of connection binding together the same set of players.

Or maybe you're the luckiest man in the universe.

I didn't know where the time machine would place me—so I'm making it up as I go—but it occurs to me that a little blood will help support my story. I pick up a fist-sized rock and smack the edge hard against my forehead.

Mierda!

I drop the rock and check the wound. My fingers come away wet.

The boy turns back to me. "There's a man out here who hit his head on a tree branch, but he says he's okay—and he's not puking."

"Yes, I'm fine," I say and attempt to stand up. "Or I thought I was." The sudden change of altitude makes my head spin, and I stumble sideways.

Sam grabs on to my arm. "I think you're bleeding, mister."

Lani shines the light in my face. "You *are* bleeding."

"To be honest," I say, fighting the vertigo, "I don't feel so hot—but I need to get to the biodome." I squint at her, shading my eyes with my hand.

"You and the Mormon Tabernacle Choir," she says and lowers the flashlight.

"My wife's in there," I say. "Or I hope she is. I need to make sure."

"They're not letting anyone back in tonight," she says. "I already tried."

"Could I borrow your phone?" I ask. "I seem to have lost mine."

"Sure," Sam says, "except the cell phone towers have been out for weeks."

I wipe the blood off my forehead. "Well, that would explain why I haven't been able to reach her."

"You can try tomorrow," Lani says, shining her flashlight back on my forehead. "In the meantime, would you like me to take a look at that cut? I'm not a doctor, but I do have medical training."

"That's very kind of you to offer," I say. "But I wouldn't want to impose." I try to take a step, but my legs are like rubber, and I stumble again.

Sam grabs on to my arm. "Whoa there, mister! I think you should let my sister take a look."

"Sam's right," she says. "At least let me clean the wound and check that you don't have a concussion."

"Perhaps you're right," I say. "I do apologize for the bother."

"It's no bother," she says and takes my other arm. "Our tent's back this way."

"Thank you," I say, trying not to wince as I step on rocks and pine needles. I don't have any shoes on—just my pair of mismatched socks—and my legs still aren't working properly.

She tightens her grip, leading me across the uneven ground. "Where's your tent?"

"Actually, I don't have one," I say, not needing to fake the embarrassment in my voice. "I was afraid I'd get here too late. So, I didn't stop to purchase camping supplies."

In for a dime, in for a dollar.

"I have a… reservation," I say, hoping it sounds plausible. "And dumb as it sounds, I had planned to walk right up to the biodome and ring the doorbell."

Sam laughs. "We have tickets to get inside too—not like all of these lolos who came here just to cause trouble."

"Shh," Lani says still leading me past more campsites. "It's not nice to call people that."

Sam groans. "But you call them that all the time!"

"No worries," I say, trying not to laugh. "I certainly feel stupid tonight. I had hoped to get here earlier, but it proved more difficult than I expected. I spoke to Dave Kirk"—I fake a cough—"excuse me. I spoke to Mr. Kirk*land* yesterday. He may be forced to seal up the biodome sooner than expected."

"You know Mr. Kirkland?" Sam says. "He's awesome! He's going to marry my sister."

"Sam!"

I rest my hand on Sam's shoulder. "Your sister does seem very nice." I look at Lani, still trying to determine if her face is scarred. "Thanks again for helping me."

"Anyone who's a friend of David's is a friend of mine," she says. "My name's Lani, and this is my brother, Sam." She unzips a tent flap and holds it open for me.

I step inside and collapse onto the floor.

A candle lamp is hanging from the roof, casting a warm glow inside.

"I'm Diego," I say and offer her my hand. "It's a pleasure to meet you, Lani." I shake her brother's hand and notice his Pikachu shirt. "Nice to meet you too, Sam. I don't know what I would have done if you hadn't found me."

"You must have hit your head pretty hard," Sam says, "because that was a loud bang."

"That'll teach me not to go running around in the dark

after Mewtwo."

Sam gasps. "You play Pokémon Go?"

"Of course," I say and ruffle his dark hair.

"Cool." He sits down on his dragon-motif sleeping bag and lets out a giant yawn.

"Back to bed, young man," Lani says, cleaning her hands with antiseptic gel.

Sam protests but crawls into his bag.

"You look really familiar," she says and takes out her medical bag. "Have we met before?"

"If I'm not mistaken," I say, watching her tear open an alcohol pad, "this is the second time I'm in your debt. You saved my fiancée's life—and probably mine as well—in that firestorm in downtown Denver a couple of years ago."

She stares at me, her eyes wide, and then gives a single nod. "I'm glad it worked out for you."

I swallow, hoping with all my being that it's true.

She nods and starts dabbing at my forehead. The shrewd, tomboy with the chopped hair and loose-fitting clothes has made a stunning transformation. Lani looks like a mod-ern-day geisha in yoga pants and a tight sweater. Her flawless porcelain skin and long black hair are the perfect comple-ment to her graceful movements.

Although she doesn't look a day over eighteen, it's easy to tell what Dave—that forty-something, lecherous old man—sees in her: youthful perfection.

All of which, she's about to lose—along with her brother—if things play out the same in this universe.

"Can you tell me a bedtime story, Lani?" Sam asks.

She glances at me. "Perhaps Diego would do the honors while I finish up?"

I make up a story about Pikachu and the three bears while Lani attends to my forehead.

When she's done, she checks my eyes with a penlight.

"No concussion," she says and offers me a bottle of water. "But you're dehydrated, and your pupil response is sluggish. I wouldn't suggest any strenuous exercise for the next day or two."

I drink the water in two or three gulps. "Thank you. I didn't realize I was so thirsty until you mentioned it." I start to get up, wondering where the hell I'm going to spend the night.

Sam grabs on to my elbow. "Do you think he can come with us tomorrow, Lani? To the biodome, I mean? Maybe he can help us get through the guard station?"

Lani looks as me, asking with her eyes if it's okay.

I nod at Sam. "Sure. As long as it's alright with your sister, I'll meet you here in the morning."

"Please, Lani?" Sam says, still holding on to my arm.

"I think that's a fine idea," she says and then turns to me. "Do you have a place to sleep?"

I shake my head. "I'll see if I can find somewhere out of the wind and—"

"He can sleep here!" Sam says, patting his bed. "You brought extra blankets, Lani, and it's only one night."

"No, I couldn't," I say. "That would be—"

"He can sleep on my side, and he can use my pillow, and he can—"

"Okay, okay," Lani says, putting the medical supplies away. "He can stay tonight."

"Yes!" Sam says and scoots his sleeping bag over so there's room on the other side.

"Shh. Go to sleep." She kisses Sam on the forehead, hands me two blankets and a jacket to use as a pillow, and then blows out the candle.

"Thank you," I say and lie down next to Sam.

I listen to Lani get into her sleeping bag, my eyelids already heavy.

She lets out a soft sigh. "Good night, Sherlock."

The sun is high in the sky when I scramble out of the empty tent, half panicked that Lani and Sam have left without me.

But they're just finishing up breakfast.

"Morning, sleepyhead," Sam says. "We saved you some food."

"Thank you."

Lani offers me a Pop-Tart and a juice box. "How are you feeling?"

"Better, thanks. Anything new happen while I was—"

"They're shutting the biodome doors!" someone shouts, and a minute later, mobs of people are running past us, some of them carrying guns.

"*Oka fefe*," Lani says, standing there with her hands on her hips. "Dave said it would be at least another week before they closed it."

She starts packing her things, but I scoop up Sam and grab her by the arm. "Just leave the tent, Lani! We need to get down to the biodome before the fighting breaks out—and the fires."

"What fires?"

"Never mind. Get your tickets, and let's go!"

She dives into the tent and comes out wearing a backpack and carrying her medical bag.

We follow the crowd, cutting across campsites and stepping on discarded protest signs. I spy an abandoned pair of loafers and stuff my feet into them, grateful to have something to protect my feet.

We tramp down the hill toward the security fence and the giant mass of desperate people. I carry Sam in one arm and hold tight to Lani with the other hand. People are throwing bottles and other trash over the fence and yelling obscenities at the men working the checkpoint.

The security forces are scanning the angry throng, guns at the ready.

I look for Dave but don't see anyone except uniformed men. The huge gate is shut, but there's a circle of jeeps parked just inside it.

We stand behind the fence for a minute, watching the chaos.

"Look," Sam says and points at a couple who have been let through the gate and are running toward the airlock. "They're letting some people in!"

"Come on," I say and start pushing through the crowd toward the checkpoint. "We need to find Dave."

We spend twenty minutes trying to push our way closer to the gate. There must be five thousand people crowded around the small entrance, and I realize it's hopeless. There's no way we're going to get anywhere near the gate. I lean over so Lani can hear me above all the shouting.

"Let's try the side entrance," I say. "The one you used before you had two tickets."

She stares up at me. "What side entrance? I haven't been here before—and why wouldn't I have a ticket for Sam?"

"You haven't been in the biodome yet?" I'm starting to get a really bad feeling about this. How much stuff has changed between this universe and the one I just left?

"No," she says. "David sent our tickets a few days ago, but they weren't good until today."

"*Mierda*," I say. "It's going to play out differently here."

"What are you talking about?" Her eyes are dark and distrustful. "Who are you?"

"An idiot." I take her hand and start pulling her back out of the mob, but she resists.

"Stop!" she shouts over the melee. "The checkpoint is

the other way! Where are you taking us? And if your wife is already inside, why aren't you in there too?"

"Look," I say, people bumping into me as they try to push past, "this mob is going to turn violent any minute, and we don't want to be in the middle of it when it does. We have to find another way to get to the biodome. Another entrance."

"Ticket holders, please approach the main gate," someone on a loudspeaker says. "Form one line, single file, and have your tickets ready."

"Fuck the tickets!" someone behind us yells. "It's reached Denver! Let us in!"

The crowd pushes in even tighter.

"Denver?" Sam says. "Isn't that where Grandma lives?"

A teenager in front of us has a boombox on his shoulder tuned to the news. "...pandemic. Unconfirmed reports out of Cheyenne, Albuquerque, and Denver suggest that the virus is spreading faster than the CDC predicted and—"

"Please," I say to Lani. "You have to trust me. There's no way we'll make it to the main gate in time. We have to get out of this mob."

"How long do we have until the virus reaches here?" she asks, not bothering to question how I know.

"A few hours," I say, hoping it's still true. "We have to get Sam inside before it does."

Lani glances up at Sam, and he nods.

"Okay," she says. "Let's go."

I take her hand again, and lead her back up the hill, Sam holding on so tight that he's almost choking me.

Two or three times, Lani is nearly torn away from me, but I refuse to let go of her.

After a minute or two, I start shoving people out of the way, ignoring their angry curses. We hear sporadic gunfire and a bullhorn telling people to move back from the security fence or risk being shot. The mob is two or three times bigger than it was when we first approached the fence, and we hear the bullhorn admonish the crowd to stop surging forward and crushing people.

We're halfway to the top of the ridge by the time we manage to break free of the hordes.

"We need something to write with," I say, trying to catch my breath. "Markers or paint."

"I have crayons in my backpack," Sam says. He pulls his small Pikachu backpack off and takes out a pencil bag.

"Good," I say and pick up a discarded "Blow Up the Biodomes!" sign. The back is covered with a caricature of Dave with a Hitler mustache. I throw it down and pick up a different one: "The End Is Near."

Finally got it right.

The back side of this second one is empty.

I draw big outlines of the letters in "LANI" and the number "215" below it.

"Help me color them in," I say.

Sam and Lani don't argue.

Once we're done, we hike up to the top of the ridge.

From this vantage point, we can see plumes of smoke rising from the city out east.

"Denver," Lani says and looks at me. "What's happening over there?"

"Doomsday," I say and force myself to look away.

The mob is pushing hard against the security fence now, and the jeeps are no longer parked by the checkpoint.

I hold up the sign and wave it around, hoping Dave or one of his minions will see it.

A covered military truck comes from behind the biodome and stops in front of the airlock. Soldiers pile out, and a minute later, they fire up flamethrowers and start using them to force people back from the fence.

We hear more gunfire, and this time, one of Dave's men

shoots back, killing a gunman on top of the pump house. There are screams, and the crowd surges forward like a rogue wave heading for the biodome.

A section of security fence gives way, and people start scrambling over it.

For a moment, I think there's going to be a massacre, but the soldiers guarding the airlock don't fire their weapons into the crowd. Instead, their brethren shift positions, forcing the mob back across the downed fence with the flamethrowers.

When the people at the front see the fire, they turn back. They rail against the mob, but it refuses to yield, unstoppable. The mass of panicked humanity is forced forward through the breach in the perimeter fence and into the flames. There are screams as the military men approach the crowd, the heat finally causing the hordes to stop pushing.

Lani gasps. "That could have been us."

"Move back behind the barrier," a familiar voice says over the loudspeaker. "Do not approach the biodome."

Dave.

The crowd erupts with boos and profanity.

"All troops are approved for lethal force," he says. "I repeat: Do not attempt to cross the barrier. We will shoot to kill."

Just as he finishes speaking, a couple breaks through the middle of the mob and starts running toward the biodome. Five or six people follow. The soldiers turn the flamethrowers on all of them and screams erupt from everywhere.

I drop the sign and pick up Sam, turning away from the carnage.

"Let's go," I say and grab Lani's hand, leading her back into the forest.

"But the virus," she says. "Where are we going to go?"

"We're both immune," I say before I can stop myself, "but I don't know about Sam. We need to get him inside."

She doesn't ask how I know, and I'm grateful for that small gift.

There are a few looters going through tents, but they pay us no mind. We make our way around the biodome, heading for the airlock that's next to the I-beam numbered 215. It's in the back—and on the opposite side from the section that's going to be blown up sometime tonight.

It takes us nearly an hour to make our way across the rough terrain, around to the other side of the dome. There's no outside access in this area, no road or pond, and we don't see anyone else as we scurry down to the double security fence.

A minute later, the emergency airlock next to beam 215 opens, and Dave Kirkland steps out—wearing a rebreather mask. He motions with his arm, and six men exit the biodome, two with rifles and four carrying tools. In less than thirty seconds, one of them cuts a door-sized U in the first fence. Two of them bend it up while the other two slip through. They repeat the process on the exterior fence and lift up the metal mesh.

I set Sam down, and the three of us wordlessly scramble through both openings.

They reseal the fences with metal clips and escort us back to the biodome.

When we get close to the airlock, Lani rushes into Dave's arms.

He picks her up like a doll and swings her around. "Fuck me, it's good to see you, Lanikins."

"See?" Sam says to me. "I told you he was going to marry her."

Dave glances over Lani's shoulder at Sam—and then our eyes meet.

For a moment I think he's going to call me *dickface* or *asshole* or even *sandwich man*, but he doesn't. He keeps one arm around Lani and reaches out to me with the other.

"Thanks," he says and shakes my hand. "I owe you one."

He ruffles Sam's hair and then escorts Lani into the airlock. Sam and I follow, the uniformed men right behind us.

Everything looks shiny and new.

"Is Isabel here?" I ask, my heart in my throat.

"She was," Dave says and starts the airlock cycle, the *Virus Detected* indicator still dark. "But she left a couple months ago. Borrowed my Tesla and never returned it."

The disappointment on my face must show because he steps closer and puts his hand on my shoulder.

"I'm sorry," he says. "I know you two had something going again."

His display of empathy catches me off guard. The last time we met in this universe, it nearly turned into a brawl.

"Any idea where she went?" I ask. "Did she mention the Magic Kingdom?"

"Why would she drive all the way to Florida?" he says and drops his hand. "The whole state is underwater." He puts his arm back around Lani and runs his hand through his hair. "Last I heard, she was headed back to that remote cabin of yours. I think she was expecting to find you there."

I glance at the airlock door we just came through. "I need to go back Outside."

"Outside?" Dave narrows one eye, looking at me like I was born without a brain. "Despite the panic, I'm inclined to believe the Feds when they say the virus hasn't made it to Denver yet—but it'll be here tonight or tomorrow at the latest. You get caught out there when it hits, and you'll be dead in a matter of minutes."

"He's immune," Lani says, looking up at Dave like he's a superhero.

A muscle in his neck twitches. "How do you know?"

"Long story," I say.

He looks more carefully at me, thinking through the implications, and then nods. "You need a jeep?"

"That would be great."

"Armstrong will get you set up," he says, "but you'll have to leave through the main gate."

"I'll manage," I say.

The inner door beeps and then slides open.

Lani takes Sam's hand. "Thank you," she says and kisses me on the cheek. I take the sheet of paper Soleil gave me out of my pocket and hand it to Lani. "If you'd make a copy of that for me, I'd appreciate it. And you're welcome to keep a copy for yourself."

She unfolds the sheet and glances at the title. "Biotechs? Is that why you're immune?"

I nod. "The ink's biodegradable. So it's going to fade quickly."

"I'll have a copy when you get back," she says.

"How come you're not staying with us?" Sam asks.

"I have someone I need to find first," I say. "But, I'll be back. In the meantime, you take good care of your sister, okay?"

Sam nods, and Lani leads him through the inner door.

"And Dave," I say, keeping my voice low. "There's a bomb somewhere in the main storage area—near beam 35. I don't know if it's inside or outside the biodome, but it's going to go off tomorrow—after the virus arrives."

He stares at me for a full ten seconds and then motions with his head toward his men. "Check it out."

The four uniforms with rifles hurry through the door.

"Thank you." He offers me his hand again and I shake it. "Good luck," he adds. He exits and disappears with Lani and Sam.

One of the four remaining men steps forward. He's

attempting to grow a blond handlebar mustache—but mostly failing. "Let's get you that jeep," he says and gestures toward the inner door.

I step into the one and only biodome in my universe...

The Girl with All the Gifts

W hen I hear the sound of tires squealing, I put the top back on the big jar of gummy bears, step over the bodies, and peek out the winda of the candy store.

A jeep that looks like Sarge from the car movie comes shootin' down Main Street, goin' way too fast for the curves up ahead.

Grammy would say *like a bat outta hell* if she weren't already gone.

I take the lid off a jar of jelly beans and scoop out a handful, trying not to get any of the black ones. I'm feeling a little sick, but I figure there's not much time until it gets dark and all the dead people come after me like in the movies.

Ain't no little girl gonna have a chance against all them zombies—and I reckon this candy is just goin' to waste.

I hear Sarge's tires squeal again—and then a loud crash.

"That's what comes a ballhootin' on them steep mountain roads," I say, pretending Grammy done said it.

I get a fancy plastic bag out from behind the counter and fill it up with some of each kind of candy—all except the black ones. I hates them ones.

"Let the zombies have 'em."

I wedge a rock in the door of the candy store and walk down the street toward the smoke. I try not to look at all the bodies, but the cats and dogs are too much. I stop and pet one of the kitties, hoping he won't turn into a zombie and come after me tonight.

By the time I get to Sarge, the man is gone.

I sit on the rocks in front of Sarge and eat my candy. After a minute or two, I see the man hightailing it up the ravine on foot, heading toward a cabin near the ridge.

"Ain't nobody gonna be alive up there," I say and go back to my sweets.

When it gets dark, I climb under a blanket in the backseat of Sarge and go to sleep.

I wake up to the sound of glass breaking, and at first, I think it must be the zombies.

But the streetlights are on, and none of the bodies have moved a whit. There's a light on in Grammy's Bar. I wrap the blanket around me and take a peek in the winda.

The man is back, and he's sittin' at the bar with a big bottle of likker in front of him, cryin' like Sissy after her boyfriend ran off with someone else.

Even though Sissy and me don't get along, the thought makes me sad.

Sissy's dead now, same as everybody else.

The man pours some hooch into a glass, takes a long swig, and then hurls the whole thing against Grammy's expensive mirror.

I watch him sittin' there, cryin' and breakin' glass, for a

few minutes, and then I sneak back to Sarge and try to sleep.

When I wake up in the morning, the birds are chirping, but them bodies are all still lyin' all over the place—even the cats and dogs.

Ain't no sign of the man.

Two days later, the whole town is stinkin' to high heaven—even the candy store smells too awful to go inside.

I walk down to the market, grab a big bag of potato chips and a bottle of pop, and head back to Sarge. When I ain't hungry and thirsty no more, I go to the library and look at the picture books, being careful not to get any dirt on them nice pages.

I don't see the man again for ages.

Actually, I'm not sure how long it's been, but the people are turning into skeletons, and if I prop open the door of the candy store, I can stand to go back inside now.

That's where I'm sittin' when I see the man walk by in the street.

His hair and beard have gone all wild—like Santa Claus if he didn't take no baths—but I can tell it's the Sarge man because he walks with a limp just like Grammy.

I follow him around for a bit, keepin' myself hidden in case he's a zombie.

He goes from Grammy's Bar to the public library, then to the po-leece station, and finally to the market. I watch him munch a whole bag of my favorite potato chips, trying to remember if zombies eat regular food.

I don't think so.

After he leaves the market, he wanders down the street, lookin' in all the shop windas and steppin' over the bodies.

And then he goes into my candy store.

I peek in the door, watching him eat the chocolates with nuts—which I hate—and some peppermint drops—which I don't like much either.

But when he takes the lid off my jelly beans, I can't stand it anymore.

"Them's mine," I say.

He whirls around, dropping the lid on the floor. "What the—"

We stare at each other for a bit, both of us sizin' up the other.

I put my hands on my hips, tryin' to look more adult. "You can have the black ones, but the rest belong to me."

He nods and runs his hands over his face and hair, lookin' spooked.

"I ain't no zombie," I say.

He picks up the lid and puts it back on the jelly beans. "Me neither."

"I knew that," I say. "Zombies don't eat potato chips."

He nods again.

"You can have the chocolates with nuts," I say. "And the black licorice and Hot Tamales." I point to the jars I'm talking about. "But the jelly beans are my favorite."

"Sorry," he says, pushing the jelly bean jar closer to me. "I didn't know there was anyone else... here."

"I saw you the first day," I say, "when you crashed the jeep. And I followed you today—in case you turned out to be a zombie."

"That was very smart of you." He squats down so we're eye to eye. "What's your name?"

"Melanie."

"It's nice to meet you, Melanie. My name's Diego."

"Why were you drinkin' all that hooch and smashing up Grammy's mirror, Diego?"

"Feeling sorry for myself, I guess." He stands up. "Because I got here too late."

"Grammy said it don't matter where you go, everybody gonna die."

He wipes his face. "Yeah."

"Except you and me," I say, taking more jelly beans from the jar. "And that man on the radio who talks funny."

"Talks funny?"

"You know, like in Harry Potter."

"You mean with a British accent?"

I nod. "He's on Grammy's radio every day beggin' me to talk to him. But even when I turn the knob all the way up, he can't hear me."

He gets a real hopeful look on his face. "When does he come on?"

"Right after it gets dark," I say. "But he says the same thing every night, and I have it memorized. Would you like to hear it?"

He sits down in the wooden chair, and puts his hands on my shoulders. "Yes."

I swallow the jelly bean I'm sucking on and stand up real straight, tryin' to make my voice deep like that British man's. "This is Matt Hudson in Deep Springs, Colorado," I say. "We have food and shelter. Is there anybody out there?"

"She's in the Magic Kingdom!" He jumps right up outta that chair, grinning like he's the happiest man alive. He picks me up and swings me around, and I can't help laughing 'cause I've been real lonely.

"Would you like to talk to that guy?" he asks. "They have a bigger radio down at the biodome. That's a—"

"I know what it is," I say and wiggle so he sets me back down. "I saw it on TV."

"Right. Would you like to go there?"

"Do they have a library?" I ask.

"Yes," he says, "and a park with swings and a slide."

"Okay," I say and take his hand. "Can I bring my jar of jelly beans?"

He smiles and stands up. "As long as I get the black ones."

THANK YOU FOR READING!

If you enjoyed the book,
I would be *very* grateful if you left a review.
Be sure to let me know by tweet:

@DL_Orton

or email:

dlo@dlorton.com

and I'll send you a FREE copy
of the next book as a Thank You!
(One free book per reader, please.)

Visit my website to join my mailing list
and get *Diego's Chocolate Cake Recipe*!

BetweenTwoEvils.com

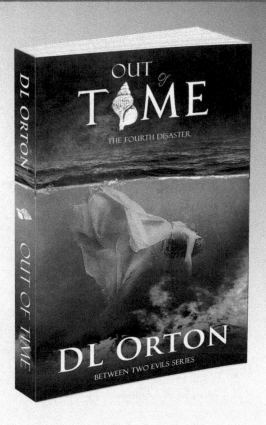

ABOUT THE AUTHOR

A ward-winning author D. L. ORTON lives in the foothills of the Rocky Mountains where she and her husband are raising three boys, a golden retriever, two Siberian cats, and an extremely long-lived Triops. Her plans include completing the five books in the *Between Two Evils* series followed by an extended vacation on a remote tropical island (with a coffee shop).

When she's not writing, playing tennis, coding, or helping with algebra, she's building a time machine so that someone can go back and do the laundry.

CPSIA information can be obtained
at www.ICGtesting.com
Printed in the USA
LVHW052320040619
620185LV00001B/156/P